War of the Seasons

Seasons

book one

the human

A NOVEL BY

JANINE K. SPENDLOVE

SILENCE IN THE
LIBRARY

War of the Seasons, Book 1: The Human
Copyright © 2011 Janine K. Spendlove
Cover and interior art by Betsy Waddell
Book design by Kelli Neier
All rights reserved.

The text for this book is set in Palatino.
Printed in the United States of America
First Printing: June 2011

ISBN-10:0983656703
ISBN-13:978-0-9836567-0-8
V3.1

FOR WILL

CONTENTS

A MAP OF
AILIONORA

Ailionora
FAERIE LAND
RED DWARF TERRITORY
MORRIGANN'S GARDEN
FORGE MOUNTAINS
The SILVER
BANNOCK
AILES
AIDAN
The DESERT of DREAMS
The AILES

AISRAS
STONEYBROOK
STONEY MTNS
STONEY LAKE
SUNSET COVE
SEA
DOGWOOD BAY
SUNSET PLAINS
SUNSET HILLS
PINEY GREEN
AILANTHU
BROWN DWARF TERRITORY
PINEY GREEN MTNS
SEA
AIBLINS
N

THE FIRST THING STORY REALIZED WAS SHE WAS SOMEHOW, miraculously, still alive. She knew this because every single inch of her body hurt; even her hair hurt. The second thing Story realized was she'd neglected an important rule in spelunking: always look up before you stand.

the human

CHAPTER ONE

THE FALL

G RAVEL SPRAYED OUT FROM UNDER THE JEEP'S TIRES AS IT skidded to a halt in front of the cave entrance. Story smiled as she saw the familiar, happy memory from her childhood. The longing—no, the *need*—to see it again had been consuming her for months. Set in a massive limestone outcropping that jutted out from the mountainside, the opening was shaped like a lopsided half-moon, as if someone had hooked the right side of the cave entrance and tugged upward. A warm, summer breeze rustled the treetops, and she took a deep breath, inhaling the sharp, piney smell of the surrounding woods.

"What do you mean *if* you go back to school?"

Story's smile evaporated, and she felt a flash of irritation over the interruption. Josh raised his fiery red eyebrows and peered over the rim of his sunglasses at her, waiting for an answer. Ignoring his question, she hopped out of the Jeep and after a quick look around noted that there weren't any other cars parked nearby.

Good.

Josh jumped out and slammed the passenger door shut before walking around to the back of the vehicle to block her access to their gear.

"I'm serious, Story. What do you mean *if*? You can't be thinking of dropping out of high school! What about your friends? What about prom? What about college?"

Story snorted. "Are you serious? Prom? College? Like those things really matter." She pushed past him and reached for her gear. "Besides, you're the only friend I have left."

Leaning into the back of the Jeep, she pulled out her day-pack and slipped a headlamp over her purple-streaked black hair. She tossed some water and snacks into the bag along with a short length of rope and a few anchor points with carabiners.

Josh picked up his daypack and mirrored her actions, but stubbornly clung to the subject. "Of course it matters. You only get to go to high school once." His face softened. "Besides, didn't we have a good time last year?" He held her gaze with his sky blue eyes and, hesitantly, as if he was afraid he'd scare her away, reached up with his hand and gently brushed her chin-length hair back, tucking a stray curl behind her ear. His thumb came down to rest on her jaw, while his fingertips grazed the side of her neck.

Story looked up at him and felt a familiar ache rise in her chest: her breath became short and shallow. But she buried the rising rush of emotions before they could fully surface. She couldn't allow herself to feel anything anymore—not even good things like Josh, because, as her father always used to say, *"You can't feel the good without the bad."*

She jerked away from Josh, as if burned by his touch, and turned back to the Jeep.

Ignoring the hurt look she saw before she turned, she threaded the string from her battered lensatic compass through one of her belt loops and then shoved its considerable bulk in her front pocket. After pausing to make sure it was secure, she pulled on a faded, black hoodie with a peeling surfing logo emblazoned across the front; it would be enough to ward off the cave's chill.

Almost as an afterthought, she picked up the knife lying in the back of the Jeep.

Her father smiled and pulled a poorly wrapped gift from his back pocket. "Merry Christmas, kiddo!" He winked and tossed it into her lap.

Story examined the oblong bundle, fairly certain she knew what it contained. Never one for trying to preserve gift-wrap, she made short work of the paper and found herself holding an old knife. Her father's old Marine Corps Ka-Bar, to be precise. She turned it around in her hands and pulled it from its brown leather sheath. It was nearly a foot long from end to end: the blade itself was seven inches in length. It was just an old, oversized knife—unremarkable in every way.

"Um, thanks?"

Her father's neck started to turn red, and he thrust his hands deeply into his front pockets as he leaned against the doorjamb. "It's not your only gift. I just wanted to give you this one now."

"Oh no, it's great, Dad, really!" She plastered a huge, and hopefully genuine looking, smile on her face. "I'm sure it'll come in handy a lot. Hiking, spelunking..."

Slamming the door on the rest of the memory, she attached the knife to her belt with more force than necessary. When she looked up, Josh was eying her warily.

"We don't have to do this today, you know—if it's too much for you." Josh stepped in closer, requiring her to arch her neck back to look him in the face, which was saying something; at nearly six feet, Story was pretty tall for a girl.

"We could just set up camp and try in the morning," he continued.

"If you keep talking like that I'm going to start thinking you're claustrophobic." Story hefted her pack and adjusted its fit. "Or a wuss." She pushed past his linebacker's bulk and walked toward the cave entrance.

She heard Josh give an exasperated sigh and, looking over her shoulder, saw him kick her Jeep's tire before picking up his pack and following her. "Just once, you could try being nice to me, you know."

"That would only encourage you," she called back at him. He rolled his eyes, and she knew she had, once again, been forgiven. For some reason, that comforted her. As much as she drove Josh away, she felt like if he ever did give up on her what little remained of the old Story would be gone for good.

Those melancholy thoughts evaporated as she neared the cave entrance. She ran her hand up the smooth, white trunk of the solitary aspen tree that flanked the opening and heard its distinctive round leaves flutter in the light wind. She smiled as she remembered her father's advice to her and the twins on one of their many trips here.

"Aspen's a terrible wood to use for a fire. Doesn't burn very hot or fast. But the inner bark can be peeled and eaten in a pinch —"

"Does it taste good?" Katie interrupted, always eager to try something new.

"It's actually pretty bitter, but if you were hungry enough, I promise you wouldn't care. That's what I learned in the Corps; why I remember back when I was in SERE School —"

"Daaaaaaad," Will whined, cutting their father off. "No more boring Marine stories!" He brandished his pocketknife. "Come on Katie, let's go try some."

Chuckling, their father winked at Story, and she smiled back.

Her younger siblings were so predictable; they always dove head first into any new thing.

"Story? Hello... Anyone home?" Josh was standing before her, waving a hand in front of her face.

Startled, she shook her head to clear away the lingering memory. "Yeah, sorry. Just making sure I didn't forget anything." Then, switching on her headlamp, she plunged into the darkness.

THE TUNNEL WAS TOO NARROW FOR THEM TO WALK SIDE BY SIDE. When she looked back to check on Josh, she saw he had to stoop slightly so that he wouldn't scrape his head.

"Don't worry, it gets bigger in a couple minutes."

"I hope so. I think I'm getting a crick in my neck." Josh's voice sounded strained. "So, what you said back there, about hating the kids who trashed the entry way to the cave."

"Yeah?" Story felt her blood boil as she remembered the scattered beer bottles and the graffiti-covered walls they'd come across before entering this tunnel.

"Well, that's pretty rich, coming from you."

"What? How?" Surprise tinged her voice. "I've never vandalized anything in my life!"

"I bet Sandy would disagree with you."

Story bit her lower lip. "Oh. That..."

"Yeah, that."

Story was standing patiently in line to pay for her bagel and cream cheese at the cafeteria. Sandy Wright was standing in front of her, carrying on a loud argument on her phone. It was impossible to ignore what she was saying.

"Seriously, Dad, you're such an idiot sometimes. I've already explained this to you like a million times—"

Story ripped the phone out of Sandy's hands and threw it against the wall so hard it made a cracking sound and broke in two. Then she calmly walked away, eating her stolen bagel and feeling better than she had in a long while. Sandy's shrieks in the background had been the icing on the cake. Or rather, the chocolate chip in her cookie—she'd never been a fan of cake.

A smile crept across her face at the memory. "You know what? I think you're right. But I'd do it again in a heartbeat."

"I know. That's what worries me."

The tunnel they'd been working their way down abruptly widened, and Josh let out a loud sigh of relief. "Finally!"

"Dude, we were only walking for like five minutes." Story raised an eyebrow at him. "Does Coach McKnight know his star linebacker is this out of shape?"

"Shut up."

"I'm sooooo telling…"

"I'm not out of shape! That ceiling was just low and stuff. Shut up." Josh tried to stalk off down the tunnel, but Story grabbed his arm and yanked him back before he could take a step. Toe to toe, they faced each other in the dark, the soft glow of their headlamps illuminating their faces. She could see a spark of hope in Josh's eyes—hope that maybe she'd dragged him all the way down here to rekindle things. For a fleeting moment, she almost gave in. It would be so easy, so very easy to do it, to be with Josh like that again. To let him try to fill the void in her heart.

But even as she thought it, she knew it wouldn't be enough. Unable to hold his gaze any longer, she dropped her eyes and stared at the olive skin of her own hand and how it contrasted with the freckled, creamy surface of Josh's biceps where she still clung. As the ache in her chest grew, she wished again for the time when life was simpler: when he was all that she needed. All she had to offer him now was the occasional friendship of an angry and bitter girl. Yet he stuck with her, either out of loyalty or misplaced affection, or maybe both.

Story stood up on her toes and kissed his cheek. "Thank you."

She turned away from him before he could ask her what for and before she could see the hurt in his eyes at being rejected by her once again. Story angled her headlamp down to illuminate the floor near their feet. "Next time, before you go charging off, remember this is a cave. We're spelunking. Always look down before you step."

Josh looked at their feet and immediately scrambled away from the craggy, wide-mouthed hole he'd nearly stepped through. He pressed himself against the wall, breathing quickly.

"Holy crap! They should put up warning signs. That's dangerous!"

Story snickered. "That's half the fun! Besides, it's a cave. What'd you expect? Well-lit paths? Guardrails? How about a tour guide and a refreshment stand?"

"Ha-ha." Josh peeled the upper half of his body from the wall and cautiously peered over the edge into the darkness below.

"There's a ledge about a foot wide along the left side of the hole that leads to another tunnel. There are some gorgeous rock formations down that way, and it eventually leads to the underground river I was telling you about before." *The river where my parents met.* A hazy image of a flighty, ethereally beautiful woman began to surface, and Story frowned, refusing to think about her mother. *My mother who left me when I was just a baby.* She felt her cheeks flush with the heat of her anger, and she pressed her sea-green eyes closed. *Sea-green eyes, just like my mother's.* Banishing the memory with a sigh, she opened her eyes and pointed out a tall, narrow tunnel that was slanted on a leftward angle, on the opposite side of the sinkhole about ten feet away.

"Um...I don't think..." Josh's voice cracked.

Story gave him a sidelong glance. "Don't worry, we're going a different way."

"I'm heartbroken."

She smirked and shrugged off her pack. "We're going down."

"I was afraid you were going to say that."

THE SINKHOLE WASN'T AS DIRE AS STORY LED JOSH TO BELIEVE. Roughly six feet deep and bowl shaped, it had craggy, pock marked walls that provided ample hand and foot holds for climbing. The twins had named this part of the cave the 'Toilet Bowl,' because of the tunnel that Story and Josh currently found themselves crawling through. It shot off the bowl at a downward angle, leading the twins to call it the u-bend.

When Story's hand dropped down into nothingness, she quickly stopped and felt Josh run into her backside. She looked over her shoulder in time to see his face turn almost as red as his hair.

"Uh, sorry. Didn't realize..."

She didn't say anything—to avoid embarrassing him more—and hopped down out of the tunnel. She let her gaze sweep the length of the massive cavern. Roughly the size of a basketball court, it was littered with holes, fissures, and crevices that led off into countless other caverns. She'd always found this part of the caves stunningly beautiful, due to the abundance of stalactite and stalagmite formations. Some had grown close enough together over the ages that they formed a beautiful pillar, narrowed at the center like an hourglass. She could hear the drip-drip-drip of water droplets around the room working ceaselessly for millennia to create these wonders.

"Whoa." Josh's voice interrupted the timeless symphony of water droplets, inadequately summing up the natural beauty around them.

Story turned to the right side of the cave and began navigating around the columns toward the far wall. There was a tiny fissure back there that she'd discovered as child. It was the only place in the caves her father had gotten upset about when she tried to explore. In fact, he'd expressly forbidden her from entering it, saying only that it was "dangerous."

Behind her, she heard Josh curse under his breath as he stumbled. When he finally caught up to her, she pointed at an unremarkable rock face in front of them with a few stones jutting out from the base.

"So what? It's a wall—am I missing something?"

"Looks like it, doesn't it?" She walked forward toward one of the bigger rock outcroppings and removed her pack. "But looks can be deceiving." She flashed him a mischievous grin over her shoulder and slipped into the shadows.

The sharp intake of breath she heard from Josh confirmed what she knew would happen. To him, it would look like she'd disappeared right before his eyes. In reality, it was just a trick of the light. Hidden in the shadows of the outcropping was a wide, horizontal slit in the cave wall that Story had pressed her body into. Built slim like her father, she was able to fit with minimal effort. It was only three feet or so deep, so she quickly slid to the other side of the fissure, into the cave beyond.

"Story? STORY?" Josh's voice was panicked, and he clutched her abandoned pack in his hands as his eyes searched vainly for her in the shadows before him.

Crouched down on her side of the fissure, she

contemplated remaining silent just to mess with him a bit more, but he was getting upset.

"Hey, quit freaking out. I'm right here." She pulled her headlamp off and flashed the light at him.

His face popped into view on the other side of the crevice; his mouth had flattened to a thin line. "Not cool, Story. Not cool. How about a little warning next time?"

"Well, that wouldn't be nearly as fun, would it?"

"I'm serious." Josh looked left, then right, eyeing the length and width of the fissure. "Also, there is absolutely no way I will ever fit through this."

"That's fine. I just want to look around a bit in here anyway." Story's legs were starting to cramp from being crouched for so long.

"I don't think that's such a good idea—you going off on your own."

Story rolled her eyes. *Great, now he sounds like Dad.* "Just pass me my pack. I'll be back in a few minutes."

For a few moments there was only silence from the other side. Then Josh grumbled something that sounded like "Fine, have it your way," and started shoving her pack through the crevice.

She felt the prickling sensation of her leg falling asleep, so she stood up to shake it out. Time seemed to slow as two things happened: She cracked her head on the ceiling or a stalactite—she wasn't sure which—and lost her balance. She felt herself fall forward as her feet slipped out from under her, and she threw her arms out to break her fall.

What she hadn't realized before was that she'd been standing on the smooth edge of a precipice. Before she had time to process what was happening, her feet, followed by her legs, slipped over the edge and down into the chasm beneath her. Her chest slammed against the lip of the opening, knocking the wind out of her.

"Josh!" she gasped out. She tried to brace her legs against the wall and push herself back up, but there was only open space beneath her. She felt the weight of her body begin to pull her down into the dark maw below.

"JOSH! Help me!"

She could hear Josh grunting as he tried to wedge his too-large frame into the crevice. "Story, hang on! I'm coming!" His voice was wild with panic, but it didn't even come close to matching the terror Story felt. Her father wasn't coming to save her; Josh couldn't save her; no one could save her but herself.

She clawed frantically at the dusty cave floor with her hands, but it only made her slide down faster.

In that last moment, as Story was clinging to the edge with just her fingertips, she realized something: she was a terrible person. She had no friends anymore because she'd driven them all away. She'd been rude and spiteful to everyone and angry at the world for the unfairness of life and death and everything in between. She'd spent this entire trip behaving horribly to the one person who'd stuck by her through the worst year of her life. Truly, Josh was her last friend in this world. The knowledge washed over her, calming her, as if admitting the truth to herself had lifted a burden she didn't know she was carrying.

"Josh?" Her voice was quiet now, calm.

"Story, just hang on a little longer—I'm going to throw you the rope!"

She heard the zipper on her bag being ripped open.

"Josh, I'm sorry."

Story's grip gave out, and she plummeted into the inky darkness below.

Chapter Two

Monsters

STORY WOKE TO THE SOUND OF THE MOST BEAUTIFUL MUSIC SHE'D ever heard. It was faint and far away, but loud enough that she could make out the melody. All around her, the woods were lit up by fireflies of different sizes, all flying off toward the music.

No, not fireflies—Faeries! Story realized as one flew past her nose.

There was no mistaking the tiny human-like form, as another one landed on her outstretched hand. It was no bigger than her finger, with delicate dragonfly wings fluttering on its back. The faeries were just like the ones from her childhood dreams, only wilder and somehow all the more real for it.

Clapping her hands with delight, she sprang to her feet and chased after the faeries, deeper into the woods toward the entrancing music. The closer she got, the more familiar the melody sounded—almost as if she should know it or had known it at one point and forgotten.

The faeries were flying in time to the music; swirling around her, beckoning her to join them in their dance. Laughing, she threw her hands in the air, swaying and twirling with the faeries. There was no fear of running into trees or losing her path; her feet knew the way, and the faeries helped guide her steps. The music coursed through her blood, and her body tingled with magic, all the way down to her toes.

The trees ended abruptly, and there in the middle of a round clearing, bathed in moonlight, sat a boy playing a gold violin. He was perched regally atop a large, flat, moss-covered stone. She guessed he was roughly her age, though his face seemed almost timeless. Barefoot, he was dressed simply in a short, green kilt that looked as organic and untamed as he did. Bits of vines and leaves and flowers wound around his body, as if he was a physical manifestation of nature itself. His skin had a faint golden hue that shimmered in the moonlight, as did his matching golden blonde hair. He was so lovely that Story felt as though she would cry if she ever had to look away.

The faeries had all gathered around him and were flying and dancing about, even more wildly than before. The music coming from the beautiful, golden violin increased in tempo and volume, building until it was so loud that Story had to cover her ears. At the final crescendo, he looked up and they locked eyes for what seemed like an eternity but could only have been a second.

Then the music came to a crashing halt, and Story woke up.

She groaned. Every muscle in her body felt like a thousand tiny needles had been shoved into them, and even the thought of moving was painful. As the dream faded, she remembered her fall down the cave shaft. She didn't know how long she had been lying there, or how injured she was. Her back might be broken, and she was at the bottom of a long shaft where it would be extremely difficult for anyone to get to her. She felt her pulse quicken, and darkness seemed to close in on her as she realized the seriousness of her situation.

She would surely be dead long before anyone ever arrived. *If* anyone ever arrived. She wasn't even sure Josh would be able to find the crevice again much less go through it. No, she couldn't wait around for a rescue.

Steeling herself, she slowly opened her eyes, wincing at the shooting pain she felt all the way from her neck to her toes.

That's actually some good news, she thought with a grimace. *If I can feel my toes, it probably means my back isn't broken.*

The bottom of the shaft was faintly illuminated, and looking up, Story could see she'd fallen a very long way. So far, in fact, that she couldn't see up to the top of the hole; it disappeared into pitch-black nothingness.

"Josh!" Yelling hurt a whole lot more than she thought it would. She paused a moment to catch her breath and tried to ignore the ache in her ribs when she called out again. "Josh! Can you hear me?"

There was no response.

Either she was so far down he couldn't hear her, or he'd left to get help. One thing was certain; she wasn't getting back out the way she'd come in.

She carefully turned her head side to side, ignoring the throbbing it caused, and looked around. Light shone from a small opening several feet above her head. It looked wide enough for her to squirm through without much trouble.

That's assuming I can actually stand.

Gritting her teeth against the inevitable pain, Story rolled onto her side and gasped. She felt like she'd been kicked repeatedly in the stomach—no, worse—like her ribs were being squeezed tightly in a vise. Grunting with the effort, she rolled over onto her knees, placed a trembling hand on the wall for support, and then shakily pushed herself up to stand.

The sudden rush of blood away from her head caused her vision to tunnel, and she nearly blacked out again. With a low moan, she leaned heavily against the wall for support. She stood there slowly breathing in and out, letting her body recover and get used to standing again. Looking at the grit and grime that coated what she could see of her body, she half-smiled. *If only the twins could see me now.*

Story stood a little straighter, wincing as her back protested the movement. She was definitely going to have bruises. Lots of bruises. She ran careful hands over her body, ignoring the shots of pain, and felt the tears that peppered her sweat-shirt along the front and back. Dust caked the inside of her mouth, and she regretted leaving her daypack behind; she'd give a lot for some water right about now. Her eyes flicked back up toward the shaft she'd fallen down, and she marveled that she'd survived, relatively unscathed at that.

Keeping her head still to avoid getting dizzy again, she moved her eyes around the space, looking for an exit other than the hole she'd have to wriggle through. About ten feet away, on the opposite wall, there was some sort of writing. Story sighed; it was probably more graffiti from the vandals in the main cavern. What could be so important that someone needed to deface nature to say it? Probably "John loves Maggie" or something else just as trivial.

Deciding to get a closer look, Story took a hesitant step forward. When she didn't collapse, she released her hold on the cool surface behind her and took another step, and then another, until she was directly in front of the wall.

With soft moonlight shining directly onto the surface before her, she could see that she'd been completely wrong. This was no simple act of vandalism; it was a mural of sorts.

It was either very old or had been made to look so: the colors were worn and faded. In the center of the mural was a simply drawn tree that resembled a cherry tree in shape, but the blossoms on it, instead of being pink, were vivid silver. In fact, the silver was the only bit of color that hadn't faded with time. The mural depicted the silver leaves falling off the tree onto the bodies of people lying beneath it. She couldn't tell if the bodies were supposed to be alive or dead. Hardly aware of her movement, Story reached out and brushed the trunk of the tree with her fingertips. As she traced the lines of the branches, she felt a connection with the tree. Somehow, she could understand it. The tree was grieving, weeping for the fallen.

And just like me, it couldn't save the ones it loved.

Tears pricked her eyes, and her chest felt like it was back in the vise again, only this time the emotional pain was far worse than the physical pain. She literally felt as though she couldn't breathe. Memories were overwhelming her. She was feeling things that she didn't want to feel—things she'd spent the last few months running away from.

Closing her eyes, she backed away from the mural carefully, forcing herself to breathe in and out with every step. And then for no reason, all pretense of calm evaporated. She whirled on her heel and moved as quickly as her wobbly legs would take her, back to the crevice that would lead her out of the cave and away from the emotions pulsing through her.

Looking up through the crack, she wanted to scream in frustration. She could see stars outside, she could feel the cool night air against her face, but she knew there was no way she could pull herself up into and then through the opening in her current condition. She was barely able to skim the edge of the crevice with her fingertips, and the wall was perfectly smooth with no finger or toeholds. It may as well have been twenty feet up for all the good it did her.

She closed her eyes and leaned her forehead against the wall. Behaving recklessly had seemed like a perfectly good idea a few hours ago. Now, she could almost hear her father chastising her, his Smoky Mountain accent coming out thick. *"What the heck were you thinkin', kiddo? Goin' into a strange cave alone, where nobody could follow you? I warned you to stay outta there! I warned you."*

She felt her cheeks flush with shame and anger at her stupidity, and before she could stop herself, she kicked the wall. Her howl of frustration changed immediately into a scream as a jolt of pain coursed up her leg to her spine. A curse word she rarely used—and never in front of her father—died on her lips as she noticed she'd left a fist-sized indention where she'd kicked the wall with her hiking boots. That shouldn't have been possible; she wasn't strong enough to pull herself up and out of the hole right now, much less make a dent in a stone wall.

Bending down to inspect it more closely, she ran her fingers over the crumbling edge of the hollow.

It's not rock at all!

It was firmly packed dirt that had broken away when she kicked it. Story felt a sudden surge of hope. She could cut away toeholds, and with the combined strength of her arms and legs, she should be able to free herself from her prison.

She unsheathed her knife, relieved to see it had survived the fall unscathed. In hindsight, she realized she was lucky she hadn't landed on it.

Blowing out a breath, Story bent over and used the blade to scrape away two small footholds. Once she was finished, she knelt down to unlace her boots and tossed them, along with her socks, through the crack. She'd put them back on once she got out, but right now she needed the traction that only bare feet could provide. She rolled up the hem of her jeans a few times to ensure her feet were free; the last thing she needed was for them to get tangled. She gripped the edge of the hole and positioned the ball of her right foot in the small opening she'd dug. Steeling herself, she took a deep and painful breath and heaved with all her strength.

Her entire body protested, and her back burned like it was being dragged across a bed of coals, but she didn't let go. She knew if she gave up now she'd never get out. She felt hot tears stream down her face as she pulled with her arms and pushed with her legs through the fiery agony, until, crying out in triumph, she was free.

Story barely had time to register her escape before the pain racking her body was too much and she lost consciousness again.

A PIERCING SCREAM JOLTED STORY AWAKE. HER EYES FLEW OPEN, and she was momentarily blinded by the bright sunlight as she sprang to her feet, hands held before her in defense. Adrenaline coursed through her, wiping away any pain her body felt.

Josh!

The yell sounded again to her left, and now that she saw nothing was attacking her, she took off running into the woods, pursuing the sound. She held her hands in front of her face, afraid of losing an eye to the branches that whipped at her as she ran. The cry abruptly ended, and she poured on speed. Lances of pain shot through the tender pads of her feet when she landed on a sharp rock or stick, but she didn't care. Josh—*or it could be someone else,* she realized belatedly—was in trouble and needed her help.

About four hundred meters later, Story ran through the tree line into a perfectly round clearing. It had to be manmade;

nothing in nature was a perfect circle. She scanned the clearing looking for the person who had been screaming but saw only a crumbling ruin of a building and a few thin tree stumps, about two feet tall, on the far side of the circle.

They must be in those ruins.

She crept closer to the decaying edifice. Broken bits of marble littered the ground, and one silvery white marble column leaned precariously against another. It reminded her a bit of an old Greek temple, only smaller. If it had once had a roof, it was long gone now. All that remained was the carving of a tree, like the one she'd seen in the cave, at the top of each column.

Her head snapped in the direction of another shout. It had come from the opposite side of the clearing, where the stumps were. Instinctively gripping the hilt of her knife, she quietly made her way to the edge of the ruin and peered around slowly.

A young man—not Josh—was bound and gagged at the base of a tree, surrounded by the three tree stumps, one of which suddenly rose up on two knobby legs. Story stifled a gasp as she realized the stumps were living creatures. Looking more closely, she could see that they had two arms that reached nearly to the ground with dozens of long, branch-like fingers.

As she watched, one of the stumps flung a rock at the man, striking him in the chest with a force she would not have believed could come from a creature so small. She heard another muffled cry of pain; the man curled into a fetal position while the tree stumps doubled over with insane laughter, their alien cackles sounding like an icy wind slicing through a hollow log.

Horror rolled over Story as she realized the creatures were just toying with him.

They had to have broken at least one of his ribs!

She grabbed blindly at the rubble near her feet and ran toward the stumps.

"Hey!" she shouted, heaving a rock at the man's three tormentors. "Leave him alone!"

In unison, three sets of burning, yellow eyes immediately opened on the backsides of the little monsters. They hadn't even turned around! They eyed her for a moment, as if sizing up their prey, and then, again in perfect unison, identical smiles split across their wooden faces. They remained there, unmoving and staring. She felt locked in their gaze, as if they were hypnotizing her into staying still. Then suddenly they were rushing toward her, cruel smiles still in place and rocks held at the ready.

"Uh-oh..."

She hastily threw the last of her rocks at her attackers. The monsters avoided them easily. Out of ammunition, she reached for her knife, frantically grappling with the strap that kept it in its holster. It wouldn't budge, and her shaking fingers weren't helping the situation. The creatures were moving with impossible speed, chattering shrilly at each other, and leering maliciously at her.

Story backed away as fast as she could, still fumbling with the strap on her knife. Then suddenly, she was flat on her back, the wind knocked out of her. She'd tripped on a jagged piece of marble half buried in the soil.

"Ouch!" A thrown rock grazed her shoulder.

They were nearly upon her now, so close she could make out the individual bark patterns in their skin—or hide—or whatever it was. She scrambled away, scooting along the ground on her backside like a scuttling crab, and they paused in their pursuit. Eyes burning, they stared down at her, and she thought—no, she hoped—that they'd decided to leave her alone.

That hope vanished when she saw the bark on their upper halves spilt into unnatural grins, and with the speed and ferocity of a pack of lions, they bore down on her once again.

CHAPTER THREE

THE COMPASS

STORY REACHED AGAIN FOR HER KNIFE AND FOUND THAT THE
holster's snap had been knocked open in her fall.

"Get away from me!" Fingers shaking, Story pulled out
her knife and waved it wildly in front of her.

The monsters stopped instantly. Shrieking and recoiling
as if they'd been burned, they dropped their remaining rocks
and backed away from her, melting into the forest like wraiths.

Still on her back, her shaking hand outstretched toward
her vanished attackers, Story scanned the tree line looking for
any signs of movement. She could feel her heart pounding in
her chest, and her mind was trying to catch up and process
whatever it was that she'd just seen.

"Ok, that was weird," she murmured. They were definitely not human, nor any animal she'd ever seen or heard of,
but they were clearly intelligent—she'd seen it in their eyes.
They'd wanted to hurt her, to cause her pain. Not to hunt her

for food or to defend themselves, but hurt her purely for enjoyment—just as they'd done with the guy they'd been torturing before she arrived.

The tied up guy!

Cautiously, Story got to her feet, her knife hand still extended. She brushed herself off with her free hand, all the while keeping a wary eye out for the return of the monsters.

Finally satisfied that they were gone—at least for the moment—she made her way over to the bound man. He was staring at her as if he was unsure what to make of her. She couldn't blame him for looking at her strangely; her clothes were torn up, she was caked in dirt, her feet were bare, and her hair was sticking out crazily everywhere. Overall, not her best look.

He's one to judge. She raised an eyebrow as she examined his appearance; he looked weirder than she did! He was dressed as though he'd just come from a Renaissance Festival. He had on suede boots wrapped up to his knees, brown leggings, and a dark green, sleeveless tunic that left his arms bare, showing off the intricate tribal tattoos that snaked up his left arm.

Story knelt before him to cut the silver-colored ropes that dug into his skin, and she saw his gaze shift to the knife. As she placed the blade against his bindings, they simply fell away, like butter being cut with a hot knife.

The man's eyes grew wide, and Story gaped at her father's old knife. She hadn't thought it was all that sharp. She felt more than heard the man jump to his feet. He backed away from her, never taking his eyes off the knife.

"Wow, that must have been some pretty weak rope to just fall apart like that. I barely even touched it." Story found herself laughing nervously and snapped her mouth shut. She had a tendency to babble when she was in awkward situations.

The man spat the gag out, and it landed with a wet thud on the ground.

"That was faerie rope. Nothing should've been able to cut through it. Nothing but iron that is."

At the sound of his voice, Story jerked her eyes away from her knife to look at him. He was staring at her, eyes narrowed, as if he was evaluating her. He had a strange accent—like a thick Irish brogue, but stronger than anything she'd ever heard in any movie. It lilted and rolled, and she almost didn't understand what he'd said.

Is he even speaking English? The thought made her smile as she swept her gaze over him; she was sure her vanilla American accent, born from years of constantly moving around the country, was just as strange sounding to his ears; unless his accent was just affected, to go along with his costume.

His build leaned more toward the stocky side, and his broad sculpted shoulders and neck showed that he spent at least a little time in the gym. His skin was a few shades darker than Story's, and she wondered if it was natural or if he spent a lot of time in the sun. Either way, his skin tone contrasted nicely with his raven black hair, cut short in a military crew cut. Overall, had it not been for the scowl on his face, Story would have thought him quite attractive.

Since he was around her height, she met his gaze easily. His eyes startled her at first: they were a beautiful, dark silver color that she'd never seen on a person before, at least not naturally. She knew they made contact lenses for every color of the rainbow these days, but his didn't look like contacts.

Suddenly aware she was staring, Story looked down and sheathed her knife while she answered him. "Yeah, well, I suppose you're lucky my old knife is made out of iron; the new models are all composite material and have a graphite coating—wait a sec; did you say *faerie* rope?" She looked back at him, one eyebrow raised in confusion.

Ignoring her, he bent over his kit and rifled through it taking inventory of his things, as if he was afraid they wouldn't all be there. She watched his muscled arms as they moved around in the pack. Her eyes followed the lines of the thick, black tattoos as they snaked their way up his left arm starting at his index finger, up around his forearm, biceps, triceps, shoulder, and disappeared into his tunic. They reappeared at his collar, thinner and more delicate, as they spiraled up his neck and eventually joined with an equally intricate, tribal-looking tattoo that encompassed his left eyelid and the cheek below it. The bit around his eye and cheek looked like it had ancient Egyptian influences. She followed the lines of the tattoo back as it wrapped itself up behind his ear.

His delicately pointed ear.

Story blinked twice and shook her head to clear it, but no, his ears—yes, both of them—still came to small but pronounced points. Either this guy was really good with prosthetics and latex, or he had a strange genetic mutation she'd never seen before. Or he was *really* crazy and had them surgically altered.

She knew she was staring again, but she didn't care. He didn't seem to either; he was so absorbed in his task—or just plain rude—he didn't even bother to look up at her when he finally answered.

"Aye, that I did."

Oh right, the faerie rope, Story belatedly remembered the thread of their conversation. She was still hung up on his ears.

He continued on, still looking away. "Though I would have thought that last bit was obvious, given what you saw when you showed up for your elegant *rescue*." Disdain coated his last few words, as he lifted his pack over his shoulders, placing it alongside a quiver full of arrows. He picked up his bow with his left hand and frowned at her. "I'll just be off now."

Momentarily shocked into silence, Story just stood there with her mouth hanging open while he walked across the clearing back to whatever Renn Faire he had come from. She cocked her head to one side, watching him in disbelief, and then hurried after him.

"Wait a minute! I saved you from the stump monster squad and that's all the thanks I get?"

He spun around to face her, meeting her nose to nose, his silver eyes momentarily darkening.

"I'll have you know I had the situation well in hand. I didn't need your meddling. Thanks, but no thanks."

He turned back around and kept walking. Story's hands clenched into fists at her side, and she pressed her mouth into a thin line, fighting the desire to scream. She didn't know where she was and needed at least a general direction to the nearest road so she could get back to her Jeep and Josh.

Josh! He must think I'm dead by now!

Sighing, she followed after the man again.

"Yeah, look, whatever your name is, you *sure* looked like you had the situation under control. I'll bet any minute you were going to magic yourself out of those ropes and scare away those freaky little tree stump things."

He didn't even acknowledge her, though she could see the back of his neck begin to darken, like he was blushing from embarrassment. Only instead of turning red, his skin took on a dark, silvery-bluish hue.

Okay, that's weird.

But she'd seen weird on this trip already, and rather than get freaked out by it, she just got more annoyed; at this point, she just wanted to find a phone, get back to her house, and get a shower. Rolling her eyes in annoyance, she reached out a hand to stop him. Her fingers barely brushed his tattooed biceps, when suddenly he had her wrist firmly locked and bent painfully back in his hand.

"Ow! Ow! Ow! You win! Let go!" She wriggled in his grasp, trying to use the technique her dad taught her—always go for the thumb, it was the weak spot—but it was like trying to bend iron.

"Why are you following me? What do you want?" Open hostility crossed his features.

"Let go of me first!" Story yanked again and on her second tug he let her go. She found herself flat on her back. Standing up warily, she brushed herself off; this was starting to become a pattern around this guy.

"Jeez, what is your problem?"

He didn't reply, but glared at her, his silver eyes flashing.

Swallowing her pride, because she really did need help, she took a deep breath. "I'm a little lost. I fell down a cave shaft and hit my head pretty hard. I'm just trying to find a way back to my Jeep so that I can get off this mountain. Do you have a phone I could borrow, or do you know of a nearby town where I could get my bearings? I don't really recognize this part of the mountain."

The man stared at her for a moment as if trying to determine her truthfulness.

"I don't have a 'phone' or whatever it is you said." He pointed back the way they had come. "There's a path along the river at the bottom of the valley that leads to a village, a few days back that way. A week at least, if you're as slow as a gnome," he paused, and his eyes moved slowly over her form. "And by the looks of it you are."

Story looked back the way he'd been pointing and could just make out a faint path between the trees leading down the slope of the mountain to a river she could hear below. But a week away? If she was as slow as a gnome? Did he mean those little garden statues with the odd, conical, red hats? Confused, she turned to ask what he'd meant, but found she was alone. He'd slipped off silently into the forest without so much as a thank you.

"Ungrateful jerk!" she yelled toward the trees. She remembered her compass and dug it out of her pocket. She wasn't going anywhere until she knew she could get back here if she needed to. She eyed the bulky, metal compass and was unsurprised to see that it appeared perfectly intact. These old things could probably survive a nuclear blast.

Story walked back to the center of the circular clearing, where she could get a better view of the sun's location. She had never been more grateful that her dad had taken her and the twins camping and bow hunting while they were growing up. Having spent all of his adult life in the Marine Corps, her dad had naturally imparted his wisdom and training on map reading, land navigation with a lensatic compass, and basic survival skills to his children. While Story was barely passable with a hunting bow, she'd taken to the compass and the outdoors like a fish to water, much to her dad's pleasure. In fact, swimming was probably the only thing she did better than land nav.

She wasn't a "survivalist" by any stretch of the imagination, but her dad had made sure that if she ever got lost or stranded in the wilderness, she could spend a night without starving or freezing and eventually be able to find her way out.

He'd tried to teach the twins as well, but they always seemed more interested in starting fires or shooting at targets with their bows. They never had the patience for "boring" subjects that involved math, the way land navigation did.

"Can you shoot things with a compass?" Will had demanded.

"Well no, but—" Story tried to explain.

"*Can you kill anything with a compass?*" Katie interrupted.

"*Again no, but that's hardly the point —*"

"*And most importantly,*" Will said, striking a heroic pose with his bow, "*does a compass look half as cool as this when you hold it?*"

At the time, Story couldn't argue with their logic and had to concede defeat, which was usually the case with the twins. But now she was very glad that she'd mastered the skill of land nav; she didn't think a bow would help her find her way back to her Jeep, no matter how "cool" she looked while carrying it.

She oriented the compass's needle to the north, and then, nearly dropping it, she gasped in surprise.

The sun was rising in the south.

That's impossible!

Her mind immediately rejected the idea, and she looked at her compass once again, shaking it for good measure. Just as before, the needle pointed directly away from the rising sun. She brought the compass near her eyes and turned it around and around, carefully inspecting it for any sort of break or flaw. There were none that she could see—the bevel ring, glass, and case were all intact. The sun was apparently rising in the south this morning.

Story could only think of two reasons for such an occurrence. Either the world's magnetic poles had shifted while she was unconscious, or she was somehow no longer *in* her world.

She wasn't too fond of either possibility.

Chapter Four

Lost

STORY HAD BEEN WALKING ALONG THE PATH FOR HOURS, BUT hadn't made much progress on her bare feet. The ground was soft enough, but it wasn't the same as having shoes; she had to keep looking where she was stepping in order to keep her feet from getting cut and bruised.

"I'm going to kill whoever stole my boots." Story winced from the pain of stepping on yet another sharp rock. She'd returned to the cave entrance—after getting over the initial shock of seeing the southern sunrise—to retrieve her shoes and socks. They weren't there. They weren't anywhere.

She was certain she'd tossed them outside the cave before climbing out last night, even though she had hit her head pretty hard in her fall and had been very focused on just getting out of her former prison at the time. Nonetheless, Story had peered inside the fissure to check and saw nothing but rocks and dirt. Annoyed, she'd searched the area outside the cavern's opening once again and then slowly walked around the small clearing.

No boots. No socks.

It was as if they'd simply disappeared. That, or someone had stolen them, which meant that now she had to hike off the mountain in bare feet. Though, if worse came to worst, she'd figured she could tear her tattered hoodie into strips and wrap her feet with them.

That was no longer an option. Either she was a lot higher up in the mountains than she'd originally thought, or a freak cold spell had blown in. It no longer felt like the end of summer but instead, based on the new growth she saw everywhere, the height of spring. She shivered as a breeze whistled through the trees, very thankful that, torn up or not, she still had her sweatshirt wrapped around her body instead of her feet. The sun was starting to set—in the north, according to her compass—and Story, cold and exhausted, stopped next to the river and bent down to get a drink.

Immediately following her encounter with the pointy-eared jerk, she'd been too full of adrenaline and irritation to really get a good look around, but after calming down a bit, she was finally able to take in her surroundings. She was in the middle of a stunningly beautiful forest that didn't look like anything back home in the Smoky Mountains. Her breath had caught in her throat as she viewed the softly waving ferns covering the forest floor and the graceful curves of the thin, black tree trunks that soared overhead. Glittering dust motes sparkled around her, floating lazily in the green-tinted sunlight that filtered through the emerald leaves of the forest canopy.

It was breathtaking.

At least it was at first. Eventually her growing thirst, sore feet, and empty stomach had dimmed even the ethereal beauty of this untouched wilderness. A wild fruit orchard had solved her hunger problem; she'd gorged herself on a tasty variety of peach or nectarine she'd never had before. They were sweet and delicious, but after the first half-dozen they were no longer such a treat, just fuel to keep her legs moving.

Her thirst had been slaked by the river she was drinking from now. Sitting back on her haunches, Story scrubbed the cold mountain water over her dirt-streaked face and hands. She pointedly ignored the state of her hair, which was an untamable mess, much like the state of her mind. Questions swirled through her thoughts. What were those things that had attacked her? Why had they left when she pulled out her father's knife? Why did the sun rise in the south? And why hadn't she seen so much as one airplane fly overhead?

Shifting from her knees to a seated position, Story dipped her bare feet in the chilly river to soak them a bit and ease the soreness. Despite the cold, she had half a mind to slip all the way in; she always felt better in the water. She kicked her feet lazily in the current and lay back against the sweet grass lining the soft bank, taking in the view of the river. It was roughly twenty feet wide and swift enough that it cut a deep furrow, leaving an embankment on either side. Rocks, boulders, and the occasional fallen tree peppered the riverbed.

She gave a half-smile. *The twins would've loved tubing down this river.*

Story could see their escapades clearly in her mind's eye: Will, all long, gangly limbs, would barely fit in his tube, constantly threatening to tip over, and Katie would be doing everything in her power to ensure that happened. But everyone knew that it would be Story who ended up capsized in the mountain water, courtesy of the twins double-teaming her. But it wouldn't matter; she had always been the best swimmer on her school team, so she did just fine. The twins had always marveled at how long she could hold her breath—far longer than a normal person could. But to Story, staying underwater for long periods of time came as naturally as... well, breathing.

She shook her head, letting go of the half-formed memories. She'd rested and daydreamed enough; time to get going. Looking around, she caught sight of a bridge a short way down the river that she'd somehow missed before.

Finally, a bit of luck!

Where there was a bridge, there was sure to be a road, and roads led to civilization. She was on her feet and jogging toward the bridge before the thought had even fully formed in her mind. Her dad would probably be harping at her for running while she was still weak and potentially injured from her fall, but that was Story's way of doing things. She never walked anywhere when she could run. Her dad always used to say she was the most impatient person he knew. Story thought she just used her time more efficiently than most.

As she neared the bridge, she realized it was not the modern concrete structure she was expecting. Instead, it was built out of a white marble-like stone with silver grain lines; it looked ancient. Her run slowed to a walk as she got closer and could make out more details.

The years had not been kind to the bridge.

Rubble was strewn across the ground: bits and pieces of marble that had obviously once been part of the bridge. The wind and rain had worn down the carvings adorning the end posts, and there were no longer any sharp edges anywhere. Examining one of the marble posts, Story thought she could just make out the outline of a tree similar to the one she'd seen painted on the wall of the cave and on the ruins where she'd encountered the monsters. She traced a finger along the faint lines of the tree and was suddenly overtaken by a wave of deep and lingering sadness.

She stared at the faint carving of the tree for one moment

more, and then tore her eyes away. She forced herself to step onto the bridge and walk across. Since nothing on her side of the river had indicated civilization, she figured following the path to wherever it led—hopefully the small town the rude guy had mentioned, or at the very least a hunter's cabin—would be better than retracing her steps back to her prison-cave.

Once on the other side, Story alternated between walking and jogging for a couple of hours, conscious of the rapidly setting sun. The trail was very narrow, and at times she nearly lost sight of it. She knew she wouldn't be able to walk safely at night, so she kept a lookout for a promising place to camp. The forest was much the same everywhere, but she eventually spotted a close-growing copse of trees that would provide some protection from the elements. Deciding that this was as good a campsite as any, she began collecting firewood. She had no matches, but her compass had a bit of flint on the cover, and by scraping her knife against it, she should have been able to spark a flame. *Should have* being the key words. It started to rain, softly at first, but then with increasing intensity.

After almost half an hour and numerous futile attempts to light wet wood, it was nearly full dark, and Story finally had to stop for fear of cutting off one of her fingers with her knife. The forest that had seemed so beautiful earlier that day was no longer so charming. The oppressive canopy loomed over her, blocking out even the starlight, and it was eerily quiet. No birds, no insects; just Story, the trees, the river, the miserable falling rain, and the terrifying feeling that she was being watched by those tree-bark monsters.

Logically, Story knew that last bit had to do with the creepiness of her surroundings and the aftermath of the day's events, but the knowledge did nothing to lessen the sensation. Even the twins would have had enough "adventure" by now and be begging for their safe, warm beds.

The enormity of the events of the last two days and her own helplessness came crashing down on her like a massive ocean wave. She screamed aloud in frustration—though she stopped herself just before she kicked at a tree. She was still barefoot after all, and breaking a toe while she was lost and alone in the woods would not be smart. Instead, she sat at the base of the tree, hoping for some protection from the cold rain, and did something she hadn't done since she was a little girl: Story buried her face in her arms and cried until exhaustion dragged her into sleep.

Chapter Five

The Elf

Story once again woke to the sound of the haunting melody from the previous evening. Just as before, the woods around her were lit up by faeries of all different sizes flying off toward the music. A smile crossed her lips, and without hesitation, she sprang to her feet on the spongy ground and joined the faeries in their wild dance.

As she twirled, the pixies swirling around her, she noticed her hair was once again hanging in soft curls, trailing to her waist. She was also clean and dressed in an airy gown. The delicate purple fabric was like nothing she'd worn before, and it shimmered and danced in the moonlight almost of its own accord.

These thoughts hardly had time to sink in before she and her winged escort danced their way into the clearing once again, the music growing louder with each step. She recognized the melody now: her dad used to hum it to her as a child, and she in turn had sung it wordlessly to the twins when they were little. But this version was far more untamed and magical; she could feel her heart beating along with the tempo of the music.

Caught up in her dance with the faeries, she only noticed the beautiful wild boy from the previous night when he stepped away from his gold violin. The instrument kept on playing without him, and he gracefully bowed his head to her. She paused, momentarily arrested both by his sudden appearance and his utter perfection.

He smiled at her, and it was so stunningly gorgeous that her breath caught in her throat. The tempo of the music increased, and her heart raced in time. His grin broadened, and before she realized what was happening, he swept her back into the faerie dance. He smelled fresh and clean, like melting snow, singing birds, and blooming flowers—like spring.

The revel seemed to last only minutes, but it surely must have been hours. Wildflowers sprouted and bloomed around them, and the faeries swirled in counter time to their dance. Finally, her head spinning, Story asked with breathless wonder, "Who are you?"

"I'm Morrigann."

His voice was like the sound of the morning breeze blowing gently through the aspen leaves. It was soft and gentle, both peaceful and entrancing. She would do anything to hear him speak again.

"Are you a faerie?" she asked dreamily, enraptured by the moonlight shimmering across his faintly golden skin and brilliant hair.

Morrigann chuckled, and Story noted somewhere in a hazy corner of her mind that it sounded like softly falling rain.

"Yes, I am a faerie, of a sort." His accent was cultured and refined—regal even.

Story inhaled his scent—he even smelled perfect; rich and earthy, with a hint of honey and citrus blossoms.

He twirled her around then caught her up in his arms. "The real question is," he paused, dipping her low, "who and what are you?"

Before Story could answer, he pulled her back up and resumed their dance, twirling her around and around in ever tighter and faster circles. She was so dizzy she couldn't think straight, and she didn't care.

"You don't look like a gnome, elf, or dryad, and I know you aren't one of the Sidhe."

Abruptly the music ended, and Story sagged into the boy's arms as he stopped their dance. Facing him once again, staring into his vivid, violet eyes, she hardly knew who she was any longer. She only knew she wanted to hear him speak again in his perfect voice.

"I'm Story," she breathed. "And I'm not any of those things. I'm just a girl."

His eyes narrowed fractionally as he leaned in close to her face, until he was only a breath away. He held her gaze for a moment then closed his eyes completely as he inhaled deeply through his nose, breathing in her scent. Time seemed to halt as he stood there, motionless.

Morrigann's eyes flew open, and he stared at her with a kind of ferocious shock. His wildness suddenly frightened her, and despite his beauty, Story felt the urge to run. But the moment quickly passed, his face was once again perfect, and his gentle smile melted her heart.

Placing his warm hand on her cheek, he gazed into her eyes.

"I'm truly glad to have met you, Story."

And then he was gone.

Story jerked awake, coated in a cold sweat, her body stiff

from sleeping sitting up against a tree all night. Groaning, she slowly unbent her limbs and got to her still-sore feet, feeling more tired than she had been before she slept. As she walked down to the river to get a drink and wash her face and hands, she noticed the sky pinking along the horizon. She pulled out her compass and confirmed, once again, that the sun was indeed coming up in the south.

She shoved the compass back in her pocket, got a drink of water, and set off down the trail once more, pulling out a peach to snack on. Squinting as the sun rose higher in the sky, she thought of her sunglasses sitting on the dash of the Jeep and sighed.

None of this makes any sense!

In the first place, how had she survived the fall down the shaft? Then, on top of all the odd things that had happened here, there were her dreams with the faeries and her father's melody, and above all else, the strange connection she felt to all the tree images she'd encountered thus far.

Oh yes, and there was also the guy with tattoos and pointed ears running around in Renn Faire garb. What was his deal? She'd helped him out, and he acted like she'd insulted his mother. She sighed again, loudly.

Men and their stupid pride.

Finishing off her peach, she tossed the pit behind her.

"Oi! Watch where you're throwing things."

Story whirled around and brought her hands up in a defensive posture. Standing before her, holding her peach pit and rubbing his forehead, she found the young man she'd rescued yesterday.

"Have you been following me?" She eyed him warily. That would certainly explain why she felt like she was being watched last night.

"Aye—I mean, no—I mean, I came back to find you."

He raised his hands in a pacifying gesture, and the peach pit dropped to the ground with a soft thunk.

"Huh?" Story remained alert.

"Look, I realize I was rude to you yesterday, and I did leave you stranded when it was pretty obvious that you were lost and more than a bit confused. Plus, you looked like you'd been attacked by an entire band of wood sprites. I shouldn't have left you, and I'm sorry." He lowered his hands slowly to his sides.

"Don't forget about the part where I saved you from the—what did you call them—woods sprites?" Story maintained her defensive posture. He'd made it quite clear that he wanted nothing to do with her yesterday, so why would he be coming back to help her now?

"Er, yes. You did distract them quite handily for me. Thank you for that." He fiddled with his bowstring while he spoke, avoiding her accusing gaze.

"Distracted them for you? Why I—oh, why do I even bother?" Exasperated, she turned her back on him and marched down the trail as fast as her legs would carry her. In an instant, he was beside her, keeping pace.

"Go away."

"No."

Sighing, she glanced at him out of the corner of her eye. He looked just as determined as she felt. That was fine; she could wait him out. Ignoring him, she trudged on.

"How did you find me?" By Story's best estimate, an hour had passed, and she asked the question more to break the oppressive silence than anything else.

"Well, for starters, you make more noise than an entire army of trolls."

Her eyebrow rose at that. *Trolls? Someone's been playing too much World of Warcraft.*

"And of course, there's the fact you were following the trail that I pointed out to you. Aye, it was *quite* difficult for me to track you down."

"You don't have to be sarcastic." She wanted to slap the self-satisfied smirk right off his arrogant face. "Why did you bother coming back? And don't say it's because you felt bad for me or anything."

"Well, I tried to tell you—I came back to guide you to the nearest village, since I happen to be on my way there anyway. It's the least I could do, with your 'rescuing' me and all." His silver eyes flashed with what she assumed was amusement, and for a moment she thought she saw flickers of orange in them.

"You shouldn't have bothered," Story replied icily. "I can follow the trail just fine on my own, thank you very much."

"Aye, I've no doubt about your ability to follow the trail. It's your ability to actually arrive at Stoneybrook that I'm worried about."

That brought Story up short. "What?"

He looked over his tattooed shoulder at her. "You'll never get to Stoneybrook by walking away from it. Unless you really wanted some more of those peaches you found yesterday."

Looking up at the sun, Story's heart sank as she realized she'd been walking away from it, rather than toward it, all morning. She sighed and closed her eyes for a moment to compose herself and to keep from kicking something—like a pointy-eared know-it-all. She took a deep breath, then turned around and began walking back the way she'd come, chin held high. He, of course, continued to shadow her.

"You're welcome," he said after a few moments.

"Thanks, but no thanks," she muttered, so quietly that he probably didn't hear his own rude words from the previous day thrown back at him. She knew it was ugly of her to be so ungrateful toward him, but she was tired, barefoot, sweaty, hungry, and she'd spent the entire morning walking the wrong direction.

And he let me!

As if to humiliate her further, her stomach rumbled loudly. Without saying a word, the man handed her a peach. Story ignored it. She could fend for herself. She'd done all right so far, hadn't she? Well, apart from her blunder this morning. And her inability to start a fire last night. But really, who was keeping track?

"Don't be foolish. Take it. You need to eat."

"No. If I eat your food, what will you eat?"

"Don't worry about me. I'm not hungry. Take it." He thrust the peach at her once again. When she pointedly ignored the proffered fruit, he responded in an irritatingly calm but firm voice. "Take it and eat it, or I will make you eat it."

Or he'll make me eat it? Who the hell does he think he is?

Turning to give him a strongly worded piece of her mind, she saw his eyes darken. She knew he meant what he'd said, and more than that, she knew she needed to eat. Swallowing her pride, Story took the peach and began nibbling on it. Apparently she was stuck with him for the time being, so she might as well make the best of the situation. Plus, he might have answers to some of her questions.

"So, what's your name?" she asked around a mouthful of fruit.

"Eirnin of the Eáchan clan. And yours?"

She stifled a laugh, and resisted the urge to ask him for his real name instead of his gaming handle. "I'm Story."

"Just Story? Have you no clan then?"

Story hesitated only a moment. "No, I have no clan," she replied flatly. She wasn't about to get into *that* with a creeper like him.

Eirnin turned to look at her, unasked questions in his eyes, but he made no response. They walked along in uncomfortable silence while she ate her peach. When she finished it, she tossed the core at his shoulder, attempting to ease the awkwardness. "So, what's up with the pointed ears and tattoos?"

Catching the peach pit before it could hit his shoulder, he stared at her curiously, as if he'd never been asked that question.

"The ailach under my left eye marks me as a member of the Eáchan clan." At Story's blank look he continued on, and offered her his left arm to inspect while he spoke.

"As for my arm, if you look closely you can see the marks follow a series of scars. Remnants of an encounter with a fully-grown mountain troll back when I was a child. The scars have grown faint with time, but I don't want to ever forget them, or what caused them." His silver eyes looked distant and unfocused, and she could have sworn she saw flickers of blue in them.

Maybe it was just a trick of the light?

She had to resist the urge to trace a fingertip along his tattoos. They were bold and delicate at the same time. If she looked hard enough, she could see very faint trails of scars under them. Considering how much the scars had faded, they had to have been decades old, especially if he'd been a child when the mountain troll... Story stopped in her tracks and looked Eirnin straight in his silver eyes.

"Wait just one second, buddy. You expect me to believe you were mauled by a 'mountain troll' when you were a kid?" she asked, making quotation marks in the air with her fingers.

Eirnin regarded her hand gestures with a raised eyebrow,

as if he'd never seen them before. "Aye, that I was. Actually I was more of an older youth, around thirty-five years old at the time—"

"Thirty-five?" Story gaped at him. "You don't look a day over twenty. Twenty-five, max. How old *are* you?"

"Sixty-four. How old are you?" he said without missing a beat, and promptly resumed their previous pace along the trail. After a few steps, he seemed to realize he was walking alone. Story, who was staring at the ground where he'd been, heard him walk back toward her.

"Aren't you going to answer me?"

"I'm almost eighteen." She answered him automatically, unthinking, her mind whirling as she added this latest impossibility to an already long list: the wood sprites, the mountain trolls, the faeries, the pointed ears, Eirnin's age... "I suppose next you're going to tell me you're an elf, aren't you?" She prayed that he would laugh at her and tell her she was being ridiculous.

"Of course I am. What did you think I was, a tall gnome?"

Story couldn't help it—she let out a giggle. "Of course you're an elf!" The giggles quickly progressed to uncontrollable laughter, and she bent over and wiped tears of mirth from her eyes.

Eirnin approached her hesitantly, placing a cautious hand on her shoulder. "Are you... all right?"

"No, I'm not all right!" Story snapped, slapping his hand away. "I fell down a shaft in that stupid cave, and I hit my stupid head, and I can't find my stupid car, and the stupid sun is in the wrong place, and someone stole my stupid shoes, and I'm stuck out here with some stupid lunatic who thinks he's a pointy-eared ELF!" She gestured around furiously, her face livid. "What part of any of that sounds all right to you? I'm probably still stuck at the bottom of that cave, slowly bleeding to death under that tree mural, and this is all an unconscious hallucination." She stomped back along the trail, muttering about trees and shoes, and occasionally throwing her hands up in the air for emphasis.

It took her a moment to realize that Eirnin was not following her.

"Where did you say you came from? What cave?"

Without stopping, Story looked over her shoulder at him and called back, "It's the one at the top of the mountain, near where I found—OW!"

In an instant, he was by her side, helping her hop over to sit against a tree trunk. "What happened? Are you all right?" The corner of Eirnin's mouth quirked up with a hint of a smile, probably remembering her reaction when he'd asked her that a moment ago.

Story smiled sheepishly back up at him. "I'm fine. I think I just stepped on a rock and cut my foot. If I ever find out who took my shoes, I'll kill them."

He lowered himself to one knee and bent over to pick up her injured foot. "I'd be willing to bet it was one of the fey. They're very territorial by nature and often take things that are left lying—"

His voice cut off abruptly, and he stiffened before jerking to his feet and backing away from her as if she had a contagious disease. He stopped only when his back hit a tree. Eirnin's silver eyes, now showing hints of bright yellow, widened in astonishment as he stared, transfixed, at the red blood dripping from the wound on Story's foot.

"What *are* you?"

CHAPTER SIX

THE KNIFE

THE FIRE CRACKLED AS A BIT OF FAT DRIPPED OFF THE REMAIN-ing meat on the spit. Story wasn't usually one for wild game, but as hungry as she was—and tired of peaches—she was not about to be picky. And the truth was, it didn't taste half bad after Eirnin had seasoned it with spices from his pack. As for the pointy-eared fellow himself, he was keeping quiet on his side of the fire.

"Stop that."

"Stop what?" He seemed genuinely surprised. She supposed he had a right to be. They hadn't spoken since the foot incident.

"Staring at me. You've been doing it ever since you bandaged my foot. And it's getting creepy." It wasn't an admiring stare. No, it was more of a "you have a horn growing out of your forehead" sort of stare. It wasn't particularly flattering.

"My apologies," was all he said. He continued to stare at her over the flames.

She sighed in frustration. He wasn't going to make this easy for her, and she needed some answers. "Look, I saw how you freaked out when you saw the blood on my foot, but you don't really strike me as the queasy type." She indicated the animal roasting over the fire and raised an eyebrow at him.

He stared at the remains of their dinner for a long time before answering. The flames reflected perfectly in his silver eyes, his irises flickering yellow and orange, untamed and alien. "I don't suppose you noticed the beast's blood when I was dressing it?"

"Um, no. Can't say that I did. I was trying not to pay attention. The twins always used to tease me; I don't do well around fish gutting or game dressing. I *am* the queasy type."

"The twins?"

"Will and Katie. My younger brother and sister." Story regretted her slip. She wasn't about to discuss her family with him, or with anyone, for that matter.

"But I thought you said you had no clan?"

"I don't. They're dead."

"Your entire clan is dead?" Eirnin's cocked his head to one side, a surprised look flickering across his face.

"Yes, and thank you for bringing up such a painful memory. Now, you were saying about the animal's blood?" Okay, technically she'd brought it up, but she fervently hoped he would take the hint and leave the subject of her family alone.

Eirnin regarded her through narrowed eyes, as if measuring and evaluating her. Finally, he stood and circled around the fire to kneel before her. He held out his tattooed hand, and Story caught herself staring at the patterns that seemed to dance in the firelight.

"I wonder if I might see your knife, please?" At Story's

hesitance, he gave a wry smile. "If I'd wanted to hurt you, I could have just left you alone to walk the wrong way and eventually starve. That is, if the wood sprites didn't get you first."

She shot him a sour look, but removed her knife from its sheath and handed it over to him. If she'd been surprised by Eirnin's request, it was nothing compared to what he did next. He carefully held the knife's blade up to the firelight and scrutinized it closely. Then he brought it up to his nose and inhaled deeply before his tongue darted out to lick the blade.

"Aye, that's got iron in it, to be sure. Downright destructive to the fey." Amazement, tinged with reverence, colored his voice.

"I know it's iron. If you'll remember, I told you that when we first met." Story didn't mean to be snitty, but he was getting on her last nerve. Why didn't he just listen to her in the first place? It would've saved them both time, and she wouldn't have his germs all over her knife now.

Ignoring her last remark, he quickly jabbed the point of her knife into the tip of his index finger. Before Story could cry out to stop him, she saw his blood shimmer in the firelight.

It was silver.

"What *are* you?" she gasped, recoiling from him.

"If *you'll* remember, I asked you the same question a few hours ago. And you know what I am. I've told you; I'm an elf." There was no condescending smirk on his face now.

"Yes, but I guess I didn't really believe you before," Story said quietly, still staring at the silver blood on his finger.

"No, I guess you didn't." A hint of a grin tugged at the corner of his mouth for a fleeting moment. "The real question is what you are. I suspect you're something other than a tall gnome with strangely rounded ears?"

She shook her head, smiling half-heartedly. "No such

luck, I'm afraid. I'm not a tall gnome, in fact I'm about average height for my kind—well, for the guys at least. I'm kind of tall for a girl. And we all have 'strangely rounded' ears."

"And your kind being?"

"Oh, sorry. Human. I'm a human." Her answer came out as distracted as she felt; this entire conversation was surreal. It wasn't every day you met an elf. A real live elf. She started to giggle.

"Oh, not this again." Eirnin rolled his eyes, clearly exasperated.

"I'm sorry, I can't help it," Story gasped between giggles. "It's just that I stopped believing in faerie tales a long time ago."

"Well, that was a foolish thing to do. Faeries are right nasty, and they'd kill you without giving it a second thought. Though they'd just as soon steal your shoes or anything else you left lying about, just to annoy you for a laugh."

Story had been working valiantly to quell her nervous giggles, but this new piece of information was too ludicrous not to laugh. "Oh come on, a little Tinkerbell faerie would kill me? Faeries are sweet, pretty things that live in flowers. Sure, they like to cause little bits of mischief, but mostly they just help nature out. But it's all a moot point, isn't it? I mean, they're just make-believe."

Eirnin stared at her, a shocked expression painted across his face, completely at a loss for words.

Story pinched the bridge of her nose in frustration. "Enough with the staring! What is it now?" Well, at least that had cured her giggles.

"I'm just trying to figure out how you're still alive. Next you'll be telling me there's no such thing as centaurs or dwarves or any of the other creatures of Ailionora."

"Ailionora?" She sounded out the strange word carefully. "Eye-le-o-nor-rah."

For a moment, Eirnin stared at her again, but he schooled his features and began speaking rapidly.

"Ailionora. It's the name of this place. Well, not just this place, but our entire world." He indicated the trees, sky, and earth beneath them with a sweeping gesture. "All of this is Ailionora."

"Oh. Well…" Story bit her lower lip, considering her next words. "The truth is, where I come from, those things—trolls and gnomes and faeries—are all just make-believe. They don't really exist." She paused, considering. "Though, I imagine they might have at one time, since we have so many stories about them."

Resting her chin in her hands, she leaned forward and stared into the fire. "I used to love faerie tales when I was a little girl. My dad always read them as bedtime stories, and then, when I got older, I used to tell them to the twins. When I was really little, I dreamt about dancing with faeries or swimming with mermaids." A smile flitted across her face at the memories. "I'd forgotten about those dreams until I had another one the other night."

Eirnin jerked his gaze up from the campfire and he looked at Story, his eyes sharp. "You did *what* the other night?"

"Dreamt about faeries. Like I used to when I was a little girl. Only these last couple of times were so much more vivid, more real. It was lovely. *They* were lovely—like little fireflies," she said wistfully, waggling her fingers toward the sparks crackling off the fire.

Eirnin frowned. "Look, there a few things you need to know about Ailionora if you want to survive and get back to wherever it is you came from. The first and most important thing is to never *ever* trust a faerie. Most especially *not* the pixies."

At her confused look, he clarified. "The 'little pretty' ones that you mistook for fireflies. I wasn't joking when I said they'd just as soon kill you as help you. They're so small and tiny that they really can only feel one emotion at a time, and usually they just want to be merry."

"But what's the harm in that?"

"No real harm at all, if all they do is bother you, pinch you, trip you, steal things from you. No, the harm comes when they push you off a cliff and laugh as you fall, or steal a baby from a crib, or.... well, you get the idea."

Story grew suddenly cold, despite the fire's warmth. Could this be true? Could they really be that nasty? The ones in her dreams had always been so sweet and nice. They were faeries, for goodness sakes!

Eirnin crouched down on one knee in front of her again and held out her knife. "But you don't have to worry. You have this."

"What does my knife have to do with faeries?"

Rolling his eyes toward the heavens, he sighed loudly. "My word, what do they teach in your land?" Story opened her mouth to let loose a sharp retort, but Eirnin pressed on with his explanation before she could speak. "Your knife. It's made of some sort of iron alloy, which is extremely rare in Ailionora. And it is the very best thing for warding off the fey. Iron hurts them, you see, and in large enough quantities, like your knife, it will destroy them. As long as you have it, no faerie can touch you."

Destroy them? Story looked at the knife with surprise. Could her dad have known? No, that was ridiculous; how could he possibly have predicted the bizarre series of events that had brought her here? Regardless, it felt like, in a way, her dad was still looking out for her, still protecting her. She could almost feel his comforting presence there beside her. Raising a hand, she quickly wiped at the hot tears pricking at the corners of her eyes.

"The knife must mean a great deal to you."

"Yes." She took the knife from his outstretched hand. "It was my father's. It was the last thing he ever gave me." Returning the knife to its scabbard, she was suddenly overcome with exhaustion and stifled a yawn with her hands.

"You're tired; you should sleep." It wasn't a question. Eirnin's eyes sought hers, but she studiously avoided them.

"No argument here." Story yawned again, while Eirnin began tracing a line in the dirt with a stick.

"What are you doing?"

"Setting up a ward against the fey so that we won't have to worry about any of our things, like shoes, going missing." He nodded at her bare feet and winked. "Or getting ourselves attacked by the little blighters while we sleep."

"Oh." Story stretched out on her side and propped her head up on her hand, watching Eirnin work. He seemed to be drawing a perfect circle in the earth around their camp. "So, a circle in the dirt means the faeries can't cross it and bother us?" She still wasn't completely convinced that they were really the awful creatures he had made them out to be. Then she remembered the wood sprites and amended that thought to just the pixies.

"Well, yes and no. Salt really works the best to repel the larger fey, but the pixies, spriggans, and other small faeries are so simple-minded that if they try to cross the circle, they end up following the line round and round until they get bored or dizzy and go away. It's a simple trick, but one that's saved me and many others a lot of time and gear. Of course, you wouldn't need the circle. Your knife would ward off any fey."

Finishing the ward, he settled himself across the fire from Story and leaned back against a tree. "Get some sleep, little human. Tomorrow will be a long day. We have a lot of distance to cross, and you walk slower than an entire family of gnomes. Babies included."

Story bristled at his patronizing tone. She wasn't entirely sure what a gnome was—at least in this world—but she was certain she wasn't slower than one, much less an entire family of them.

Throwing Eirnin a scowl, she flopped onto her other side and turned her back to him. Then exhaustion claimed her, and she fell fast asleep.

CHAPTER SEVEN

NAMES

S O TELL ME, WHAT KIND OF NAME IS STORY EXACTLY?"

"Huh?" Story jumped, startled by Eirnin's voice. She'd been deep in thought, wondering why she hadn't dreamt about Morrigann or the pixies last night.

"Will, Katie, and Story? I don't understand your naming convention."

"Naming convention?" Story ducked under a low-hanging branch without taking her eyes off the trail; she didn't want to cut her foot again. "I'm not sure I understand what you mean."

Eirnin blew out an irritated breath. "What I mean is, how do you come up with names for your children and places? What do they signify?"

"Oh. I don't really know." She shrugged. "I suppose my mother was going through a hippie phase when she had me."

Eirnin opened his mouth as if to ask what she meant by that, but snapped it shut when she glared at him.

"Anyway," Story continued. "She was long gone by the time my dad, Milton, adopted the twins a few years later."

"So, Milton, Story, Will, and Katie." Eirnin repeated the names as if he were trying out the sounds in his mouth to see if he liked them. "I still don't see a pattern. How do you tell the genders apart?"

Story paused for a moment to consider his question. "Well, some names are girl names like Nicole or Candace, and other names are boy names like Bryan or Brent. But then you have some names like Jordan or Dani that could be either." Eirnin's eyebrows knitted together as he mulled over her words. She was glad that, for once, *he* was the confused one.

"So what you're saying is that you have to come up with a new name for every person, and then you have to memorize these names and which gender they are attributed to, except that sometimes they can be either?" Eirnin looked appalled.

"When you put it that way it sounds like a complete mess. But no, we don't have to learn loads of names since we all share."

"You *share* your names?"

"Well yeah, with a few billion humans there's no way we'd each get our very own unless we just started stringing random letters together." Story tried to suppress her laugh; his obvious distress at the concept of name-sharing was kind of adorable.

"But then how do you tell one Story apart from another in writing or in speech?"

"That's what middle and last names are for. For example, my name, while unusual, is certainly not unique. There are bound to be dozens of other Storys out there. But I'd bet I'm the only Story Melissa Sorenson." She paused, and then amended, "At least currently living."

"How does one get these other names? Are they also chosen at random by your parents?"

"No, my last name is my family name."

"Ah! So your last name is your clan name." He glanced over at Story quizzically, and she knew what he was thinking. *I said I had no clan.*

Well, she didn't want to talk about it. She'd already informed him that her family was dead, so she pointedly ignored his unasked question. Subject closed.

He looked away, and after a few awkward moments of walking in silence, he pulled himself up easily over a large, moss-covered tree trunk that blocked their path. Story found herself staring in admiration as his taut shoulder and arm muscles flexed under his skin, the tattoos on his left arm further highlighting the lines of his defined musculature.

Eirnin turned back to Story and held a hand to help her up. They locked gazes, and for a brief second, she swore she saw her own sea-green eyes reflected in his brilliant silver. The connection was almost like magic. But then he ruined the moment by talking.

"Well I must say, your human way of naming things is very inefficient and quite confusing."

At his condescending tone, she pulled away from him and finished climbing over the log on her own. "And I suppose your way is better?"

"Aye, that it is." Seemingly oblivious to her annoyance, he jumped down off the log and pressed on. "The elf naming convention is quite simple. Male names begin with 'Ei' and female names begin with 'Ea'."

"Fascinating."

Eirnin either missed the sarcasm in Story's voice, or he didn't care. "Names beginning with 'Ai' are reserved for very special things, because it implies 'life.' Hence, 'Ailionora' for

the name of our world and 'Ailes' for the 'Life tree' and—"
He cut off abruptly and narrowed his eyes, scrutinizing Story
again.

"Seriously, no more staring!" Story pushed past him in a
huff. What was his deal? She self-consciously reached up and
patted her hair, but dropped her hand when she realized it
was a lost cause. What she wouldn't give for a hairbrush right
now instead of her useless compass.

The trees abruptly ended in a small meadow, and she
had a clear view of the morning sky. Out of habit, she pulled
out her compass, then shook her head at the southern sun.

"What are you doing?"

Story was so startled she nearly jumped out of her skin.
Eirnin was practically breathing down her neck. She took a
large step away, clutched at her chest with her free hand, and
spun around to face him. "Holy crap! How about a little warning next time? Are you trying to give me a heart attack?"

He raised an eyebrow. "No." Then he looked down at her
hand pointedly.

"It's a compass." She unhooked it from her belt loop and
passed it to him.

Eirnin turned it around in his hands and looked at it
closely. "I know *that*. What is this one's purpose?"

Story moved in closer to him and indicated the face of the
compass, trying not to sound like she was explaining this to a
child. "The same as any compass. It always points to the north.
It's what I use for land navigation."

Eirnin studied the compass for a moment, then snorted
and passed it back. "No wonder you got lost. That particular instrument is worthless. The sun rises in the east, not the
south."

She was thoroughly confused now. Though she supposed

this world could have east/west magnetic poles, which could explain the way her compass was pointing…

Eirnin's face appeared before her and he waved a hand in front of her face. "Hello?"

Story shook her head. "Sorry. This place is just… different."

"Aye, I'm sure it is from your point of view. Look, can you stay on the path? I need to go hunt for us, and you are taking a rather long time. Are all humans as slow as you?"

She had to grit her teeth to keep from yelling at him, and the smirk on his face was making matters worse. She suspected he thought he was being cute or endearing, but mostly he was just obnoxious. "Yes, I can stay on the path. I'm not completely helpless, you know."

He didn't reply, just looked pointedly back the way they had come. Story glared at him. She'd been lost in the woods one time in her life, and of course, *he* had to be the one to find her.

"And I'm not slow. You just walk incredibly fast."

"That is not an answer."

"Yes! Go hunt or gather or…whatever it is you do." Story motioned toward the trees. At Eirnin's raised eyebrow she gritted her teeth. "I. Will. Be. Fine. Just go!"

"Very well. I'll meet you at sunset. Try not to dawdle, though; at this rate we'll never make it to Stoneybrook." He tossed her a bundle of jerky held together by twine, and before she could come up with a retort he was gone, melting into the woods like a shadow.

HOURS LATER, STORY RESTED ON A FALLEN LOG, WORKING VERY HARD to ignore her ravenous hunger. She'd long since finished off the food Eirnin had given her, though she'd tried to make it last. Eirnin, on the other hand, had not eaten anything for breakfast that she could see, and it hadn't seemed to bother him at all.

Perhaps that explained his age and appearance. Maybe elves just had very slow metabolisms, so they didn't need as much food—or sleep for that matter—and aged slowly. Like turtles. Maybe they were just human-looking turtles.

Or maybe I hit my head way too hard, so I'm thinking up crazy things.

Either way, she was still starving, and the sun was at least an hour away from setting. As if to punctuate her thoughts, her stomach let out a very loud rumble.

"I know, I know. I'm hungry. Thanks for the reminder. My feet hurt too. Care to remind me of that as well?"

Levering herself off the log, Story resumed her trek. Her respite hadn't been nearly long enough, but the faster she walked, the faster she'd get to food, rest, and heat. It grew surprisingly chilly as soon as the sun went down. She wanted to ask Eirnin if the seasons were the same here too, but after the embarrassing episode with the compass she was in no hurry to show her ignorance again. At least not today.

She pulled out the compass to look at it in the waning light. She should probably chuck it, for all the good it did her now. But she couldn't; it was one of the few remaining links she had to her world.

"No idea how I'll get back there now. I'm pretty sure there are no phones in Stoneybrook." She held the compass up to her face, addressing it gravely. "What about you? Any idea? Maybe you're pointing the way back for me?" She shook it gently and watched the needle spin. "Or maybe I've gone completely bonkers, and now I'm talking to inanimate objects." She returned the compass to her pocket, thankful that Eirnin wasn't there to witness her slight lapse of sanity.

As for the elf, he perplexed her. One minute he was funny, sweet, and nice, and the next he was arrogant, rude, and condescending. Other times, it almost seemed like he was afraid of her. She was grateful to him for helping her, but she also wasn't quite sure she trusted him. Granted, the constant staring had a lot to do with that. What was his deal, anyway?

Then there was Morrigann. She smiled unconsciously at the thought of him. He was nice. And gorgeous. And a gentleman. And gorgeous. Of course he was only in her dreams, but... they seemed so very real. *He* seemed real. If she closed her eyes and focused, she could almost see him shimmering in the moonlight and smell his sweet scent wafting toward her. Everything about him was magical and seductive.

This is no time to daydream, Story. If she closed her eyes right now, she'd probably trip over something, and besides, she had bigger problems. Now that she was alone and had some time to contemplate the enormity of her situation, she had to struggle not to freak out.

She was in another world.

A world where creatures of mythology and fantasy were commonplace. If anything, *she* was the fantastical creature, being—as far as she knew—the only human in existence in Ailionora. She had no idea how to get back to her own world, other than attempting a climb out of the chasm she'd fallen through. For that, she would need rope and other climbing supplies, none of which she currently possessed. So for the time being, letting Eirnin guide her to Stoneybrook seemed like her best option.

Something fluttered off to her right, just in the corner of her vision. Looking around, she realized that dusk was settling in. A chill crept up her spine, and the distinct feeling of being watched returned. Her heart began to race as she picked up her pace on the trail.

There's nothing out there. It was just a bird. Besides, you've got your knife, and Eirnin said it would protect you from faeries. Then a horrible thought struck her. *What about trolls? Did they count as faeries?* Scanning her surroundings quickly, she gripped the hilt of her knife, more for reassurance that it was still there than anything else. Feeling calmer, she was about to slow down to a normal walk when the hairs on the back of her neck stood on end.

Something was definitely watching her.

She pulled the knife out of its scabbard, her arm shaking, and turned around slowly to peer into the tall shrubbery beside the path. A pair of glowing, red eyes gleamed up at her. She stared back, momentarily rooted to her spot but desperately willing her legs to move.

The eyes, slightly lower than her head, blinked and were suddenly closer.

A shriek ripped from Story's throat as she spun around and tore off running down the trail. She barely had the presence of mind to hold the knife behind her back as she ran, so that in her haste she wouldn't accidentally trip and fall on it. Too scared to look back, she could only pray she was outrunning the creature.

STORY CRASHED INTO THE CAMPSITE AT A DEAD SPRINT AND NEARLY fell into the fire.

"Whoa there, careful." Eirnin swiftly caught her and led her over to the tree trunk he'd been leaning against. He removed his cloak and wrapped it around her shaking form. "What happened? You look as though an entire horde of goblins was after you." He clasped her arms reassuringly, and she could see firelight reflected yellow in his worried eyes.

"Eyes! There were red eyes…" Her voice drifted off as she looked over her shoulder and saw… nothing. Nothing was chasing her. Nothing had followed her into the campsite. Nothing but her own wild imagination.

Shrugging off his hands and cloak, she moved closer to the warmth of the fire. Story felt quite foolish. Here in the light and protection of the fire, her nighttime flight seemed childish and unwarranted. Surely all she'd seen was the reflection off some little animal's eyes.

"I'm fine, actually," she continued after a moment. "I just figured a little jog would be nice. Besides, you always complain about how slow I travel." She bared her teeth in a forced smile.

Eirnin narrowed his eyes, clearly suspicious, but evidently decided not to press the issue. Instead, he bent over to pick something up off the ground and joined her next to the fire. He thrust a bundle at Story, and her hands automatically reached out and took it. Looking down, she saw that she was holding a pair of plain, leather moccasins. Her eyebrows furrowed together, questioning.

"I made them while I was waiting for you. They aren't anything fancy, but they should keep your feet from being cut to ribbons the next time you decide to go for a 'jog' in the woods."

"I—I don't even know how to thank you." Story bent over and slipped them on. Taking a few experimental steps, she realized they fit perfectly. She stared at her feet, then at his hands, and finally at his face. Warmth spread to her heart when she realized he'd gone through quite a bit of effort to make these for her. He'd probably had to cannibalize something in his own kit to get the leather.

Eirnin met her gaze, his silver eyes glinting purple. They stood there for a long moment as the flames illuminated his face, making the tattoo around his eye dance in the firelight. She smiled hesitantly at him, and he responded in kind.

He's really not bad looking at all, especially when he smiles.

His face was only a few inches from hers, and the air between them felt charged with electricity. The purple flickers in his eyes flared brighter.

Suddenly Eirnin turned away and quickly moved to sit down on the opposite side of the fire. "Well, now you don't have any excuse for walking slow and holding us up."

Story felt like she'd just been doused with a bucket of cold, river water.

Probably for the best. The last thing she needed was to get attached to this place, or anyone in it. Still, her cheeks were flushed, and she felt pretty stupid.

"I've left you something to eat over by my gear. Hopefully it's enough." He stage-whispered the last part to the surrounding trees.

"I heard that." Story shot him a scathing look as she shuffled over to retrieve the food. Her new shoes felt wonderful, but her feet were still pretty sore. "Honestly, I don't eat that much. You make me out to be a cow or something."

He leaned forward, resting his elbows on his knees. "You mean your race generally eats more? How can there possibly be enough food to feed billions of you? You must spend your entire existence looking for food, and when you aren't finding food or eating it, you are sleeping!"

"You know what would be great? If you would stop judging me by your race's norms. I'm not an elf."

"That's the truth if I've ever heard it."

Story sighed and began eating the dandelion salad he'd put together. There was no use trying to explain it. Again. "Remember how you said the other night that my knife could destroy the smaller fey?"

Eirnin blinked his eyes against her abrupt change of subject, pausing for a moment before answering. "Aye, that I do."

"I was wondering about your choice of words. You said 'destroy' rather than 'kill'. Why?"

Eirnin just stared at her in response, his mouth half open in surprise.

Story rolled her eyes. "Look, let's just assume from here on out that I'm from another world and don't know anything at all about yours. First off, because it's true, and secondly, because that should make our conversations go a lot smoother. And no more staring! It's really creepy."

"I apologize. I'll stop." Eirnin obediently looked away from her face into the fire. "I simply find your lack of basic knowledge to be both fascinating and mildly amusing."

"Well I'm glad I can *amuse* you. How about we go visit my world next, and I'll watch you try to drive a car?"

Eirnin raised both hands in a placating gesture. "That's not what I meant. What I was trying to say was... Oh, never mind. Back to your question. I said your knife could destroy the smaller fey because they can't be killed."

"You can't kill a faerie?"

"No."

"How is that even possible? I don't get it; aren't they alive?"

"I suppose they are alive, but in a different way than you and I are."

Story set down her food and pressed her fingers against her temples. She was getting a headache. "I don't understand."

In response, Eirnin returned to her side of the fire. He held out his hand and took one of hers. "You and I are flesh and blood. The fey are not."

She regarded their joined hands for a moment, feeling the blood pulsing beneath his warm skin. She was trying to process what he'd said, but his touch was more than a bit distracting. *Get a grip, Story!*

Eirnin sat down next to her without letting go of her hand. "I don't fully understand the fey. No one does. But they're said to be the physical embodiment of Ailionora's magic and nature. So when you destroy one of them, they can't really die because they aren't really alive. They just sort of… cease to exist. Whereas when we die, our essence, the magical part of us that can't die, leaves our bodies and…" He trailed off, a slight frown tugging at the corners of his mouth.

"And what?" Story leaned in closer to him, leaving only inches separating their faces.

Eirnin withdrew his hand from hers and stood up, gazing into the fire. "Goes to join the others across the Ailes Sea." Bitterness tinged his voice, and Story was taken aback. He'd been cocky, smug, and rude in turns thus far, but this was the first time she'd seen him bitter.

"But you don't believe that last bit." It wasn't a question.

He ignored her and moved to gather more wood for the fire. Story bit her lower lip, debating whether or not to push the subject.

Well, it can't get any more awkward than it already is, can it?

"I was raised with a similar belief." She looked up at him to gauge his reaction. He continued piling wood methodically, as if he hadn't heard her. "That when we die, we join our family in the hereafter. Some call it Heaven."

Eirnin snorted. "And you believe that?"

Story stared into the fire. "I don't know. I want to. In some ways, I have to. I can't imagine never seeing them again."

Closing her eyes, she tried to bury the memories that were surfacing unbidden. Will and Katie jumping up and down on her bed to wake her up on a Saturday morning. Her dad teaching her to always lace left over right on her shoes. The twins staging mock sword fights in the backyard that always degenerated into the hedges getting smacked around like piñatas.

She picked up the cut of game he'd set out for her and resumed eating, but it was only to give her something to do. Her hunger had evaporated, and the food tasted like sand in her mouth.

Eirnin paused as he placed a fallen branch in the fire, regarding her guiltily. "I'm sorry, I didn't mean—"

She held up a hand to stop him. "Don't, just don't. I don't need your sympathy."

A shocked look flickered across his face; her anger had surprised him. He continued piling more wood on the fire for a minute, then stopped, apparently satisfied. When he finally responded, the condescending tone was back in his voice. "Look, I've got to get a bit of sleep. Less than you, mind you," he said, leaning up against a log opposite hers. "The circle's already been drawn, and if you can manage to stay awake for the next hour or so and keep watch, that would be rather helpful."

And with that he closed his eyes, leaving Story alone with her demons once more.

CHAPTER EIGHT

THE AILES

S HE DIDN'T DREAM ABOUT FAERIES OR MORRIGANN THAT NIGHT or the next. In fact, she didn't dream at all. Eirnin kept them going at such a fast pace it was all she could do not to collapse and fall instantly asleep as soon as they made camp. The only thing keeping her awake was her ravenous hunger at the end of each day.

Elves might not need to eat and sleep much, but this human certainly does.

Her belly full of the simple, yet filling, meal of salad and wild game Eirnin had prepared, Story licked her fingertips clean and gave a contented sigh. Despite his promise, Eirnin was staring at her, probably in disgust over her "gluttony," but she didn't care. Actually, she was kind of getting used to it.

"It's a good thing we'll be arriving in Stoneybrook day after next. Keeping you fed is turning into a full time job."

"Ha ha."

"Really, you eat as much as a troll." He winked to let her know he was only teasing.

"One more comment about how much I eat, and I'll show you just how troll-like I can be." She bared her teeth at him in what was meant to be a ferocious grin but quickly morphed into a jaw-splitting yawn. Eirnin took the hint and got up to draw the circle around their camp.

For the last two days, he'd been constantly peppering her with questions about her world and how humanity functioned. He wanted to know everything, no matter how inane it seemed to her. Truly, he would have put the twins to shame with his incessant responses of "but why?" to every answer she gave him. Though he tried to feign nonchalance, it was clear that he had a voracious thirst for knowledge of "earth" and "humans." The most annoying thing about it was that he left little room for her to ask her own questions in return.

"So what exactly are Gnomes? You keep comparing me to them." She settled back against a mossy tree stump and held her hands out toward the fire. "In my world they're these tiny garden statues with tall, red, cone hats. I'm assuming that's not the case here." She made a face. "At least I hope not."

Eirnin snorted and settled down across the fire from her in his now-customary spot. "Your world is very odd."

"I know. You've told me that several times. The gnomes?"

Pulling his bow toward him, he removed the string and began inspecting it for imperfections. "Gnomes are the earth people of Ailionora. All the races have a bit of magic, you see, and theirs is tied to the soil and growing things. They're mostly farmers, and they produce the bulk of the food in Ailionora. You'll like them." He flashed a grin at her. She gave an obligatory eye-roll, but felt her mouth quirk into an involuntary half-smile.

"Aside from the fey, they're the most populous race in

Ailionora. They're simple folk, but generally quite happy. Unfortunately, the fey, especially spriggans, love to torment them. Most of the tricks we elves use to keep the fey away were learned from the gnomes long ago, right after the Change."

She could hear the capital "C" in the word. "The Change?"

Satisfied that his string was in good repair, Eirnin began rubbing a chunk of beeswax along its length, slowly and methodically. "The old legends say that a thousand years ago, before the Change, elves used to be immortal. We could be killed of course, but this was hard to do since none of the fey could get near us, so it was a rare occurrence—"

"Why couldn't the fey go near you?"

Eirnin gave her a measured look, red flickers of irritation in his eyes.

"Sorry. Please keep going."

He frowned at her across the flames. "Look, it's a rather long story, and the truth is, I'm not even sure I believe it, so I won't bother trying to tell it if you're just going to interrupt me with questions every few seconds."

Story almost pointed out that he'd had no compunctions about interrupting her with dozens of new questions while she was answering his endless queries about her world. But she was truly curious about the "Change," so she mimed zipping her mouth shut, and looked at him expectantly.

He quirked a puzzled eyebrow at her.

Right, probably no zippers in Ailionora. "Um, that means I'll be quiet."

"How could that possibly… never mind," he said, shaking his head. "As I said before, all the creatures of Ailionora have magic, and the faerie folk have the most. But it's said that this wasn't always the case. Before the Change, the elves were the most magical. They were the 'guardians' of the realm, so to speak." His voice was changing, taking on a storyteller's lilting speech pattern.

"The fey were wont to do as faeries do. Peace never sits well with them, and they hungered for mischief and mayhem. The Faerie Prince was the worst of them all. He had long been jealous of the elves and our power, for we were the only ones who could call the cold iron from the depths of the earth. Not even the dwarves could mine the iron, so deeply was it buried. So it fell to us to use our magic and forge the iron into weapons of defense or amulets of protection from the faerie magic and the Chaos they threatened to release."

Story heard another capital "C" and wanted desperately to interrupt again, but sat on her hands—literally—instead.

"But the fey were not the only creatures with a weakness—we elves had one too." He restrung his bow, set it back with his kit, and stood up to get more firewood. "Our magic was the strongest, but it was tied to one source: a great silver tree in the center of our capital city. It was called *The Ailes*, for it alone was the source of our immortality and magic. If anything happened to the tree, we would lose both. Of course, that knowledge was a closely guarded secret. To outsiders, it was only one of many beautiful trees that grew on our islands."

"Hold on, this tree..." Story bit her lip, thinking. "Did it... did it happen to have silver leaves too?"

"Yes?" He dragged out the word, turning it into a question.

"And did they all fall off with the Change? When it happened?" Her heart rate picked up; why was this suddenly so important to her?

"Supposedly." He sat back down across from her. "How do you know so much?"

"I saw a cave painting when I first got here. I was just wondering."

He narrowed his eyes. "You're sure that's it? That's all you've seen?"

She didn't understand his question or why it mattered; she just wanted to hear more about the tree and what happened to it. "Yes, I'm sure. So, what happened? I'm assuming the fey figured out your weakness?"

"Aye, that they did. Through treachery and seduction, the Faerie Prince tricked a naïve elf maiden from one of the mage clans into revealing all. He cursed the *The Ailes* to never bloom again, condemning us to extinction."

Story was so completely wrapped up in the tale Eirnin was spinning that she nearly missed that last sentence. "Wait... how did he do that? Not curse the tree, but condemn you to extinction?"

She half-expected him to bite her head off for interrupting him again, but surprisingly he didn't. Perhaps he'd finally recalled that she was, in fact, from another world.

"Ah. Each elf male can only father one child, with the occasional rare set of twins. That's not really a problem when your race is immortal—in fact, it keeps you from overpopulating. But if you are mortal, it will lead to extinction." His voice was flat, emotionless, much as hers was when she spoke of her family.

"Oh, I'm so sorry—"

"Thanks, but we don't need your sympathy," he bit out, flinging her own words back at her. Her cheeks flushed, and she looked away. Had she sounded that rude?

He leaned forward to gaze into the fire, pale, blue sparks flashing in his silver eyes.

Questions and thoughts swirled through Story's mind. Who was the Faerie Prince? Could he be Morrigann's ancestor? The golden boy from her dreams was clearly not a normal faerie. But, most importantly, why did she feel such a connection to the tree?

"You said you're not sure if you believe in the legends. Why?"

Eirnin shrugged, keeping his eyes on the fire. "They've always seemed like an excuse, I suppose. Something for us to lay all our problems on and avoid taking responsibility for our actions. Or rather, inaction." He poked at the fire with a stick, sending up a scattering of sparks. "The legends say that once upon a time we were a benevolent and wise race. The protectors of the realm. Now you're lucky to see an elf outside of our city, and when you do, they're afraid of everything and everyone—leaving the few of us who do care to risk our lives and die alone."

"Did you know someone... who died, protecting the realm?"

"Aye." He jabbed the fire savagely, dislodging a burning stick.

Story didn't ask him any more questions. Eirnin didn't seem ready to talk about it, and he never pressed her when she did the same. Instead, she stretched out on the ground and pillowed her head in her arms. As her eyes drifted shut, she watched the fire slowly die in the fallen stick and tried not to wonder about the death that had scarred Eirnin even more deeply than the Troll wounds on his arm.

Chapter Nine

Betrayal

Story awoke to an eerie silence and saw that the fire had burned down to glowing embers. She reached for the handle of her knife and found only air. Looking down, she found that she was once again dressed in the gauzy, purple gown. She was dreaming again. Her heart fluttered—that meant Morrigann was near!

Soft violin music wafted toward her from deep in the woods. She recognized her lullaby from the previous nights, but it sounded sadder somehow, more melancholy. She was on her feet and gliding toward it without even realizing she'd moved. Morrigann was waiting for her in the clearing, perched majestically on the flat center stone. He smiled sadly at her and kept playing his forlorn-sounding violin, beckoning to her with a nod of his head.

Entranced, Story made her way to his side and sat cautiously on the wide stone next to him, never taking her eyes off his perfect features. This close, she could see that his blonde hair was streaked with darker gold, shining in the moonlight. She didn't doubt for a moment that he was related to the Faerie Prince that Eirnin had spoken of.

Morrigann bowed a final few melancholy notes, then gently placed his violin to the side before turning to face Story.

"Why did you stay away so long?" she blurted, then clapped a hand over her mouth in mortification. Unruffled by her outburst, Morrigann smiled radiantly down at her. She felt her skin grow warm, her fingers and toes tingling as if she were sitting in a sunbeam.

"Where are your pixies tonight?" she asked, more to cover her embarrassment than from true curiosity. Though she still liked the pretty little faeries and missed seeing them, despite what Eirnin had said. There was no way they would hurt a fly, much less a person.

"I'm afraid we can't have our faerie dance tonight, Story. I've just discovered some grave news, and I need to talk with you about it."

Story was so enraptured by the sound of Morrigann's voice that she nearly missed the serious tone underlying it. "What's wrong? You're acting like someone died…" Her chest clenched, and it was suddenly hard to breathe. Please, not that. She couldn't take it, not again.

Morrigann gave her a sad half-smile. "Interesting choice of words, fair one. Tell me, when the elfling was telling you about the Faerie Prince's curse, did he bother to mention just how the curse could be lifted?"

"No, he didn't—wait a sec… how do you know about that? Were you following me?" She leaned away from him, fists on her hips, anger flashing across her face.

Morrigann took both of her hands in his, brought them up to his mouth, and kissed her knuckles gently, silencing her protests. "Dear, sweet girl, of course the fey have been following you. The Faerie Prince is very concerned about your welfare, especially now that he knows who and what you are."

"He is?" Story struggled to make her voice sound even, having been rendered momentarily breathless by the simple kiss to her hands. She knew that she should be more curious about the Faerie Prince's identity, but all she could think about was Morrigann and his inviting lips.

Morrigann smiled beatifically at her. "He's the caring sort."

Story grinned foolishly back up at Morrigann until his words finally broke through the fog that clouded her mind. "But... if the Faerie Prince is such a caring fellow, then why did he curse the elves and leave them all to die?"

Morrigann dropped her hands, making her instantly sorry that she'd said anything.

Sighing, he turned to gaze up at the moon and ran his fingers through his golden hair, sending sparks of magic flickering off the ends. "Story, I'm afraid it's not that simple. You must understand that the Faerie Prince is just that: the Prince of the Faeries. He has a responsibility to them, to look out for their welfare and protect them from harm. They are his family. Surely you understand how important it is to protect your family?"

Story stared down at her hands and swallowed around the lump growing in her throat. Yes, she understood that very well.

"Before the Change, the elves were cruel to the fey. They hunted the faeries down, destroying them with their iron swords and arrowheads. Unlike the elves, we fey don't get to go someplace else when we die. For us, this is it. It's all we have," Morrigann finished quietly, turning back and taking Story's hands in his own again.

Any confusion she felt was wiped away at the touch of his hands. Sympathy for the faeries' plight and anger at Eirnin and the rest of the elves rolled through her body. How could she blame the Faerie Prince for trying to protect his family? And how could the elves so callously seek to exterminate the fey? Especially the helpless pixies? It was unforgivable.

Then, a half-formed memory burned through the mist in her mind: the tree creatures cruelly tormenting a helpless Eirnin. Story pulled her hands away from Morrigann's again and raised them in front of her, palms out, keeping him at arm's length. "Why should I believe you over Eirnin? He says it was the other way around—that the fey were constantly causing problems for the people of Ailionora and the elves were the guardians of the land. And when I first met him, he was being attacked by some wood sprites, who then promptly turned and attacked me!"

Morrigann slid toward her, ignoring the barrier of her arms, and placed his own arm around her shoulders to draw her close against his side. "Fair one, you mustn't blame them. They thought you were an elf and broke away as soon as they realized you were not."

"But that doesn't explain…"

"Shhh." He placed a shimmering fingertip against her lips, and Story had to fight the urge to sigh contentedly at his touch. "There are far more important things to discuss right now. The elfling never told you how his kind intend to restore their immortality, did he?"

She shook her head slowly, her gaze locked on his glittering, violet-colored eyes. They were absolutely hypnotic.

"There is an old prophecy, Story. It says that with a sacrifice of blood from another world to the *The Ailes*, the elves' ability to manipulate magic fully—and therefore their immortality—will be restored."

It took a moment for his words to sink in, but they hit Story like a blow to the gut.

"You mean… they want to sacrifice me?"

He nodded sorrowfully. "The elves will stop at nothing to restore their lost power."

Story looked down at her lap, completely at a loss for words. It all made a sick sort of sense. Eirnin hadn't come back to help her because he felt sorry for her; he only wanted to sacrifice her to get his precious immortality back! It also explained the constant staring and unending questions; he'd been trying to confirm that she was indeed from another world.

Her mind felt slow and clouded like she was trying to wade through thick mud, but a tiny, insistent voice was floating up through her cloudy mind. Hadn't Eirnin said he wasn't sure if he even believed the old legends? And he had been kind, in his own way—looking out for her, feeding her, answering her questions. And there was his gift of the moccasins; would you do that for someone you were intending to kill?

Morrigann seemed to sense her inner turmoil and lifted her chin up to look at him again. "Remember, Story, the elfling has told you how obsessed his people are with restoring *The Ailes*. You will see that I am right. Tomorrow, he will suggest that instead of dropping you off at the gnome village, perhaps you should travel with him all the way to the queen's isle and meet her personally. He will tell you that she will be able to help you return to your world better than anyone else in Ailionora."

He leaned in even closer, his sweet scent wafting across the inches between them. "He will lead you to your death, if you let him. They need your blood." He placed his hot hand against her cheek, and Story closed her eyes, leaning into his touch. Her heart raced with fear and excitement. "The Faerie Prince can protect you. He is powerful enough to send you back. But you must come to him tomorrow night, willingly."

"I don't know the way…" Her protest was half-hearted, and they both knew it.

He chuckled lightly. "You've danced it often these last nights, but no matter. Tomorrow night, after the elfling is asleep, the pixies will arrive to guide you." His face turned somber. "You must leave your iron knife behind, for it is too strong to allow the Faerie Prince to work his magic." He leaned in still closer, nearly touching his nose to hers.

Story hardly dared to breathe. He was so close; all she had to do was cross that last inch…

As if he could read her mind, Morrigann closed the gap and laid a light, but lingering, kiss on her lips.

She closed her eyes and breathed him in, tasting honey and vanilla. His kiss was better than she'd imagined it would be, could ever be. She wanted more. Needed more. Opening her eyes, Story leaned in to kiss him once again, but found that he'd begun to fade away, glittering in the moonlight.

Panic rose in her chest. He couldn't leave yet! "Wait! Don't go! When will I see you again?"

As he disappeared into the starlit night, his ethereal voice caressed her, leaving goose bumps across her skin. "I will always be in your dreams, so long as you welcome me."

TO SAY THAT THINGS WERE A BIT AWKWARD THE NEXT MORNING would have been an understatement of epic proportions. The air was thick with one-sided tension, and Story fought a constant inner battle over how to act toward Eirnin. Part of her wanted to demand that he explain the elves' persecution of the fey and, more importantly, what they intended to do with her. Another part of her worried that if she said anything at all, he'd truss her up like livestock and haul her away to the queen's island to be sacrificed. And one small part of her kept pointing out that Eirnin, while often condescending and rude in his manner—though he seemed to think he was just being funny—had done a lot more to help her and keep her alive thus far than the Faerie Prince had. She sighed and shook her head. This was maddening.

And on top of it all, she was truly tired of walking. "How much longer until we reach Stoneybrook?"

Eirnin glanced back at her, plainly surprised she'd spoken; his earlier attempts to engage her in conversation had been met with silence. "At our current snail's pace, never." When Story didn't even crack a smile, he rolled his eyes and turned back to the trail. "Mid-morning tomorrow."

"Fantastic. By the way, time to stop again. The human needs to rest awhile."

Eirnin made a sour face, but he stopped and found a perch atop a small boulder. Story dug out some jerky from her pocket, sat on a moss-covered log, and began eating.

He watched her eat in silence for a few minutes then casually asked, "What will you do when we get to Stoneybrook?"

"Find a way to get back to my world, of course."

"Aye, but originally you wanted to find a 'phone' and your...'car', was it?"

Goodness, that had been ages ago, hadn't it? She'd revised her plan considerably since then, once she'd accepted that she was most definitely no longer in her world. She couldn't just call a cab and get a lift to her Jeep.

"Well, I figure I'll get some rock climbing gear, or whatever counts for that around here, buy some fresh provisions, head back to those caves, and climb out the way I came in."

Eirnin blinked at her in disbelief. "Are you saying that

you intend to return to Aisras and climb your way out? That is, of course, assuming that you'd even survive the trip back through the Stoney Mountains without an escort." He paused. "Are you *quite* mad?"

"No, as I've told you countless times, I'm not completely helpless." *Plus I know the faeries aren't out to kill me, which is more than I can say for you.* "I can walk around in the woods all alone without dying, and I even know how to use a bow, thank you very much." True, she wasn't the greatest at archery, but what he didn't know wouldn't hurt him. Then something he'd said caught up with her. "Wait a sec... what's Aisras?"

"The elvish ruins you encountered where we... er, first met."

Story snorted, but Eirnin didn't rise to the bait. He jumped off his perch, walked over to where she sat, and began tracing a rough map in the dirt with his fingertip.

"It's one of the old elf cities from before the Change. There are several spread throughout Ailionora: Ailanthu in the Piney Green Mountains to the east, Aiden at the edge of the Desert of Dreams in the west, and Aiblins in the Ailes Sea to the south." He indicated each location with a finger as he spoke. "They've all been deserted for centuries. Most of us call Ailes, the cluster of islands in the heart of Ailionora, our home."

Here he pointed at the center of the crude diagram, where a narrow neck of land was bisected by a wide river. "Most elves consider the ruins to be holy sites, and on the rare occasion that an elf leaves Ailes, it's generally to make a pilgrimage to one of these places and 'feel the old magic' again."

"Is that what you were doing when we, um, 'first met'?"

Eirnin snorted. "Absolutely not."

Story frowned; none of what he was saying was adding up. Elves only left Ailes to visit the old elf ruins and commune with magic, or whatever it was, and they were obsessed with recovering their immortality. But here Eirnin was out roaming around with no apparent agenda and no belief in the old legends. She looked up at him through suspicious eyes. "Then why were you there?"

"I... look, it doesn't matter why I was there. Just count yourself lucky that I was." He stood up straight, brushing the dirt off his hands, then looked down at her with a cautious expression. "I'm not so sure trying to climb out the way you came in is such a good idea. Portals between worlds follow the rules of magic, not logic."

"I thought you didn't believe the old legends."

A corner of Eirnin's mouth crooked up. "I don't. Believing in magic and believing in the legends are two very different things. I'd be a fool not to believe in magic when it is woven into the fiber of every creature here, and of Ailionora itself. Even we elves still have a bit of magic left in us; we couldn't exist if we didn't."

She had to admit he had a good point about climbing out: there was no guarantee that going back up the hole would return her to her world. But that didn't mean she wasn't going to at least try.

He crouched before her and cocked his head to the side, his gaze lingering on her rounded ears. "Look, I've been giving it a lot of thought. Perhaps you should consider coming with me all the way to Ailes to meet with Queen Eánna. I think she'll be able to help you get back to your world. At the very least, it would be safer than trying to climb through an enchanted passage. Magic portals and doorways have a tendency not to work when forced."

Story froze, her mind clouded for a moment, and then Morrigann's words from last night sounded in her head, as if he was there speaking them himself. And he'd been right!

Eirnin was trying to convince her not to leave this strange

land, but to continue straight to its heart, to the queen's isle. Like a pig to the slaughter. Anxiety seized her, and it was all she could do not to bolt right then and there. She forced a laugh to cover her reaction. "I thought you said your people didn't have access to your magic anymore? How do you propose to help me? What could your queen do for me that I couldn't do on my own?"

Eirnin avoided her gaze and stood back up. "Truth be told, I don't really know. But the queens have always had access to far more knowledge and understanding, especially in the matters of magic, than anyone else. She may know of another passage to your world. Just because we can't manipulate magic doesn't mean we don't understand how it works. We've had a millennium to study it, and the queens have always passed their full knowledge onto their daughters. If anyone can help you, Eánna can."

Yeah, help me right onto a sacrificial altar and then plunge a knife in my heart. She plastered another smile onto her face. "Well, if that's really what you think is best…"

"I do." He gave her a relieved grin in return and extended his hand to help her up. It took all of Story's strength to keep her fingers from trembling in his grasp. As they returned to the path, she caught Eirnin surreptitiously glancing her way, and only the knowledge that the Faerie Prince's fey were shadowing them, protecting her, kept her calmly walking toward her impending death.

Just gotta play along until tonight, she reminded herself. Then she would make her escape from Eirnin's "help" and hopefully be back at her Jeep by sunrise. Feeling Eirnin's eyes on her again, she turned and beamed at him with an encouraging smile.

Just until tonight.

Chapter Ten

The Faerie Prince

STORY STARED AT THE FIRE, ABSENTMINDEDLY TURNING HER
father's knife over and over in her hands. Eirnin was on
his side of the fire, apparently asleep, though she couldn't
really be sure since he slept so rarely. Curled up under his
cloak, he looked peaceful, almost childlike. She had to fight
the urge to make sure the cloak was tucked in snug around
him like she used to do for Will and Katie. Like her father used
to do for her.

*He's not the twins. He's not your family. He wants to kill you.
He's the enemy.*

Her concern for his comfort vanished.

As she watched him sleep, she had to admit that he was
not at all how she'd expected an elf to be. Not that she'd ever
actually expected to meet an elf, but from everything she'd
read and seen, elves, unless they lived in the north pole,
were supposed to be very tall and willowy, kind, wise, and

incredibly magical. Essentially, everything that Eirnin said his sort of elves were before the legendary "Change".

Though according to Morrigann, that wasn't exactly the case.

It sounded like the elves were more like bullies, abusing their power and running roughshod across Ailionora. Even Eirnin admitted that most elves now only cared about their own race's survival, to the exclusion of everything else. He himself was as fickle as a cat, one minute implying that guiding her was a burden, and the next acting like nothing was more important than her well-being.

The tattoos on his face danced in the firelight, making him look exotic, almost alien. They were also a bit of a shock, his tattoos. They were lovely and intricate, true, but when he wasn't smiling, they lent him an air of menace. Quite the opposite of her demure, majestic mental image of elves. Either way, the only things about Eirnin that seemed to jive with her preconceived notions were his pointed ears.

Story sighed, shifting her gaze from Eirnin's sleeping form back to her father's knife. The pixies would be here any moment, and when she left with them the knife would have to stay behind. Her stomach clenched at the thought.

It's just a stupid knife.

But even her logical side knew that it was much more than *just a knife* to her. It was a memory of her father; it was how she had kept him with her during this last year. The thought of leaving it behind nearly made her sick.

She reminded herself forcefully that the knife was not worth getting sacrificed over. Though the very fact that she'd even considered staying, even if only for a fleeting moment, revealed to her just how fragile her psyche still was.

Blowing out a resigned breath, Story continued to turn the knife around in her hands. No, when the time came she'd go with the pixies and leave the knife behind. She was, for all intents and purposes, an adult. It was time to start acting like one.

SHE WOKE WITH A START. DESPITE HER BEST EFFORTS, SHE'D STILL drifted off to sleep. The long days of walking were taking their toll on her. By her estimation, Eirnin had them hiking fifteen to twenty miles a day, and while she was a fit person, it was still bodily exhausting. The really annoying thing was he never seemed to tire at all.

Glancing over at him, she saw that he was still asleep.

Then I can't have been out for that long myself.

She heard a soft giggle behind her and turned to see a handful of adorable little pixies flitting around just outside the circle that Eirnin had drawn. They beckoned her to follow them. Story hesitated and looked over at Eirnin's quietly slumbering form one last time. A shade of doubt clouded her mind for a moment, but then she remembered: *he wants to kill me.* She stood and stepped outside of the circle.

Instantly, the pixies zipped away from her and gestured madly at her waist. Her father's knife was still fastened at her belt. Removing it from the scabbard, she looked at it regretfully and caressed the smooth finish with her fingertips; this was harder than she'd thought it would be. She pressed a soft kiss to the blade and then set the knife down on the ground.

"Goodbye, Dad." Tears pricked at the corners of her eyes, but she wiped them away and squared her shoulders. Taking a deep breath, she followed the pixies away from the light of the campfire and into the dark reaches of the forest.

At first she was completely disoriented in the oppressing darkness that claimed the woods, but just as Morrigann had promised, things began to look and feel familiar. More pixies joined the ones already flying around her, and before long, she had a whole host of faeries dancing wildly through the air to the faint strains of music playing in the distance.

It was, of course, her childhood lullaby. Smiling softly, she felt her spirits rise, and she took a dancing leap along the path. The pixies encouraged her with tiny smiles and excited waves of their hands. Feeling a bit foolish—it was a lot different to dance in a dream—she cautiously placed her hands in the air and swayed her hips along with the melody. The faeries obligingly swirled themselves around her in time with her tentative dancing. Feeling better by the minute she increased her tempo while the music did the same. Grinning, she threw caution to the wind and danced with the exuberance of a child.

The music was much louder now; she was getting close, she could feel it. Story danced into the clearing, and just like in her dreams, Morrigann was awaiting her arrival. The moonlight reflected off his skin with sparks of magical energy, and he beamed at her. As his arms opened in a clear invitation, she raced across the springy grass into his comforting embrace.

She knew she'd made the right decision. Morrigann was here, and he would get the Faerie Prince to help her, and then she could leave this place, and then maybe... maybe Morrigann would want to come with her? The thought of never seeing him again caused her breath to quicken and her palms to sweat. Anxiety coursed through her. A small voice in the back of her mind reminded her that this was irrational behavior—she barely knew him! But then he smiled, banishing the thought completely.

Maybe he can visit me in my dreams there too?

The music's tempo picked up again, and Morrigann was twirling her round and round in their now familiar dance. Magic coursed off of him and left a trail of golden sparks in their wake as they waltzed about the meadow. The little pixies flew in effortlessly to weave flowers into her hair, and Story felt like a faerie princess.

Nearing the center of the clearing, he maneuvered her over to the stone they had sat on in her dream the night before. A seductive smile on his face, he peppered her neck with soft kisses trailing down to her collarbone. She sighed with pleasure, and Morrigann smiled down at her as he tenderly tipped her back against the stone surface. It was as soft as a bed of roses since the faeries had covered it in petals. They were, even now, settling a flowered crown on her brow.

She wasn't exactly sure what was going on and had no idea how any of this was going to help her get back, but the truth was she couldn't make herself care. Her mind was completely enraptured by Morrigann. His feel, his scent, his deliciously seductive lips and kisses, and mostly his warm, magic-filled hands as they caressed her skin making her feel more alive than she had in a very long time.

Her eyes began to feel heavy, and she stared up at Morrigann dreamily as he placed one hand firmly, yet gently, on her shoulder, while the other hand reached behind him.

"I am truly sorry about this, Story." He leaned in close, his nose almost touching hers, and his sweet breath intoxicating her senses. "You seem like a delightful, if simple, girl." He kissed her lightly on her lips, and she soaked in the feeling of him—all freshness and rebirth of nature. And then he was pulling away and standing over her again, his grip on her shoulder tighter, almost painful.

"But I can't risk the elves getting their hands on you. I'm sure you understand."

Before Story's muddled mind could take in what he'd just said, he raised his right hand high above her. An obsidian blade gleamed, poised directly over her heart, and even if she'd had the time or the mental capacity to move, the flowering vines that had grown over her held her securely in place.

A small voice in the back of her mind screamed that this was wrong. That she should not just lie on this altar, smiling dazedly up at the man who was trying to murder her. But as she stared up helplessly at the black knife in his hand, time seemed to slow. The shiny blade came down, and she did nothing.

Suddenly Morrigann cried out in pain and dropped the blade, clutching at his hand. She heard the knife clatter harmlessly off the rock and fixed her gaze on his hand. The blade of another knife—*my knife!*—protruded from the flesh of his palm. Smoke started to rise as the skin around the wound began to blacken and burn away.

The vines holding her in place began to wither, and she felt the fog in her mind clear. Sitting up, she looked across the meadow and could see Eirnin fighting off pixies. They were dive bombing him with stones and anything else they could get their hands on.

He must have thrown the knife in order to stop Morrigann from killing me!

That realization cleared away any lingering magic that the faerie had spelled on her mind. Seething in anger, she glared down at Morrigann. "You tried to kill me, you jerk! I trusted you." She didn't mean to sound so plaintive and betrayed.

Bent over in pain, he clutched at the hilt of the knife trying feebly to pull at it. The black wound was growing, charring more and more of his hand. Free from the vines that bound her, Story jumped off the boulder and slapped his hand off the hilt.

"Don't you DARE touch it! You have no right!" Tears escaped the corners of her eyes, and she didn't bother wiping them away.

He looked up at her, and she saw that his once beautiful face, while still perfect, was marred by the cruel sneer that crossed his features.

"Why not?" he coughed weakly, while slowly standing up. "You were so willing to trade your father's memory for a few stolen kisses and a dance in the moonlight, you stupid little girl."

Her eyes blazed. Rearing her hand back, she let it fly forward and punched Morrigann right in his perfect mouth, knocking him back down to the ground.

"Don't call me stupid." She stepped down hard on his right wrist, pinning his arm to the ground, ignoring his pain-filled cry. "And don't you EVER mock my father's memory again." She twisted her heel, grinding his hand into the dirt and rocks. "You are nothing compared to him." Leaning over she grasped the hilt of the knife and yanked it out of his hand savagely.

"Story, no!" Eirnin yelled from across the clearing, but it was too late.

Smirking up at her, Morrigann blew her a kiss and then promptly disappeared.

A HAND CAME DOWN ON HER SHOULDER, AND SHE WHIRLED around, pulling away from it. Facing Eirnin, she held her knife out in an aggressive stance. "Don't you touch me!"

His eyes looked like fire, the silver almost completely masked by bright red and yellow swirls of color. This time it was no reflection from the firelight. He was angry.

"Are you completely mad? What were you thinking going off alone into the forest with a bunch of fey? And the Faerie Prince himself no less!" He jabbed a finger in her direction, punctuating his words. "And then, just when we have him, you let him go!" He threw his hands up in the air and started pacing. Eying the knife she still had pointed at him, he rolled his eyes. "What are you pointing that thing at me for? I'm not the one who tried to kill you!"

"Yet! You're not the one who tried to kill me *yet*," she bit out as she maneuvered away from him.

"What are you going on about?" He stopped pacing and glared at her.

"Just what it sounds like. I know all about your elvish prophecy. You know, the one about getting a 'blood sacrifice' from someone from another world." She'd managed to position the stone altar between them at this point, and began backing toward the tree line, keeping Eirnin in her line of sight the entire time.

"Story, wait! It's not like that. You don't understand!" He moved to intercept her. "I don't know what the Faerie Prince told you, but it clearly wasn't the truth."

She paused and lowered her knife. "Faerie Prince? You mean Morrigann was…"

Eirnin nodded and took a hesitant step forward. She immediately brandished her knife again. "Stay right where you are, elf-boy. At this point I don't trust anyone, least of all you. How do I know you aren't going to cloud my thoughts the way that faerie bastard did?"

He sighed and closed his eyes. "For the last time, Story, elves can't use magic. If we could, I'd have sent you back to your own world long before now." He pinched the bridge of his nose before muttering, "Believe me on that one."

"Well, then why don't you explain what the hell just happened?"

"Fine, I'd be happy to. Only please put the knife away, and let's get out of here."

"No way. Start talking. Now. I'm not going anywhere until I have some answers."

"Really, Story, a Faerie Ring is not the safest place in the world to sit down and have a chat. Can we please go back to the campsite?"

It was not his words but the hint of desperation and fear in his voice that convinced her to trust him, at least for now. Eirnin had yet to show any discomfort in their travels, but it was obvious that being inside the meadow was making him anxious. His eyes kept darting around as if he expected to be attacked at any moment.

"Alright." She sheathed her knife at her side and pointed a finger at him. "But don't think this means I trust or believe you."

The walk back to the camp was surprisingly quick, if awkwardly silent. Ultimately, she was grateful for how short it was since she found herself first dwelling on, and then berating herself for, her stupidity concerning Morrigann. How could she have been so naïve? Perhaps she could forgive herself for trusting him since, as a general rule, she tended to assume the best of people.

Unless, like Eirnin, they start out as a jerk. She watched his broad shoulders bob up and down as he walked the path ahead of her, and she let out a sigh; even then she tended to give people a second chance.

What she couldn't forgive herself for was not realizing that Morrigann and the Faerie Prince were one and the same.

And more importantly, that he was so obviously manipulating me. A five-year-old could have figured that out.

I should have known better!

They arrived back at their campsite and, after building the fire back up, sat down in their customary spots. As they stared at each other across the flames, Story raised an expectant eyebrow at him.

"Okay, elf-boy, start talking. Why does it seem that everyone here in Ailionora wants to kill me?"

"The only person who wants to kill you is the Faerie Prince. He believes your very presence puts his curse in jeopardy of being broken." He raised a hand to forestall her inevitable questions. "Please, this will go a lot faster if you just let me talk. I promise I will answer all your questions when I'm done."

She nodded, so he continued. "I never lied to you—I just didn't tell you the whole story. Though in hindsight..." He sighed and scrubbed his face in his hands.

"As I told you before, after the Faerie Prince cursed *The Ailes*, the silver blossoms fell from the tree, and the elves themselves fell down to the earth and *Changed*. Many wept, for they knew what had happened, as they felt cut off from the life-giving essence of Ailionora, from magic itself.

"One among them wept the most; she was the maiden who had fallen in love with the Faerie Prince and had been tricked by him into revealing the source of our power. In her grief, and with her last ounce of magic, she was unable to remove the curse, but to add a small loophole: with the sacrifice of blood from another world, willingly given, the tree would be restored."

"So you *do* want to kill me!" Story was on her feet and moving away from him as quickly as she could, but she was too slow.

"Story, wait!" He grabbed her wrist, pulling her to a gentle stop. "No, it's not like that at all. To begin with, the blood has to be *willingly* given, otherwise it's pointless. It won't work."

"Well, I'm *not* willing, that's for sure." She tugged at her trapped wrist, but it was useless; his grip was like an iron vise.

"And the other thing is that it only takes one drop. No one wants to kill you." He dropped her wrist. "Well, no one but the Faerie Prince, that is." Eirnin moved back to the fire and sat down on his haunches, resting his chin against his knees. "I don't want to kill you. I don't even care about immortality.

I hate how wrapped up about it my race has become. They're so worried about living forever they've forgotten how to live."

He looked up at her with worried, yellow eyes. "I'll take you back to your cave and even help you climb out if that's what you want. Just promise me you won't go running off with any faeries again."

She stared at him from the edge of the camp, completely torn. Logic dictated that he could be making all this up, just as Morrigann had. But something inside of her, that little voice in the back of her mind that had warned her away from Morrigann, believed the elf. Or maybe it was the simple fact that Eirnin had made her shoes.

"Why didn't you just tell me all this in the first place?"

He snorted. "For starters, I really didn't believe any of it myself. I still don't know if I do." He eyed her with a mixture of curiosity and confusion. "But it's clear that you aren't from Ailionora, and that the Faerie Prince believes you are the fulfillment of the prophecy."

She walked back toward the fire and slumped down next to him, a resigned look on her face.

"He really does want to kill me, doesn't he?"

"Aye, that he does."

"Figures. I find my way into a magical world and manage to run off with the one guy who wants to kill me." She sighed loudly. "And then I threaten the one guy who tries to help me."

Eirnin nudged her shoulder with his own. "Don't be too hard on yourself. You were under a faerie spell, after all. Plus, you did land a splendid punch on his arrogant face. So there is that."

"Hmph. Yeah. There is that, I guess." She shook out her hand—it was starting to get sore. *So worth it!*

Looking at Eirnin out of the corner of her eye, she

half-smiled. "I still don't know why you didn't just tell me the whole story to begin with. All this could have been avoided."

He let out a short laugh. "I can see it now: you would've broken the Faerie Prince's hold on you, and instantly believed me right?"

Story chuckled. "Oh come on. I wasn't that far gone for him."

He raised his eyebrow at that. "I hate to point this out, but you willingly lay down on the sacrificial altar. You all but drove the blade into your own heart."

"Well, yeah. But I mean besides that. I was so totally *not* into him," she said wryly.

Eirnin barked out another laugh. "I could tell. Well, aside from all that, it would have been a bit of an awkward conversation, don't you think?

It was her turn to raise an eyebrow. "Awkward how?"

"Well, it's quite something to say to someone you've just met. 'Hello! I think you are the Ailesit. Could I please have a wee bit of your blood to save my entire race?'"

"Okay, yeah. I guess I can see how that could be a bit awkward." She chuckled, and then looked over at him, curious. "The Ailesit... what's that? It sounds like it has the name for that tree in it."

"Aye, that it does." He poked at the fire with a stick. "The Ailesit quite literally means 'the one who will restore Life.' Or in simpler terms, 'savior'."

She shot to her feet and, putting her hands up, backed away a few steps. "Whoa there, elf-boy. I'm no one's savior. Jeez, I can barely save myself right now."

The bemused expression on his face didn't help any. "I know. Trust me, you're not what anyone is expecting."

Story's face clouded. "And what the heck is that supposed to mean?"

Just because she didn't want to be this Ailesit savior person, or whatever it was, that didn't mean she wanted to be viewed as "not good enough."

Eirnin placed his forearms behind him and leaned back. "Just that the Ailesit has to be powerful enough to defeat the Faerie Prince. Most have assumed the Ailesit would be a great warrior, overflowing with magic." He fixed his now green-eyed gaze on her. "Definitely not a lost girl who clearly doesn't want to be here and who nearly got herself killed by the Faerie Prince himself within her first week of arriving."

Story paced back and forth in front of the fire. "You're damn right I don't want to be here! I didn't ask for any of this. I don't want anything to do with faeries or elves or any other mythological creatures." She gestured wildly with her hands to punctuate her words. "I most certainly don't want to be any prophesied tree savior or whatever the heck it is. I just want to go back to my world, and back to school, and live my life my own way!" She kicked at a rock and it clattered off loudly into the depths of the forest.

Eirnin was staring at her again.

"What is it this time?" She bellowed, throwing her hands up in frustration. "Do I have a horn growing out of my forehead or something? We've already established that I'm not from Ailionora."

"Oh, it's nothing like that at all, though your hair has started to take on some interesting characteristics over the last few days." He winked, and she wanted to kick him. She wasn't in the mood to be teased.

"No, I just find it interesting that whenever you talk about going back, you never talk about going home."

His words shot through her like an arrow straight into her heart, and a memory rose unbidden.

Her dad used to make the best apple cider in the world. It

was simple really. Just apple juice thrown into a crockpot with cinnamon sticks and cloves for a bit of flavor, but after a day of simmering, it smelled wonderful. It smelled like home.

Why was she so desperate to leave when she had no home left to go back to?

Chapter Twelve

Gnomes

Story woke with a groan. She'd slept fitfully, constantly afraid that Morrigann would come to her in her dreams again and put her under another spell.

He hadn't come, and she could only assume that it was because he was no longer welcome in her dreams. That, or he was busy planning some other means to kill her.

Sitting up, she winced as pain shot through her right hip.

That's what I get for trying to sleep on my side on the ground. What I wouldn't give for a real bed!

She put her right hand down to steady herself and her fingertips brushed against something soft and yielding. Looking down she saw that Eirnin had thoughtfully left her some fresh fruit for breakfast.

Eirnin!

Her eyes darted around their campsite, but apart from the cold remains of the fire, there was no sign of him. He'd left her, and she didn't blame him after the way she'd behaved. Her cheeks heated as she recalled everything she'd said and done the night before, and moaning loudly, she buried her face in her hands.

She was worn out, grimier than ever, and desperately craving a soak in a hot bath. But more than anything, she wanted Eirnin back so she could apologize to him.

"Amazing! You can even manage to sleep while sitting up."

She peeked through her fingers. Eirnin was standing a few feet away, a sardonic grin on his face. "And you haven't even touched your breakfast yet. Who are you and what have you done with Story?"

Lowering her hands, she smiled sheepishly up at him, relieved he was there.

His eyes softened toward her, comforting green flickers of color dancing in them. "Well, are you going to sit there all day? Let's get going; I'd like to reach Stoneybrook at some point today." With another teasing grin in her direction, he turned around and started walking down the trail, leaving Story to scramble after him.

THE WALK WAS A RIOT OF EMOTIONS FOR STORY. FOR STARTERS, SHE was still completely embarrassed about being so easily manipulated and taken in by Morrigann. Eirnin was, surprisingly, kind enough not to mention it and, apparently sensing she needed quiet and time to think about things, didn't try to force a conversation.

Of course there was also the figurative "elephant in the room." The whole Ailesit business. She hated to admit it, but it all seemed to make an odd sort of sense now. Why she'd felt drawn to the caves in the first place, and why, even now, she felt inextricably drawn forward, as if following Eirnin to the city of Ailes was the right choice. The very thought of going back to Aisras made her stomach churn. That said, she wasn't keen on going off in search of some stupid tree, just so she could go bleed on it for a bunch of self-absorbed elves.

It's not fair!

She felt like she had no choice in any of this. At least she knew that the blood had to be willingly given, so that mollified her somewhat. She was just going to go to the city of Ailes, get the queen to help her out, and go back to her own world.

Story gazed at the gradually flattening land around her. The forest had thinned out and she could see fields filled with new growths of crops dotting the surrounding landscape. She sighed; it frustrated her that Eirnin had been able to see something about herself after just a few days of traveling together that she hadn't noticed. Even now she couldn't bring herself to say she wanted to go "home." Though going home was what she wanted most, she just didn't know where home was anymore.

Shaking her head and trying to clear her mind of such depressing thoughts, she called out to Eirnin, who was, as usual, walking ahead of her.

"Oi, what's that?" He turned to look back at her. "Don't tell me you're hungry already."

Story felt the blood rush up to her face, and she swallowed her snippy retort. She was a bit hungry, but that's not why she'd called out to him. "No, not really. I guess I was just curious about something is all."

With half a smile and a knowing shake of his head, he tossed her a peach from his kit. "When we get to Stoneybrook, the first thing we're doing is getting you a big bag, so you can carry your own food. I'm not a pack animal you know."

Story caught the peach, stuck her tongue out at him, and then bit into the juicy flesh.

"Then we're getting you a bath." He wrinkled his nose at her and waved at the air in front of him. "You stink worse than a troll."

"Always the gentleman," she said around a mouthful of peach. "Besides, you don't smell so great yourself."

Taking an exaggerated whiff of himself, he pretended to choke on the smell.

She chuckled, but then returned to her question. "So, seriously, I want to know two things. The first," she held one finger, "What season is it, because it's summer where I came from, and with the chill and the new fields, I'm thinking it's spring here. The second," she raised another finger, "Why I haven't seen any bugs, or am I just blind?"

"Aye, it is spring, which makes things a bit more dangerous for you." He pushed down one of her raised fingers. "As for the second, I'm not quite sure I follow."

"What did you mean by spring being dangerous for me?"

"What did you mean by bugs?"

Story pursed her lips together, annoyed. "You know, bugs. Insects? Flies? Bees? Cockroaches?"

He continued to look blankly at her.

"The creepy crawly things that live in nature? Actually, they're kind of essential to any eco-system. They pollinate the flowers, break down and decompose dead things, eat trash; you know, the fun jobs. If insects weren't around we'd live among piles of dead things and trash, and there'd be no living plants." She indicated the fertile, green farmland around them.

"And no food for you either," Eirnin quipped, barely ducking out of the path of the peach pit she threw at him. "We do have those things, what did you call them? Insects? Well, here they're called faeries."

Story's jaw dropped. "No way!"

"Aye, the pixies and other smaller faeries pollinate the flowers; the wood sprites tend to the forests, and less savory fey eat garbage and other things. There are more fey than I could possibly list. Much like your insects I assume."

"So wait, you're saying that faeries are the bugs of Ailionora?" She barely stifled a giggle; for some reason this struck her as immeasurably funny. "I was going to ask why your ancestors didn't just destroy all the fey back when they had the chance, but it's obvious now."

"Aye, it would kill our world. As annoying as they are, we can't survive without them. So we've just devised ways to live with them, but to keep them at bay."

Story nodded her head. It made sense. Didn't she put bug spray on every time she went hiking? And millions were spent each year by governments spraying for mosquitoes and other insect pests. But everyone knew you couldn't just kill off all the world's bugs and still continue living yourself.

As they walked, the path eventually turned into a wide and rutted dirt road. They were bordered by farmland as far as the eye could see; the Stoney Forest and Mountains were only at their back now.

"So, elf-boy, why is spring a bit more dangerous for me?"

Eirnin didn't answer, but paused, staring intently into the distance.

"What now?" She clutched at the hilt of her knife.

He looked back at her, his mouth quirking into a half-smile. "Calm down. It's not the fey. You're about to get your wish and meet your first gnome."

Relaxing, she followed his gaze. If she squinted she could see a dust cloud forming ahead. She watched as it resolved itself into a small wagon pulled by a diminutive pair of oxen that matched the small person driving the cart proportionally in size.

Ah, he must be the gnome.

As he got closer, she was able to make out more details. He looked, for all intents and purposes, to be human, only shorter, maybe as much as a foot shorter? Nothing at all like a dwarf. She noticed that his ears were also larger and distended at the tips. Story didn't know if his leathery skin and thick build were the norm among his kind, but she left off her observations of him when he pulled up next to them and came to a halt.

"Good morning, Mister Jord. How are you this fine day?" Eirnin inclined his head at the smaller man, who, in turn, tipped his wide-brimmed straw hat back at the elf.

"I'd be doing much better if the spriggans would stay away from my crops." He frowned deeply. "Their last whirl-wind took out a full quarter of my corn field." His accent was thick and heavy, almost Germanic sounding to Story's ears.

"I'm sorry to hear that." Eirnin dug into his kit and pulled out a leather pouch. He tossed it at the little man who caught it handily. "Here's some more salt. It's not much, but it should help."

The gnome's sun-darkened face split into a wide smile. "Thank you, lad. I do appreciate this." Pulling out a rough canvas bag, he tossed it to Eirnin. "It's hardly a fair trade, but it's the best cornmeal you'll find this side of the Sunset Plains, I assure you."

Mister Jord looked like he was about to say more, but then shifted his gaze to Story, raised one eyebrow curiously, and tipped his hat once again to Eirnin. "I'd best be off now. It was nice to see you again, Mister Eáchan."

Eirnin raised a hand in goodbye and then shrugged when he turned to Story as Mister Jord pulled away. "He's never been the talkative sort." Handing the burlap bag to her, he grinned. "You get to carry the food for once."

They continued on like this for the rest of the morning, encountering the occasional gnome farmer on the road and filling their bag with more food. A couple potatoes here, some carrots there, and given freely to Eirnin for past kindnesses done by him. This showed a new side of him. He may not have the ability to wield magic anymore, but unlike the rest of his people, he didn't let that keep him from helping out those who needed it, and for no other reason that Story could ascertain than he wanted to.

The few gnomes they passed on the road to Stoneybrook who didn't have something to give to him still tipped their hats, and he greeted most of them by name. The majority of them ignored Story the way Mister Jord had, and the few who did look at her stared more at her unkempt appearance than anything else. This actually surprised her a bit; Eirnin and Morrigann had both been completely fascinated by her origins, whereas the gnomes didn't seem to pay her any real mind at all.

"Don't any of them wonder who I am, where I came from, or why I'm with you?" she finally asked.

Eirnin smirked. "Really, Story, it's not *always* about you." She smacked his shoulder playfully, and he laughed. "Okay, the truth is, you're much taller than them, and they can't see your ears because of your mad hair, so they just assume you're an elf."

He looked at her as if that should explain it, and when she looked back at him blankly, he continued. "Like I said, elves don't travel much, and when they do, they tend to keep to themselves."

"You're an elf."

"I knew I'd be able to convince you of that eventually!"

"They all know you and talk to you."

He shrugged. "That's because unlike the rest of my kin, I actually travel. I belong to the hunter clan—there used to be a day when we were everywhere. We loved to explore; though you wouldn't know it to look at us these days. *I* like to see the world, and I do like to help my fellows where I can." He kicked a stone, knocking off the road. "I think my people idolize the wrong bits of our ancestors. Any idiot can be immortal. What's important is what you do with your life."

"Is that how you happened to come across me? You were just out wandering?"

Eirnin sighed, as if he'd known this conversation was coming and hadn't been looking forward to it. "Remember how I told you that the queens have always had great foresight and knowledge—actually, most call it prophecy—even after the Faerie Prince cursed the tree?"

She nodded her head.

"Well, a few months back Queen Eánna asked me to go to Aisras and await the arrival of the Ailesit."

She stopped walking. *Huh*, Story thought, *I didn't see that coming.*

"So you knew... you knew all along who I was?"

"No, remember I left you at first? It never even crossed my mind when I met you that you were the Ailesit. For starters, I didn't believe such a person existed, and then when we did meet, you didn't really look like a great warrior."

"Then why did you come back for me?"

An exasperated look crossed his face. "It's like I told you when you asked the first time. I felt bad—you were clearly lost." He raked his hands through his hair. "I'm not the villain you seem to think I am, Story. I didn't even begin to suspect anything until you cut your foot. And even then, I didn't know what you were."

She pinched the bridge of her nose, feeling a headache coming on. "I thought... well, I hate to sound like a broken record, but I thought you didn't believe any of the old legends? Why would you do it? Why willingly go into dangerous, faerie-filled lands, all alone, to await the arrival of someone you knew wasn't coming?"

Eirnin sighed again. "As I said before, most elves won't leave the city of Ailes these days. Queen Eánna knew that I would."

"That only explains why she asked you to go not why you agreed to do it."

"I said yes because Eánna is my queen, and in addition to that, she's my cousin." Stopping, he looked her in the eyes, and she could see the familiar flickers of bright yellow in them that seemed to appear whenever he was worried or anxious. "I promise I'm not taking you back to be sacrificed. We would never do that. I only went because she's family. I didn't actually expect to find you."

Story smiled briefly at him and patted his arm before continuing down the road. "I know, elf-boy. I believe you. I think I would have gotten a better reception from you had it been otherwise." She looked over her shoulder and smirked. "Now, explain to me how in this world you and the queen are cousins? I thought you said elves could only have one kid, which kinda negates siblings, and therefore uncles, aunts, or cousins."

"Oh, that." He let out a breath, as if a potential crisis had just been averted. "That's easy. Our grandfathers were twins. Like I said, very rare, but they do happen on occasion."

His silver eyes now had calm, sea-green swirls in them, and she was glad that he seemed to have relaxed some. It was as if he thought she was going to bolt whenever he revealed anything new. Though, had it been yesterday, she probably would have. The evening's events had done a lot to change her perspective. Well, that, and having her mind finally clear of Morrigann's spell. She felt her cheeks flush again at the thought of her mortifying behavior.

Stupid, stupid, stupid!

She was interrupted from her personal tirade by Eirnin pointing down the slope of the small hill they were on to the intersection of two rivers. "Not sure if your human eyes can see it yet, but if you look really hard, you can see the outskirts of Stoneybrook."

Chapter Thirteen

STONEYBROOK

As they entered the village, Story tried not to stare. It was difficult—everything around her was so vastly different from what she'd come to expect from a town. She felt excited and anxious as she took in every detail. It was like she was in the most accurate Renaissance Fair village ever built; except that this was real life to these people. All around her there was movement, hustle and bustle, trade and commerce. Children chased dogs, farmers led livestock to market, women walked around with babies on their hips and baskets full of fresh bread or produce from the farmers' market.

I really am in another world!

She watched as two women paused in front of a shop window and pointed at some vividly-colored orange cloth before stepping inside to get a better look. She could hear their laughter; she could hear everyone's laughter all around her.

One thing was certain; the gnomes were definitely not the little garden statues that populated lawns back in her world. On the other hand, they were obviously not elves or humans either.

Now that she could see several of them all at once, she confirmed what she'd assumed in her encounters with the solitary gnome travelers on the road. They were all short in stature, around five feet in height, plus or minus a few inches on either side. If Eirnin was an example of the elves' typical dimensions, the gnomes were a shorter and hardier bunch—thick set and sturdy. Story thought that actually might have more to do with the nature of the labor-intensive farm work than anything else. They all had weather-beaten, sun-darkened skin, many as dark as the earth itself, and every one of them managed to look serious, yet all were quick with a laugh. Ultimately, the gnomes struck her exactly as Eirnin had first described them to her: earth people. They even smelled earthy.

"Hey, elf-boy, why are so many of them wearing their clothes inside out?" The gnomes all had on vivid and earthy shades of red, orange, brown, and yellow. Most of them also had tiny bells woven into their hair, or beards if they had them, which caused a constant, yet pleasant, tinkling sound in the background noise of the village.

"It's another trick to keep away the fey. Same with the bells." Eirnin inclined his head and greeted another gnome, who thankfully had no produce to give him. The bag of food Story was carrying was heavy enough.

"Ah, you mean it's like bug spray."

He cracked a smile. "Aye, if that is what you use to keep the fey in your world from bothering you, then yes, it's just like bug spray."

Starting about a mile before the village proper, the dirt road had gradually been replaced by a smoothly paved road. The paving stones themselves were gorgeous white marble with silver grain lines, just like the stones used for the bridge and building she'd encountered on her first day in Ailionora—at least from what she could see of them. The road was mostly covered by a thin layer of dirt, straw, and animal feces: the typical things you'd expect to encounter on a village road.

The buildings in the town were small, practical edifices made of wood siding, logs, and wooden shingles or thatch for roofs. Signs hung above all of the shops, each one with a picture describing the nature of the business carried on within: a milliner, cobbler, blacksmith, and many others. Despite its grimy and shabby appearance the road looked out of place—overly refined and artistically very different from the rest of the village.

"The gnomes didn't build this road did they?"

Eirnin's eyes widened momentarily, orange flickering through them. "Very perceptive. No, they didn't build the roads."

"The elves did. Back before the Change, I'm guessing." It wasn't a question; she was certain of this.

"Are you sure you've never been here before?" He sounded like he was only half-joking, so she pointed at her bandaged foot. "Oh, right." He smiled wryly at her. "How could I forget? Well, you are correct, little human. Back before the Change, the elves built and maintained roads from Ailes to all of our cities. All that remains of them now are the bits that are kept up by the gnomes in their villages. The rest have long since been reclaimed by the forests."

"I don't see how you can disbelieve that the Change happened now, with such solid proof before your eyes."

"Story, I never said I didn't believe the Change happened; I just don't believe that we were these magically powerful immortal beings. We did change as a people, and not for the better." Eirnin turned away, but Story had already caught the flashes of blue swirling in his silver eyes.

He walked purposefully toward what was easily the largest building in the town. It was two stories in height, with a wrap around porch, covered balcony on each story, and a wood-shingled roof. A sign hung over the main doors with a mug of ale and a bed painted on it.

An inn! A bath! A real bed!

Story quickened her steps; she could hardly wait to get inside and check in!

Suddenly a new realization slammed into her: she had no money, or whatever passed for currency in this world. Her stomach sank.

Was it asking too much to hope that Eirnin would loan her the amount needed for a room? He'd done so much for her already, and she couldn't figure out how she would pay him back even if he did. Her hand brushed her knife, and looking down she realized that she had at least one thing that was worth something in this land. Though bartering it would be her last resort.

Eirnin pushed open the heavy, main door and held it so she could walk inside. Setting her bag down, she peered into the room, letting her eyes adjust to the dim light. The room was vast, taking up the entire main floor of the inn. Tables were scattered throughout, some occupied by gnomes eating lunch, drinking beer, or smoking a pipe, while others sat empty and waiting. The quiet roar of a dozen conversations carried on, while a girl sat in the corner playing a stringed instrument that looked like a wide-necked guitar. Its melodious harmonies were unobtrusive and relaxing, perfect for a lunchtime respite in a common room at an inn.

"Good afternoon, Mister Eáchan." A thickset middle-aged female gnome stepped in front of Eirnin and grinned up at him in delight before holding open her arms in a clear invitation.

His face broke into a hesitant smile as he cautiously leaned in to hug her. "Good afternoon, Missus Bryggeri. It's good to see you ag—" His words were cut off as she crushed him in a tight hug.

"Can't breathe…" he gasped, straining against her, and Story stifled a giggle.

"Oh, sorry!" Missus Bryggeri let go of him. "I forget how fragile your kind is." She turned her shrewd eyes to Story and gave her a quick appraisal. "Who is your friend?" she asked with the same loosely Germanic accent to her voice that Story noticed Mister Jord and the other gnomes had.

Bent over, hands on knees while catching his breath, Eirnin pointed at Story with one hand and then at the robust woman before him. "Story, I'd like to introduce you to Missus Brygerri, the innkeeper here. Her husband is the town's brew master. Missus Brygerri, this is my traveling companion, Miss Sorenson."

Story held out her hand out to the innkeeper. "Nice to meet you, Missus Brygerri."

The gnome looked at Story's proffered hand curiously, but reached for it anyway. Before Story knew what had happened she was in a bone-crushing hug and gasping for breath.

"Likewise, Miss Sorenson." She released her none too gently, and Eirnin reached out to steady Story before she could fall. "My stars! You both smell worse than my Mister B, and that's saying something. Let's get you in a room and then out to the bathhouse."

Story's stomach chose that moment to rumble loudly, and she squeezed her eyes shut knowing the smirk Eirnin would be giving her. It was bad enough that she could hear him chuckling softly.

Clucking her tongue loudly, the innkeeper put her hands on her hips. "On second thought, perhaps we'd best get some food in you first, dear." Then she directed her piercing gaze to Eirnin. "And shame on you for bringing her to me half-starved."

A wounded look crossed his face, and he raised his hands in protest. "But I—"

"I'll not hear your excuses, Mister Eáchan. You just take her to that table over there, and I'll be around in a bit with two bowls of my eternal soup."

"Better bring three just for Miss Sorensen," Eirnin softly quipped, but the innkeeper didn't hear him. Story's stomach rumbled once again as they sat down at the table, and she buried her head in her hands, mortified and cursing her traitorous stomach. She really didn't eat that much! At least, not for a teenage, human girl.

She steeled herself for what was undoubtedly going to be another conversation that involved Eirnin poking fun at her while she futilely tried to verbally spar back, but luckily, the guitar player chose that moment to begin singing.

Her voice was light and airy and flowed in perfect harmony with the melody her instrument produced, and Story's attention was immediately riveted by it. All the conversations in the room silenced immediately as everyone focused on the music wafting through the space. Story couldn't understand the language in the song, but her heart felt a sudden longing for whatever it was the girl was singing about. She would do anything for it. Anything at all. Then as suddenly as the song began, it was over, and Story could breathe again.

She turned to look at Eirnin. He was smiling contentedly, and his eyes were nearly solid sea green in color. She watched as they faded back to their usual silver, hints of green flashing only occasionally. She had a theory about that but for now had more pressing matters to discuss with him. She leaned in and lowered her voice. "That girl is a siren!"

His eyebrows shot up at that, but before he could speak another voice with the same rolling accent as Eirnin's answered for him.

"Actually, she's only half-siren. Or, more accurately, she's only half-dryad."

Story looked up, and where she expected to see a gnome head only saw a set of slim, masculine shoulders. Her gaze continued up until she saw his thin, angular face and the beginnings of crows feet around his eyes. He had a head full of long, stick-straight, silvery white hair that brushed over his shoulders like a curtain. One side was tucked up behind his delicately pointed elf ear, and he too had a tattoo near his eye. His was different from Eirnin's in that it was located over his eye and had four thick, intertwined, blue strands leading up to his hairline.

"Eilath!" Eirnin jumped to his feet and grasped opposing wrists with the other elf. Eilath placed his free hand on Eirnin's shoulder, and Eirnin did the same. They smiled at each other, and Story could see vibrant green and orange swirls of color in Eirnin's eyes, while Eilath's eyes remained a clear, perfect silver.

"Eirnin! How have you been? And who is your friend?" Eilath turned his liquid silver gaze to her and smiled, instantly putting her at ease. There was kindness in his face, the sort that you couldn't fake; it was a reflection of caring and gentleness manifested in his very aura from years of behaving that way. She trusted him completely, and knew this was no faerie trick clouding her mind. Eilath was a good person.

She stood up, held out her hand in the same way Eirnin had, and answered him. "My name is Story, sir. Eirnin found me a bit lost and turned around. He's trying to help me get back to where I came from." He took her outstretched wrist and gripped it though he didn't place his free hand on her shoulder.

Maybe that's something they only do with close friends?

Eilath studied her face, focusing in on her sea-green eyes, and with a sudden flash of bluish-green in his own eyes, smiled at her. "Is he now? Well, young one, once my Adair finishes playing her faolán—if it would be all right with you— we should head out to our campsite. I'd be very interested in hearing the full tale."

"Eh, what's this Mister Eásphor?" The innkeeper bustled up to the table, a large tray in hand with three bowls of soup on it. "You're not going anywhere until Miss Sorenson here's had a bite to eat. And then only if you promise that Mister Eáchan will get a bath." She waved at the air in front of her face and pinched her nose.

Eilath laughed rich and full at Eirnin's sour expression. "Don't worry Missus Brygerri. I think the da'nan would run off if they had to smell him for too long." This seemed to mollify her, and she left with smile and a "You be sure to eat up all of that" for Story.

She looked around the table and saw no spoons or anything to eat the soup with. She was about to ask Eirnin if he had an extra one near him, when she saw both he and Eilath pick up their bowls and tip them to their lips.

Ahhh, so it's like Medieval Times. The twins would love this! Well, here goes nothing…

Picking up the bowl, she brought it beneath her nose and inhaled. It smelled wonderful, a perfect blend of herbs and spices, and something like a butternut squash soup base. She took a swallow and confirmed that it was, in fact, just as delicious as it smelled. Tipping the bowl back she drank it all down as fast as she could, and only stopped when her body cried out for air. She smacked her lips as she set the bowl down and looked up to see two bemused elves staring at her.

"What? It's really good..."

Eilath started laughing again, and Eirnin joined him. Even Story couldn't help cracking a smile; Eilath's good humor was contagious. He was not at all what she expected in meeting another elf. Sure, he looked every bit an elf, more so than Eirnin did. He was well over six feet in height, very lean and slim, dressed elegantly—yet simply—in finely cut, blue travel clothes, and he carried himself with calm dignity and refinement. Yet Eirnin had led her to believe that all elves were xenophobic, self-absorbed, isolationists. This elf was anything but.

Feeling her eyes on him, he stopped laughing, but the smile was still on his face, and his eyes still held their greenish-blue swirls of color. "What is it, child?"

"Uh, sorry." Story thought fast, unsure of what to say, so instead latched onto his appearance. "I didn't mean to stare. You're just the oldest looking elf I've ever seen. Not that I've met a wide range..."

This brought a soft chuckle from him. "No, I don't suppose you have," he said with a wink. "Well, I assure you that my hair color is natural. I've always looked old and gray. And don't worry about me falling over dead here on the table. I'm only two hundred and three, and I fully intend to eek out at least one more century before I sail across the Ailes Sea."

Eirnin rolled his eyes, and Eilath smacked him lightly on the shoulder. "Respect your elders, boy. Besides, you never know, it could be true."

Eirnin snorted, but kept his comments to himself. Just then the girl who had been playing the music bounded up behind Eilath, hugged him around his neck, and planted a kiss on the crown of his head. Then she reached out and flicked one of Eirnin's ears with her fingers before she threw herself into the remaining empty chair. Her fiery red dreadlocks flew about her head wildly with her every movement.

"Oi, Eirnin, nice to see you again. How are you?" Then without waiting for him to answer, she fixed her gaze on Eilath. "How was I today, Da? Was I better? Did you like my new song?" But before he could answer she looked at Story with her liquid silver eyes. "Who's this? You don't look like a gnome or an elf. And what did you do to your hair? Are you friends with Eirnin?"

Story's mouth hung open in confusion, even after she was able to sort out what the girl had said in her thick Welsh-like accent. For starters, Story didn't know which question to answer first, and secondly, she wasn't sure if the girl was done talking yet. Eirnin saved her from having to figure out what to say. Hand still clutched at his ear, he turned to the girl, a mildly annoyed look on his face. "Well Adair, I see you haven't lost your propensity for getting right to the heart of an issue. I suggest we move this conversation to your camp, Eilath. That is, if Story is done eating."

Story motioned a hand at him. "Lead the way, elf-boy. I've still got a bag full of food to munch on—that should see me through at least the next hour."

He winked at her and left to go find Missus Brygerri and pay for their meals. Story felt a tug on her shirt and turned to see Adair less than an inch from her face, frowning at her intently. She was so close that Story could count each of the freckles splashed across her nose.

"No really, what did you do to your hair? It looks like it hasn't been brushed or taken care of in over a week!" Adair looked at her seriously. "But there is hope you know."

"Oh, is there?" Story leaned away from her, a worried expression on her face.

Adair clapped her hands together gleefully. "Yes! As a matter of fact, I'm pretty good with hair." She stood up and grabbed Story's arm, yanking her from her chair. "Let's go!" As an afterthought, she turned and waved at her father who waved back, seemingly unconcerned by his daughter's actions.

Story sent Eirnin a beseeching look when Adair pulled her past him, but he just shrugged and held up his arms in a hopeless gesture. Then he grinned at her.

Adair smiled at her excitedly. "This is going to be fun!" She opened the Inn's door and tugged Story outside.

Chapter Fourteen

The Dryad

"Wait! Hang on." Story pulled against the girl and found that she was surprisingly strong, especially for her size and build.

Geez, what's in the water here?

It seemed like everyone in Ailionora was ridiculously strong. In the bright sunlight, Story could see that Adair was a couple inches shorter than herself, making her easily taller than a gnome, but much shorter than an elf. She clearly took after her mother in her looks; Adair had full hips, a tiny waist, and very large breasts, with not much covering her up. She was wearing a short, green sarong tied around her waist, a piece of the same fabric tied around her chest that barely kept her contained, and she was barefoot. Aside from her father's pointed ears, and what Story assumed was the standard set of silver-colored elf eyes, she looked nothing like him; except when she smiled. Her laughter and smiles were identical to her father's.

As Story appraised her, the girl continued to pull her down the road, oblivious to her struggles, and chattering on incessantly about several different topics, most of which Story could barely keep up with, much less understand. She pulled again, harder this time.

"Seriously, STOP."

Adair did stop, but didn't drop Story's arm. Instead she turned to look at her, a wounded expression on her round face and hints of blue in her eyes. "But... don't you want me to fix your hair?"

Story eyed Adair's hair warily and noticed that her first impression had been wrong. The girl didn't have fraying dreadlocks but dozens of well-kept braids, some with colored ribbons woven throughout and others with seashells and bells in them.

"Yeah, that's fine. You can help me get my hair tamed. I just don't need to be dragged is all."

Adair promptly dropped her arm, leaned in close, and smiled. "I like the purple in your hair! I wish I had purple hair sometimes. Other times I wish I had blue. Or green. Or yellow." She continued on like that and turned to walk toward her camp. Story obediently followed, unconcerned since Eirnin didn't seem to be. Plus, she really was longing to finally brush her hair, and it seemed pretty harmless to let Adair have her way in this case. She could certainly do no worse than the mess that currently sat atop her head.

Once they reached the outskirts of Stoneybrook, Adair turned off to her right and walked down a gentle hill toward their campsite. Story squinted into the bright afternoon sunlight and could make out a wagon that looked like a huge technicolor barrel mounted on top of four wooden wagon wheels. There was one chestnut-colored horse grazing untethered on the grass in front of the wagon and another set of horse legs peaking out from behind.

As she got closer she could see that the riot of colors on the wagon was not haphazard, but instead, a stylized depiction of an underwater seascape. Multi-colored fish were portrayed swimming all over the round wagon against the brilliant blue background. "Who painted the wagon?"

"Oh, I did. Do you like it? My da lets me paint the wagon whenever I get to feeling like it. I usually do underwater scenes so that we can bring the sea with us wherever we go. Though Da does try to keep us near water as much as possible so I don't go mad."

She would have kept on like that had Story not let out a loud and very surprised, "Oh!" The other horse had come around from the other side of the wagon. It looked unremarkably similar to the first horse... until her eyes locked on the massive ram's horns on its head. The horse walked directly over to Adair and began nuzzling her, and the other one soon followed.

"Oh, you two! I don't have any treats for you today." She gently pushed against them, but they stubbornly held their ground. "Come on. You'll get me in trouble with Da! He says I'm not supposed to give you sweets." When it was clear they weren't moving, she sighed in resignation and dug into a pouch she had tied around her hip. "Fine, but don't tell Da, okay?" She pulled out something bright pink and gave a piece to each of them. They took it gently from her fingers with their massive horse teeth and then ambled away to continue grazing. Adair, popped a piece in her mouth and belatedly handed one out to Story. "Oh, sorry. Taffy?"

She shook her head quickly, not keen on eating horse treats. "Adair, what are those? They look like horses... but... the horns?"

Adair danced to the rear of the wagon, opened the door, and bounded inside. "Haven't you ever seen a da'nan before?"

"No; haven't heard of them either."

Adair's head popped out from the wagon's doorway, a perplexed look on her face. "Never heard of them before? What, have you been living under a rock your whole life?"

"Uh, you could say I'm not from around here."

Adair seemed to take this in stride and jumped out of the wagon with a bag in her hand. She grabbed Story's arm and tugged her down to the river's edge. "Da'nan are not horses. You obviously are familiar with horses."

Story nodded, so Adair continued. "They look like horses but are a bit 'other.' They're right smart beasties, too; you can see it in their eyes."

They'd arrived at the river's edge, and without hesitation, Adair pulled off the scraps of fabric that constituted her clothing, dropped them on the grass, and stepped in the water. She continued her lecture on the da'nan as if nothing abnormal had happened. "You don't pick da'nan, they pick you, and they will leave you if they don't like you anymore, and nothing you do can get them back. Are you going to get in the water? We need to wash your hair." She stood in the waist deep water holding a bar of soap in one hand, leaving her free hand down at her side. She was clearly comfortable with her nudity.

Story looked everywhere but at Adair, but not staring at her only seemed to make her nudity more obvious. She felt her face flush; they were in a fairly public place, and Adair seemed completely oblivious. Anyone could walk by and see her!

"Well?"

"Uh, I'm coming." She slipped off her moccasins and fumbled with the button on her jeans, tugging them down awkwardly. They were stiff with dirt and grime, and pretty foul smelling from all her sweat. She stripped off her hoodie and the t-shirt beneath, which were in the same condition as the jeans. Here she stopped. She refused to take off her sports bra or panties out in the open; she didn't care what the local customs were.

"Hand them here, and grab another bar of soap from the bag. I'll start on your clothes, and you start on yourself." Adair wrinkled her nose. "You smell—"

"I know, I know, I smell worse than a troll."

"Actually, I was going to say you smelled worse than Eirnin." Adair flashed Story a grin, and she smiled back easily. Grabbing the soap, Story stepped into the cool water, and her smile broadened. Holding her breath, she plunged all the way in and immediately felt better.

I should have done this days ago!

As always, the water soothed her worries away, and she felt the tension leave her shoulders. As a toddler, her dad could never get her out of the tub. As she got older, she practically lived in the pool. She smiled wistfully as she thought of her father trying to get her younger siblings to bathe. Hah! That had always been a disaster in the making. As she lathered her body up, she realized that Adair was once again talking about the da'nan and hoped she hadn't missed much.

"They don't like the fey, and the fey don't like them. They're a natural ward against them, I suppose." She pursed her lips to consider and then continued. "They enjoy work and get bored when there is none to be had, and so they also may leave you for that." Adair stepped out of the river and spread Story's jeans out on the grass to dry. "We'll move your clothes next to the fire later to dry them faster if you want."

Story nodded her head and focused on scrubbing the dirt out from under her fingernails, determined not to stare. She was all for "when in Rome" but surely having a fully developed teenage girl running around completely nude was not a normal thing, even in this strange land.

"Adair?"

"Yes?"

"How old are you?"

"Fourteen." Adair cocked her head to the side. "Why do you ask?"

"Doesn't your dad mind the way you dress and how you just kind of run around naked in a semi-public place?" Story's last words came out in a rush, but she couldn't help herself. If Katie had been running around like that Story would have had a fit, and their father would have been beside himself.

Adair's expression looked curious for a moment, then her eyes widened in understanding. "He does, actually. That's why he made me start wearing clothes in public after I learned how to walk on my own. I don't mind it so much anymore. I understand why now; not everyone is a dryad after all. So back to the da'nan."

"Wait." Story held up a hand and turned to look at Adair, who was now back in the river with Story's shirt in her hands. "Dryads run around naked everywhere?"

She laughed. "Of course not!"

Story let out a sigh of relief.

"We swim naked everywhere. Clothes are a hassle under water."

Story's eyes bulged, and Adair kept right on talking about the da'nan. She'd finished with the rest of Story's clothes by now, and moved behind her with a hairbrush in one hand and a different bar of soap in another. "Now let's see what we can do about your hair."

She continued chattering on like that about a dozen different subjects, all the while washing, brushing, and tugging on Story's hair.

Story closed her eyes and enjoyed the sensation of the cool water flowing by, the warm sun on her face, and the gentle breeze tickling her skin. For the first time since arriving in this strange world, she felt relaxed and comfortable. She didn't realize how much she missed having someone she could enjoy being with. Not that she didn't enjoy being with Eirnin, but that was often stressful. She never knew quite where she stood with him. Whereas Adair obviously liked her and wanted her around. Plus, her never ending babbling had a calming effect—there was no pressure on Story to say anything in response. And it was nice that she cared about Story's hair. Still, Eirnin had made her shoes.

Maybe she wouldn't go back to the cave just yet. What could it hurt to explore this world a bit more? To meet this Queen Eánna? Maybe she really could help her get back. Plus, maybe Eirnin was right; forcing her way through a magical portal was probably not the smartest thing to do. She didn't know much about magic, but that much made sense.

"Do all your people have purple in their hair? What are your people? I've never met one before. Your ears don't have points, did you know that?"

Story blinked her eyes open and saw Adair was, once again, only a few inches from her face.

"Ah!" Story leapt back and placed a hand over her speeding heart. "Don't DO that! Please, you're going to give me a heart attack." The girl truly had no sense of personal space. "In answer to your first question, no, we don't all have purple hair—I've just always had the purple streaks, which made it awkward for my dad when I was little, but now everyone just thinks I dye it."

Adair passed her a small hand mirror. "All done. I hope you like it. I used purple ribbons to match your purple hair!"

Adair clapped her hands excitedly and looked at Story in earnest.

Story took the mirror and looked at her own reflection for the first time since arriving in this world. What she saw surprised her. A young woman stared back at her, and Story hardly recognized her own face. Her eyes were harder, more cautious. Her mouth looked like it hadn't truly laughed in a long time, and all traces of the happy teenage girl she remembered were gone. She looked like a shell of a person, hollow and empty.

How long had she looked like this? Surely it was longer than just the week or so that she'd been in Ailionora. No, this had to have been months in the making, most likely starting the day of the accident, when she'd first walled off her emotions. No wonder all of her friends had eventually stopped calling. Only Josh had bothered, and even he looked at her with a constant mixture of worry and unease. She really couldn't blame them; she wouldn't have wanted to hang out with a lifeless zombie either.

A lump rose in her throat, and she struggled to keep the tears at bay. She hadn't cried about her loss yet, and she wouldn't start now. She had bigger, more important things to worry about. Like avoiding getting killed by a megalomaniacal Faerie Prince. *Prince of the bugs is more like it*, Story grimaced.

"Oh no! You hate it! I'm so sorry." Adair's lower lip quivered, and she looked like she was about to start sobbing.

"No! No! It's not that at all!" Story eyed her newly braided hair quickly and realized that it actually did look great. At the very least, functional and low maintenance. Adair had plaited it into dozens of braids just like hers, and had tied little silver bells on the bottom of one braid near the front.

Wow, either she braids really fast, or I was napping without realizing it!

Adair's lower lip had stopped quivering, but she was still eying Story expectantly.

Story beamed at Adair. "I love it!"

Adair launched herself at Story, hugging her exuberantly. "I knew you would! I just knew it." Then she grabbed Story's hand and yanked her out of the river. "Come on. Da and Eirnin are almost here, and we need to get a fire started before the sun goes down."

Story looked behind her and noticed that the sun was low in the sky. They had been there for a lot longer than she'd realized. She leaned over and picked up her nearly dry clothes and began tugging them on, frowning at the scratchy feel of the stiff fabric. At least they were clean now.

"Guess I'd better get dressed too." Adair frowned grumpily at her pile of fabric in the grass and then looked longingly back at the water. Story hated seeing her look so sad and, before she even realized what she was saying, found herself promising to go swimming with the girl the next day.

"Really?" Adair's face filled with hope and excitement, and her eyes sparkled orange.

"Uh, yeah, sure. I love swimming. Sounds like you do too." Just sitting in the water this afternoon had done her a world of good; she could only imagine what going for a long swim would do.

Chapter Fifteen

The Swim

Story blew on her burnt fingertips while Eirnin sat next to her, laughing softly.

"Didn't anyone ever teach you to let the food cool down a bit before you make a grab for it? Really Story, how did you make it past childhood?"

She stuck her tongue out at him, and he grinned in return before handing back her now cool piece of corn bread. "Careful, or you'll burn your tongue too if you leave it hanging out like that."

Adair and Eilath both joined the laughter this time. They were eating together around the campfire; Adair was surreptitiously sneaking bits of her food to the da'nan, and Eilath was playing a soft tune on his faolán. That was the instrument that Story had mistaken for a guitar earlier. From what she could see, it had eight strings, the top six being very much like a regular guitar's, while the bottom two were very large and deep sounding.

She could pick out a tune on a guitar, but was far from skilled enough to even attempt adding two strings. Eilath made it look effortless and his fingers danced across the strings as if they were part of the instrument. In a way, she supposed, they were. He had made the faolán, and you could tell music was his passion.

Eirnin tugged gently on one of Story's braids, drawing her away from her thoughts. "I sort of miss your old look. It was very… carefree."

She elbowed him in the ribs lightly. "I can't believe you let me walk into Stoneybrook looking like that, elf-boy."

"How was I to know that wasn't some traditional human way to wear your hair?"

She just shook her head at him and laughed. It felt good to laugh and to mean it. She felt light and airy. Safe and secure. Eilath smiled at her from across the fire and stood to pass the faolán to Adair.

"Why don't you play us a song, little one? The da'nan have had plenty to eat."

Adair looked up guiltily and hid her hands behind her, hastily cleaning them off on her sarong before reaching out to take the instrument from her father. For once she was tongue-tied, embarrassed at being caught.

He smiled down at her kindly and tousled her brilliant red braids. "You know you'd be better at the faolán if you would swim less and practice more." His voice was soft and lilting, like his music.

She made a face at him before retorting good-naturedly, "You'd be better at the faolán too Da, if you would spend less time making them and more time actually playing them."

Everyone laughed, and Eilath patted his daughter on her

shoulder before returning to his seat. Turning his eyes back to Story, she noticed that apart from the first time they met, his eyes seemed to remain a steady shade of greenish-blue, whereas Eirnin's were constantly flickering and sifting through colors on their liquid silver canvas.

"And now, my new friend, we need to discuss your situation," Eilath said as he settled down comfortably.

Story sat up straight and looked at Eirnin, who wouldn't meet her eyes. "What did Eirnin tell you?"

Eilath held up his hands in a calming gesture. "I'm not looking to sacrifice you either, if that's what you're worried about. I would like to see you safely home."

Story eyed him suspiciously, forcing herself to distrust this kind elf. "Why?"

Eilath looked confused. "I'm afraid I don't understand the question?"

"Why do you want to help me?" She jerked her thumb toward Eirnin. "He says that all elves are isolationists and only worried about their own problems. So why help me and most likely get on Morrigann's bad side in the process?"

Adair's soft music filled the silence as Eilath composed his thoughts. Steepling his fingers together before him, he once again met Story's gaze. "I'm afraid I have no answer to give you other than to confirm what Eirnin has told you about our people." He smiled sadly, and his eyes became a darker blue. "I suppose you remind me very much of my little Adair in some ways, and I would hope if the situation were reversed, your father would do what he could to help her."

Story felt tears welling in her eyes, and she fought to keep them from escaping. She looked into the fire and saw her father's face in her memory. He was smiling and tousling her curls while telling the twins he used to have hair just like their big sister—that is, until they came along. Rather than being horrified at the thought of causing their father's receding hairline, the twins had whooped and high-fived each other in triumph.

She felt Eirnin's hand rest on her shoulder, and she fought her instinct to shrug it off. It felt kind of nice, comforting, and familiar in a way. So instead, she hugged her knees tight to her body and rested her chin on them before glancing furtively toward Adair and then back to Eilath. "Yes, he would have."

EIRNIN WAS SITTING CROSS-LEGGED UNDER A LONE TREE ON A hillock overlooking the slowly flowing Stoney River. The water was deep and wide here and nearly a part of the great Stoney Lake itself. The cloudy skies parted overhead and allowed moonlight to peak through and illuminate the bow resting in Eirnin's hands. Story walked up quietly and leaned against the tree. She folded her arms across her chest and gazed out across the river, enjoying the peaceful view for a moment before looking down at him.

"How much did you tell Eilath?"

Eirnin answered without looking up. "Not much. I didn't have to. Eilath's intelligent, and you don't exactly blend in."

She nodded her head absentmindedly.

But Eirnin wasn't finished talking. "Besides, there's not much to tell. I don't really know anything about you."

"That's not true!" She protested. "I've answered every question you've ever asked."

"Aye, that you have. Yet you still tell me nothing about yourself. And you don't ever ask anything about anyone else either—well, nothing that's not superficial." He paused and looked up at her, his eyes swirled with dark blue. "You're afraid to get close to anyone. To trust anyone. And you don't think too much of yourself either. At least, you don't think you're worth talking about."

Story balled her hands into fists and had to resist the urge to rip Eirnin's bow out of his hands and hurl it into the water.

How dare he? He doesn't know me! What makes him think he has any right to try to psychoanalyze me?

She fumed inwardly, angry at Eirnin and his presumption. "Why should I bother getting to know people when all they do is go and die on you? What's the point?"

Eirnin was very still, and Story realized that she was crying. Wiping at the traitorous tears that had fallen, she turned and fled back to the camp and away from Eirnin's piercing gaze.

STORY'S EYES FLUTTERED OPEN, AND FOR A MOMENT, ALL SHE COULD see was a hazy, silvery-orange mist. Then the mist coalesced into two round blurs, and Story tried to bring them into focus. It wasn't until Adair spoke that she realized the blurs were eyes.

"Finally! I was wondering when you were going to wake up. You sleep a lot, did you know that?"

Story jerked back and sat up quickly, cracking her head on the bottom of the wagon.

"Please don't do that, Adair." The girl had more exuberance in her than the twins combined, and that was saying something. She raised her hand to rub the bump forming on her head and winced. When Adair had tugged her under the wagon last night, proudly proclaiming that she had set up a perfect bed for Story, she had been too exhausted, both emotionally and physically, to say anything.

As it turned out Adair hadn't been lying. The blankets

she'd laid out for Story were warm and comfortable, and Adair and Eilath had stayed up late into the night playing their faoláns in harmony. With Adair's siren song allaying all of Story's worries and fears, she had slept a deep and dreamless sleep, warm and safe.

Adair giggled, then shoved a hot, buttered roll into Story's yawning mouth.

"Hurry up and eat. Eirnin says I have to feed you a lot." She held another roll at the ready.

Story rolled her eyes and choked down a bit of the roll. "Did he now?"

Adair nodded her head quickly and handed Story another roll.

"Not just yet, sweetie, but thanks. Let me finish this one first." Story started inwardly. Sweetie? Where had that come from? She used to call the twins that on occasion. When they weren't being hellions, which was a rare occurrence. She shook her head; she was obviously still drowsy. "Where is Eirnin anyway? Probably out foraging or something, or doing whatever it is he does while I'm sleeping and/or eating."

"No! He and Da went back to town to get some ropes and things for your cave expedition."

Story sat there for a moment in surprised silence. They had meant it. They were going to help her get back. She was a complete stranger, causing them more hassle than she was worth, and they were going through all this trouble to help her. Not only that, but they were helping her despite the fact that she wasn't willing to donate a measly drop of blood in the off-chance that their legends were true. She swallowed thickly, trying to quell the small stone of guilt she felt developing in her gut.

Suddenly she was jerked out from under the wagon, and Adair was pulling her toward the lake.

"Wait! Where are we going?" She didn't bother pulling against Adair, knowing how futile it would be.

"You looked like you were done eating, and you said we could go swimming today, and now it's today, so let's go swimming. The river here is fun and exciting, but slow moving enough that you don't have to worry about bad currents." She stopped and looked at Story seriously. "And even if there were, you wouldn't have to worry. I'm an excellent swimmer!" She giggled and wiggled her toes.

Looking down at her feet, Story noticed for the first time why Adair went barefoot. Her feet were much longer than her height proportionally would need, and her toes were abnormally lengthy, three inches at their longest, with a thin membrane of webbing between each one.

They were at the river's edge, and just like the day before, Adair was out of her clothes and into the water before Story had time to blink. She surfaced and blew a delicate fountain of water out of her mouth before splashing at Story. "Hurry up and get in! I'll be right back. Wait here."

"But…" It was useless; Adair was already gone, so Story pulled off her clothes and stepped into the water. She yawned and stretched and then brushed at the goose bumps the breeze had raised on her arm. She looked around furtively. Now that she was alone, she felt a little silly, standing in waist-deep water in nothing but her underwear. She was debating getting back out and telling Adair that they'd go swimming later, when a slime covered hand rose out of the water, grabbed Story's arm and yanked her down into the murky depths below.

Chapter Sixteen

The Fuath

Story flailed around in the water, kicking and punching, but it was no use. The hand on her wrist had a steel grip, and no matter how hard she yanked she couldn't get loose.

"Calm down!" It was clearly Adair's voice, but Story had heard it directly in her head, not out loud—which would have been impossible underwater anyway. She turned her head wildly and waved her free hand, hoping Adair would see it and come over and help get her away from whatever was trying to drown her.

"Seriously, Story, stop struggling! I've got you."

Despite the fact that she was rapidly running out of air, she stopped flailing and let the bubbles and currents settle long enough for her to make out the form of Adair grinning before her, her hair haloed out around her in the water, making it look like flames were flying off her head in every direction.

"I've got something to help you breathe underwater. Hold still."

She raised her free hand, and Story noticed that it was filled with a nasty looking, greenish-black slime. Her eyes widened as it came closer to her face, and she started jerking away again. Adair clung on and moved her hand with lightening speed, not slowed by the water at all, and smeared the ooze over Story's nose and mouth. It seeped into her pores and sealed itself to her skin like it had been fused there.

"Breathe, Story!"

How could she possibly breathe now? Story panicked. She was out of air, and Adair had just put something over her nose and mouth that would prevent her from inhaling even if she could make it to the surface again.

"Story, stop being foolish! Trust me. BREATHE!"

Story's vision was tunneling, and her body began convulsing. Her lungs screamed from the lack of oxygen, and, unbidden, her mouth opened and tried to draw in a deep breath that she knew would never come.

Except that it did.

The sweetest tasting oxygen she'd ever inhaled filled her lungs, and she felt her body relax. Her vision started to return as she focused on simply breathing in and out. Somehow the slime over her mouth and nose was acting as a filter pulling oxygen from the water.

Adair's face coalesced in front of hers, and she was smiling broadly. *"I told you to breathe, didn't I?"*

Story found it more than a bit disconcerting to hear Adair's words in her mind as clearly as if she'd spoken them, yet not see her mouth move at all.

Of course! This must be how dryads communicate underwater. Telepathy! I wonder if Adair can read my mind? I wonder if it works on the surface too?

Adair shook her head. *"No, it only works under water. And Dryads can't read minds. We can only project our thoughts to each other, and it's limited by line of sight. Kind of."*

She stared at Adair, her eyes wide. *"Oh my gosh! You read my mind!"*

Adair pulled away from her, surprise on her face as well. *"No I didn't. It's impossible."* Then she drifted in closely to Story again, her eyes searching Story's face curiously, as if trying to unravel the mystery hidden in there. *"You must be projecting your thoughts to me somehow. That's the only possible explanation."*

"So that's something common then? The elves and gnomes can do it too, right?"

Adair shook her head, causing her braids to wiggle in the water like Medusa's snakes. *"No. Only dryads and other water creatures can. And now I guess humans."* She grinned broadly and caught Story in a hug, swirling both of them around. *"Isn't it wonderful? It's perfect! I knew we were going to be the best of friends the moment I saw you, and now it's even better! It's like we're sisters!"* She let go of Story and beamed at her. Story smiled back; Adair's enthusiasm was hard to resist.

"This is pretty neat. Thought projection." Then another thought occurred to her, and she looked at Adair, worry crossing her features. *"Wait, you can't hear EVERYTHING I'm thinking can you?"*

Adair opened her mouth in a silent laugh. *"No silly! Weren't you listening? I can only hear what you want me to hear. Nothing more."*

"Oh good." Story relaxed. *"Hey, how come you don't have to have this nasty slime on your face to breath? And what is this stuff?"* She poked at the mask on her face; it felt rubbery under her fingers.

Adair turned to her side and brushed the braids by her ear out of the way. Story looked closely and could see three, one inch vertical slits parallel to each other nestled behind her ear. They were gills! *"Ah, of course!"*

"As for the ad'har mask... Maybe it's best if you didn't know." Adair grimaced. *"Suffice to say that only water folk can get it for the earth folk, and it only lasts until it dries out, which all depends on the salt content of the water."*

"Why drag me under the water and nearly drown me though?"

"Well, you can't take ad'har out of the water or it instantly dries out and becomes useless."

"Yes, but you still could have at least warned me what you were going to do. You scared me to death!"

Adair hung her head. *"I'm sorry... I just didn't think..."*

Any anger Story had toward her instantly evaporated, just like it did whenever the twins behaved so chagrined. She extended her hand and patted Adair on her shoulder. *"It's ok... just try to remember that not everyone is as daring as you."* Story smiled at the younger girl fondly and realized with a start how quickly she'd slipped into the same mothering/big sister role with her that she'd had with the twins.

"You're right. I need to think more about what I do before I do it. My da is always telling me that." She smiled sheepishly at Story and then grabbed her hand and yanked her down deeper into the river's depths. *"Come on! I want to show you something!"*

As Story felt her arm nearly get pulled out of her socket, she made a mental note to talk with Adair later about thinking before she acted and not being so impulsive. Then she grinned; it was just like being around the twins again... and she realized that she loved it!

"So those right there are white sea lilies that only bloom in the moonlight." Adair pointed at some softly waving, leafy green

stalks on the river's floor. They'd been exploring the depths for at least half an hour, and Story was in heaven. It felt so natural and freeing to be weightless under the water, though it was a bit humbling to swim with Adair. While Story had been the fastest on her school's swim team, she couldn't hold candle to Adair, who darted from place to place like a fish. Which, Story realized, she kind of was.

"I wish you could see them, Story. They're so pretty! I've only seen them bloom once when my Ma took me swimming when I was little. Da won't let me swim at night. Too many dangerous things come out then, he says. I think he just uses it as an excuse to make sure I practice my faolán though." Adair shrugged her shoulders jovially and then turned around, guiding them back toward the shoreline by their camp.

Story peered into some of the craggy holes and caves in the rocks below as she followed Adair past the lilies. The murky caves were creepy and made her feel like she was being watched again, and this time there was no staring Eirnin to blame. She thought of all the monsters that lived in her own world's oceans and shuddered. Sharks alone were enough to make her think twice before she went for a swim on the beach. *"He's probably right. Who knows what lurks in the dark down here."*

"Oh, I know he's right. Ma has taught me all about the fey that live down here. She says there are all sorts of nasty things that would love to eat a little dryad for a snack." Adair sounded downright cheerful as she talked, and Story marveled at her attitude. Either the girl was crazy, or just a naturally peppy person who didn't let much worry her or get her down.

Story was going to let Adair continue in her ramblings when she remembered what Eirnin had said to her last night— about being afraid to get close to anyone. She frowned and then looked at Adair's swimming form. Well, it appeared that any walls she'd erected, the girl had busted down. She found that she'd already become attached to Adair.

"*You said your mother 'says,' in the present tense.*"

"*Yes.*"

"*I just assumed… since you live with your father…*"

Adair somersaulted over and eyed Story quizzically. Understanding dawned on her face. "*Oh! No, Ma's not dead. She lives in the Silver Sea with the rest of our kind. I see her occasionally. She's very flighty though. It's sometimes hard to keep up with her train of thoughts or what she's doing.*" She resumed swimming toward their camp at a conversational pace. "*She says that I take after my da with how serious and calm I am.*" A hint of pride crept into Adair's voice as she said that last bit, and Story had to stifle a mental laugh. Adair's mother was too energetic for her? Adair was calm like her father? The girl's mother and, Story assumed, the rest of the dryads, apparently had the market cornered on attention deficit disorder.

"*So, why do you live with your father and not your mother? And, if you don't mind me asking, why don't they live together?*"

A school of brightly-colored fish swam by, and Adair paused to run the tips of her fingers along their silky bodies. "*I don't really know the full story. Da just says that Ma gave me to him after I was born, and that was more than enough to make him happy. Except for sometimes when I look at him, I can tell he's really sad and missing someone he cares for a lot.*" Adair worried her lower lip with her teeth for a moment before continuing. "*As for Ma, the one time I managed to ask her, she looked at me like I was mad. I guess I can understand her now that I'm older. Dryads don't ever settle down and stay with one partner.*" Adair shrugged as if that was explanation enough.

"*So you think your dad is sad because your mom won't stay with him, and he misses her?*"

Adair shook her head, her braids flailing around in slow

motion. *"No, I don't think that's it. He and my ma... well, you've heard me sing. Imagine my ma doing that."*

She was surprised by Adair's candor and realized how dangerous a weapon a full-blooded dryad's siren song must be. *"So she seduced your father, had you, and then abandoned you both?"* She was both appalled and livid. It sounded like both their mothers were cut from the same cloth.

Adair's mouth opened in her silent laugh. *"No! Well, yes. Kind of. They're very good friends, but my ma's a dryad. She loves many, and they love her. She has lots of children. Though I'm the only half-elf."* She preened, taking pride in this fact. *"I actually used to split my time with them until a few years ago. Ma has her family, a whole community with her. Da has no one but me—elves can only have one kid you know. His traveling life is a lonely one. So I stay with him."*

Story stopped swimming and watched as the girl continued toward the nearing shoreline. She didn't know what to say. Adair didn't seem bothered in the slightest by her mother's behavior, taking it as a matter of course. She didn't appear to have any resentment or abandonment issues. In fact, she seemed to completely enjoy and embrace the life fate had dealt her. She was by far the most hyper-active teen Story had ever met and, at the same time, the most mature. Cocking her head to the side thoughtfully, she realized she could learn a thing or two from Adair.

Scaly, webbed fingers curled around her ankle, and Story looked down just in time to see burning yellow eyes peer up at her from a man-sized crevice in the boulders below. She kicked at the hand with her free leg and reached for her knife. A sinking feeling lodged itself in her gut as she realized with horror that she'd left it hanging off the branch of a tree on the riverbank. The creature wrapped another bony hand around her leg and began to slowly pull her down into its hole.

Adair was still swimming off ahead, nearly to the shore-line, chatting about dryad culture and what life was like living on the road with her father, oblivious to Story's distress. Panicking, Story opened her mouth in a silent scream, thrashing against the monster below her. She was at the cave mouth now and splayed her arms across it, refusing to get pulled any further.

"Adair!"

Story kicked again, and this time, she contacted the torso of the creature, feeling its long shaggy fur beneath her toes. It momentarily loosened its grip on her, and she shot out of the hole like a cannonball.

"ADAIR!" The girl was nowhere to be seen, and she'd said that the thought projection was limited to line of sight.

At least she's safe!

Fire ran up her leg, and it was paralyzed immediately. Looking down she saw a long, thin, hairless tail wrapped around her calf. Attached to the tail were hundreds of tiny barbs embedding themselves in her skin. She followed the length of the tail to its owner, hidden in the shadows. She could see enough of it to tell that it was covered in yellow fur and looked simian in form, yet lacked a nose. It more than made up for that in its disproportionately large mouth filled with row upon row of razor sharp teeth. If it could have hissed at her, Story had no doubt that's what it would be doing.

All this flitted through her mind in a moment, and she kicked with her free leg yet again to dislodge the creature. Or at least, she tried to. With rapidly increasing horror she realized that the barbs in her leg were pumping her body full of some sort of paralyzing agent, and she could no longer move anything from the waist down.

She reached out with her hands to get a rock to throw at the creature, but they were slow to respond. Her lungs began to burn as the agent spread upward to her heart.

Well, at least I won't get eaten alive.

The edges of her vision began to darken, yet she still moved her hands feebly trying to swim away from her attacker, who was content to lurk in the shadows and watch her slowly die. Whether it was just hungry, or sent by Morrigann to kill her, she didn't know and found it funny that she should care about such a thing in these, her final moments.

Unable to draw breath any longer, she floated limply in the water staring into the creature's malice-filled eyes.

A beam of sunlight shot into the dark recess where the monster was hiding, illuminating it perfectly in all its horror. She saw its eyes widen momentarily, and then the fire in them went out. The tail wrapped around her leg went limp and dropped off into the water below. Her attacker dissolved into nothingness.

Strong fingers wrapped around her wrist and pulled her away from the river bottom toward the shore. The motion tilted Story's limp head back, and in her hazy, oxygen deprived vision, she could see the backlit form of Eirnin hovering above her in the water. Adair's small mirror was in his free hand, reflecting the sunlight down. She smiled weakly up at him, and then the toxin paralyzed her lungs, and everything went black.

CHAPTER SEVENTEEN

MORRIGANN'S GARDEN

WARM WATER LAPPED AT HER TOES, AND STORY SAW THAT she was standing on the shore of a smooth, glassy lake. On the far side were pine-covered mountains abutting the lake's edge. Snow dusted the highest peaks, yet down where she was, it was surprisingly warm. A light breeze, with the exquisite scent of citrus on it, ruffled the hem of her long, purple gown.

Great. Please don't tell me I'm dreaming about him *again.*

Story glanced over her shoulder warily, but no one was there. Instead, there was a sprawling fruit orchard; a shoulder-height, wooden fence penned it in. The fence actually looked like it had grown there; flowering limbs sprouted off a fence post here and there down the line. She found herself walking toward the open gate without commanding her feet to do so—as if she was being drawn to it.

Once inside she could see that the orchard spread for

miles. Every sort of fruit tree she could imagine, and some she couldn't, were there in various stages of growth. Some had flowering blossoms on them, others had mature fruit ready for picking, while still others were young saplings, with only a dusting of leaves. Despite the fact that it looked completely untamed and random, there was something methodical about it—as if it were organized chaos.

But because of the chaos, she couldn't find any sort of path. So aside from wondering why she was even there to begin with, she didn't really know where to go now that she was inside the orchard. She wished for her compass because—even though it wouldn't really do her much good since she had no known landmarks to navigate off of—it would at least be comforting to have.

With her next step, she felt a slight weight and bump against her hip. Looking down she saw her compass hanging off the sash around her waist. Had it been there all along? Or had it appeared because she'd wished for it?

"Man, I sure wish I had a cold Barq's in a bottle right now." She was disappointed, but unsurprised, when no root beer appeared.

Well, it was worth a try. At least I have my compass now.

She untied the lanyard from her waist and brought it up near her face, aligning the needle to point north, and out of habit checked it against the sun's position. She blinked in surprise; the sun was where it ought to have been—in the east! Story shook the compass for good measure, and just as before, once the needle settled down, the sun was rising in the east, not in the south.

Was she back in her own world? Had Ailionora's magnetic poles shifted while she was swimming with Adair? Her mind raced, and then a thought struck:

What if the compass was pointing at a fixed object instead of a magnetic pole? And now that I've moved position somehow...

She set off briskly in the direction her compass was pointing. She felt it then, for the first time, the pull on her soul. She really had no other way to explain it—it was simply that. Something was tugging on her very essence; it was similar to what she'd felt when she'd seen the cave painting of the tree, only exponentially more powerful. Story had no idea where she was going or what the compass was leading her to, she just knew that it was the right way. Magic coursed through her veins, and she felt every hair on her body standing on end as if she'd just been shocked by an enormous charge of static electricity.

She picked up her pace and began to jog, eventually breaking into a full run, all the while moving toward the center of the orchard. Fruit trees flew by faster and faster as she ran, much faster than she'd ever been able to run before, yet as her speed increased, so did the tugging on her soul.

The needle on the compass face started to flicker back and forth erratically, then suddenly it was spinning. She stopped running and groaned. "Great. Now what am I supposed to do?"

"You could try eating an apple. I assure you they're quite delicious."

Story whirled around to see Morrigann emerging from the trees behind her. As he walked by he tossed her one of the two apples he was carrying. She let it fall to the ground, untouched.

"Suit yourself." He settled himself onto an ornate, wooden throne in the center of the clearing that, just like everything else, looked as though it had grown there. He casually slung a bare leg over one arm of his chair, leaned his back against the other arm, and bit into his shiny, silver apple.

"What are you doing here, Morrigann? You're not welcome in my dreams anymore." She glared at him and tried to keep her voice from shaking. "Or did you need me to blacken your eyes to match the fat lip I gave you last time?" She didn't feel any of the bravado she was spewing, but she was determined to avoid being put under another spell.

He straightened, a defiant look on his face. "What am I doing here? My dear, I *live* here." He raised his empty hand and gestured sweepingly at the trees surrounding them. "Welcome to my garden, Story." Then he took another bite of his apple. It was so crisp she could hear it crunch from where she stood.

There was only one tree in the clearing, a few feet behind Morrigann's throne. It wasn't flowering and it had no fruit or leaves; in fact, it looked quite dead. It was so out of place in the beautiful garden, she couldn't understand why he kept it there. Then she took in the familiar lines and shape of the tree, and she gasped.

"Oh yes, a little souvenir from the elves." Morrigann had a self-satisfied smirk on his face as he followed her gaze to the tree behind him.

"Then it's real." She took an involuntary step toward it and then hesitated, looking warily at him.

"Oh, by all means please go look at it. You can't do anything to it here. Just like I can't do anything to you. Otherwise, I would have killed you the first time we met in your dreams."

He said it so nonchalantly that Story was momentarily taken aback. Would he really have killed her so callously? Remembering the altar on which he'd tried to sacrifice her not two nights back, she decided that yes, he would have killed her without a second thought.

"Why did you bring me here?"

Morrigann stood up gracefully and walked toward her

slowly. Flowers grew in every step he took, and the sunlight shimmered off of him making him look ethereally beautiful. "I thought that would be obvious."

He stopped in front of her only a foot away, and despite her obvious loathing of him, she felt her heart begin to race and her palms sweat. She wondered if he was trying to put her under another spell, or if she was still stupidly attracted to him.

His warm fingers brushed against her cheek, and she felt a hot line of magic trail down her face. He leaned in, his sweet breath filling her senses. "But then I remember, you are rather simple, aren't you?"

He dropped his hand and turned away, walking back toward the tree, his hands clasped behind his back. Despite her better judgment, Story followed him. If only to get close enough to smack him.

"You still haven't answered my question. Why am I here?"

He barely spared her a second glance, the scorn evident on his face. "My dear, you are here, because I wished it." He examined his nails, cleaning a non-existent bit of grit out from under them. "I want it known that I have won, and that you, or rather, the elves, have lost."

She looked at him in confusion. "You've won what? I don't understand. I thought you wanted to kill me so that I couldn't fulfill the prophecy." She glanced at the dead tree. "For this thing." Then she shrugged nonchalantly. "Hate to break it to you, but I'm still alive."

His fingers brushed lightly against the rough bark of the trunk, and he smiled. "Ah, but that's where you are wrong, simple-minded one. The elfling knew enough to use sunlight to destroy the fuath I sent to kill you, but it was too late. It had already injected you with the paralyzing toxin. You only have moments left to live before your heart stops."

Story balled her hands into fists by her side. "So what, you brought me here to gloat? How old are you again?"

"I am older than the trees."

She rolled her eyes. "It was a rhetorical question. Besides, it's not like someone else from my world can't come down that cave shaft and be the Ailesit if you kill me. So really this was all kinda pointless." Story had no idea what had come over her. She thought she ought to be afraid or angry over her impending death, but found that instead, she was disgusted with Morrigann. How had she ever been attracted to him? Any residual feelings she may have had were definitely gone now.

A knowing smirk crept across his face. "That won't be a problem, I assure you. My wood sprites caused a rather large landslide over the entrance of your cave, and then I sealed it. That portal is no longer a viable option. I doubt the elves will be getting their prophecy fulfilled any time soon." He was positively gleeful about it.

Her eyes narrowed, incredulous. "Then it's all true. You were jealous of the elves, so like a petty little child, you took away their life essence. All because they had something you didn't."

He looked at her and scoffed. "What? Immortality? Magic? In case you haven't noticed, I have both."

Watching him stand there, like a toddler breaking a toy to make sure that no one else could play with it if he couldn't, Story had a flash of intuition. She walked over to him and looked directly into his violet eyes, holding his gaze until he turned away.

"I think it goes beyond that. You didn't want the elves' power. You were jealous of the fact that they not only had immortality, but that they also had real bodies of flesh and blood, and more importantly, souls. Souls that gave them the ability to truly laugh and love, because they could also experience sadness and despair. Like my dad always said, you can't have one without the other."

His hands tightened into fists, and his face grew hard.

"You've been just as you are throughout all the ages, never changing, never growing, and never truly feeling anything beyond the most basic of emotions." She suddenly felt an overwhelming wave of pity for the creature before her.

He chuckled, but it sounded hollow and false to Story's ears. "So that's your big theory, is it? The sad, little faerie who wanted to be a real boy, but decided that since he couldn't, he'd make everyone else pay?" He snorted. "And to think, I actually thought *you* were the Ailesit." He wagged a finger at her mockingly. "I'd say that next time you should probably get the full story before you make assumptions, but you won't be having a next time will you?"

Story was about to retort when she felt a tugging at her navel, as if something had hooked her from behind and was dragging her away. She looked behind her and saw nothing, but suddenly she was at the edge of the clearing while Morrigann was still at the tree.

"What?" His eyes widened. "No!" He lunged for her.

She felt another tug, and this time trees sped by so fast they blurred into darkening streaks, and Morrigann was left far behind.

STORY'S EYES FLEW OPEN, AND SHE TOOK A DEEP, RAGGED BREATH. Coughs racked her body, and she rolled over onto her side to throw up onto the sand on the river's edge. Warm hands patted her back as her body convulsed, and she could feel the rough weave of Eirnin's cloak as it slipped over her skin.

"It's a side effect of the anti-toxin. I was afraid we were too late, so I may have given you more than was needed," Eilath's gentle voice sounded from behind her.

She opened her mouth to respond, but found another wave of nausea came instead. After feeling like she had thrown up all of her internal organs, Story flopped onto her back limply. She squinted up at the sun, amazed to see that it wasn't even fully up yet. It felt like years had passed since Adair took her swimming that morning.

Eirnin's face eclipsed the sun as he hovered over her. A worried expression was plain on his face, and his eyes were solidly yellow with anxiety. "Are you ok? I'm sorry I wasn't there sooner."

She coughed again, and then nodded her head. Seeing that she would live, his face became stern. "What were you thinking, going swimming without your knife? This is the second time you've done this; you say you don't want to be killed, yet your actions don't support that."

Struggling to sit up, Story wheezed, "S-sorry. I wasn't thinkin'." She looked around, worried. "Where's Adair? Is she—"

"She's fine. She's back at camp getting a bed made up for you in the wagon." His expression softened, and the yellow in his eyes slowly faded to a light green. From what she could tell, he wasn't mad at her, just worried, and relieved that she was okay. "Don't try to get up just yet. You're still weak—you nearly died."

She lay back obediently, but only because she was too exhausted to do anything else. Her mind felt fuzzy, but not like she was under a faerie spell. Instead it was like she'd just taken some really strong over-the-counter cold medication. Glancing back up, she saw that Eirnin's eyes had settled down into their usual liquid silver color, only now they had swirls of bright green through them.

"Eirnin?"

"Yes?"

"Why do your eyes change color? I've a theory about that, but I just wanted to check first."

Yellow flooded back into his eyes, nearly obscuring their silver base. "You can see my eyes changing color?" He shot a quick glance to Eilath, who only chuckled in response. "Do Eilath's eyes change color for you too?"

"N-not really. They mostly stay greenish-blue. I think it's 'cause he stays mostly happy, but with a tinge of sadness I haven't figured out the cause of yet." She knew her babbling was completely due to her weakened and medicated state, but it was like the floodgates had been opened. Plus, he *had* said that she should take more of an interest in the people around her, right?

Eirnin's eyes were solidly yellow now, and Story reached up and patted his tattooed arm. "Don' be worried. I think it's kinda sweet ya wear your emotions so clearly in your eyes. I haven't figured out what all the colors mean yet, but still, it takes a lotta the guesswork out for me." She smiled sloppily at him, and began tracing a fingertip along the lines of his tattoos. "Now I know when you're trying t'be funny, or when you're jus' bein' a jerk."

Eirnin turned away from her gaze, but Story had already seen a flash of purple swirl through the yellow in his eyes. He sighed, and Eilath only laughed harder.

"Did I say somethin' wrong?" Her words were starting to slur together.

Eilath patted her shoulder. "No, child, it's just that most elves work very hard at building walls so their emotions can't be read. It takes a fairly strong—"

Eirnin cleared his throat noisily and glared at him.

The older elf sighed and looked down at Story apologetically. "Well, never mind. Let's get you back to the wagon and into bed."

Eirnin reached down and gently lifted her into his arms.

"I can walk!"

He gave her a cynical look. "I'm not taking the chance. The fuath did a right nasty job on your leg. It will be a few days at least before you can put any real weight on it. Which means that you'll need to convalesce for a little while before we can head back to your cave."

"What? No!"

"Story, I won't budge on this. You can't walk right now." He strode purposefully toward the wagon, refusing to put her down.

"No, that's not what I meant." She flailed her arms weakly trying to punctuate her words. "I'm not going back to the cave. I couldn't even if I wanted to—Morrigann sealed it off. I need to see the queen. I know where *The Ailes* is! At least, I think I know how to find it."

He stumbled and nearly dropped her. "What?"

Eilath reached out to steady him, but remained calm and silent, listening intently.

"Yeah, remember my compass that we both thought was broken?"

Eirnin looked down at her, confusion on his face. Then understanding washed over it. "No!"

"Yes!" She nodded her head enthusiastically. At least she tried to. Her neck wasn't really listening to her right now. "I think my compass points to the tree." Story chewed on her bottom lip as she pondered everything she saw in Morrigann's garden.

"Are you certain?"

"Yeah, it lead me right to it. Morrigann showed me the tree when I was dying. He's like a bad James Bond villain." Whatever was in the anti-toxin was making her babble even worse than before, and she was finding it hard to focus. "I thought everyone knew that ya don't reveal your master plan to the story's hero before ya kill 'em. Ya jus' kill 'em."

Eirnin just raised his eyebrows at that comment, not bothering to ask for clarification. They were at the wagon now, and he managed to maneuver both of them through the small door at the back without bumping Story against the frame, though she doubted she would have felt it if he had.

He set her down on a bed, and she felt a twinge of sadness when his arms slid out from under her. His embrace had felt nice. Comfortable and soothing. Her eyes began to flutter, and she was losing the battle against the medication in her system.

Eilath placed a hand on Eirnin's shoulder. "Come, my friend. Let her rest. I need to tell Adair about our change of plans, so we can move out, hopefully within the hour. She'll need to talk to the da'nan and see if they are willing to go with us on this journey."

"You don't need to come, Eilath. I know how difficult this is for you. For both of you." Eirnin might have been talking to Eilath, but his gaze never left Story's face. His eyes were a yellow-green and she felt like she could swim in them.

The last thing she saw before she drifted off to sleep was Eilath looking back at her, his eyes solidly dark blue. "Aye, but some things are more important than the past. And unless you happen to have a wagon to carry the girl, this really is the only way."

Then the door to the wagon closed, and Story succumbed to the sleep pulling at her.

Chapter Eighteen

Recovery

Story struggled to open her eyes. They felt like they'd been cemented shut. She raised her hands weakly to them and began rubbing gently, relieved that at least her arms worked.

"Hey," Eirnin murmured in his now familiar rolling accent.

"Hey." Her voice was dry, and her throat felt like it was coated in dust. Her tongue was swollen and had the consistency of sandpaper. How long had she been unconscious?

"I knew you liked to sleep, but this has to be record, even for you."

She pried her eyes open and blinked up blearily at him. He had a full mug in one hand and used his other arm to gently prop her up so she could get a drink. Her hands were still too feeble to hold the cup on her own, so Eirnin guided it to her lips and helped her tip it back.

It felt like the drink was putting out a hot brush fire, and she was immediately more alert and a bit stronger. She detected a hint of lemon and honey on her tongue and finished off the cool beverage greedily, surprised when she tipped the cup back and found it empty.

"What kind of water was that?"

Eirnin refilled her mug from a matching clay pitcher on the small table next to him. "While you were asleep Adair brewed you some tea to help you recover. She said it's a secret dryad recipe her mother taught her to help combat the side effects of the anti-toxin Eilath gave you." He held the mug out before her, but when she reached for it, he moved just out of her reach. "Slowly now this time. You're very dehydrated, and you haven't had anything to eat in over a week. You drink too much right now, and you'll just throw it all up. We're nearly stopped for the day and we'll heat you up some broth. I'll bet you're ravenous."

As if on cue, Story's stomach rumbled. Heat raced up her neck and flushed her cheeks, and he grinned broadly.

"I'll drink slowly, I promise. Now hand it over." Eirnin raised an eyebrow, and Story rolled her eyes and chuckled. "Pleeeease..."

With a quiet laugh he handed the mug over, and she began sipping the tea gratefully, careful not to spill any despite the wagon's jostling. Looking around inside the wagon, it was just as she'd expected it to be. While the outside was wild and colorful like Adair, the inside was sedate and gentle like Eilath. Soft shades of green and blue alongside the natural browns of the wood were everywhere. Faoláns hung securely on the wall, and a few half-finished ones were on a workbench near the back door.

It was a traveling home, barrel-shaped with a quaint table and stools next to the narrow, yet comfortable, bed she lay on.

Based on the placement of the half-folded table, she surmised that the bed also doubled as bench. A hammock rocked overhead, and she guiltily realized that while she'd been sleeping here, someone, most likely Eilath, had been displaced and forced to sleep outside. She hoped the weather had been good. She'd been lucky in that, other than her first night in Ailionora, it hadn't rained at all.

She passed the empty mug back and sat up slowly against the back of the wagon. "How long was I asleep? A week, did you say?"

"A little over. Nine days to be exact." He set the mug on the table next to him.

"How am I still alive?"

"The anti-toxin Eilath gave you, of course. He had some prepared just in case this sort of thing ever happened to Adair. Though, it's a bit surprising that the fuath went after you at all. They don't normally risk coming out in daylight hours."

She waved his answer away. "No, I know all that." She paused and thought about what she had just said. "Okay, actually I didn't know that stuff about the fuath. Though, to answer your question, it's because Morrigann sent it after me." Eirnin's eyes flashed red, and Story hurriedly continued. "What I meant was, how am I still alive after not eating or drinking for so long? The human body can only take a few days without water before it dies."

"Oh… that little detail." His eyes calmed, and he refilled her mug. "We've been giving you drops of Adair's tea through a sponge. As long as we kept the amount we put in your mouth small enough, you swallowed it reflexively. It was enough to keep you hydrated, though only just. You really had me—us— worried these last few days. I was afraid you were never going to wake up."

She smiled at him and wagged an admonishing finger,

before taking the mug from his outstretched hands. "Careful. Or else I'm going to start thinking you actually care about me."

His face turned serious, and a swirl of yellow, blue, red, and dark purple clouded his eyes. He was experiencing so many emotions simultaneously Story couldn't make any sense of them. She reached out her arm and placed it gently on his biceps. "Hey, I was only joking; there's no reason to get upset."

Eirnin squeezed his eyes shut. When he finally opened them, they were a sedate silver once again. "So, *The Ailes*, it's real then?"

Well, that was quite the subject change. She frowned at him, but didn't push the issue, nodding her head instead. "Yup. Sure is. Kinda makes you rethink all the old legends, doesn't it?"

He ignored her teasing jab at his beliefs, or rather, the lack thereof. "Where is it?"

"Morrigann's garden," she yawned. How could she possibly be tired again? She'd been sleeping for over a week.

Eirnin groaned. "Of course it is."

"Is that a problem?"

"You mean, aside from the fact that it's in Faerie Land and doesn't have a fixed location?"

Story stifled a giggle. "It's called Faerie Land? Seriously?"

He raised an eyebrow. "What else should we call it? The fey haven't named it, and we have to call it something. And since it's their land..."

She burst out laughing. It was a combination of the ridiculously childish name for Morrigann's domain and Eirnin's serious take on it.

He frowned grumpily, still not getting the joke. "And that doesn't really solve the problem of finding the tree. Like I said, his garden moves around inside his territory." He drummed his fingers against the tabletop. "It was theorized long ago that this is where *The Ailes* was kept, but no one could ever find his garden. Most elves who went on a searching expedition never came back. Half a millennia ago, they simply stopped searching."

Story shifted to a more comfortable seated position in her bed, waving away Eirnin's assisting arms. "Problem solved. My compass points to the tree."

He leaned back and crossed his arms across his chest. "Aye, I thought you were merely delusional when you said that before. Are you certain?"

"Yes! It guided me all the way to the clearing in his garden, and there in the middle was *The Ailes*. It worked perfectly until Morrigann showed up actually. His presence sent the needle spinning." She shrugged; she wasn't completely sure how it all worked.

Eirnin's brows furrowed together, and he cupped his chin in his hand. "If that's the case then your compass is also a useful warning for when the Faerie Prince is near." He looked at Story seriously. "You sound as if you've chosen to go on this quest. To restore *The Ailes*."

She chewed on her lower lip and looked away, picking her words carefully. "Well, I don't really have a way to get back to my own world right now. Your queen seems to be my only option, and if she can't help me, then I'm stuck here. Meanwhile, Morrigann's going to try to kill me any chance he gets." She took an absentminded sip of the cool tea before continuing. "What happens if I ever lose my knife? You can't protect me forever, and I won't live in fear. It seems like the only solution is to restore the tree." Her face darkened. "Plus, what he did was wrong - it's genocide! If I can help you, I will." She shrugged as if to say that's all there was to it, that it was a simple matter—but deep down, she was terrified.

Eirnin seemed to sense that and placed his hand on her

shoulder. "Only if you want to. We can look for another way to get you back. You don't have to do this."

She smiled softly over her mug at him, and despite his attempt at control, she saw small green and purple flickers in his eyes.

"I... I want to." And in that moment she knew she truly did. She lowered her mug into her lap and looked at him shyly through her eyelashes, suddenly quite aware that they were alone in the wagon together.

They stared at each other like that for a few moments, and the silence grew. Story felt herself subconsciously leaning toward him—*just to get a better look at his eyes*, she told herself. His hand moved slowly from her shoulder to cup her neck. She felt his thumb tracing small, hesitant circles on the sensitive skin behind her ear.

She leaned into his hand, and her heart began to flutter. There was definitely magic in the air, but a good, natural kind—not the manipulating, controlling kind Morrigann had used on her. Eirnin bent toward her, slowly, giving her every chance to pull away, to say no, all the while his eyes darkening to a solid purple.

She didn't lean in to meet him, but she also didn't stop him. She didn't know what to do. She liked him a lot—usually—and was definitely attracted to him, but the last person she'd let kiss her...

Her stomach rumbled loudly, and they jerked apart, the magic between them evaporating. Eirnin's hand dropped to his side as if burned, and she was blushing furiously. An awkward silence hung in the air until she couldn't take it anymore and was suddenly giggling nervously.

Eirnin shook his head, laughing softly. "I'll ask the da'nan to stop. It sounds like you really need to eat. We've probably traveled far enough for one day." He winked at her, and Story couldn't decide if there had been some sort of hidden meaning in his last sentence. He got up and moved to the door.

"Wait!" Story cringed at the tone of her voice. She sounded panicked.

Eirnin turned and looked earnestly at her, eyes searching her as if she'd been hurt or was in some sort of danger he'd missed. "What's wrong?"

She blushed again under the heat of his gaze. "Um, where are my clothes? All I've got on is one of Adair's sarong thingies, and, well…"

He visibly relaxed, leaning against the door. "Oh, yes… Well, you see, you, um, didn't put a ward up around your clothes after you took them off to go swimming…" He shrugged at her helplessly.

"THEY'RE GONE?" Story shot straight up in bed, clutching the blankets to her chest. *But my shoes!* She thought. *The shoes he made me, gone.* She struggled not to cry.

Eirnin raised his hands placatingly. "Your knife and compass obviously weren't taken, and we can pick you up some new things in Piney Green. We should be there in a few days. You'll just have to make do with what Adair has until then." Then he grinned mischievously. "I promise I won't mind!"

She threw her pillow at him, but he ducked safely out the door, laughing.

STORY FELT BOTH FULL AND CONTENT AS SHE SAT BY THE FIRE THAT night. Eirnin had tried to limit her to drinking only broth, but Adair had managed to sneak her a few sweet rolls. It had hurt her mouth to chew them, but it had been worth it—her stomach was finally full.

Adair felt terrible about what had happened and fretted

over Story from the moment she emerged from the wagon, supported by Eirnin's strong arm around her waist. She tried telling her not to worry, but all it took was Adair getting an eyeful of her bruised and battered leg for her to begin again in earnest. Eilath finally sent her off on the pretext of seeing if the da'nan needed anything.

As it turned out, the sarong that Adair had lent Story was not as skimpy on her as she thought it would be. It was a single piece of large cloth, roughly the size of a beach towel and dyed in interesting patterns and symbols that looked similar to the tattoos that Eilath and Eirnin had around their eyes. It was, of course, purple, since Adair had insisted on matching it to her hair. She had also shown Story how to wrap and secure it around her neck in such a manner that all of her torso and her legs down to her knees were covered, leaving only her shoulders and part of her upper back bare. Story felt a bit odd wearing it, since it seemed more appropriate to lounging on a beach in Hawaii, but she had to concede that it was very comfortable.

She and Eirnin were reclined against a wagon wheel listening to Adair sing while Eilath accompanied her on his faolán. Father and Daughter were a perfect match, both of them a master of their respective instruments. The mixture was potent, and Story was completely drawn into the song Adair was singing about a dryad who fell in love with one of the elf queens of ages past. Because she would not abandon her obligation to her people, she could not return his love until her term as queen ended. Sadly, he died before she was free to go to him, and in despair, she took her own life.

Adair's voice was so soulful here that Story felt tears streaming down her face as she listened. She would have been embarrassed, except one look showed her that her two elf companions were similarly affected. The song actually had a happy ending: as the queen sailed across the Ailes Sea to her soul's final resting place, she saw his soul swimming there, waiting for her. Without thinking, she dove into the water to join him, and they were finally united, never to be separated again.

The song finished, and Story dabbed at her eyes. She whispered to Eirnin, "Wow... better warn the elf boys about her voice. She'll have them all wrapped around her little finger in no time!"

His smile melted away from his face, and he looked uncomfortable. "That won't be a problem."

She glanced over at him—something about his tone of voice tipping her off that there was more to this than she saw. She lowered her voice and leaned toward him. "Why? Does it have anything to do with what Eilath said the day I got hurt? About some things being more important than the past? He doesn't seem especially excited to go to back to Ailes."

Eirnin's face had a resigned look on it, and he bent his head toward hers, keeping his voice low as well. "You could say Eilath's a bit of an outcast among our people. You know how I told you that elves were obsessed with preserving our race?" Story nodded her head. "You've obviously noticed that Eilath's one child is not an elf."

"She's part elf!"

Eirnin gestured for Story to keep her voice down, and wincing at her mistake, she lowered her voice again. Eilath and Adair were still playing their faoláns, seemingly oblivious to her outburst. "Besides, what does it matter? She's wonderful!"

"I agree, but most elves wouldn't. There are no laws against bonding with others outside our race, but it's simply *not done*. What he did was near unto blasphemy according to them—he sped up the extinction of our race."

"Well, maybe there just wasn't any elf he fancied." Story bit her lower lip. Had Eirnin really been trying to kiss her inside the wagon? *I'm not an elf...* "And then Adair's mom came along and sang to him..."

He was shaking his head again. "No. That's not it. He did have an elf that he loved, still loves actually. They wanted to bond, but he wanted to travel around Ailionora as a minstrel for a bit, and she wouldn't go with him. So they parted, and he hasn't been back since. That was over fifty years ago."

That explained the blue sadness that she always saw in Eilath's eyes. Whether he missed his lost love, or regretted leaving her, she wasn't sure. Maybe it was a bit of both. At least she was certain of what brought the green happiness and contentment to his eyes. He'd never regretted having Adair.

"What are you two talking about so secretly over there?" Adair called from across the fire. Her faolán was silent in her lap, and Story and Eirnin looked up guiltily. Eilath just smiled at them, oblivious to the content of conversation, and apparently pleased by whatever it was he saw.

"I was just explaining to Story a little about the queens of old. She didn't understand how someone could stop being queen." He looked at Story meaningfully, and catching the hint, she jumped in.

"Yeah, I thought once you were a queen, you were one until you died."

"That's only been a more recent development, in the last thousand years or so," Eilath said. "Elf queens are born into their job. There's an unbroken line of queens to this day that span the millennia. Before the Change, they were only queen for a few hundred years, and then, when they were ready, their daughter would take over. At that point the old queen would join the clan of the elf she was bonded to." He shifted in his seat, and picked out an atonal tune on his faolán. "After the Change, they remained queen until they died." His eyes were momentarily a deep blue, before he let out a breath and started playing a happy jig. "Well, that's enough talk. Shall we play another?"

"Yes please!" Story leaned back against the wagon wheel and was very much aware that Eirnin was still as close as he had been when they were whispering to each other. She found that this did not bother her one bit.

Chapter Nineteen

Piney Green

THE NEXT FEW DAYS WERE A BLUR FOR STORY. WHEN SHE wasn't sleeping or eating (or rather, having food shoved down her throat by Adair), she was sitting on the wagon's front bench alongside Eilath, enjoying the warm sun. Even though the bruises on her leg were healing nicely, she wasn't allowed to walk anywhere yet. She still had trouble putting her full weight on it, and ugly, puckering, pink scars wrapped around her right leg from where the fuath's tail had grabbed her. She traced her fingers along them absentmindedly, seriously considering Adair's offer to paint over them in patterns the way Eirnin's arm was covered.

A bird fluttered off to her right, and she looked up. The landscape around them was drastically different from what she'd last seen in the woods around Stoneybrook. According to Eilath, they were traveling through the Sunset Plains, toward the Piney Green Forest and a gnome settlement of the same name. Gently rolling hills, covered in waist-high, waving grass, spread out as far as she could see. There was the occasional cluster of trees located around small pools of water that broke up the endless plains.

Story thought it was all starkly beautiful, especially when the wind ruffled the tops of the grass. Adair held a very different opinion; she was going stir crazy with no water to swim in—the pools hardly counted since they were rarely deeper than her knees. So, at Story's suggestion, Eirnin had spent the last couple days taking Adair hunting. Just as she thought, Adair loved the bow and had taken to it with as much enthusiasm as the twins had—though without their exuberant penchant for destruction and chaos. She hadn't actually managed to hit anything yet, but that would come eventually.

This left lots of alone time with Eilath, and Story found that she enjoyed it. He was very easy to be around. He didn't feel a need to fill up the silence with useless chatter (not that Adair did, but like the twins, her exuberance could be wearying at times). Eilath reminded Story of her father in many ways; not that they were alike in personality or anything. No, it was something about the way they both made her feel: warm and protected, comfortable, and above all else, loved.

"I wanted to thank you for everything you've done for Adair." Eilath's gentle voice broke into her thoughts.

"Uh, how do you mean? I think she's done more for me actually. It's a good thing my clothes were stolen; I don't think I could button my jeans anymore with as much as she's been force feeding me."

"Aye, my daughter has never done anything by halves," he chuckled. "No, what I meant was, thank you for being such a great mentor for her. She doesn't get to see much of her mother anymore, and I'm afraid that I let her get away with nearly anything she wants to."

She smiled, thinking of all the times he turned a blind eye to Adair feeding sweets to the da'nan, or how she'd convince him that she didn't *really* need to practice her faolán right then. "Yeah, you are kind of a push over." She smiled at him to let him know she was teasing. "But really, I should be thanking you. I know how hard this must be for you to go back..."

She left the unasked question hanging, not wanting to pry, but also wanting him to know that she was aware of and grateful for the sacrifice he was making.

He shrugged and smiled wryly at her. "I've avoided the past for far too long. My daughter is nothing for me to be ashamed of, and I don't wish to set a poor example for her. I'm not too stubborn to see when I'm wrong."

His answer was pretty cryptic, but Story didn't want to push him, so she shifted the conversation to the subject of elf society. The last thing she wanted to do was to commit some sort of social faux-paus when she had her audience with the queen.

"Eirnin told me a while back that Ea names are girl names..." Eilath nodded to confirm this, so she continued. "So his clan name, and yours as well, are female?"

Whether he noticed the abrupt subject change or not, Eilath didn't indicate. "Aye, elves are a matriarchal society." He strummed idly on his faolán while he spoke, since there was no need to guide the da'nan. "While the clan elders are an elected position and can be held by either gender, we only have a queen, and never a king. When she chooses to bond with another elf, he becomes her consort, but he has no more rights or privileges than any other elf in the realm."

She stretched out her injured leg and began gently kneading her thigh muscle. It tended to fall asleep if she sat in one position for too long. "Do elves bond for life then?"

"Aye. Most of my kind typically find someone to bond

with between the ages of one hundred and two hundred. It all really depends on the elf and the situation, though. As for me, I'm just an old bachelor." He grinned at her and winked.

"So... would that make Eirnin a young bachelor?" She hoped she sounded casual.

Eilath smiled broadly. "Eirnin is not bonded to anyone, if that's what you're asking."

Her cheeks blush a brilliant red, and she hastily changed the subject. "I've figured out that the tattoo, sorry, I mean your ailach, over your eye is different from Eirnin's because you're from different clans. What happens after elves bond?"

"The ailach changes to reflect the elf's new clan, that of his wife's." His strumming took on an airy sound, providing a soft background for their conversation. "The bonding ceremony is actually one of the few areas of magic we still have control over. I've always thought that was because of the inherent magic of love that permeates it." He winked at Story. "So, no matter how powerful the Faerie Prince is, he'll never be able to take love away. It's the deepest magic there is."

She nodded her agreement. As cheesy as it all sounded, Eilath was more correct than he knew—this little fact, the "magic of love" had to be a huge thorn in Morrigann's side. Yet another thing he could never have.

"How many of you are left?"

Eilath stopped strumming his faolán and was silent.

Story instantly regretted her question. How callus could she be asking a member of a dying race how many of his kinsmen were left? "I'm sorry, I shouldn't have..."

"No, it's fine, child. I was just trying to do the math in my head. It has been a while since I've thought about it, you know." He smiled gently at her to let her know he wasn't upset. "I imagine that there are about a thousand of us remaining these days. If you figure that every two to three hundred years our numbers half themselves, that means we've got roughly one thousand years left before we're entirely extinct." He shrugged his shoulders casually, as if he'd already accepted the inevitability of it.

"Well, that remains to be seen," she said stubbornly.

He looked at her out of the corner of his eye, but didn't say anything. She couldn't tell if he approved of her choice to go on the quest, but he hadn't said anything against it. It seemed, more than anything, he just wanted her to be happy.

"You said something before about clan elders. How many are there? What do they do?"

Eilath chuckled and strummed a cheerful tune. "My, you are full of questions today."

"I'm sorry. I just want to be sure I understand." She held up her hands helplessly. "Plus it's all pretty interesting. You're all so different from my own people, and yet, in some ways, we're very much alike."

"Curiosity is a good thing, child. You just have to be prepared to accept all the answers you get, whatever they may be."

She eyed him curiously, not fully understanding his, yet again, cryptic answer.

"There are twelve ruling clans that are, in turn, assembled into three different higher clan groups—allies, if you will. Each of the twelve clans has a different specialty or trade. My family specializes in music." He nodded at his instrument. "Others are warriors, some are builders or inventors. There are three mage clans, each one a part of a different higher clan." He glanced at Story, and she smiled her encouragement. "Each family also has their own elected family matriarch or patriarch who is the clan's embodiment of power. For example, Eirnin's clan leader, Eáchan is not merely a hunter, but *the* Hunter. The clan leaders' main role, aside from taking care of their families, is to serve on the council as the queen's advisors."

His eyes darkened, and the tune he was playing became more solemn. "As for the queen, she only gets involved in governing when she is needed. If anything, she's more of a spiritual guide, a seer—if you will—for my people." He looked at Story to make sure she was following, and she nodded her head for him to continue. "Though just because she's queen, her power is not absolute. As a unanimous body, the council can overrule her, though it's never been done before."

Then he tossed her a peach. "Now it's my turn. How old are you, child? What is the typical human lifespan? And most importantly, how much of your day is dedicated to finding, preparing, and eating food?"

Story laughed, bit into her peach, and spent the rest of the ride regaling Eilath with tales of her world and the way things worked there. As the sun slipped over the horizon, she could just make out the waiting forms of Adair and Eirnin on the side of the road and, behind them, the outskirts of the Piney Green Forest.

THE NEXT DAY SAW THEM ENTER THE VILLAGE OF PINEY GREEN. IT was similar to Stoneybrook in appearance and setup, only on a much larger scale. Adair was bouncing around in her seat excitedly, looking forward to seeing old friends and performing in the common room of the main inn. Story exchanged bemused looks with Eirnin who was walking beside the wagon's bench, and they both chuckled quietly.

Gnomes called out greetings to Eilath and Adair, and a few also greeted Eirnin. None even gave Story a second glance, though she'd expected as much. Upon reaching the inn (which made the one in Stoneybrook look like a barn), Adair leapt off the wagon before it came to a complete stop and ran to the main entrance.

Eirnin reached up and, despite Story's protestations that she could walk unassisted now, gently lifted her down before placing her on her feet. He kept a steadying hand on the small of her back, and even though she didn't think she really needed it, she didn't tell him to move it. She felt a blush creep up her neck and stared straight ahead, reluctant to look at Eilath or Eirnin. She was afraid of the knowing smile she'd see on the former's face and what she might not see on the latter's.

A woman, who looked like a much younger and, if possible, thicker version of Missus Bryggeri, burst out of the inn and scooped Adair up in a massive hug; the girl in turn squealed with delight and hugged back just as hard.

"Ah, Miss Adair, it's been so long since I've last seen ya! Where has your da been keeping you? I know you've been visiting my sister, but what's wrong, don't you love me anymore?"

Eilath leaned forward, and placed a hand on her shoulder, taking care to stay safely far enough away from her crushing arms. "Missus Borgmester, my apologies for staying away for so long. As it is we'll only be staying the night, since we have urgent business in Ailes."

Missus Borgmester's face fell.

Story looked at Eirnin and mouthed "Borgmester?" He leaned over and whispered "Her husband is the mayor," as if that explained everything.

Meanwhile, Eilath was trying to calm the innkeeper down. "I promise my daughter and I will perform in the common room tonight."

Missus Borgmester's face beamed.

"Wonderful! I'll have my Mister B spread the word. There will be quite a crowd tonight!" She turned around to dash back into the inn, her hand wrapped around Adair's wrist (though Story didn't know who was pulling who). After a few steps, she paused to look back. "Oh, sorry Mister Eáchan, it's very nice to see you again. Your friend is welcome here of course." And with that she hurried inside to find her husband.

"Eirnin, I'll lead the da'nan around back and park the wagon near the stables. Missus Borgmester's sons will help me get set up for tonight and move our things to our rooms."

Her eyes nearly glazed over at the thought of a bed, a *real bed*. Meanwhile, Eilath's lilting voice continued. "Why don't you take Story to the tailor? He still owes me for the faolán I gave him two seasons back."

That got her attention back. "Wait, what? No! I can't let you pay for new clothes for me. You've done enough already."

Eilath's hand came down gently, but firmly on her shoulder. "Child, let me do this for you. It would make me happy."

Story chewed on her lip worriedly and glanced over at Eirnin for help. He inclined his head in a subtle nod, and so, when she looked back at Eilath, she nodded her head. She felt like a mooch, but if it really would make him happy…

Still, if only to show just a bit of independence, she stepped away from Eirnin's steadying hand and strode purposefully down the street. She figured if she could keep her momentum up, she wouldn't wobble back and forth as much. Her leg didn't hurt really; mostly it just felt tingly, as if the circulation in it was struggling to keep up with her. She only went a few feet before she realized that she was alone. Stopping abruptly, and nearly falling on her face when her leg threatened to give out, she turned and looked back at the elves.

Eirnin was working at keeping a knowing grin off of his face and coughed into his hands while he hastily looked away. Eilath just crossed his arms and shook his head.

"Let me guess. It's the other way?" She pointed the

opposite direction she'd been walking. Eilath nodded, and she let out a loud sigh.

Of course!

She started walking back the other way, albeit, a bit more unsteady this time, and Eirnin was instantly by her side. He didn't try to support her, though, seeming to understand that it was important to her to walk at least this bit on her own. She'd had enough of being bossed around and coddled over the last few days.

STORY LAUGHED AND CLAPPED HER HANDS IN TIME TO THE MUSIC as she watched Adair dancing gaily in the middle of the inn's great room floor. Tables had been pushed off to the side to accommodate the dozens upon dozens of villagers who were all dancing a sort of jig. It looked very chaotic to her, but she could see that there was some sort of pattern to it. The couples wove in and out, trading partners, faster and faster, as the music sped up.

Adair danced by, waving and giggling, Eilath played the faolán masterfully, and the natural acoustics in the room reflected the music loudly over the crowded room's hum of voices. Story felt a breeze swirl her skirt, or rather, kilt, as a set of dancers nearly collided with her table. Her new clothes were clean and comfortable, and much to her surprise, she quite liked them.

The tailor, Mister Tilpasse had given her a cream-colored ladies' peasant blouse and a lavender archer's vest to wear over it. The vest had looked like a corset at first, which Story would have immediately rejected, but it just laced up the front, as loose or as tight as she wanted, with no boning in the vest to cut off her breath. Mister Tilpasse had flat refused to give her a set of trousers or leggings, saying "It is indecent for a lass to dress like a lad," but Story balked at wearing a long skirt, adamant that it would restrict her ability to move quickly. Just because she couldn't move quickly right now, didn't mean that she wouldn't need to in the very near future. So, they'd compromised on the knee length kilt she now wore. He hadn't seemed too happy about it, but she'd stubbornly held her ground until she got her way. The tailor then topped her entire ensemble off with a calf-length, hooded, wool cloak for the cooler evenings and inclement weather. She decided to skip getting shoes from the cobbler—she found she was enjoying being barefoot, and the days were generally warm enough now for it.

Eirnin met up with her after she was done, and he too had a gift for her: a bow and a quiver full of arrows. Before she could protest, he pointed out that she'd mentioned she knew how to use one, and that if she persisted in leaving her knife lying about, she needed another form of self-defense.

So, she found herself now in this happy hall, tapping her feet along with the music. The crowd in the room didn't feel oppressive or confining. The anxiety she'd felt around people she didn't know ever since the accident happened was gone. The gnomes, once properly introduced to her, were perfectly amiable and friendly.

Her thoughts were interrupted when Eirnin stepped before her grinning, bowing at the waist. He extended a hand.

"No way." Story backed her chair up against the wall and shook her head. She was itching to dance, but knew she'd fall flat on her face the moment she attempted it. She was only graceful in the water, or while running, and a sore leg wouldn't help things.

"Please?" His expression had now turned into a playfully sad pout.

"Bad things happen when I dance."

"Like what?"

"Like tripping, and falling, and stepping on my partner's feet."

Eirnin indicated the dancers. A good portion of them tripped around, a few fell, and many feet were being stepped on. The dance was pure joyful exuberance.

Before she could come up with another protest, he pulled her to her feet and swung her out on the dance floor. This was nothing like dancing with the Faerie Prince. While that dance had been wild and *other*, it was also structured and elegant. *And all part of a plot to kill me,* Story thought sourly. This dance, on the other hand, was the definition of fun. She realized quickly that there was no wrong way to dance it and, with Eirnin's support, no chance of her falling. She threw her head back and laughed and let the joyful feeling in the room fill her.

Chapter Twenty

Confession

ONE DAY HAD TURNED INTO THREE, PARTLY DUE TO MISSUS Borgmester constantly insisting that they needed just one more day of rest. Eilath, despite what he'd said upon their arrival, seemed in no real hurry to move on to Ailes. Still, it seemed that they would be leaving tomorrow (Eirnin insisted upon it), and Story found that she would be sad to say goodbye to the gnomes.

After that first night of dancing with them in the common room, they treated her as a long lost friend, and she was constantly greeted whenever she went for strolls through the village. She enjoyed taking in the new sights, sounds, and smells—so very alive and vibrant. The walks also helped her stretch her leg out, and she could feel it was slowly getting strong again.

Story paused in her current walk when she felt her leg twinge; it still had some stiffness and sensitivity to it. Leaning against the Milliner's store front she curled and uncurled her toes. It seemed to help and took her mind off the pain darting up her calf, so she focused on that simple act, smiling at the lavender and black swirls that were painted up her leg. She'd finally given in and let Adair paint over her scars with a semi-permanent dye that she'd sworn would wash off after a few weeks. She had to admit, it looked pretty cool—*though Dad would have lost his mind if I did it permanently*. She chuckled at the thought and looked around at the gnomes bustling about with their daily business, smiling and nodding at each other and occasionally at her.

Without warning, the scene before her made her feel like she'd been punched in the stomach.

She thought being here in another world, and so many months after *it* had happened, that she couldn't be affected like before. That it would be safe to let her guard down.

Apparently, she'd been wrong.

It was a simple thing really. Some young boys were taunting some young girls walking home from school. One ruddy-cheeked boy dropped a frog down the back of one prim-looking girl's dress. Rather than scream or run, she'd turned around with a handful of mud and made him eat it.

It was so Will and Katie.

A searing fire tore through Story's heart like it was being fed gasoline. Gasping for breath, she ran back to the inn as quickly as her legs would carry her and fought the tears that threatened to spill.

Not here, not now, not in public!

A soft knock sounded at the door of her room, and Story ignored it. She wanted to be alone. She *needed* to be alone.

Swinging her legs lazily in the open air below them, she leaned her forehead against one of the wooden poles that was part of the balcony's railing. The sunset over the forest was beautiful, and she thought that maybe if she just focused on that for a while her lungs would stop feeling like they were burning, and she'd be able to breathe normally again. Or at least without hiccupping sobs.

"You didn't come down for dinner." Leave it to Eirnin to intrude on her solitude.

"I wasn't hungry."

"That's a first."

She stiffened her shoulders and didn't answer; she was in no mood to be teased. The silence built, and finally, she heard the door close, and she breathed a loud sigh of relief. He'd taken the hint and left.

Relaxing her shoulders, she slumped forward again and focused on breathing in and out, slowly, methodically. Someday, it wouldn't hurt. Someday, she would be able to do this without thinking about it. Someday, she'd be able to live a normal life without the fear of being blindsided by hurt and loss.

Someday.

"The first year is always the hardest, you know." Eirnin sat down next to her, threading his legs through the railing. He let them swing idly back and forth in time with hers.

She wasn't sure if she was more irritated, surprised, or relieved that he'd remained.

"How did you... never mind." She bit her lower lip, considering her next words carefully—almost afraid to say them. "Do you want to know what happened?"

"Only if you want to tell me."

She didn't want to tell him. She didn't want to talk about it with anyone. But a large part of her wanted—no, *needed*—him to know. She took a deep, calming breath. This would not be easy.

"It was last winter, over the holidays. That was when my dad gave me…" She swallowed hard and gripped her knife's handle tightly. "Anyway, we were all staying at the cabin for Christmas, like we do every year—me, my dad, and the twins. I left early to go to a party. My dad told me to drive carefully, that there was a lot of ice on the roads." She paused, remembering how he'd leaned over her window and wagged an admonishing finger at her. She'd rolled her eyes and stuck her tongue out at him in response. At least she'd told him she loved him before she tore off down the mountain. "He was right; there was a lot of ice on the roads. Especially the next day, when he and the twins left the mountain." She glanced at Eirnin and saw confusion flicker through his eyes. "Cars move very fast—faster than anything I've seen in your world. If they hit ice, they can spin out of control and crash or flip." Her voice broke and she paused until she'd regained control.

"I knew. I knew as soon as I saw the police lights outside…" She took a deep breath and fought to keep her voice even. "There was no surviving the wreckage."

She didn't dare look at him as she asked, "Will I ever—will it ever stop feeling this way? Stop hurting like this?"

She gripped the round, wooden poles with her hands and felt her fingers convulse around them. She squeezed her eyes tightly until they burned.

I will not cry, I WILL NOT CRY!

"Yes… and no." Eirnin stared steadfastly out at the orange horizon, seeming to understand that Story did not want to be looked at, or pitied, at the moment. "Eventually you'll be able to think about them with a smile, and you won't feel like your heart is constantly breaking." He gave her a sidelong glance;

his eyes swirled in dark blue and yellow, sadness and concern for her vying for preeminence in them. His hand settled gently on her shoulder. "But you'll never stop missing them."

Story's resolve cracked and a wave of emotion—regret, longing, and mostly, relief crashed over her. She covered her face with her hands and felt her hot tears leak onto them. Her shoulders shook as the sobs threatened to overtake her again. Strong arms encircled her as Eirnin pulled her onto his lap. He rocked back and forth gently and simply held her as she buried her face in his neck and cried.

Chapter Twenty-One

The Troll

W HEN YOU SAID YOU KNEW HOW TO SHOOT, DID YOU, IN FACT, mean with a bow?" Eirnin crossed his arms across his chest and raised an eyebrow quizzically at Story.

She let out a sigh, slung her bow over her shoulder and marched over to the tree trunk that had her still-quivering arrow buried in it. She ran her free hand along the surface of the bow, marveling at its smooth texture and exquisite construction. It was a composite bow, made out of horn and sinew on the back of a wooden core. Its construction gave her the pull and power of a longbow, without the bulk and size. It was the finest bow she'd ever used; the craftsmanship was perfect.

Too bad it didn't help her any with her aim. Her arrow was two trees over from her intended target, a large oak that a blind squirrel could have hit with a nut.

"If I'd been surrounded by wood sprites, I'd be doing just fine, thank you very much." She grasped the arrow and yanked. When it didn't budge, she wrapped both of her hands around the shaft, braced her left foot against the trunk of the tree, and pulled hard. She overdid it; the arrow jerked out of the bark, and she fell down hard onto her backside.

Eirnin tried to hide a laugh with a cough, but the amused orange flickers in his eyes gave him away. "Aye, and if you'd had a wood sprite behind, you'd have squashed him. Interesting tactics you employ." He held out a hand to help her up.

Ignoring his hand, she glared at him while she got to her feet. She dusted the dead leaves off her bottom and flounced back to her original shooting position.

"Well, if you're so perfect at it, why don't you come show me how it's done?" She gave a toss of her hair and crossed her arms across her chest expectantly. She wasn't really mad, and he knew it. Mostly, she was just embarrassed; she'd never really excelled at archery.

"Alright." He stepped in front of her and raised his own bow, a slightly larger version of her own. "Proper archery techniques begin with a proper stance and end with a proper follow through." He continued talking through the different steps of shooting and said something about how a proper mental checklist was really what would help her with her aim.

Story tried to focus on what he was saying, really she did, but watching the lean muscles of his back contract and move under his sleeveless tunic was too distracting. She followed the lines of his shoulders to the swirling tattoos on his arm that seemed designed to emphasize the musculature there. Her appraising gaze had just made it down to his hand, when he let go of the arrow. It flew true and hit the fist-sized knob on the tree they'd been targeting.

Story gulped in a deep breath and felt her pulse quicken. *Get a grip, girl! He's just a guy!* Yeah, just a guy who'd gone out of his way to keep her alive time and time again, despite her often sour attitude toward him. And there was the thing with the crying the other night... He wasn't the sweetest guy she'd ever known, no, he was too sarcastic and teasing for that, but he had the truest heart. And a cute backside too.

She realized then that she was well on her way to falling in love with him—if she hadn't already—and the thought terrified her.

"And that's how you *properly* shoot a bow." Eirnin turned around to look at her, a smug grin on his face. When he saw the frightened look on her face his eyes instantly clouded into swirls of yellow. "What's wrong?"

She squeezed her eyes shut and ducked her head. *Stop acting like an idiot! He's just a boy, and you're just a girl. It's simple. Quit trying to make drama!* She had to remind herself that her eyes didn't change colors to betray her emotion; she then forced herself to open them and smiled weakly.

"Nothing. Archery was just the twins' thing is all. They were always a whole lot better at death and destruction than I ever was." Story found that it was easier to talk about her family now, at least with Eirnin.

He chuckled at her comment, and his eyes melted back to silver. "I don't know about that; you seem pretty good at destruction yourself."

He reached out his hand toward the side of her head, and she stilled, her heart fluttering. *Stop that!* she ordered herself, feeling like an idiot all over again. He pulled a crushed leaf from her hair and held it in front of her eyes.

"See? What did this poor mangled leaf ever do to you?" A smile tugged at the corner of his mouth, and his eyes glittered with orange flashes of amusement. A breeze blew between them, and the little green leaf flittered off into the forest on the light current.

She tore her gaze away from his and shook her fist play-fully at it. "Yeah that's right! You'd better run!"

Eirnin laughed and called, "Go, little leaf! Flee from this hideous monster."

"Hey! Who are you calling hideous, elf-boy?" Story slapped at his shoulder, and he caught her hand in his.

"Oh, the leaf. Definitely the leaf. You're absolutely not hideous. In fact, you're quite the opposite." Purple sparks joined the orange in his eyes, and he interlaced their fingers together.

Story stepped in closer and felt the tingly, magical feeling around them intensify. Or maybe that was just the butterflies in her stomach. "What's the opposite of hideous?"

"Beautiful." His lips pressed against hers softly, stealing her breath away.

She felt herself lean toward him, closing the remaining few inches of space between them. Her free arm encircled his neck, and she ran her fingers up into his short, silky hair, luxu-riating in its feel. He smelled like cinnamon and apples, and she inhaled his scent deeply.

He let go of her hand and wrapped both of his arms around her, pulling her in tighter. She marveled at how per-fectly their bodies fit together, as if they were two puzzle pieces finally rejoined. Her mind was perfectly clear, and it was let-ting her know that it definitely liked this. The kiss lengthened, and she both heard and felt his lips part in a contented sigh.

That was when a tree crash-landed, splintering to the side of them, and nearly crushed them both. Breaking apart breathlessly, they looked at the tree they'd been shooting at.

It was gone.

In its place was the strangest, and by far the scariest, crea-ture she'd ever seen. It was a twenty-foot tall, roughly human-oid-shaped, moving pile of rocks. Its long arms hung down past its knees, and it was using them to pull up another tree, as if it were picking a flower.

Eirnin shoved Story roughly behind him and nocked an arrow.

"Story, RUN!"

She didn't need to be told twice, but she also wasn't about to let him get killed either. Whatever that thing was, it didn't strike her as something that was friendly. Grabbing his biceps, she yanked Eirnin nearly off his feet, causing his arrow to fly awry and miss the stone monster completely. It opened the maw in the lower portion of what she assumed was its head, and roared at them. The noise it made sounded like rocks being torn in two; it chilled Story to her very bones. Still hanging onto Eirnin's arm, she tore off running through the woods, leaving him no choice but to follow.

"What do you think you're doing? I had him!" He jerked his arm out of her grip, but kept pace with her. Meanwhile, the ground started to shake as the monster began to pursue them, leaving a trail of decimated trees in its wake.

"Shut up and keep running, elf-boy. What, did you think you could shoot a rock with an arrow and kill it?"

A tree exploded over their heads, showering them with leaves and splinters.

"Aye! If I could hit the troll's weak spot." He glared at her and ducked another flying tree limb.

"Oh, is that what that thing is?"

Eirnin ignored her question and glanced behind them. His eyes widened, as he took in the rapidly approaching troll. "Keep running toward the stream and get in the middle. You'll be safe there." He stopped and faced the troll, nocking another arrow. It was only a hundred feet away now.

"What? No! Not without you!" She stopped short and stubbornly crossed her arms.

"Story, GO. I don't have time to explain, and I can't do this if I'm worried about you." He spared a glance in her direction to punctuate his words. That was a mistake.

"Look out!"

He whirled around and dove away in time to avoid the bulk of another flying tree trunk. Story ran toward him to help him up, but the troll roared again, freezing her in her tracks. It was much closer now.

Eirnin looked at her, frustration and pain painted across his face. "Story, please go!"

"No! I won't leave you."

"Stop trying to be a hero. My leg is pinned. RUN!"

The ground shook like an earthquake, and the troll got closer. Sixty feet. Fifty feet. She tore her eyes away from it, and looked down at Eirnin. His eyes were all yellow and red flames, and there was no way she could leave him here to die.

Story stepped in front of him and pulled her knife out, holding it out before her as she took a defensive stance. Why she hadn't thought about this before she didn't know, and prayed that her idiocy hadn't caused Eirnin's leg to be broken.

Thirty feet, and the troll stopped short as it looked at her. It focused on the knife in her hand, and then bellowed at her.

"Yeah, that's right big ugly. I got iron. How do you like them apples?"

"Story—"

"Don't worry, elf-boy. I got this."

"But Story—"

The troll took another step forward, and then another, and then another.

"—Mountain trolls aren't fey. Iron doesn't hurt them!" Eirnin gasped as he struggled to move the tree off his leg.

"WHAT?" Her eyes were fixed on the troll as it got closer and closer. It appeared to have decided to forgo the trees and crush her with its bare hands instead. There was no way she could get Eirnin out before the troll got to them and killed them both. "Then what the heck DOES hurt them?"

"Water."

"We're fresh out of that right now. I need options here..."

"Aim for just below the knee, it's their weak spot."

"Right, because that makes perfect sense." Story tried to remember what her dad had taught her about throwing a knife. It was all in the stance; left foot in front, with her two feet forming a forty-five degree angle, and both knees bent, especially the front one. She leaned back and rested her weight on the ball of her back foot and took a deep breath. She would only get one shot at this.

Twenty-five feet, twenty feet. *Wait for it... wait for it...*

She tensed, and swung the knife behind her back. Suddenly the male da'nan burst out from the trees. He reared up on his hind legs and then came down, horns aimed for attack. The da'nan hit the troll full force in its knee, and then backed up, ready to charge again, but it was unnecessary. The Troll roared in surprise and then was abruptly silenced as it fell apart into a heap of boulders.

Story stood there, still poised to throw her knife and watched as the da'nan stepped over to the rock pile. He snorted air out of his nose as if to say "hah!" and then turned to face her. She lowered her arms slowly and looked into the intelligent, brown eyes.

"Thank you." That seemed so inadequate, but she didn't know what else to say to him.

The da'nan simply stared back at her, swished his tail, and then turned and trotted back toward the campsite. She stared after the creature in shock, still trying to process what she'd just witnessed.

"Lucky for us, he smelled the troll," Eirnin gasped, trying

to heave the tree off his leg. Story rushed over to his side, and between the two of them, they were able to move the trunk enough for him to free himself.

"Are you okay?" Story eyed him worriedly, but he seemed to be bearing weight on his leg normally.

"I'm fine." He finished brushing himself off and then looked westward. "But we have bigger problems now."

"We do?"

"Aye." He looked at her, the worry clear in his eyes. "I'd hoped that by traveling with the da'nan the fey would stay away, and Morrigann would be unable to track you. That's obviously not the case."

"Who cares if he can track us? He can't hurt me."

"Not directly, no. But remember the fuath? And he clearly had enough sway over that troll to get it to come down off the mountains and attack you, even in the presence of the da'nan. We're just lucky it was a youth. It would have taken a herd of da'nan to bring down a fully-grown mountain troll."

Story felt her mouth go dry. "That thing... that was just a baby?"

"Aye."

Her jaw hung open as she stared at him.

"What?" He raised an eyebrow.

"It's just that you said... when you were a kid..." She looked down at his arm and began tracing the scars under his tattoos with her fingertip.

Chagrined, he smiled at her. "Aye, that. Yes, I foolishly attacked a fully-grown mountain troll when I was young and reckless. I'm fortunate this is all that happened."

"Why did you do it?"

"It killed my parents."

"Oh."

They stood there awkwardly for a moment, Story's

fingertips hovering over his arm, avoiding each other's eyes. Finally, Eirnin pulled her into a hug, and her body began shaking, the realization of what she'd just faced finally catching up to her mind and scaring her nearly senseless.

"Story?"

"Yes?" Her voice came out as a squeak.

"Next time I tell you to run, will you please run?"

"That depends."

"On what?"

"If you're running too."

She both felt and heard him sigh in frustration. "You'll be the death of us both."

"At least we'll be in good company."

His only response was to pull her closer to him, and she wrapped her arms around him tightly in return.

CHAPTER TWENTY-TWO

THE CITY OF AILES

THE MORNING AIR WAS CRISP AND COOL, LEAVING STORY quite thankful for her warm cloak. She fingered the soft, green wool and forced herself not to look over at Eirnin while they walked. Even the thought of him made her cheeks flush and a small smile cross her lips.

After the troll attack yesterday, Adair had come bursting through the trees before they'd had a chance to talk about, well, anything. She'd grabbed Story by her hands and pulled her over to the mound of rocks that had been the troll, demanding she tell her everything that happened. Eirnin chuckled and promptly abandoned her to go recover her bow if it had survived the attack—which it had.

The evening passed in the usual way: with Eilath and Adair singing and playing while they all sat around the campfire eating sweet rolls and a stew made from the wild game Eirnin had caught. Eirnin was attentive as always and sat next to Story, as was customary, betraying nothing of what had passed between them both before and after the troll's attack. She would have gone to bed believing she'd imagined the entire kissing event if, just as she was settling down for the night, he hadn't pulled her behind a tree and stolen a quick goodnight kiss.

She'd had a hard time falling asleep after that. Her mind kept replaying the events—well, the kisses really—over and over again. She had long since given up on berating herself for being a "silly girl." She *was* a girl after all, and this is what a girl did when a boy kissed her. Girls over-analyzed everything and also tried to remember every single moment of what passed.

Despite her lack of sleep, she was not groggy in the least. The cold air and her pointed awareness of Eirnin's location and proximity to her at all times kept her alert. She didn't want things to be awkward or weird, and from what she could tell, he was completely at ease with the way things were between them now. The problem was she wasn't sure what they were exactly. When they weren't teasing or purposefully baiting each other, it seemed pretty clear that they liked each other. But beyond that, she didn't know.

A terrifying thought struck her—had they "bonded"? Was that all it took? A simple kiss? No, Eilath had said something about a ceremony, so that couldn't be it. And besides, she didn't think it was allowed. What had Eirnin said? Bonding outside of the elf race was simply *not done*. She frowned at that memory. So what was he playing at, flirting with her and kissing her? It couldn't be to manipulate her into restoring the tree; she'd already decided to do that on her own.

Though if she restored the tree wouldn't the social taboo of being with someone outside the elf race be lifted? Since they'd be immortal again? But that only brought up another problem—she'd eventually grow old and die, while Eirnin stayed forever young.

Really, you're jumping the gun here, Story—you're only seventeen, and you barely know the guy, and already you're considering future compatibility? It was just one kiss. Ok, two actually.

She sighed; this entire train of thought was pointless. Regardless of how she might currently feel about Eirnin, she was going to leave Ailionora eventually—so it was a relationship ultimately doomed to failure. It would probably be best to nip things in the bud now before they both got too attached.

"You're rather introspective this morning." Eirnin grinned at her, and Story nearly lost her balance—he'd caught her off guard.

"Uh…" She blushed.

"And less verbose than usual."

"Uh…" She blushed again.

He peered at her, still smirking. "Are you all right?"

Say something! Anything but UH!

"Uh… yeah. I'm fine. Just had a hard time sleeping last night." Well, at least that had been the truth, even if it did sound completely lame.

He furrowed his eyebrows together, and she could see flashes of yellow in his eyes—and, did she just detect a hint of brown? That was a new color for him.

"No bad dreams, I hope?" He looked overly concerned, for something as simple as a bad night of sleep.

She raised an eyebrow at him, confused for a moment, but when he continued to look worried, it clicked. "If you mean the sort that involve a sadistic Faerie Prince trying to seduce and/or kill me, then no."

"Good." Eirnin's mouth tightened and his eyes became solidly brown.

Was it jealousy? *So much for staying free of attachments.* The thought of Eirnin being jealous of Morrigann made her feel giddy, frustrated, and a little scared—but in a good way. *Ugh, why are emotions so complicated?*

Eirnin's eyes bored into hers, and she watched as swirls of purple displaced the brown. She should turn away. She should stop this. This was the opposite of what she needed to do. But she couldn't—for once, she felt happy. Or rather, like she remembered what being happy felt like. He leaned toward her and cupped her face with his tattooed hand, his thumb tracing the line of her jaw.

"Story, look!" Adair was pointing straight ahead over the hill.

They broke apart, and Story, both irritated and grateful for an excuse to avoid Eirnin's piercing eyes, jogged up to the crest of the hill. She looked down the slope where the trees thinned out and followed the line of the road as it led to a wide, glassy sea. Eirnin had told her that it was the Ailes Lake, but she couldn't see the other side of it—it was massive!

Adair grabbed her hand and squeezed it excitedly. "The City of Ailes!"

They were gliding across the water on elegantly carved, white gondolas, steered by Eirnin and Eilath. Originally Adair had wanted to swim across, but one look from her father had silenced her. Eilath had become quieter of late, and his eyes were almost solidly blue these days. Upon first sighting the islands they'd also acquired a yellow tinge. Adair had also become somewhat subdued. Story could tell that she was excited, but also a bit anxious. This was her first visit to Ailes as well.

As for Story, she was torn between excitement and anxiety. She couldn't wait to see a real elf city, but she was worried about what the elves would think of her. She kept remembering Eirnin's words to her from a few weeks ago:

"Trust me, you're not what anyone here is expecting."

She traced her fingers over a tree carving on the prow of the little boat and gazed out at the city before her.

"That's the queen's island in front of us." Eirnin indicated with a nod of his head. "There are thirteen primary island clusters that make up the city of Ailes. One for each clan, and then of course, the queen's."

Story looked at the island spread out before her. It wasn't overly large, maybe nine or ten miles, though it was completely covered in buildings, and as they got closer, she could make out dozens of canals and rivers leading into and out of the island.

"It kind of reminds me of Venice. Not that I've ever been there, but what I've seen in pictures."

"Venice?"

She looked over her shoulder back at him and smiled. "Sorry, I forget sometimes that you aren't human. It's a city in my world made up of over a hundred tiny islands. The roads between them are all canals and rivers, so everyone gets around on boats and such."

Eirnin's mouth curved upward into a smile. "See, our worlds are not so different. This is our Venice."

He wasn't too far off, Story noted. As they entered one of the canals, her gaze followed the lines of the tall, sweeping, white marble walls and intricately carved bridges. *The Ailes* tree was depicted absolutely everywhere but wasn't overdone. The architecture was all in the same style of the bridges and elf structures she'd encountered thus far, only on a much grander scale.

"It's pretty lonely though isn't it?" She thought she'd said it too quietly for anyone to hear, but she'd discounted Eirnin's sharp elf ears.

"A millennia ago our islands were swarming with life and industry. Now each family has less than a hundred living members. The queen's island is nearly empty, since she has no family of her own. It's just her and her twelve handmaidens, one from each family."

It was eerily quiet, with only the lapping of the water against the gondola and the sound of Story's breath filling her ears.

"Are there no faeries here either?"

Eirnin's mouth twisted. "No. There's enough salt in the water here that they don't like to linger. Wards set up throughout the city keep them out as well. Places like Queen Eánna's royal palace are protected by our last remaining iron."

"Wait, so the fey aren't in the oceans? And how have you managed to keep the iron around the palace from rusting after all these years?

"There are no fey in the seas that claim any allegiance to the Faerie Prince." Eirnin's eyes flashed brown, and he looked straight ahead. "As for the iron, as you can imagine, the mage clans haven't had much to do over the years, so they take meticulous care of what's left."

They glided to a stop at the base of a large courtyard that had an enormous palace on the opposite end of it. The palace followed the same architectural theme as the rest of the city, white marble, multiple arches, strong columns, domed roofs with spires on top, and lots of intricate carvings, statues, and decorations—only on a much grander scale. Story was struck by how delicate and, well, *feminine* the palace looked. It was clearly the residence of a queen.

Eirnin stepped out of the gondola and secured it to a pole, then bent over to help Story out of the boat. She could see out of the corner of her eye that Eilath was doing the same thing with Adair, who was still quiet. Her eyes were wide as she took everything in; her father simply looked resigned and indicated with a nod of his head that they should go. Eirnin gave Story's hand a quick squeeze that set butterflies off in her stomach, and they all strode toward the palace.

They went down three black marble steps into a recessed courtyard and Story tried to focus on her task at hand instead of the giddy sensation she was feeling after holding Eirnin's hand so briefly. She schooled her face and tried to do the same with her emotions.

Quit acting like an idiot! He's nearly Granddad's age, for goodness sakes!

Except her granddad was dead, just like the rest of her family. She frowned and pushed that thought out of her mind. Looking at Eirnin's back, she mused that even though he was technically a senior citizen by human measurements, by his own race's standards he wasn't much older than her. Still, it was kind of weird when she thought about it.

Probably best not to try to make sense of it, she thought with a wry smile, then frowned again. She should not even be considering any of this—not if she wanted to keep Eirnin at arm's length.

In the center of the courtyard stood a solitary marble bowl filled with rich brown earth and nothing else. The bowl was framed by three sweeping archways on the other side of the courtyard. Story walked up to it and, leaning her hip against the lip, picked up a small handful of the damp soil. Her fingers tingled, and she felt the echo of something. She couldn't quite ascribe a name to it, but she felt a hazy connection to the bowl, almost as if she was trying to rebuild the memory of a memory. *That makes no sense, not even in this place.* She gave up on trying to figure out what she was feeling and let out a breath she didn't even realize she'd been holding.

"This is where it was, isn't it?" Story let the dirt slip through her fingers back into the planter.

"Aye, that it was—before the Faerie Prince took it away as his prize." Eilath placed his hand gently on her shoulder. "Come child, we're nearly there."

Her stomach lurched, and she felt as if she was leaving a piece of her heart behind in that lonely old courtyard. A cool hand cupped hers and gently pulled her away from the bowl.

"Thank you, Adair."

The dryad didn't answer, just squeezed her hand and then caught back up to her father. Eirnin steered them toward the center archway, up the three steps leading out of the courtyard, and onto the broad landing under the archway. The smooth, black marble tiles under Story's bare feet were polished to such a high sheen she could almost see her own reflection in them.

Like the rest of the city, the palace was eerily quiet. She knew there weren't many elves left, but the fact that they hadn't run into a single guard or servant or anyone at all struck her as very odd. She would have thought the vast palace with its sweeping ceilings and long open corridors was quite lovely, if its lack of life hadn't been so oppressively creepy.

"It's like a ghost village," Adair whispered in her ear, causing Story to jump a little in surprise; she hadn't heard the girl come up next to her. She nodded her head in agreement with Adair, but otherwise kept silent. They followed the main corridor; the only sound was the faint echoes of Eilath's hard-soled boots.

As they approached a white tiled intersection, Story heard soft voices from the left corridor and felt her stomach turn into knots. Was she about to meet some new elves? They reached the intersection just as the other group did, and for a moment both groups froze and all talking ceased.

There were twelve of them, all dressed according to their family trades, and each with drastically different tattoos over, under, or around their eyes. The female elf in the center of the group stepped forward and took in Story's party. When her eyes lit upon Eilath and Adair they narrowed slightly before moving on and finally settled on Story, lingering on her ears.

Story felt instantly like she was under a microscope and forced herself not to shuffle her feet or look away. She realized belatedly that the elf scrutinizing her had the same ailach under her eye that Eirnin had.

Another member of his clan!

Eirnin stepped forward and inclined his head respectfully toward the elf in front. "Eáchan, my apologies. We did not mean to interrupt a council meeting."

Eáchan cocked her head to the side, and her short-cropped, inky black hair gleamed as streams of sunlight hit it from overhead stained-glass windows. She flicked her silver eyes back and forth between Story and Eirnin before narrowing them slightly. Then her gaze settled on Story as she addressed Eirnin, completely ignoring Eilath and Adair.

"Eirnin of my clan, you have nothing to apologize for. We were just walking." She turned to indicate her fellow clan leaders, and Story caught a glance of an iron tipped bow strapped on her back, next to a quiver full of arrows. "But tell me, what brings you here? I thought you were away on a mission for Queen Eánna?" She continued to stare at Story, her eyes seeming to drill into Story's, as if she had evaluated her and somehow found her lacking. In fact, more than that, Story got the feeling that Eáchan didn't like her. It was nothing tangible, just something about her; she absolutely exuded hostility.

A charcoal-skinned elf standing on Eáchan's right side

stared at Story similarly, while the bespectacled male on Eáchan's left looked at her with open curiosity. Story watched as he surreptitiously exchanged glances with a silver-robed female at his side, and she slipped away from the main group.

Eirnin, his eyes still inclined toward the floor, answered his clan leader. "Aye, Eáchan, I was. I have completed it and am now here to report back to Queen Eánna."

Eáchan's eyes finally left Story and fixed on Eirnin as if he had a bull's-eye painted on his chest. "But the queen sent you out to find the Ailesit..."

Story instantly felt all eyes on her and stepped forward, keeping her back as straight as she could manage. She hoped they couldn't see her trembling. She opened her mouth to speak, but Eirnin cut her off with a glance before he turned back to his clan leader, eyes still cast down.

"Aye, that is correct, Eáchan."

The eight remaining clan leaders stood behind the three in the forefront, as if waiting for their reaction before deciding on their own. Story wondered if these three held some sort of higher place among the other clan leaders. She looked at them unabashedly; why should *she* avert her eyes? It's not as if they were her clan leaders.

The elf on the right crossed his thickly muscled arms across his chest and looked thoroughly unimpressed. The elf on the left continued to look at Story over his glasses and, unless her mind was playing tricks on her, winked at her. As for Eáchan, she snorted derisively and looked at Story like she was a bit of dirt under her nails.

"You think that this... this insubstantial girl is *the* Ailesit?"

"I do." Eirnin's voice was calm, but Story could tell that he was talking between gritted teeth. There was obviously no love lost between him and his clan leader.

"She looks like an overgrown, pasty-skinned gnome to

me," the clan leader on the right rumbled. Story glared at him and noticed the silver blocky tattoos around both of his eyes. Because he was bald, she could see that they wrapped all the way around the back of his head as well.

The clan leader on the left continued to look at Story, a bemused expression on his ancient face, but otherwise remained silent. The light blue wave like tattoo under his left eye would have looked like tears had he not a perennially cheerful expression on his face.

"With all due respect Eíswin," Eirnin began saying to the large elf on the right, but Eáchan cut him off.

"Eirnin of my clan, we all know that you have never shared our beliefs of the Ailesit, and I will not allow you to make a mockery of this. Of us. Of *me*." She gave Story a scathing look. "This girl is obviously no warrior; she could never defeat the Faerie Prince. You will take her back to wherever it is you found her and leave her there." She sliced her hands horizontally through the air with finality, and Eirnin swallowed hard. It was clear that he wanted to say something but was either at a loss for words or could not bring himself to openly speak against his clan leader.

Eilath stepped out and, keeping his eyes averted as well, held out both of his hands in open supplication and addressed the older, smiling clan leader on the right. "Eídolin, I ask you to please listen to Eirnin of the Eáchan. He speaks the truth—"

"SILENCE TRAITOR!" Eíswin roared, his silver eyes flashing a vibrant red. "You have no standing among us. Do not presume—"

Before Story fully thought it through, she had her knife out and poised against the flesh of her palm. She could feel her eyes burn with anger at their words, so she stepped forward and met each clan leader's gaze fully.

"I *am* the Ailesit." She sliced into the skin of her hand; it hurt like hell, but at the moment she didn't care.

If she'd wanted to make an impression with the clan leaders, she'd done it. There was an audible intake of breath from all of them as the bright, crimson liquid dripped from her open palm onto the once pristine white floors.

Every jaw dropped; even Eilath and Adair stared. Eirnin winked at her, and Story felt triumphant.

"Ailesit," a silvery, feminine voice sounded from behind Story. "We have awaited your arrival for a long time."

CHAPTER TWENTY-THREE

THE QUEEN'S GARDEN

STORY FROZE, ALL HER PREVIOUS BRAVADO GONE IN AN INSTANT. She slowly turned and took in the form of a female elf that could only be Queen Eánna. She was flanked by the elf whom Eídolin had sent off earlier. The queen was taller than Eirnin; Story noticed most of the other elves were taller than him.

Eirnin is short for an elf?

She had long, wavy hair, which fell well below her hips, and was pale blonde scattered with red and gold highlights that glittered in the light. Her forelocks were pulled back into a braid that entwined around an intricate wrought-iron circlet that rested on her brow. Unlike every other elf Story had seen, the queen had no ailach. She was dressed in a simple, sleeveless, white shift that reminded Story of the sort of clothing the ancient Egyptians used to wear. The only ornamentation on the dress was a low-slung belt on her hips that had a panel of fabric hanging down the front with twelve different symbols embroidered in gold on it.

The elf clan symbols.

Story realized two things: one, she was gawking, and two, everyone but her was kneeling before the queen. She hastily got down on one knee and bowed her head. This elf was not someone who Story felt like she *had* to show respect for, but someone she *wanted* to show respect for.

A soft hand slipped under Story's chin and raised her eyes up to meet the queen's. She smiled down at her, filling Story with peace and calm.

"You kneel to no one, Ailesit." The queen pulled Story gently to her feet and then turned to the others. "Eáchan, thank you for looking out for our well being. We know you would never purposely seek to interfere with one to whom we have given a mission." Her tone remained gentle, but even Story could hear the blatant rebuke in the queen's words.

Eáchan's face colored, and keeping her head bowed, she answered in a meek voice. "No my queen. I would never... I just did not think—"

The queen cut in, still keeping her voice soft. "Perhaps next time you will try to think. You and Eíswin may go now."

Eíswin's dark skin made it impossible for Story to see if he'd blushed in embarrassment too, but his body language made it obvious that he was mortified. The two lead clan leaders and the six behind them rose to their feet, bowed, and hastily exited the corridor.

Story turned back toward the queen and found she had pulled Eirnin up to his feet and was greeting him in the same manner Eilath and Eirnin had greeted each other in Stoneybrook, one hand on his shoulder, the other clasping his hand firmly. She leaned forward and whispered something in his ear. He laughed softly and nodded in response.

Releasing him, the queen turned to Eilath and, still smiling, said, "Please, get up. Thank you for helping Eirnin on his… oh—" She stopped abruptly once Eilath raised his head. Her eyes widened momentarily in recognition and then flicked over to Adair who was peeping out from behind her father shyly.

Story hoped that the queen reacted better to the "traitor" and his daughter than Eáchan had.

She shouldn't have worried.

Turning smoothly to the elderly clan leader, the queen gestured toward Eilath. "Eídolin, this elf and his daughter are clan of your clan. We all owe them our thanks for aiding the Ailesit in her journey, and they will be treated as our most honored guests."

Eídolin nodded and gestured at the female elf behind him who shared Eilath's silver hair and clan tattoo. *Eásphor*, Story realized. Eásphor indicated that they should follow her, and Adair, with a quick wave at Story, obediently did so. Eilath looked at the queen with solid yellow eyes one last time before inclining his head in a final respectful bow and followed his clan leader out.

The queen turned to Story and placed a hand on her shoulder. "Ailesit, you look tired. One of our handmaidens will show you to your rooms and help you get settled. Once you feel rested, we would speak with you."

Story nodded her head—as if she would say no—and a young female dressed in a simple white shift seemed to materialize next to her. With one last glance at Eirnin, who gave her an encouraging smile, Story followed the girl down one of the corridors. She tried very hard not to over-analyze everything that had happened and instead focused on the task at hand—which was to somehow get to Morrigann's garden, bleed a bit on a tree, and presto, save the entire elf race.

Easy day.

THE BATH WAS LUXURIOUS; THE LARGE STONE TUB NEARLY LARGE enough to swim laps in. As usual, the water was just what Story needed to relax and clear her mind. It was with a large amount of reluctance that she finally got out of the tub and dried herself off with a white linen towel that the handmaiden had left out for her.

The bathing room was linked to the bedroom by a large archway, giving the rooms an airy feeling. The high-columned ceilings added to the scale of the room and the broad balcony overhanging the water below had an inviting hammock and small wooden table with two chairs.

She found a white shift on a low, wide bed, and put it on; her traveling clothes having disappeared. It was as simple as the handmaiden's, ending just above her knees, and was soft as silk against her skin. She rubbed her hands over her bare arms, feeling a bit chilled. She wished they hadn't taken her cloak; she was sure the palace would be cool and drafty at night.

A simple meal of assorted fruits, cheeses, and crackers was laid out on a small dining table in her sitting room, but preferring the evening breeze, she wrapped herself in a light throw from the foot of the bed and watched the sun set from the balcony while she ate. She didn't have much time to think or reflect on anything (and by anything, she actually meant Eirnin), because as soon as she finished eating, the handmaiden reappeared and beckoned her to follow.

Doesn't anyone talk around here?

As they walked back through the palace, Story looked around but found that it all looked much the same. Sweeping arches, white marble, stained-glass windows above to let in the light from the setting sun. Beautiful, but the same.

It's a good thing I've got a guide—I'd get lost in this place.

Story focused on the girl in front of her. She was small and waif-like, and her skin was a dark olive color. Her thick, black hair was as straight as a board and hung like a velvet curtain down her back. She looked like she was only twelve years old, but for all Story knew, she could be forty-five.

"What's your name?"

The girl glanced over her shoulder at Story briefly before responding, and Story noticed that her ailach was a simple cluster of dots and swirls of color by the corner of each eye.

"Eavon." Then returned her gaze forward and didn't say anything else.

Okay... Clearly Story was going to have to carry on the conversation or walk in silence. Before she could ask another question, Eavon paused in front of an archway and indicated with her hand that Story should enter.

She stepped through the archway and down into an atrium. Tall columns loomed overhead, and clear glass made up the majority of the dome that topped the room. It was very warm in there, and she was grateful for her airy shift now. The room was filled with all sorts of exotic plants and birds. The perfume of thousands of flowers hung heavy in the air, and the tinkle of multiple water features played in the background.

Story looked around for the queen but couldn't see her. She stood around awkwardly for a moment, afraid to go somewhere she shouldn't, but she also didn't want to keep the queen waiting. Story took a few hesitant steps forward and peered around a massive fern on her left just in time to see Eirnin smile broadly at Queen Eánna, kiss her extended hand, and then pull her into an exuberant hug. The queen looked surprised by his enthusiasm, but returned the hug.

"Just tread carefully." Story heard the queen say.

"Of course. And thank you." He exited out of the garden near a door Story couldn't see from her vantage point.

Story watched him go curiously. *What could he have been so excited about? What's he supposed be careful of?* She stared at the space she'd last seen him, wishing he was there, waving and smiling at her.

"Ailesit." The queen's lilting accent sounded across the garden, and she raised her arm to beckon Story over.

Story took a deep breath, composed her expression into one of calm she wasn't feeling, and walked over to the queen, picking her way around the small streams that wound around in grooves on the floor.

The queen was standing in the middle of a small cluster of paving stones that had water flowing freely around them. Story noticed that there were thirteen stone clusters arrayed on the floor.

"It's a representation of the clan islands, Ailesit."

"Please, your highness, call me Story."

The queen paused for a bit and looked at Story curiously before nodding. "Only if you will call me Eánna."

Story raised an eyebrow at that, but nodded back. "Okay... Eánna." It felt weird saying it, but the queen smiled at her when she did.

"Thank you. Nobody's called me that in a very long time." Her voice instantly sounded more relaxed, less formal.

"I would imagine being the queen is quite lonely." Story snapped her mouth shut, shocked that she'd just said that. *Awkward much?*

"It can be. Thankfully, I have a few dear friends, like Eirnin, who I can be myself around. Walk with me, Story." Eánna stepped off toward one of the paths winding through the garden. Story moved to her side and kept in step with the taller female, who maintained a slow, sedate pace.

"Eirnin tells me that your race is called 'human'."

"Yes."

"He also tells me that you wish to restore *The Ailes*."

Well, she certainly doesn't beat around the bush does she?

"I—yes. I do." Even though most of the elves she'd met here in Ailes had been rude and judgmental, if she had it in her power to right a wrong done to Eirnin, Eilath, and Adair, she would do it.

The queen stopped under the bough of a tropical tree and looked at Story directly in her eyes. "You don't have to, you know."

Her words stunned Story. After nearly a thousand years of waiting, and facing the extinction of their race, Eánna wasn't pressing for her to go. And yet, Story could tell that she meant it.

The queen continued, "I am not completely power-less, and if I'm unable to find a way to get you back to your own world, I can afford you plenty of protection here from Morrigann."

Story felt her eyes widen at the queen's casual use of Morrigann's name. So far everyone but herself always called him the Faerie Prince. "Thank you, but no. I really am quite determined. If only for my friends' sake." She chewed on her lower lip, considering her next words. "And, if I did stay here, I'd be a prisoner in a way."

"But it's nearly the spring equinox, meaning Morrigann will be at the height of his power. You could at least wait until autumn. You would be safe here until then."

"What, and give him time to come up with a way to kill me the second I set one toe outside of here? No way. Besides, what good is safety, if I can't live? And if I did restore your tree, you'd get all of your magical abilities back, right?"

"In theory, yes."

"Which means you'd be better equipped to help me get back to my world. So again, thank you, but no."

Eánna sighed and resumed her tour down the path. "Well, if you are quite determined…" She actually looked sad, as if she didn't like the idea of Story going on the quest.

"Look, if you're worried that just because I'm not some great warrior, Morrigann will defeat—"

Eánna raised a hand, and Story instantly silenced. She may have dropped her queenly formality and treated Story like an equal, but she still had power in her every gesture.

"I'm not worried about your competency or veracity. I simply do not like the idea of you putting your life in danger for my people." She closed her eyes and her voice softened. "It isn't right. What I wouldn't give to trade places with you." Her voice dropped so low Story could hardly hear it. "I should be the one to do this."

What am I supposed to say to that? 'Sorry your blood isn't red like mine?' Because this isn't awkward enough already…

The queen's eyes opened, and they were still sedately silver, like a glassy lake. No betrayal of her emotions there.

"Eirnin tells me that you have a compass that points toward *The Ailes*."

Story nodded.

"And that currently Morrigann's garden is on the shore of a large lake bordered by mountains."

"That's all true."

"Do you think you'd be able to see it?"

"Uh…" Story was confused. What did she mean by that?

Eánna saw the look on her face and explained. "Previous expeditions that should have found his garden never have.

And it's not because his garden was moved before they got there—that takes a lot of magic." She paused, as if gathering her thoughts. "I'd imagine that Morrigann can only manage to move his garden about once a century. So my fore-mothers and I all believe the entrance somehow has been made invisible to our Ailionoran eyes."

She regarded Story with her implacable silver gaze. "So, I ask again, do you think you'll be able to see it?"

She considered for a moment before answering. "Yes, I do. My compass will guide me to it, and I'll be able to see it. I'm sure of it." Story had no idea how she knew; she just did. The same way she knew she had a connection to the tree the first time she saw it depicted. "Can I ask a question now?"

Eánna nodded.

"It seems not all of the clan leaders think I'm the Ailesit."

The queen's mouth twisted into a half-smile—and she still managed to make it look beautiful. "Hm, yes, I do suppose that would have been hard to miss." She let out a soft sigh. "The simple answer is that they are afraid. They're afraid of change. They're afraid of being let down. They're afraid to hope." She brushed her hand lightly through a small trickling waterfall. "Fear can lead even the wisest of people to make foolish choices." She looked at Story pointedly then, and Story looked away, embarrassed and not sure why. She decided to change the subject.

"Why does everyone treat Eilath like he's a terrible person?"

The queen froze in the act of picking a blossom from a flowering bush.

"Excuse me?"

"Eilath is possibly the nicest person I know and a great father too. Then there's Adair, who should be embraced by her own people, yet your clan leaders wouldn't even acknowledge her existence!" Story could feel her anger rise. "You know, if it weren't for those two, I wouldn't even be here, and all everyone can do is treat them like they're worse than dirt. It's not right." She knew she wasn't being fair, that the queen had made sure to welcome Eilath and Adair, but she was still upset by their reception by everyone else. This, in turn, made her worry about things with Eirnin. She'd told herself to avoid any attachments here, but to know this culture wouldn't even accept the idea of the two of them being together, well, it made her angry. Here she was risking her life for them, yet she couldn't be with Eirnin if she wanted? And who were they to judge Eilath? And Adair, who'd done nothing to deserve their censure.

The queen straightened and smiled sadly at her, yet her eyes still betrayed nothing. "Centuries of culture is a hard thing to overcome, Story. They're only elves after all." She sighed. "But yes, I do agree, it's not fair, and it's not right. But come, you've got enough to worry about. Let's not add elvish politics to your plate, shall we?" She indicated an archway, the one Story had entered through, and Eavon was suddenly there waiting.

Story inclined her head respectfully to the queen, who in turn inclined hers. She then followed Eavon back to her rooms determined that she would not lay awake all night over-analyzing absolutely everything.

Yeah, like that'll happen.

Chapter Twenty-Four

Dreams...

SHE WAS STANDING IN THE MIDDLE OF A VAST ORCHARD: A WILD orchard, with trees in various states of growth and blossoms falling from their branches like rain, softly carpeting the earth below. The wind rustled Story's hair, causing it to brush against her elbow. She sighed loudly.

"Not again."

Warm arms wrapped around her waist from behind, and she was pulled tightly against a broad, firm, bare chest.

"Hello, Story," Morrigann's husky voice whispered in her ear. "I did not expect to see you here again. At least not so soon." He sounded cocky and smug. Her blood boiled, and raising her right foot, she smashed it down on his instep.

His arms instantly loosened, and she stepped away from him before whirling around.

"What are you doing here?" she demanded. This was a complication she did not need or want.

Morrigann was seated on his throne in front of *The Ailes* rubbing his right foot with his hands. "That hurt. You really should learn some manners, especially when you are a guest in someone else's home." Then he looked up at her, his violet eyes glittering. "As for your question, why don't you tell me?" Letting go of his foot, he stood up and walked over to her once again, leaving only a few inches between them.

"You aren't welcome in my dreams any more." Story fought the urge to back away from him and the even greater urge to close those last few inches and kiss him.

What the heck is wrong with me?

This jerk had tried to kill her on at least three occasions (that she knew of), and now she was thinking about kissing him?

He leaned over and brushed his lips lightly against the shell of her ear as he answered. "Obviously some part of you wants me here." Then he pulled away and smiled knowingly. "What's wrong, trouble with the elfling? I'm not surprised; he's a child." Morrigann moved behind her and whispered in her other ear. "Whereas I could make you a queen. All this could be yours to rule." He gestured with his arm at the magical wood before them. "The pixies would be your friends, and you could dance with them every night."

His lips left her ear and began trailing soft, fiery kisses down her neck. Story felt warmth spread through her. She could hear music, her father's lullaby, playing quietly in the background, and felt her hips began to sway along with it. Morrigann's hands slid down from her shoulders over her arms and slowly to her wrists before finally entwining his fingers with hers.

He pulled her tight to him, wrapping their joined arms around her chest tightly, and swayed with her for a few beats before spinning her around to face him. Sparks glinted off his golden hair, and his skin shimmered, radiating magic. Story smiled dreamily up at him and he pulled her close again. Cupping his broad hand behind her neck, he stared down at her, his eyes smoldering.

"See, isn't it better when we're nice to each other?" His lips brushed lightly across her mouth, teasing her.

She gripped his shoulders with her hands and smiled against his honey sweet lips. "Mmmm," she murmured pleasurably before thrusting her knee into his groin. The loud groan he gave was one of the most satisfying sounds she'd ever heard.

"Fool me once, shame on you. Fool me twice, shame on me." She shoved him roughly in the chest. "I *don't* want you here."

The scene shifted before he even hit the ground.

She was sitting at the square log table in the cabin's kitchen. The smell of fresh waffles wafted through the air, and Story's stomach rumbled.

"Whack for my daddy-o, Whack for my daddy-o, There's whiskey in the jar," a familiar voice sang.

Story twisted in her chair to look behind her. A tall, lanky man, whose olive skin and what remained of his dark curly hair mirrored her own, was standing with his back to her in front of a waffle iron.

"Dad?"

He flipped a piping hot waffle onto a plate before turning around. "Here you go, kiddo. Just like you like 'em. Raisins, bananas, and oats. No nuts." He set the plate in front of her and turned back to the waffle iron. She watched as he scooped some more lumpy batter into it with a measuring cup. Her dad's waffles might look gross, but they tasted as delicious as they smelled. Usually Story couldn't wait to start eating them, but today she couldn't tear her eyes off of her father.

He sprinkled a generous handful of chopped walnuts and almonds on top of it all and then closed the iron's lid. Her dad walked back over to the table and, sitting down in the chair to her right, looked pointedly at her full plate.

"You gonna let that get cold?"

Story picked up her fork and spread some fresh strawberry preserves on the whole wheat waffle, all the while trying not to stare at her father. She took a tentative bite and closed her eyes in ecstasy. They were every bit as delicious as she remembered. A burning sensation erupted on her tongue, and her mouth abruptly formed an "O." She blew air out before fanning her mouth with her hand. Her dad handed her a glass of milk that she eagerly swallowed, and it soothed her seared tongue.

"Where are the twins?"

"Outside buildin' a city of tiny snow people so they can stomp through like Godzilla and Mothra and smash 'em all."

Story laughed around another mouthful of waffle, and her dad got up to pull his off the iron. He settled back down next to her and spread some boysenberry jam on his.

"Why're you here, kiddo? Not that I mind. I'm just surprised to see you is all." He cut a large piece, speared it with his fork, and popped it into his mouth. Immediately he reached for his glass of milk and downed it.

"I… I don't know. I guess I missed you. And the twins. I miss home." She picked at her food, her appetite abruptly gone. Her father stopped eating, reached one battle-scarred hand over to hers, and squeezed it.

"Be strong, Story. You always have been. You'll find home. Have faith."

Tears pricked her eyes, and she stared down at her half-eaten waffle. "I'm scared, Dad."

"I know."

"Can't I just stay here with you?"

"This is just a dream, kiddo."

Her eyes flew open, and Adair's face was mere inches away.

"Ah!" Story jerked to the side. "DON'T DO THAT!"

Adair held out a hot scone which Story took automatically.

"Queen Eánna was surprised by how much you sleep too, did you know that? She came to visit me and Da last night. They're old friends, did you know that? I finally went to sleep because they were being boring, but before I did I swam in the big tub in our rooms. I saw you have one too. I like Queen Eánna. She's really nice. Have you had enough to eat yet? Everyone's meeting in the throne room, and they're waiting for you." She finally paused to take a breath, and Story shoved the scone in Adair's mouth before she could talk again. She threw her covers off and sprung out of bed, grabbing at her newly returned clothes.

"Eavon?"

The girl materialized from the adjoining room and inclined her head respectfully.

"Yes, Ailesit?"

"Please take me to the throne room." Story straightened her kilt and shirt and was thankful for the braids Adair had put in her hair. Though they required some weekly maintenance, on the whole they were quite convenient.

Eavon nodded and walked silently out the door. Story wrapped her hand around Adair's wrist and, for once, was the one doing the dragging.

"I can walk on my own!" Adair protested around a mouthful of scone as soon as they reached the corridor. Story gave Adair a pointed look before dropping her hand. Adair blushed and dropped her eyes in response. "Alright, I get it."

They followed Eavon in silence, which gave Story some

time to think about her dreams—she was certain they were dreams, no matter how real they felt. She clicked her tongue in annoyance and gasped—for a fleeting moment it felt like her tongue had been burned!

Her mind reeled. Had she really seen her father again last night? Or was it just some crazy part of her subconscious? She didn't know, and she didn't care. For a few minutes she had been home. Her heart picked up its pace, and she thought about what he said to her.

"You'll find home. Have faith."

She nodded to herself resolutely and gripped the handle of her father's knife. She would find her way.

Then she recalled her encounter with Morrigann and couldn't help but frown. Whatever part of her subconscious had invited him into her dreams was in serious trouble. How could she still be attracted to that creep? It disgusted her. At least he hadn't been able to put her under another one of his spells. She smiled broadly as she recalled the look of pain on his face after she'd kneed him.

That led to thoughts about Eirnin and all her confusion there. Why hadn't he come to see her last night? Story realized with a pang how much she'd gotten used to having Eirnin around, and she hadn't seen him since yesterday evening.

She missed him.

Oh great, now I'm becoming one of those stupid girls who can't be away from their boyfriend for any amount of time.

Story shuddered at the thought of being a clingy, co-dependant girlfriend but then somberly remembered she and Eirnin weren't exactly anything as of yet. *Probably for the best,* she told herself. She didn't need any attachments here, especially not emotional ones. *Besides, loving someone is the surest way to heartbreak.*

Eavon stopped in front of a massive, wooden door that

looked like it would take about ten strong men to pull open. She pulled gently on the ringed handle, and it swung out with ease. Either it was counterbalanced on its hinges remarkably well, or Eavon was freakishly strong. Story hoped it was just a miracle of engineering; she already felt inadequate enough around everyone here when it came to speed and strength.

She stepped inside a large marble hall with an enormous dome looming overhead. At the end of the hall thirteen identical marble thrones were arranged in a half moon. The thrones were surprisingly Spartan, with no ornamentation. They clearly were not meant to be comfortable, as was evidenced by the posture held by each clan leader who sat in one. The center throne, the one that Eánna sat in, was slightly higher than the others on a small, raised dais.

Behind her throne was a massive square tapestry that had to be twenty feet in height. It depicted *The Ailes* growing in the palace courtyard covered in silver blossoms. Just as always, Story felt drawn to it.

The queen raised an elegant arm, and all eyes fixed on Story.

"Ailesit, your presence is most welcome. Come, we have a plan."

Chapter Twenty-Five

...*and Schemes*

STORY WALKED TOWARD THE THRONES ARRAYED BEFORE HER. She kept her back straight and resolutely met the gaze of each of the clan leaders. As expected, eight of them regarded her with a range of negative emotions—mostly disbelief. Some of them, like Eíswin, wore openly hostile expressions. Four of them, led by the broadly grinning Eídolin, were looking at her with a mixture of curiosity and excitement.

She was grateful for their support, because she knew that without it the council of twelve could overrule the queen, and by the look on Eáchan's face, she would do it given half the chance. Out of the corner of her eye, Story saw Adair join her father at the side of the room. Then she had to stop herself from looking at him again—he had his old smile on his face, and seemed perfectly at ease.

Okay...

Story stopped in front of the elf leaders and inclined her

head respectfully to each one in turn before finally facing the queen.

"I'm sorry I'm late, your highness. I was unaware my presence was required."

Eáchan squeezed the unforgiving armrests on her throne, and her eyes bugged out. Had she spoken, Story had no doubt she would have said something along the lines of "it is *not* required, pretender!" But one pointed look from the queen kept her mouth firmly shut.

"Please Ailesit, do not apologize. We were warned about how much sleep and nourishment you need." She grinned and indicated Eilath with her head, and Story couldn't help but chuckle, especially after seeing the shocked glances at the queen from many of her opposers.

The queen looked to Story's left and raised an elegant hand, sending a dozen plain silver bracelets jingling down her arm.

"Eirnin, if you would, please?"

He entered the hall pushing a large, wheeled table assisted by two other elves. Story peeked at him through her lashes, unwilling to make any sort of eye contact with him here—there was no way she'd be able to keep her bearing if she did, and she needed to focus. So instead, she stared at the table, eyeing it cautiously.

It was a rectangular box, six feet by four feet in size, and was much taller than a normal table—obviously meant for standing rather than sitting. Four-inch walls circled it and inside was a very realistic terrain representation of a portion of Ailionora. In the center were the island clusters that made up the city of Ailes, to the north and south were the Silver and Ailes seas, and to the east and west were the Piney Green and Forge mountain ranges. Blue sand represented the oceans, lakes, and rivers, and tiny trees dotted the landscape. It was a work of art, and Story wondered which clan was responsible for making it.

Queen Eánna, the three main clan leaders, and Eirnin gathered around the table, and after a moment's hesitation Story joined them. The remaining nine clan leaders arrayed themselves loosely around the table, looking over shoulders and between bodies at the terrain diagram. Story stood on her side of the table alone facing the queen, Eirnin and Eídolin to her right, Eíswin and Eáchan to her left. The hostility emanating from that quarter was palpable, and Story had to resist the urge to stick her tongue out at them.

Probably wouldn't help things—but I'd sure feel better.

"Council, it has come to our attention that the Faerie Prince has made at least three attempts on the Ailesit's life thus far." Queen Eánna paused to allow her words to sink in, and Story could see all of the clan leaders on her left fidgeting awkwardly. Clearly they had not heard about that—even if they did not believe she was Ailesit, it was obvious Morrigann did, and that had to count for something.

"It appears he will stop at nothing to prevent her from reaching *The Ailes*. In light of that, we have asked Eirnin to come up with a plan for getting the Ailesit safely to the Faerie Prince's garden." The queen locked eyes with Story. "After that, Ailesit, it will be up to you."

Eirnin opened his mouth to speak but was cut off by a fierce-looking elf who had an angry, three-inch wide, solid red tattoo across his eyes stretching from temple to temple. He pushed his way forward between Eáchan and Eíswin and gripped the edge of the table with his massive hands with such force Story was afraid the table would splinter.

"Did you have something to say, Eíbhilin?" Queen Eánna turned her implacable silver eyes toward the large man. His eyes were as red as his tattoo as he made no attempt to hide his anger.

"Yes, my queen. As leader of the warrior clan it should have fallen to me to make the tactical assault plan." Shirtless, except for the barest of a beaded chest shield which looked like it was more for decoration than actual protection, Eíbhilin's muscles spasmed in irritation underneath his bronze skin.

The queen regarded him curiously and cocked her head to one side. "And if we had asked you to do so? What would your answer have been?"

His nostrils flared, and the feathers that adorned his long mohawk and braided forelocks quivered, but he kept his silence.

"And so the responsibility fell to a hunter instead."

Eáchan's eyes flared at what Story assumed was the queen's subtle insult. She'd said "a hunter" not "the Hunter"—but Eáchan chose to keep silent since nothing she could say would ease either her embarrassment, or clan of her clan's—Eíbhilin's.

The queen turned to Eirnin. He had kept his eyes averted the entire time, since he was not a clan leader and had no official standing here other than as the queen's guest. She gestured at the table with her open hand, silently asking him to proceed.

Keeping his gaze firmly on the table, Eirnin produced two small ships and two similarly-sized, elf figures, all carved out of wood. He placed the ships in the river to the north and south of Ailes and one elf figure on each shore on the east and west side of Ailes.

"The plan is simple," he began in a strong, yet respectful, voice, and Story made herself focus on his words and not the sound of his voice. "We will send out four groups, one toward each cardinal direction with a decoy elf who is dressed like the Ailesit hidden in each group. The Faerie Prince will be forced to use a massive amount of assets to follow each group, leaving *The Ailes* relatively unguarded. Eámonn's clan will lead the sailing groups, and Eáchan's clan will lead the groups on foot. Hopefully the red and brown dwarves will be willing to assist both overland groups. Or at the very least not hinder them."

He moved each figure on the table to indicate the general movement of their journey. Then he produced a fifth wooden figure and placed it back in Ailes. "At that time, the Ailesit and I will depart Ailes and journey together on our own to Faerie Land." He picked up the figure and moved it to an area in the northwest quarter of the table.

Eáchan's frown deepened, and she crossed her arms across her chest firmly. "And just how do you intend to fool the Faerie Prince? As soon as she sets one toe out of the city one of his little pests will see her and report her location, and you will have wasted precious elf assets on this farce."

"I have a way to hide them from fey senses, Eáchan." Queen Eánna looked around the table. "Does anyone else have any questions?"

Brilliant green eyes and fiery red braids peeped out from behind Story.

"Oi! I've got a better idea."

Silence resounded as the elves on Story's left pointedly ignored Adair's presence, and the elves on Story's right regarded her with caution. Eánna looked at Adair a little surprised but beckoned her forward nevertheless. Eirnin just raised an eyebrow at her and then shot Story a quick wink. She tried not to blush.

Adair pushed her way in front of Eáchan, whose eyes flared red momentarily before she moved out of the way. Adair picked up the boat that was sailing to the north and brought it back to Ailes.

"See, what we could do is leave with Eámonn's north

group on the boat and sail toward this island, what's it called? Ainen?" She indicated a large island northwest of the opening of the Ailes river, in the Silver Sea.

"Then, they keep sailing around like they're looking for the garden, and Eirnin, Story, and I slip over the side and swim to my ma's house which is right near there. I don't think Da should go with us since he's not a very good swimmer. The Faerie Prince won't be able to find us on the boat with whatever trick it is the queen has, and he won't be able to track us under the sea. We'll be able to breathe because I can get them ad'har, and of course, I've got my gills, but then you already know that. So when we get to my ma's house, we can borrow some of her selkies which will swim us up the coast and into Faerie Land's main river and eventually the lake that borders the garden much faster than we could ever sail or swim ourselves."

Making a mental note to ask Adair what the heck selkies were, Story watched as Adair stabbed a finger into the blue sand of the lake in Faerie Land and then looked up at the queen expectantly. The queen, in turn, looked at Eirnin.

"It is a good plan, my queen. A much sounder plan than mine and has a much greater chance for success."

The queen turned back to Adair and regarded her seriously. "We mean no slight when we say this, but can Almera be depended on to help?"

Adair's face became confused. "I don't understand the question. Why wouldn't she help?"

Story could tell that Eánna did not like where the conversation was going, and only Eáchan and Eíswin were bothering to feign ignoring the conversation by this point. The queen shot a quick glance at Eilath, but he merely shrugged.

"We were under the impression that she did not like us very much."

"Oh, that!" Adair rolled her eyes. "That was forever ago. She doesn't hold grudges. Probably doesn't even remember, and even if she did, she wouldn't care. She's not an elf, you know."

Story blinked and looked away quickly, just like everyone else. Adair seemed completely oblivious to the insult she'd inadvertently given the queen and, well, pretty much everyone in the room other than Story.

"So, when do we leave? I'm already packed."

The queen composed her features and smiled down at Adair kindly. "We are certain you are. But the rest of us need a little time to prepare a few things for your journey. You will leave in two days' time." She looked around the table and met each eye firmly. "Unless anyone has any objections?"

No one did, at least none that they voiced, but by the way Eáchan's eyes burned when she looked at Story, she had a feeling things were far from settled between them.

Chapter Twenty-Six

Hello Goodbye

Éachan didn't wait long to confront her.

After the meeting, Story went back to her rooms, accompanied by Adair, to finish the breakfast she'd abandoned in her haste that morning. She'd also promised to go swimming with Adair afterwards, and she was looking forward to it—if anything would help her sort out her feelings about Eirnin and calm her fears about facing Morrigann again, that would.

"Ailesit." Eavon entered the room. "The Hunter is here to see you." Éachan swept around the handmaiden, flanked by another elf bearing the same ailach as the clan leader. He was dressed in a similar fashion to Eirnin and Éachan and also kept his muddy brown hair cropped short.

I wonder if that's a hunter clan thing?

"Leave us." Éachan didn't even spare a glance at Eavon as she dismissed her from the room. She completely ignored Adair and fixed her icy gaze on Story. "I need to talk to you. Now."

Story cocked an eyebrow and finished filling her plate with assorted fruits, rolls, and cheeses. "I don't know how you were raised, but my daddy always taught me that you catch more flies with honey than with vinegar."

Eáchan's brows furrowed together momentarily, and the elf at her side mouthed the word 'flies' with a questioning look on his face.

"Oh, right, no bugs here." Story indicated the spread of food before her. "Hungry?"

"No, I am not." The clan leader folded her arms across her chest and glared, not bothering to the hide the flickers of red annoyance in her eyes. "I need to talk to you. Please."

Story could tell it took a lot out of her to say that last word, so with a flick of her head she indicated the doors leading to the balcony outside. Eáchan turned to the other elf and handed him her iron-tipped bow and quiver. "Eisrus, wait here."

Story didn't know if she should take that as a good or bad sign. On the one hand, with no weapons, Eáchan couldn't fly into a murderous rage and kill her, but on the other, why had she felt the need to doff them? Perhaps it was some sort of strange protocol she didn't know about? Just to be on the safe side, she pulled her knife out of its scabbard and passed it over to Adair, who took it from her solemnly. "Wait here please, sweetie. This won't take long."

Both elves were staring at the knife, and only when Story cleared her throat and walked outside did Eáchan break her gaze and follow.

Story sat down at the table for two and dug into her food. She never thought well on an empty stomach, and this wasn't going to be good, she could tell. She only hoped it didn't get too loud.

Eáchan stood facing the water, hands clasped at her back, completely formal in her bearing. Story kept eating, waiting for her to say something, as she'd been the one who'd barged into her room demanding they talk right this instant. Story wasn't about to make it any easier on her.

"Have you and Eirnin bonded?"

Story's hand froze halfway to her mouth, her cheese topped cracker forgotten. This was not the conversation she thought they would be having. "Excuse me?"

"Have you and Eirnin bonded?" Eáchan turned to look at her fully. "Don't lie to me. I must know."

"What? No! That's crazy to even think that—we've only known each other a few weeks."

Relief flickered across Eáchan's face and eyes. "And do you promise not to bond with him, ever?"

Story felt her hackles rise. Just because she thought it was too soon to even begin thinking about that level of commitment with Eirnin, especially as she wasn't even sure where things were going, she certainly was not about to promise to never even give them a chance.

"No." She bit into her cracker and savored the sweet and salty taste of the creamy cheese.

"No?" Eáchan leaned over the table, placing both hands on its surface. "No? Do you even understand what you're saying? How dare you—"

"How dare I?" Story stood up and pointed at her. "How dare you! Who do you think you are, barging in here and telling me whom I can or can't be with? What gives you the right—"

"I am Eirnin's clan leader, and that gives me every right."

Story snorted and rolled her eyes. "Whatever. Look,

you're not my clan leader, and I am going to do whatever I think is best for me, regardless of what you think. So you can just save us both a bunch of time and leave. Then maybe I can finish my breakfast in peace." She sat back down and took another bite of her cracker.

Eáchan just stared at her for a moment then resolutely folded her arms across her chest. "You selfish girl."

Story's anger flared again. "Selfish?"

"I thought you actually cared for him."

"I do care for him. A lot!" She realized then that she cared for Eirnin a whole lot more than she'd even been willing to admit to herself before now.

Eáchan ignored Story's protests. "Because if you did, you would end it. Look at Eilath. Look at his daughter. Is that what you want for Eirnin? To be shunned by his people? To be looked upon as a traitor and treated like an outcast?" She looked Story directly in her eyes. "Because that is what would happen if he stayed with you."

"Only because you allow and encourage that sort of treatment and mentality to permeate your culture."

"Wishing it were otherwise will not make it so." Eáchan turned and walked to the door where she paused and looked back at Story one last time. "If you really do care for him, don't make him choose between you and his entire race." Then she stepped through the door and was gone.

AVOIDING EIRNIN OVER THE LAST TWO DAYS HAD BEEN DIFFICULT— Story had essentially barricaded herself in her rooms and was either "sleeping" or "bathing" anytime he came by to see her. She knew it was rude, but as much as she didn't want to listen to Eáchan, how could she not? She didn't want to cause Eirnin pain. Regardless of how prejudicial his society was, they were still his family. Who was she to make him choose between them? Especially since she would just be leaving anyway.

Or dying on my quest.

Regardless, both scenarios involved them not ending up together, so why make things more difficult now? Attachments always ended with heartache.

The logical course of action was to pretend the kisses hadn't happened. To go back to just being friends and travel companions. The problem was, that was easier said than done. He was pretty hard to forget, and her burgeoning feelings for him were proving hard to bury. So she'd avoided him, removed any temptation from being around him since she seemed incapable of thinking straight when he was near. She'd hoped that by the time the boats were ready she'd have things sorted out in her mind.

No such luck.

The wind rustled her kilt, bringing her thoughts to the present. She wished she'd worn her cloak, as the docks near the palace were chilly this spring morning, but it was already on the ship with the rest of her kit. They were waiting to board the gondolas which would carry them out to their ship, and Story was doing everything in her power to avoid looking at or talking to Eirnin. Since he was standing directly to her left that brought an awkward tension to the air. Adair was on her right, and she too was keeping unusually quiet.

There were four distinct groups arrayed around the queen and her council, each with a pair of elves who were dressed like Story and Eirnin and who, from a distance, would even pass as them. Story's group also had a pair of look-alikes, since, once they left the ship the deception would have to continue.

Eánna walked forward flanked by several handmaidens, each of whom held a different item on a silver pillow in her hands. The group stopped in front of Story. The queen motioned, and Eavon came forward carrying a carved wooden box. The queen opened it and removed an iron amulet on a thin silver chain. The amulet itself was about the size of a quarter and, from what Story could see, looked like several delicate iron circles worked around each other to form an endless knot.

"This necklace will blind you to the fey. They will not see you, hear you, or sense you. Even to the Sidhe, should you encounter any, you would be hazy and difficult for them to make out." The queen passed the necklace in her hand to Eirnin and then pulled out another. "As such, they were incredibly difficult to make and are one of the most powerful remaining magical items we still have." She handed Story a necklace and then pulled a third one from the box.

"Before the Change, the mages spent centuries constructing these, and at one time, there were thirteen in existence." She placed the final necklace in Adair's hands and then closed the box. Eavon walked away with a bow of her head, and Eánna turned back to face them.

"Unfortunately, many were lost—along with the elves who wore them—on previous expeditions to find *The Ailes*. Now only these three remain," she said with a gentle motion of her hand toward each of their necklaces.

Story paused in the act of putting the amulet around her neck. She instantly felt guilty about taking such precious items from the elves, and judging by the expressions on most of the council members' faces, she could tell they weren't very happy about it either. Only constantly smiling Eídolin and his small group didn't seem to mind.

He winked at her, and Story returned a chagrined smile

before closing the clasp around the necklace. Giving it back was pointless—the mission would fail without them—they had to convince Morrigann that they were nowhere near his garden.

The queen then stepped in front of Eirnin and motioned another handmaiden forward. Judging by the red-stripe of her ailach and the feathers adorning her hair, she was from the warrior clan. The girl carried a broad, velvet pillow, but that's not what caught Story's eye. It was what was on the pillow that piqued her curiosity, especially in a world where metal was rare and precious.

A shiny, bronze sword gleamed in the sunlight next to a matching leather scabbard. The blade was leaf-shaped, narrowing near the base, and roughly two feet long. The hilt was constructed with the tang sandwiched between layers of wood, and leather wrapped around it all to secure it.

Eánna took the pillow from her handmaiden and held it out to Eirnin.

"This is Aiolus."

Story heard everyone, including Eirnin, draw in a surprised breath. Mohawk and feathers quivering with his obvious rage, Eíbhilin looked like a blood vessel beneath his eye was going to burst. Eirnin reached out a tentative hand and gingerly picked up the sword by the hilt.

"It is not pure bronze but has been forged with iron. This sword will bite the fey, and as its name implies, it is quick and nimble." She handed the pillow back to her handmaiden and stepped in front of Adair, leaving Eirnin to swing his new sword experimentally.

She smiled down at Adair and placed a hand on her shoulder.

"You are very brave, young one, to go on such a quest, especially for those who do not recognize your birthright. You honor us all."

Adair blushed and mumbled something indecipherable. The queen then reached down and removed a short dagger that was hanging from her own hip. She pulled it from its intricately carved wooden sheath, and Story could see that it too gleamed bronze down to its very sharp point. Eánna placed it in Adair's hand.

"We hope you never have to use this."

Adair's mouth opened and closed wordlessly as she stared at the priceless gift she held. Then, in one swift motion, she threw her arms around the queen and gave her a fierce hug. Eánna's eyes widened momentarily, and she shot Eilath a bemused look. He shrugged his shoulders helplessly and winked back.

Finally, extricating herself from Adair's clinging arms the queen stepped in front of Story, placing one hand firmly on each of her shoulders. Story looked up at the taller female and thought she saw flashes of blue in her eyes before they settled into their eternally liquid silver.

"Ailesit, we can give you nothing greater than the protection your father has already blessed you with." She glanced down at Story's knife before locking eyes with her once again. "Instead, we will give you our blessing." She lowered her voice and leaned her forehead against Story's and closed her eyes. "Let Ai guide your steps. Let her heighten your senses. Let her bestow upon you the grace she has given me."

Queen Eánna then pressed her pale lips against Story's forehead, and she felt a jolt of energy running through her body. The change was subtle, yet immediate. She felt like things were brighter and sounds were clearer. It was like she'd been walking through Ailionora with sunglasses on and ear-plugs in, and the queen had removed them with a simple kiss. It was amazing.

She blinked her eyes, trying to get used to the brighter sun, and then inclined her head to Eánna, who bowed hers in return.

"Thank you." The words seemed inadequate, but there was really nothing else she could say. Turning, she boarded her gondola and tried not to panic at the thought of her up-coming trials.

CHAPTER TWENTY-SEVEN

*U*NDERWAY

STORY HAD HER COMPASS OUT AND WATCHED AS IT POINTED DUE east, perpendicular to their current northerly course. She set the compass down and let it hang from the lanyard on her waist before looking back out at the water before her. The sun was low in the sky, casting orange and purple streaks through the scattered clouds overhead. It was amazing how many colors she could see in the prism of a simple white cloud now, thanks to Eánna's magnificent gift to her.

She leaned against the guardrail at the front of the ship and felt it gently rock and sway beneath her. The salt spray whisked in the air around her, and the ropes overhead cracked and snapped as the wind blew at her back.

"I thought you'd get tired of being cooped up in your cabin eventually."

Story stiffened as Eirnin leaned against the railing next to her. She still wasn't ready to talk to him. She didn't know what to say or how to say it.

"Uh, actually I was just going..."

His hand wrapped around her wrist, and she could tell by the way Eirnin's tendons flexed under his tattoos he had no intention of letting her run off.

"Have I done something wrong?" His tone was light, almost uncaring, but his soft yellow eyes gave his worry away.

"No." She bit her lip. "Yes." Then squeezed her eyes shut and shook her head. "No."

He raised a confused eyebrow at her and let go of her wrist. She sighed and looked out at the water again, knowing she lacked the courage to say any of this if she looked him in the eyes.

"No, you've done nothing wrong exactly. I guess I just assumed a few things. Well, one thing really. But, you know, it's nothing. *We're* nothing. And that's okay." The words came out hesitantly at first and then in a rush. There, she'd ended it. Now they could go back to just being friends, and someday her heart wouldn't feel like a mountain troll had just torn it apart.

He placed a hand under her chin and guided her face to look at his. "How can you even think that?"

His eyes were a deep blue, and his entire countenance was so sad that she dropped her gaze, lest she lose her nerve. Why did he have to make this more difficult for her? "You should be with someone else. Someone like you, another elf." A moment of inspiration hit her. "The queen!"

He cocked his head, confusion plain on his face. "What does she have to do with any of this?"

Story couldn't believe that he was going to make her spell it out for him. He obviously knew what would happen if they pursued this relationship, how he'd be treated. Why was he playing dumb?

"You love her."

"Aye, of course I do. She's my cousin." He shrugged. "But that's it—she's family. There's nothing romantic there, and there never will be."

So much for that tactic.

She took a step back from him, sliding her hand along the railing, needing space. His nearness confused her and made her irrational and unable to think about anything but running her fingers through his silky, short hair.

Stop that!

"Look, you're an elf. I'm a human." How much more clear could she make it?

"Your point?" He looked a bit irritated.

"It'll never be accepted. *We'll* never be accepted."

"Are you really worried about what they think?" He folded his arms across his chest, the exasperation clear in his voice.

She lowered her eyes, whispering her words. "I won't put you in a position where you have to choose between me and your people."

He snorted. "Well, if that's the problem, then don't worry, I've already chosen." He looked at her pointedly, orange and purple flickers beginning to overtake his irises.

Happiness soared through her as she realized what he meant, but was instantly buried by guilt. "No! I won't allow—"

"Story, just stop. You can't tell me what to think or feel." He quirked a corner of his mouth in a smile. "Besides, it won't even be a problem once you restore *The Ailes*."

"You don't even believe in *The Ailes*."

"I believe in you." He took a step toward her, sliding his hand along the railing, like she had.

He'd managed to knock down what she thought was their biggest barrier, because he was right: she couldn't control his feelings any more than she could control her own. But there was still the problem of her leaving—they were still doomed for heartbreak in the end. "Why can't we just be friends? I'm just going to leave when this is all said and done. We should end things now before they become too... complicated."

His eyes clouded for a moment, a swirl of emotions, and then settled back to the excited orange sparks on purple irises.

"Why don't I uncomplicate things for you?" He took another step closer. "I could go back with you. After."

Story's heartbeat quickened, and she stepped back right into the ship's prow.

"You can do that?"

He moved forward, sliding his hand along the railing, stopping just before his fingers met hers. She could feel the electricity arcing between them and glared at her traitorous fingertips as they ached to close the distance.

"Why not? If you could come here, why couldn't I go there?"

"Why would you *want* to?" Ailionora was amazing and beautiful; why would he want to leave this world and head to a place filled with noise and industry? *And cars and phones*, she thought wistfully.

The corners of his mouth turned up into a sly grin, and he slowly moved his hand over hers. He paused, but then continued. His fingers slid up her bare arm, leaving trails of fire in their wake, before settling warmly on her shoulder. His other arm followed suit, but instead of resting on her shoulder, he placed his hand firmly on the wooden beam behind her head, effectively penning her in.

Her breath quickened, and she opened her mouth to say something, *anything*, but he quickly silenced her by covering her mouth with his. Eirnin's kiss seared through her, and it was better than she'd remembered. Sweeter and hotter all at the same time. Any coherent thoughts she had flew away on the ocean breeze, and her hands did just as they'd been itching to do from the moment he'd arrived at her side. She buried one in his hair, and the other wound around his neck pulling him, and his kiss, in tighter.

He leaned against her, pressing her against the prow, and ran his hands down her sides slowly, finally resting them on her hips. Story thrilled at the feel of him and wanted to be closer—needed to be closer. She drank him in and hoped the kiss would never end as she poured every bit of feeling she'd tried to keep hidden from him into it. He pressed in tighter for a moment and then pulled away gasping, his eyes a swirl of bright purple and orange flames.

"And you wonder what possible reason I could have for wanting to go with you?"

Her heart was racing, and she was both dizzy from and disappointed by the end of the kiss. *So much for being just friends.*

"Be serious," she teased, and leaned in for another kiss.

Eirnin pulled back, with what looked like considerable effort, and placed two staying hands on her shoulders.

"I am being serious. Completely." His smile softened, and he was suddenly shy. "Haven't you figured it out yet? I'm in love with you, Story Melissa of the Sorenson clan. I don't want to live in a world without you, so the answer is simple; I'll just go to whatever world you are in."

Story's mouth hung open in shock. She didn't know what to say. She knew that he liked her, but love... well, that was an entirely different level of "like." As far as she knew, love meant marriage (or bonding in the elves' case), and marriage was something adults did, and Story, much as she liked to think she was, was not an adult yet. Or maybe she was jumping to the wrong conclusion. Maybe he didn't want to marry her. Wait, why was she even thinking about marriage?

Being a girl is so frustrating sometimes.

Eirnin's eyes started to cloud over yellow with worry, or fear—maybe both, and she realized she had to say something.

"Um, thank you?"

Eirnin dropped his arms from her shoulders and cocked an eyebrow at her. "I tell you that I'm in love with you, and all you can say is thank you?"

"Thanks a lot?"

Eirnin balled up his fists and pressed them into his eyes. He took a deep breath and, when he let it out, looked at Story and calmly said, "Let me ask my first question again. Have I done something wrong?"

"What? No! You're wonderful. More than wonderful." A hopeful expression dawned on his face, so Story quickly pressed on. "But, you're like, almost fifty years older than me. Isn't that weird, at least to you? Because when I think about it..."

"Then don't think about it." He leaned in to kiss her, but she pressed her hand against his lips.

"Please be serious."

Exasperated, he took her hand in his and shook his head. "No Story, I'm not bothered by it at all. You've a grown-up soul inside of you. You're older than your recorded years. Life has seen to that." His eyes tinged with blue momentarily. "Besides, a fifty year, or more, age gap in my culture is also fairly common. Queen Eánna is well over a hundred years older than me, and you didn't seem to think that was a problem."

"Okay fine, the age thing is a non-issue. But what about once I restore *The Ailes*—"

"If it exists."

Story glared at him for interrupting, and he glared right back at her, fighting a smile the entire time.

"Fine, *if* it exists. What happens after I restore it? Besides it being ok for us to be romantically involved."

"I don't follow?"

She let out an exasperated sigh. "You'll be immortal."

"So?"

"What do you mean 'so'? You're going to live forever. You'll never age. You'll never die."

Eirnin frowned at that. "Sounds boring."

She slapped his biceps. "Pay attention!"

He rubbed at his arm. "Alright, no need to get violent. Aside from boredom, why is my immortality a bad thing? I'd assumed you weren't hoping for my death, at least not lately..."

She leaned her head back against the ship's prow and sighed again. Guys were thick-headed no matter what race they came from, it seemed.

"My point is *I* won't be immortal. I'm going to grow old and die. And soon, at least relative to what you're used to."

"All the more reason for me to spend as much time with you as possible."

He was persistent; she'd give him that.

"I'm high maintenance."

"Yes, you are. Good thing I like maintaining you."

"I'm bossy and rude and I jump to conclusions. Usually the wrong ones."

"But in a good way." He leaned in close again and whispered in her ear, "I love you because of your flaws, not in spite of them." He placed a soft kiss on her jaw. "I love that you sleep more than any living being should have a right to." He trailed his nose down her neck and kissed her on her collarbone. "I love that you can eat more than an entire family of gnomes in one sitting." He moved his mouth to her shoulder and pressed another kiss there. "I love the way you aren't afraid to take action and stand up for what you believe. And I love it when you look at me the way you are right now—like you think I'm completely mad."

He stepped back and looked at her with a confident smile.

"Face it, Story, I'm not going anywhere. I know that this is overwhelming and a lot to take in. And I also know that you're scared to death to emotionally tie yourself to anyone after what happened to your family." He took one of her hands in both of his. "So I guess you have a lot to think about. I'll still be here when you sort it all out."

With that, he bent over her hand—just as he had with the queen—but instead of kissing the back of it, he flipped it over and pressed his lips to her palm, all the while never taking his eyes off of hers. In some ways it felt more intimate than any of their other kisses had.

Then he was gone, leaving Story to stare out over the ocean alone. She clutched the hand that he'd kissed close to her heart, still feeling the lingering sensation of him there. He was right; she did have a lot to think about.

CHAPTER TWENTY-EIGHT

UNDER THE SEA

THE WATER WAS COLD, BUT IT DIDN'T BOTHER STORY. THEY'D left the ship without any fanfare, slipping into the ocean at an hour so early it may as well have been considered part of the night. She glanced to her left and saw Adair swimming ahead of them in the murky darkness of the sea, making her thankful yet again for Eánna's gift. She scratched at the ad'har on her face absentmindedly. They were on their third set of the stuff, and it was almost time for a fourth.

Adair had said they were near her mother's home now, which was a good thing, since after three hours of swimming, she was exhausted. She'd always been a natural swimmer, and after all the walking she'd done around Ailionora, her endurance was better than it'd ever been before. But even Eirnin looked like he was starting to flag a little, and that was saying something. Or maybe he just didn't like being under water. Story wasn't sure which, but he had eyed the ad'har with more revulsion than was really necessary before Adair had smeared it on his face.

She glanced surreptitiously in his direction, and that was a bad idea. The muscles in his bare shoulders and back moved fluidly under his skin while he swam, and she imagined how they would feel under her hands.

Stop that!

Story shook her head to clear it, sending up a cascade of bubbles to the surface far overhead, and tried to focus on what Adair was saying—she had, of course, been talking non-stop since they'd submerged. But it was a pointless venture. Her mind kept going back to what Eirnin had told her two days before.

He loves me!

She was flattered, scared, excited, nervous, happy, and very unsure of how she felt all at the same time. How could a person feel so many emotions at once and not explode? She knew that she cared about him—that much was obvious—but she didn't know if she was in love with him.

She'd never been in love before, so she had no frame of reference. She'd always figured, at least based on many of the movies she'd seen and books she'd read, that she'd know instantly if she met *the one*. But with Eirnin, it was all so slow and gradual that she didn't even realize she had feelings for him until they were in the middle of it all. She still wasn't sure what "it all" was.

He also had a tendency to purposefully irritate her—though he'd probably call it teasing.

But in a good way, she thought with a half-smile, remembering his words to her.

Maybe it was just a bizarre elf way of flirting? Though—if memory served her—in elementary school, little boys were always mean to girls they liked. Mostly because they didn't understand what they were feeling and being mean was the only way they knew how to cope.

And maybe I'm just over thinking things. Again.

Eirnin was as good as his word and didn't act like anything was any different between them. He had been just as attentive as before but without the kissing and cuddling, which—she realized with a blush—she really missed. What there had been was plenty of staring, and not just from him this time. She was hyper-aware of him at all times and tracked his movements with her eyes like some crazy, obsessed stalker. Except it couldn't be stalking if he liked it—could it? He had said that he liked her looking at him…

I am an idiot. She flushed, suddenly very grateful that no one could read her thoughts.

No wonder men didn't understand women. Heck, she didn't even understand herself. What hope was there for them?

"Hey, I just asked if you wanted to shave off your eyebrows and you said 'uh-huh'." Adair swam up next to Story, her sarong fluttering lazily in the ocean currents, blending well with the small school of brightly-colored fish clustered around her. She'd fought wearing anything initially, stridently informing Story that she was a dryad, and dryads swam naked. It took Story pointing out that she couldn't go prancing around the Faerie Prince's garden in her birthday suit before she agreed to put anything on. So, they were all swimming in minimal clothing, carrying the rest of what they needed in a pack on Adair's back since she was the strongest swimmer. Neither Eirnin nor Story liked that much but had eventually agreed that it made sense.

"Now I see why you're so distracted." Adair followed Story's gaze and stared at Eirnin's muscular back for a minute before looking at Story with a broad grin. *"When do you think you two will move past the staring stage into the kissing stage?"*

Story's eyebrows shot up to her hairline. *"Shhhh! He'll hear you!"*

Adair looked momentarily perplexed before opening her mouth in a silent giggle, releasing a stream of bubbles.

"Oh Story, he can't hear us unless we want him to."

"Wait...We can do that? Control who hears our thoughts?"

Adair looked exasperated, as if they'd already covered this before. *"Yes, you can control who you send your thoughts to. Remember, we can't 'read' thoughts, we can only send them."* She looked from Story to Eirnin. *"That's why he can hear us but we can't hear him—he's not capable of sending his thoughts."*

Story eyed him carefully, but though they were only a few feet from him, he appeared completely oblivious to their conversation.

She looked at Adair. *"Eirnin, can you hear me?"* He didn't so much as glance over his shoulder, so she fixed her gaze on him and repeated herself. This time, he stopped swimming and looked at her and nodded.

"Um, never mind. Sorry about that. I was just testing something."

He looked confused, but shrugged and resumed swimming.

"You don't have to be looking at the person to make it work, you know. But if that helps you..." Adair shrugged like Eirnin had and took her guiding place up ahead again.

"So, when do you think he'll finally kiss you?"

Story blushed and remained silent. She was not about to kiss and tell. Besides, no matter what Adair said, "talking" about this with Eirnin only a few feet away was weird.

"Slippery selkie, he's already done it, hasn't he?" Adair swirled around, peering at Story intently with a wide grin on her face.

Story fought back another deep blush. *"Turn around before he realizes what we're talking about!"*

"Only if you promise to tell me all about it."

"Fine! Just turn."

Adair turned around obligingly, and thankfully, Eirnin appeared none the wiser. Before Story had a chance to say anything though, Adair was already running away with the conversation.

"Yes! I knew it! Da and I both knew it. The way he looked at you and you at him. It was all so obvious. We kept wondering when the two of you would figure it out for yourselves. Even the queen asked if the two of you were planning on bonding, and Da told her—"

"Okay, stop, stop, stop. Wait right there—you, and everyone else, are getting way ahead of yourselves. Just because we kissed like once—or twice—okay, a maybe a few times... But it doesn't mean that we are going to run off and get bonded or that we are anything other than just friends. Who sometimes kiss." Her eyes strayed over to Eirnin again, and she felt a goofy smile creep across her face before she hastily looked back at Adair, who was, in turn, smirking knowingly over her shoulder.

"Look, believe what you want, but we aren't anything other than friends."

"Why not? Doesn't he want to be?"

"Well... yes, at least I think he does. He asked if he could come back to my world with me."

A high-pitched squeal sounded in Story's head, and she glared at Adair.

"That hurt!"

"Sorry." Though she didn't look the least bit sorry. *"So, did he tell you he loves you yet?"*

Story sighed, releasing another stream of bubbles to the surface. It appeared that Adair was not going to give the subject up.

"*Yes.*" She braced herself for another exuberant onslaught of thoughts, but thankfully Adair seemed able to keep her squeals contained this time.

"*And?*"

"*And what?*"

"*And what did you say in return?*" Adair peered at Story over her shoulder again, a dreamy look on her face, as if this were the perfect romantic story to her. "*You told him that you loved him back, right?*"

"*Uh...*" Story looked worriedly over at Eirnin, who still seemed oblivious. "*Actually, I told him 'thank you'.*"

"*But THEN you told him you loved him back, right?*"

"*Well... not exactly...*"

"*What? Why not?*" Adair demanded and shot Story an appalled look. "*If you love him, you should have told him!*"

"*Yes, well that's the problem. I don't know if I do.*" Story held up two placating hands toward Adair's disbelieving look. "*What I mean to say is, yes, I do love him. But I love you and your father too. I just don't know if I'm IN love with Eirnin, which is a totally different kind of love.*"

Surprisingly, Adair was silent, as if truly pondering Story's dilemma. Hoping that was the end of it, Story let her eyes wander but kept them firmly away from Eirnin's backside. The ocean floor rose before them in an underwater mountain, and she could see an old shipwreck at the mountain's peak. They were still too far away for her to make out any details, so she had no clue as to how old it might be, or what race had built it.

"*Do you think about him all the time?*"

Story furrowed her brows together. She knew whom Adair meant, but she wasn't sure she wanted to follow this line of questioning. Still, it might help—as long as she wasn't afraid of the answer she'd get.

"Yes."

"No, I mean allllll the time. Like it keeps you up at night."

"Yes." Story blushed again. At this rate she should paint her face red permanently.

"Do you feel like you can be yourself around him? Like really, REALLY be yourself? Say anything, feel anything, or do anything?"

Story's mouth quirked in a half-grin. "Yes, definitely. Poor Eirnin doesn't get any sort of filter from me at all."

"I'm assuming you two have no problem with the kissing thing, so I won't ask about that."

"How old are you again?"

"Don't try to change the subject. Last, but not least, do you miss him when he's not around? And does your stomach get all fluttery when he is? Especially when he smiles at you?" Adair sighed, looking like a hopeless romantic.

Story swallowed hard, reluctant to answer this one.

"Well?"

"Yes, but—"

Adair snorted, and giggled. "Face it Story, you're in loooooove."

She strung out the word "love" as only a teenage girl could and clasped her hands at her heart before batting her eyes and puckering her lips exaggeratingly.

Story realized she had nothing to say to counter Adair's words. Nothing logical, at least. She looked at Eirnin and realized he was looking at her. By the crinkles near his eyes, she could tell he was smiling at her, and her stomach flip-flopped.

"Adair you didn't—"

"Well, I'd better swim down and get you and Eirnin some more ad'har. Yours are nearly dried up." Adair waved at Story brightly and in a flash was swimming down toward the ship below them.

She watched Adair go and felt the water ripple as Eirnin swam up next to her.

"You heard everything, didn't you?"

He shook his head no.

"But you heard Adair."

He shrugged and then nodded his head slowly, confirming her suspicions. Whether he'd heard her answers or not, Adair's final statement was damning enough. She glared at him and could make out a broad grin beneath his ad'har. She wanted to punch him. Or kiss him. Both actually.

"Only people you really care about are capable of making you really upset," her dad once told her when she was venting to him about the twins and their most recent shenanigan, which involved a muddy beagle and her once clean bedroom.

Eirnin's hand slipped into hers, and he gave it a quick squeeze. He did not let go, and Story was glad for that. Somehow having him close by made her feel a lot less foolish about everything.

A massive jet of bubbles shot right in front of them, and they both followed it up to the water's surface with their eyes. It went by with such force that Story imagined that it must have caused a small geyser on the ocean's surface.

Good thing the ship was safely far away.

Eirnin tugged her hand to get her attention and started pointing down frantically. She followed his gaze and would have gasped in horror if she could.

Creeping out from inside the ruined ship's hull, like the under-sea spider it was, Story beheld the largest crab she'd ever seen. Its black and red mottled carapace was easily the size of Eilath's wagon, with each of its legs twice that length and covered in gleaming armored spines. It scuttled over the side of the ship, its eye-stalks waving lazily in the ocean current. The eyes, each the size of Story's head, were trained intelligently on the blissfully unaware Adair, who was trying to extract her sarong from the jagged wooden beam she'd gotten snagged on—probably cursing Story for making her wear clothes in the water.

Eirnin already had his sword out and was swimming toward the crab as fast as he could. What he expected to accomplish with the sword against that armor she didn't know, but she was right behind him, her knife firm in her grip.

"ADAIR!" The girl ignored her, either concentrating on her stuck clothing or too irritated with Story to respond.

Even swimming as fast as they could, it was clear they weren't going to make it in time. The monster was nearly on her, its massive right claw reaching out menacingly. Story took a deep breath and willed her worn out arms and legs to swim faster—or rather, she tried to take a deep breath. She nearly choked on the ad'har before it peeled away from her face, completely dried out and worthless. It floated lazily in the current next to Eirnin's. She hoped he could hold his breath as long as she could.

"ADAIR!"

The girl looked up and frowned at Story while she tugged helplessly at the fabric.

"Next time I'm swimming naked, I don't care what you—"

"BEHIND YOU!"

Adair looked behind her, eyes burning yellow with fear. "Kraken..."

She stopped tugging on her sarong and focused on trying to unwind herself out of it, but between the backpack and the wood of the ship, she was firmly stuck. All she could do was sit there like Andromeda and wait for the kraken to arrive and consume her. Unfortunately, neither Story nor Eirnin happened to be carrying Medusa's head with them. Adair wasn't one to sit still and be a sacrifice to a hungry crustacean, so she pulled out her bronze dagger and began hacking at the fabric that bound her.

Time seemed to slow as Eirnin, Story, and the kraken converged upon Adair almost simultaneously. Eirnin went straight for the monster's one weak spot, its eyes, and Story, her chest tight and beginning to burn from the lack of air, darted toward the trapped dryad. The kraken paid them no mind; both its eyes were trained completely on Adair and the flame red hair that swirled around her with every tug she gave on her sarong. The monster snapped at her with its larger right claw, and she ducked out of the way just in time. The pincer came away with only a few red braids for its trouble.

Story watched as Eirnin barely avoided being skewered by one of the spines on the kraken's many legs as he continued to press his attack on the monster with his bronze sword. She tried not to worry about him (though that was difficult) and focused instead on helping Adair. Story reached the massive claw that had nearly decapitated the girl and stabbed at what she hoped was a chink in its armor. The kraken swatted her away like she was a fly, and she flew right into the ship's broken mast. She hit so hard that what remaining air she had left her chest in a scatter of bubbles.

Adair turned to look at her, and that was her mistake. The kraken's smaller, and therefore ignored, pincer grasped her by her right biceps and tried to pull her into its gaping maw.

Story tried to swim to Adair, but her limbs moved clumsily, and her vision began to tunnel from lack of oxygen. A roaring sound filled her ears, like static in a radio.

Why do I drown every time I go swimming in this world?

Her eyes blinked closed, and she struggled to open them back up. Each time she managed it the picture was vastly different.

She saw Adair, finally free of the pincer, but missing her right arm from the shoulder down, a cloud of silver blood spreading around her.

Blink.

She saw several harpoons fly through the water and spear the kraken in both eyes and in invisible chinks in its armor as it tried to scuttle away.

Blink.

She saw Eirnin's limp body being tugged away by a blue-skinned man, who had equally blue hair drifting lazily around him in the ocean current.

Blink.

She saw her knife gleaming on the ship's deck as she floated in the ocean current a few feet above it.

Blink.

She saw black.

Chapter Twenty-Nine

MOTHER

WATER SPEWED OUT OF STORY'S MOUTH AS SHE COUGHED in a deep breath of moist, warm air. Judging by the hacking and gagging coming from the side of her, it sounded like Eirnin was conscious as well.

"I don't think I like swimming any more." The words tore at her throat like sandpaper. Eirnin groaned his agreement before returning to clearing salt water out of his lungs.

Story got up on her hands and knees, looking for Adair; she needed to make sure the girl was okay. She nearly fell right back over again. The surface they were on was silky smooth to the touch and quite slick. It gleamed pinkish-white and reminded her of the coloring and texture of the inside of a seashell. Movement and low, melodic voices to her left caught her attention, and she looked toward them, careful of the placement of her hands for stability.

It was like looking at a rainbow. Arranged around Adair—who was lying on the floor and protesting loudly—were half a dozen male and female dryads, still wet from their underwater rescue. Story knew which ones were male and which ones were female since none of them wore a stitch of clothing. She felt her cheeks heat up, and so she focused on Adair, who, despite her missing right arm, seemed to be doing just fine.

"Just let me go! I need to speak with Ma. I'm fine!"

But squirm as she might, an orange and black-striped female dryad held her shoulders firmly down while a yellow and blue-spotted male held her kicking feet. A brown-skinned female, with electric blue dreadlocks, knelt beside Adair's right shoulder and scooped an iridescent paste out of a shell.

"Noooooooo!" Adair jerked away before she could put the paste on her bleeding stump, and silver blood sprayed across the other dryad's knees. "It stings! I don't want it, I don't want it, I don't want it! You can't make me!"

But she was wrong; they could.

Eirnin was done clearing out his lungs by now, and he joined Story in watching the paste congeal and harden on Adair's wound, effectively stopping the bleeding. Adair, meanwhile, was shrieking loudly and, judging by the way some of the other dryads were flinching, swearing profusely in their dialect.

Just then a short, silvery-white-skinned female with hair so red it looked almost neon dashed in and moved toward the group quickly. Apart from the dryads being more colorful in their pigmentation than a school of tropical fish, it seemed that long, hip-length hair was about the only thing they all had in common. This new dryad, and the few who accompanied her, at least had the barest of sarongs tied around their hips but were still naked from the waist up.

Story blushed again and peeked at Eirnin, wondering if he was as uncomfortable with all this as she was. He wasn't even looking at the dryads; instead, his eyes were trained on her and tinged with worry. She smiled at him and was about to tell him she was fine when the most intoxicating voice she'd ever heard came from the female who'd just thrown herself down by Adair's feet. Both Eirnin and Story's heads swiveled toward the speaker, and they stared unblinkingly.

"Oh my dear, sweet, precious girl, what has that kraken done to you?" Her voice was so spellbinding Story felt like she'd do anything it asked her to do. Swim a thousand miles, jump from a cliff, anything.

"Ma, I'm—"

"The fishers will bring it back, and we shall have it for a feast tonight!"

"But Ma—"

"It's a shame about your arm, but you are young enough, and since Keelin got the sh'yla on it in time—no doubt with you screaming your head off, though you know it only stings for a bit—your arm should hopefully grow back good as new. Until then, you will just have to stay with me. I don't want your father to think I can't take care of my own pup. Which brings me to another point, what possessed you to go swimming in the open ocean unescorted? What possessed your da to let you? Oh! Does he not know? Did you swim away from home? Why would you do that? Were you not happy? You know you're always welcome here, right? This is your home, too."

She finally paused for a breath, and Eirnin and Story shook their heads trying to clear them. It was no wonder Eilath fell for her hook, line, and sinker. And thank goodness none of the other dryads had spoken to them directly—their voices could be dangerous weapons it seemed.

"Ma, calm down! That's what I've been trying to tell you. I'm on a mission—"

"What kind of mission? Did your da approve of this?"

Adair sighed and rolled her eyes, red flickers of irritation showing.

"I'm helping the Ailesit get to the Faerie Prince's garden so she can restore *The Ailes*." Adair pointed at Story, and Eirnin helped her get to her feet.

The musical undercurrent of murmuring voices from the other dryads stopped, and they all turned to gaze at Story curiously. Almera, who up until then had her back to Story and Eirnin while she was speaking to her daughter, stood up and, despite her diminutive size, still managed to fill the room with her presence. She turned around, and Story was not surprised to see a pearl and coral crown woven through her long red tresses. Apparently Adair's mother was either the queen of the dryads (she certainly carried herself like one), or someone who ruled this group of them.

"Welcome to Vevila. Any friend of Adair's is always welcome in my city." Almera cocked her head to the side and narrowed her eyes slightly as she scrutinized the two of them. This time Almera's musical voice had no effect on Story, since she felt like all the air had gone out of the room. She was staring at a pair of sea-green eyes that mirrored her own, and she'd know that face anywhere—she'd seen it in a framed picture sitting on her dad's bedside table every day of her life.

"Mom?"

Almera's eyes widened first in surprise and then in recognition.

"Story?"

"How did you know it was me? I mean, you left when I was just a baby." Story fought to keep the bitterness from her voice, but judging by the wounded look in Almera's eyes, she was unsuccessful.

"You look just like your father. Except far prettier and more feminine of course," Almera said with a sad smile. Her hand strayed to an old water-stained photograph set inside of a seashell-bedecked frame. Story realized with a start that it was her father, back when he was young, holding a chubby toddler with short purple and black wispy curls in his arms.

Me.

Story's eyes moved from the photo to her mother. The word sounded odd in her head. "I always thought your name was Mera. At least, that's what Dad said it was."

"Your da always did like pet names. He shortened it to Mera almost as soon as we met." She traced a finger along the glass of the photo and hummed a melody that Story recognized as her childhood lullaby: the one her father always used to sing to her.

"I haven't been called Mera in a long time. Not since I left."

There was the awkwardness again, hanging in the air like it had immediately after they'd recognized each other. They were now in Almera's personal chambers, which happened to be at the very top of the massive conch shell that made up the main structure in Vevila. Almera had Adair moved to her quarters to rest before she could work herself up again from the excitement of learning she had a new sister. Eirnin, perceiving that the two of them needed to talk alone, had gone with the fishers to bring back the kraken so that it could be prepared for the feast (apparently they were notoriously hard to find and quite the delicacy). Story had also asked him to retrieve her father's knife from the deck of the shipwreck while they were out. She was trying not to panic at the thought of losing it, and if anyone could find it, Eirnin would.

And so, she found herself, once again, facing a situation where she didn't know what to say. What did you say to someone who abandoned you right after you were born? Someone you'd never expected to see again? Someone you'd grown up resenting for being absent when you needed a mother? Someone who was gone when you needed her the absolute most—when everyone you loved was suddenly taken away?

Story felt that even if she'd had years to prepare for this moment she still wouldn't know what to say. She decided to start out with the one question she'd always wanted answered.

"Why did you leave?"

Almera let her hand drop from the photo, and she turned sorrow-filled eyes toward her daughter.

"I had to. I had a responsibility to my people as a leader. I couldn't just disappear and leave them forever, much as I would've liked to at the time."

This was definitely not the answer Story had been expecting. She'd always assumed that her mother had been a flighty woman who hadn't wanted the burden of raising a child, not a woman who'd left a relatively small responsibility of one child to be the figurative mother of countless others.

Story sat down heavily on a stool fashioned out of driftwood and coral, trying to process it all. It was nearly too much to meet your long-lost mother and then find out she wasn't the villain you'd always presumed her to be. She never realized how much a part of her these "facts" had become. To see that they were no longer true... well, it turned her world on its head more than showing up in Ailionora had.

"Tell me everything. Please."

Story's mother adjusted the sarong around her waist before sitting opposite her on an accompanying stool.

"There is so much to tell. But where to start?"

"At the beginning."

Almera bit her lower lip, the same way Story did, and nodded her head.

"Nineteen years ago, right after the old king died—he was four hundred and twelve, and a shark got him—I was elected the new queen of our people. The fact that I had no desire to be the queen didn't matter. I was elected, and that was that. I'm one hundred percent certain it had everything to do with my singing voice."

At Story's questioning eyebrow, Almera waved a hand.

"No one ever said dryads were rational beings." She smiled tightly before continuing. "I didn't much like the idea of being in charge. At fifty-three years old, I was young and flighty. It didn't seem fair that I would be condemned to be the one serious dryad among us all for my remaining centuries. So I left."

Now this was the mother Story had always imagined, one who ran away from responsibility. Though, in truth, she almost couldn't blame her. She wouldn't want to be saddled with ruling an entire race either.

"I found a series of underwater caves that I'd never seen before, so decided to explore them—"

"And you ended up in the underground river in the caves where Dad found you," Story finished for her. She'd heard that half of the story many times from her father, only now it had a very different light to it. "You showed up naked and helpless… you're lucky Dad was the one who found you."

Almera shot a quick glance at the photo on her table. "Indeed I was. Milt was the kindest man I ever met. He took me in and didn't ask any questions—well, I take that back, he did ask me to marry him eventually." She looked down and fingered a small pearl ring on her left hand that Story hadn't noticed before. "Dryads don't get married, so I said no. After we had you, something changed in me. I realized that I couldn't run away from my responsibilities. I had to come back."

"So you ran away from me and Dad instead?" Story balled her hands into fists angrily.

Almera leaned over and placed a gentle hand on Story's knee. "I asked your da to come back with me. He said no—he'd made a commitment to defend his country. He couldn't leave, and I couldn't stay." She looked Story in the eyes, willing her to understand. "I couldn't take you away from him either. He loved you so much. It would have killed him to lose us both."

Story looked away, unable to maintain the eye contact which made it impossible to disregard her mother's words; she wanted to ignore them. She stood up and took several angry steps away.

"Well now he *is* dead." The words were hateful, vindictive, and aimed to hurt. They had the desired effect. Her mother stared at the empty stool, mouth slightly open in shock. Story immediately felt guilty. She'd purposely meant to hurt her, but now that she'd done it, she wished she could call the words back. Being mean to her mother hadn't made her feel better; it made her feel worse.

She walked back over to Almera and placed a hand on her shoulder.

"I'm sorry, I shouldn't have—"

"No, it's okay," Almera interrupted. "I knew it would happen someday—human lifespans are so short. I guess I had always secretly hoped to see him again at some point before it happened." She took a deep breath and wiped the tears away.

Standing, she turned to face Story and placed both hands on her shoulders before smiling hesitantly up at her.

"Daughter, you have siblings and cousins here; Adair is just one of many. Should you desire to stay, we would welcome you with open arms. Nothing would make me happier." Then her face turned serious. "But should you desire to return to your world now, I can show you the way."

Story didn't flinch at her touch, but she didn't move to embrace her either. This was going to take some time. "Thanks, I might do that—come stay with you for a while. Maybe get to know you. But for now, I have a mission to finish. The elf race to save. You know, no biggie."

"You really are the Ailesit. Many times over the last seventeen years I've imagined what you looked liked and all the things you would grow up to be someday. I'll admit that this was not one of them."

Story looked down at Almera and half-smiled. "Me neither. I always thought I'd grow up to be an Olympic swimmer or something. Fulfiller of an ancient prophecy was definitely not on the list."

Almera laid a hand on Story's cheek. "Please promise you'll be careful. Morrigann is no fool and is filled with all sorts of nasty tricks."

"I know what I'm getting into—"

"I know, I know, but I can't help it. You are my daughter after all. Mothering comes naturally, even to dryads." She smiled weakly. "Adair will need to remain here to convalesce while her arm grows back, but I will have two of my best selkies take you and your elf wherever you need to go when you are ready to finish this."

Story blushed and ducked her head, which was completely ineffective since her mother was at least six inches shorter than her.

"He's not *my* elf…"

Almera gave a very unrefined snort.

"Seriously." Story said with warning tone.

"Whatever you say, Daughter. It's just that your da used to look at me like that—"

"Drop it…"

Almera laughed and raised her hands in defeat. "Fine, I won't say another word. Except that I like him. And he has a cute behind."

Story pinched the bridge of her nose with two fingers and squeezed her eyes shut. "I did *not* need to hear that." Then another question occurred to her.

"Actually, I was wondering… why don't I have gills or webbed toes like Adair does? She's only half-dryad too." *Whoa*—it hit Story for the first time that she wasn't completely human. It was kind of thrilling and weird all at the same time. Though it did explain a lot: the purple streaks in her hair, her natural affinity for the water, and her ability to "speak" under water.

"Yes, I have given that some thought. I suspect that human genes are more dominant. Which is why you look more like your father than me, much the same way I suspect dryad genes are more dominant than those of the elves. Though don't tell them that," she said with a laugh. "Of course, that's all purely conjecture. As far as I know there aren't any other human/dryad or elf/dryad children out there. So it could just be that's how it all happened to work out."

Story stared at her with her mouth half opened. "How do you know about genetics? I mean, no offense, but Ailionora seems kind of primitive…"

"I did spend well over a year in your world, Story. And I wasn't about to leave my little pup behind in a world where scientists would have dissected you if it was obvious that you weren't fully human—give me some credit, please."

Almera then cocked her head to the side and studied Story's tired face. "You look exhausted, and I'll bet you're hungry—I remember how much humans need to eat! It's been a big day for you. Come on, let's get you some food, and then I'll take you to your room."

She put action to words and interlaced her fingers with Story's before tugging her out of the room.

Chapter Thirty

*U*NRESOLVED

S TORY TOSSED IN HER BED, UNABLE TO SLEEP. THE BED WAS comfortable enough—it was made of sea sponges after all. The light from the softly glowing pearls in the room was quite soothing. She was tired—no, make that *exhaust-ed*—enough to fall asleep. The problem was simply that she couldn't get her brain to shut off.

After their conversation in her quarters, her mother had taken her to a kitchen and the hot pink and lime green-striped dryad there served her up a plate of what looked like sushi. Story wasn't normally one for seafood—and definitely not into eating raw fish—but she was hungry. The meal turned out to be quite tasty, once she got over the somewhat slimy texture.

Her mother had led her out of the main shell (the palace, as it were), and they'd swum to a much smaller shell nearby that was just large enough to house a bed, a stool, and a small table with a polished rainbow abalone surface. A kaleidoscope of shells, rocks, and coral were affixed to the wall, and an overly excited Adair was in her bed. The beginning nub of new growth was already protruding out of the stump from her arm, and Story would have, under normal circumstances, probably thought it was gross and weird—if it hadn't been so darn fascinating. She'd idly wondered if she'd inherited that handy gene from her dryad mother, but wasn't willing to sacrifice an appendage to test that theory.

Adair had chattered on excitedly about finally having a sister—all of Mera's other children were boys—and how she'd always known she and Story were somehow related, essentially leaving Story and Almera to just nod their heads in agreement every so often. This went on until Adair finally fell asleep—a side effect of the herbal tea her mother had given her to help with the healing of her arm. The queen then led Story out through the water opening in the floor, and took her to the shell adjacent to Adair's. It was similarly outfitted, though somehow a bit morose without Adair's spectacular artwork on the walls. Just outside the floor's water opening was a bucket-sized snail shell filled with ad'har. This way Story could come and go as she pleased without having to wait for a dryad to come get her.

So here she was now, unable to sleep, because in light of everything: her quest, this different world, being reunited with her mother, a sister discovered (and several half-brothers), all she could do was think about Eirnin and worry that he wasn't back yet. How long could it take to bring back a giant, dead crab?

She sighed and rolled over onto her stomach. The truth was she missed him. Not just the last few hours, but in general. His snarky comments and his sweet kisses. His arrogant grin and his tender eyes. His obnoxious sense of humor and his reassuring presence. As cheesy as is sounded, she felt complete when he was near her.

That wasn't to imply that she was incapable of functioning without him around, just that she preferred it when he was. Admitting this made her wonder, why was she so afraid to attach that simple little four-letter word to what she was feeling? Because she was pretty sure that's what she was feeling. Even without thinking of the actual word, just knowing that she felt that way for Eirnin made her both giggly and scared.

If she had to pin down why she was scared, she was fairly certain that Eirnin had nailed it. It was commitment, or rather, being willing to open herself up that much to another person—it implied risk, a lot of risk. Someone could only hurt you if you let them in too close. Though in all fairness, there wasn't much, if anything, she'd kept from him at this point. Still, she wasn't ready. Yet. She needed time, and he was willing to give it, so why push things?

Story flopped onto her back and smiled, finally able to quiet her mind somewhat by feeling resolved to be unresolved. For now. Her eyes closed, and she was finally drifting off to sleep when the splash of someone surfacing through her shell's entrance got her attention.

Eirnin!

Story's heartbeat quickened, and she felt a familiar flutter in her stomach when she saw him. His eyes were closed tightly, and he was in the process of peeling off his ad'har with one hand while he used the other to heave himself onto the edge of the opening.

She sat up, wide awake now, and searched his hands for her father's knife. It wasn't there. Maybe he'd left it with the rest of his stuff before coming here.

"You can open your eyes. I'm decent."

Free of the ad'har, and blinking his eyes against the salt

water running down from his glistening, black hair, he grinned at her. "I very much doubt that. You're never decent."

She rolled her eyes, but grinned despite herself. "Did you find it?"

His smile melted from his face, and his eyes turned a sorrow-filled blue. That was all the answer she needed. Tears welled in her eyes unbidden, and she fought back the lump in her throat. It was just a stupid knife after all. She looked down at her hands unable to meet his gaze. She would surely cry if she did.

In two steps he was next to her, and wrapped his wet arms around her.

"I'm so sorry," he whispered into her hair. "We looked everywhere for it, Story. Everywhere that I could think of and everywhere they could think of. It's gone. I'm sorry."

Those words of finality broke through Story's weak control, and hot tears slid down her face. Eirnin pressed a kiss into her hair, and she buried her face in his chest allowing the tears to fall where they would.

"It's ironic isn't it?" her muffled voice sounded.

"What's that?"

"I find my mother and lose my father all in the same day. Perhaps I was never meant to have two parents at once."

He patted her back gently. "Now you're just being silly. A knife is not a parent."

"I know." She looked up at him and smiled weakly. "But now I have to do this without him. I don't know if I can." Her smile faded, and the tears welled up again.

Eirnin pulled her tightly to him and stroked her hair softly with one hand while the other cupped the side of her face.

"I'm here. I'm not going anywhere."

She stared up into his sea-green eyes that mirrored her

own, not just in color but in feeling, and before she could stop herself, she leaned in hesitantly for a kiss.

He didn't pull away, but he didn't lean in to meet her either. Instead, he let her take the lead, seeming to understand that she needed to control something in her life right now. That initial kiss turned into a series of soft, exploring kisses, as if they had all the time in the world to do just that.

She drank him in—the feel of his soft, yielding lips against her own and the smell of cinnamon and apples that lingered on his skin despite their prolonged exposure to the sea. His hand ghosted down from her hair to rest on her upper back, where her sarong left her skin bare. That simple touch sent a jolt of heat right down to the tips of her toes.

Gentle exploration time was over for her, and she leaned against him, all the while never breaking off their now more forceful kisses. His hand on her face slid down her neck to her shoulder and then eventually to her hip, leaving a trail of heat behind it as he pulled her in tighter to him. She raked her fingers though his short hair and stroked the back of his neck and shoulders, reveling in the feel of his bare skin under her hands.

Story left off kissing his much-abused lips and moved her explorations to his shoulders, tracing the lines of the tattoos on his shoulder with her fingertips and placing a hesitant kiss on the pointed tip of his ear. This was apparently quite a sensitive spot because Eirnin, who up until then was following Story's lead, seemed to shift gears.

In one fluid motion, he moved her off his lap and tipped her back onto the bed. He followed her down, pressing demanding kisses against her mouth, neck, and shoulders, kisses she more than willingly returned.

His touch felt wonderful, and she craved more. A small corner of her mind was starting to sound a warning that this probably shouldn't go any further, but she willfully ignored it. Right now the only thing she cared about was how good Eirnin felt against her and how much both of them seemed to be enjoying this.

At that moment, Eirnin dragged his lips from Story's and sat up. He ran a hand through his wet hair before letting out a deep breath.

"I think I should go."

Story's lips were puffy and felt bruised, and her mind was reeling from the sudden stop, but when he stood up to leave, she knew she couldn't let him go—not yet, not like this. Had she done something wrong? From what she could tell he sure seemed to be enjoying himself too.

"Wait, why do you want to leave?" Her voice sounded demanding even to her own ears.

Eirnin chuckled, and in the dim light, she could see that his irises were solidly purple. He sat back down on the edge of her bed, making sure to keep from touching her.

"I didn't say I *wanted* to leave, Story. Just that I thought I probably should. Before things get completely out of hand." He peeked at her out of the corner of his eye, and Story blushed when the implication of what he was saying hit her.

She sat up against the back wall and pulled her knees to her chest, wrapping her arms around them tightly. Yeah, she definitely wasn't ready for *that*. Not yet. Not for a long while. She leaned her forehead against her knees and groaned loudly. "I'm sorry, Eirnin. I shouldn't have—"

"No, I'm the one who's sorry." He placed a tentative hand on her foot, and she peeked over her knees at him.

"What can I say? I'm mad about you." He gave her his roguish, lopsided grin, and Story giggled.

"Do you think maybe you could stay for a bit? At least until I fall asleep? It's kinda soothing having you around." She felt very shy at saying the words out loud to him, yet they were true.

His eyes, nearly back to sea green again, took on a yellow tint along the edges, and Story hastily grabbed his hand to prevent him from leaving. "I promise I'll be good! No more kissing or anything else. At least not tonight." She said the last bit with a wink, and Eirnin visibly relaxed.

"Aye, that suits me just fine and fits nicely into my plan to spend as much time with you as possible." He moved to sit next to Story on her bed and draped his arm around her shoulders while she happily snuggled in close to him.

"Eirnin?"

"Hmm?"

"How do you know you really love me and that it's not just my dryad half luring you in with my evil siren song?"

Her head bounced lightly against his chest as he chuckled.

"Well, I don't guess I'll ever know for sure. You are an evil temptress after all. You take right after your mother in that regard. You must have left a whole string of broken hearts back in your world when you left."

Story snorted at that, and then sat bolt upright.

"Josh!"

"Who?"

"Josh. I can't believe I've completely forgotten about him! He was hiking with me when I fell down the cave shaft. He must think I'm dead by now and probably blames himself for it—because that's the sort of guy he is. Oh my gosh, he is going to need so much therapy for this. Especially after I show back up alive and well."

Story then noticed that Eirnin wasn't saying anything in response, and while he hadn't physically withdrawn himself, it felt like he had emotionally, and that was worse. She looked at him and noticed that his eyes were solidly brown.

"Hey, there's no reason to be jealous, or insecure, or whatever it is brown means." She squeezed his hand reassuringly. "Josh was just a friend. That's all."

Eirnin cocked an eyebrow. "The way we're just friends?"

Story recalled her words to Adair from earlier that day and winced. "You're going to make me say *it*, aren't you?"

"No." His eyes became a contented sea green again, and he grinned. "I doubt anyone could ever make you do anything you didn't *want* to do."

Her mouth quirked into a half-smile, and she snuggled back into his arms. "Well, if anyone could, it'd be you. You did *make* me eat a peach when we first met."

His eyes widened momentarily, but wisely, he didn't comment. It had been a pretty large admission on her part, and the surprising thing was that it didn't scare Story nearly as much as she thought it would. She sighed contentedly and closed her eyes sleepily.

"Story?"

"Hmm?"

"Don't promise to be good again. It doesn't really suit you. Besides, I prefer it when you're naughty."

She stifled a tired giggle. "But then you won't stay."

"Let's leave it to me to be the good one then, shall we?"

Story leaned up and kissed the tip of his ear quickly before flashing him a wicked grin. "You sure about that?"

Eirnin's momentarily purple eyes faded back to green, and he smiled down at her before pressing a soft kiss to the top of her head. "Absolutely. See? Completely in control. Now you should try to get some sleep."

Since she was exhausted and completely happy at that moment, curled up against him, she did just that.

Chapter Thirty-One

Friends

STORY'S EYES BLINKED OPEN SLOWLY, AND SHE STRETCHED OUT into a catlike yawn. Her fingers brushed a face. Eirnin's face! He was still there, and that fact alone made her smile.

"Good morning, little human/dryad chaotic abomination."

Story peeked up at him through sleep-filled eyes and stuck her tongue out. "Who you calling little, elf-boy? Last I checked you were shorter than just about every other elf I've ever met."

"Aye, but you haven't exactly met a wide range now, have you?" He stuck his tongue back out at her, and she made a grab for it with her hand. He snapped at her fingers with his teeth, and she jerked them back just in time and giggled.

Eirnin cocked an eyebrow and then grinned at her wickedly. "You know what I've wondered for a while now?"

Story propped her chin up on his chest and smiled up at him. "No..."

"Are you ticklish?"

Before she could respond he rolled her beneath him and started tickling her furiously. Story shrieked with laughter and tried to capture his hands in hers to make him stop, but he was too strong, and her loud giggling and squirming only encouraged him to double his torturous attack.

So Story attempted a different tactic. Forcefully taking his face in both of her hands she pulled him into a deep kiss. The tickling stopped almost immediately, and when they both finally came up for air, Eirnin's eyes were a swirl of purple and orange.

"You know, you're very lucky my dad is already dead, because if he caught you here with me like this, he'd kill you. Slowly." Story made sure to smile to let him know that she was just teasing him. And strangely enough, joking about her father with Eirnin wasn't painful. It felt nice to be able to do it.

Eirnin rolled onto his side and propped his head up with his arm. "Is that so?"

Story nodded emphatically and leaned in for another kiss.

"Because your mother doesn't seem to mind." He looked over Story's shoulder meaningfully.

She froze millimeters away from kissing him, sat straight up, and looked over at Almera. She was seated casually on the only stool in the room, and Story had no idea how long she'd been there. A blush burned from Story's hairline to the tips of her toes.

"Good morning, Daughter," she said brightly, completely at ease. "I came by to see if you wanted breakfast—you humans do seem to always be hungry—but you were sleeping so peacefully that I didn't want to disturb you, so I've been getting to know your elf a bit better." Then she leaned forward and stage whispered, "He's a keeper!"

Story wanted to crawl into a hole and die of embarrassment. Her mother and Eirnin had been chatting for who knew how long, while she lay there snoring. And then, when she woke up, she'd...

Story buried her face in her hands. *I think I liked it better when I didn't have a mother.* She took a calming breath and looked up at Almera's beaming face.

"It's not what it looks like. Eirnin's not *my* elf. He's just... we're just..." She looked over at him for some help, and he simply quirked an eyebrow up at her in response—as if daring her to say they were "just friends."

The silence hung awkwardly for a moment before Almera graciously filled it.

"You, dear girl, are wound way too tight. Relax. No one here is judging you, least of all me. You are among dryads after all. No one cares if you and your elf have—"

"Just stop right there!"

Almera laughed lightly, her voice sounding like tinkling bells. "Fine, fine, I'll stay out of it. But you are an adult and therefore old enough and, from what I've seen, mature enough to make your own decisions and deal with whatever consequences may arise from them." She rose smoothly to her feet and stepped toward the hole in the floor. "I'll meet you later to finalize the things you'll need to complete your journey." And with that she dove nimbly into the water and was gone.

Story whirled to face Eirnin and pointed an accusing finger at him.

"You! You knew she was in here, and you let me act like a... like a..."

"Like a girl who was happy and carefree for once?"

He was still lounging languidly, stretched out across her bed, wearing only the pair of cut off leggings he'd swum to the city in. Given their current company they were both over-dressed, but that fact didn't help her any when her eyes kept straying to take in his long lean muscles and flat stomach. She jerked her eyes to his smirking face and frowned sourly.

"Look, I might be half-dryad physically, but I'm all human in my head. My father raised me a certain way, and I'm more inclined to follow his advice than my mother's."

Eirnin, sensing that she was truly upset, stood up and walked over to her. He met her eyes with his, and she could see his concern in them.

"I'm sorry. I wasn't trying to make light of the situation."

"Yes, you were. You always do. You always joke about everything. And usually I love that about you, but this time I felt like you hung me out to dry. I don't give my heart away easily, Eirnin. I put a lot of trust in you."

He pulled her into a gentle hug. "Again, I'm sorry. I didn't realize... There's still so much about you I need to learn." He kissed her forehead. "And I look forward to spending years doing just that."

She relaxed and returned his embrace, resting her chin on his shoulder. "I'm sorry for freaking out. I shouldn't expect you to know everything about me. That's not very fair of me. I certainly don't know everything about you."

Eirnin snorted. "Since when was your sex *ever* fair?"

She smacked his arm playfully.

"Ouch! See, you've just made my point."

Story chuckled. "Touché." She pulled back from him and cocked her head to the side. "My mother did bring up a good point though."

"What's that?"

"Well, we can't go around calling you 'my elf'—"

"Why not? I rather like the idea."

Story glared at him teasingly. "Would you please be serious for like five minutes?"

"Does it have to be all together?"

"Yes!"

"Well, if I must…" Eirnin plastered a serious expression on his face, the ridiculousness of which nearly sent Story into a fit of giggles.

"So, back to my original question. What exactly are we?"

"Well, I thought we were just friends." Eirnin sat down on the stool and coolly leaned himself back against the wall with his hands behind his head.

Story shot him an unamused expression. "Of course we're friends. I think a good friendship is essential to any romantic relationship—"

"So you do admit that we are in a romantic relationship."

"Don't interrupt."

He mimed zipping his mouth shut, and Story rolled her eyes and plopped herself down on his lap. She leaned her forehead against his and sighed. "What am I going to do with you?"

"Whatever you'd like. Just so long as it involves me being with you."

"I thought your mouth was zipped shut."

"I don't even know what a zipped is."

Story laughed and rested her head on his shoulder. He wrapped his arms loosely around her and leaned his cheek against her head.

"Alright, in all seriousness, elves do tend to take romantic relationships quite a bit more seriously than dryads do. In my culture, I would be officially courting you now."

"That sounds so formal."

"It is. You have to get the permission of both sets of parents first. In our case, my parents are dead, so normally it would revert to my clan leader, but I've got Eánna's permission to court you which overrides whatever Eáchan has to say in the matter. And your mother just gave me her formal consent while you were sleeping."

Story was silent. She didn't need anyone's permission to date someone, and she didn't like the presumption it all implied.

"Of course, I'd court you with or without anyone's permission. But don't tell them that." He winked at her and any irritation she felt melted away.

"So what happens now?" Story hoped that he didn't say they went and got bonded or something. She was definitely *not* ready for that!

"We get to know each other."

"For how long?"

"For as long as it takes. Among elves it can take years, often decades."

"Hmpf." Story let out a halfhearted laugh. "Humans work a bit faster than that. We usually only date for a few months— several years on the extreme end—before we decide whether we want to stay with that person or not. We don't have the benefit of a three-hundred year lifespan to work with."

Eirnin hugged her tightly and kissed the top of her head. "Then we'll do things your way. What is your way, exactly?"

Story shrugged. "It's not really that much different from your way, except for the whole permission thing. That's a bit old fashioned—at least in my culture. It's different in other cultures around the world. Where I grew up, we'd be considered to be 'dating' right now. Or in other words, you'd be my boyfriend." The term seemed somehow completely inappropriate when applied to Eirnin. He was so much more than just a "boyfriend" to her; at least, he meant more to her than any of her previous boyfriends.

"Ah, so we're back to being 'just friends' again are we?"

Story shook her head and chuckled. "No, silly. 'Boyfriend' implies a romantic relationship. Human girls typically only have one boyfriend at a time, whereas they may have several friends who are boys at the same time. Do you see the difference?"

Eirnin began nodding his head and then shook it in a definite 'no'.

She gave a resigned laugh. "Fine, we're courting."

He grinned and kissed the tip of her nose. "I knew you'd see it my way."

"Oh really?" she asked while sliding her fingers stealthily up his ribcage.

"Yes, really."

"We'll just see about that!" She let loose a torrent of tickles up his side, and Eirnin, surprisingly, was ticklish. Laughing, he tickled her just as forcefully, until they were both squirming and laughing so hard they fell off the stool.

Story landed on top of him, knocking the air out of both their lungs in a woosh and leaving them breathless and momentarily startled; then they both started laughing again. That is, until Eirnin wound his fingers through Story's braids and pulled her face down for a kiss. Any thoughts of breakfast vanished as soon as Eirnin's lips touched hers. She grinned against his mouth.

"Yes, definitely courting."

Chapter Thirty-Two

Selkies

AFTER A HEARTY LUNCH OF KRAKEN SUSHI, Story and Eirnin met up with Almera and Adair in the large main chamber of the massive, central Vevila shell. Dryads wandered through lazily, stopping to chat with each other, and always said goodbye with a hug and a kiss. On the lips. The first time a new cousin kissed Story goodbye, she'd turned brilliant red with embarrassment. That was until he then proceeded to bid Eirnin goodbye in the same manner. Story had never wished for a camera more in her life than at that moment; the look on Eirnin's face was priceless. But he took it all in stride, easily adapting to the situation like he'd always done.

Dryad culture was completely different from the elves and gnomes—so very at ease and laid back. That wasn't to say they didn't do anything; fishing and, strangely enough, cloth production (both primarily for trade with the surface dwellers) took up much of the dryads' free time. Even Queen Almera helped with the weaving and fishing as time allowed.

The difference was that while the gnomes seemed to run around constantly busy on the surface, working through every bit of daylight available, the dryads took things at a much more sedate pace. There was no sense of urgency under the sea. Nothing had to be done *now*, and the company of others should always be savored and enjoyed. Story didn't necessarily see anything wrong with this ideology—it certainly seemed to work well for the dryads—it just wasn't her at all; she liked to be busy, to always have something to do or accomplish. Vevila would be a nice place to visit, but she could never live here.

She was jarred out of her thoughts by a cold, wet, and whiskery nose sniffing her neck. She shrieked and jumped behind Eirnin, who was trying to stifle a laugh with a cough. Behind her were two of the largest seals she'd ever seen, both easily the size of a da'nan. They'd surfaced out of the water behind her and must have found her scent interesting because they were both still eagerly stretching their necks toward her while blowing air in and out of their nostrils loudly.

"Pinni! Ped! There you are." Almera swept over to them and started to scratch one of them around its furry earflap—which was quite a stretch up for her. Adair pounced on the other seal and started scratching its back and neck vigorously with her single arm. The seal clearly approved and rolled on its back to allow for its belly to be rubbed. She nimbly moved around the seal as if this was a normal occurrence, and Story belatedly realized that it must be. There was still so much about this world she didn't know.

"I'm guessing these are selkies?" She looked at Almera, who was currently getting a tongue bath on her face from the seal she was petting.

"Okay Pinni, that's enough for now. Pinni!" The seal finally stopped licking the queen and instead thrust its head under her hand to encourage her to resume scratching its earflaps. "Yes, Daughter, these—as you have figured out—are selkies." Pinni let out a loud bark of indignation and Almera absent-mindedly began scratching its head again. "They're not the smartest creatures ever, but very good natured, fiercely loyal to their masters, and also the fastest things under the sea."

Pinni's tongue lolled out of its mouth, and it lay down happily at Almera's feet, finally satisfied by the attention she'd given it. "They should be able to get you to the lake outside Morrigann's garden in about two days."

In two days? Story glanced at Eirnin, and even he looked surprised.

Adair looked up from petting Ped's belly and grinned broadly. "Ma did say they were fast, after all." She turned back to Ped. "Aren't you boy? You're the fastest selkie ever!" If Ped had had a tail, Story was certain he'd be wagging it.

"They'll also accompany you once you get to the garden to afford you another layer of defense, such as it is. I'd send an entire army of dryads if I thought it would help, but I agree with Eirnin that a smaller party will most likely have greater success at sneaking in."

Story eyed the selkies speculatively. She didn't doubt they were fast in the water, their streamlined, muscular bodies and large, powerful sets of flippers attested to this fact. But regardless of their ability to turn their hind flippers forward and hop around the shell's surface on all fours, they were still hopelessly slow and clumsy out of the water. Then a memory of an old faerie tale she'd once read as a child surfaced in her head.

"Wait, do these selkies remove their seal skin and become people on land?"

Everyone stopped what they were doing and looked at Story, making her feel like she'd just said the ocean was red or something else equally ridiculous. Ped whined and nudged Adair with a flipper, and she resumed scratching his belly.

Story furrowed her brows together as she tried to recall the faerie tale. "It's just that I remember a story about female selkies turning into human women after they removed their seal skins. Then if a man stole them, they would be forced to marry them unless they could find their skins and return to the ocean in their seal form."

Adair giggled, and Story felt heat rush to her cheeks. Eirnin casually wrapped an arm around her waist and gave her a quick squeeze and an encouraging smile.

"I'd forgotten how wrong your world got things about Ailionora," Almera mused almost to herself.

"What?" Story looked at Eirnin, and he shrugged his shoulders in confusion.

"Yes, well, you don't think that I'm the first person to ever visit your world, or that you were the first person to visit ours do you?" Almera pursed her lips as she pondered her next words. "It's not common knowledge, of course, especially since for nearly a millennia it was thought that all of the passages between our worlds were gone—filled or closed by Morrigann. I guess he missed a few." She grinned at Story. "My point is, thousands of years ago, our worlds did see the occasional traveling visitor. When I visited your world, I found the legends—what you would call faerie tales—that remained about Ailionora were amusing at best, and glaringly wrong at their worst."

"So they don't shed their seal skins and turn into women?" Story eyed the unwieldy selkies again.

"No, but don't worry, they'll be able to keep up with you and Eirnin quite easily once you get on dry land. Though this girl," Almera nudged Pinni with her toe, "is easily distracted by schools of fish and flocks of birds."

Eirnin and Story exchanged a look, but didn't say

anything. There was no point in arguing. They could just leave the selkies at the lakeshore outside Morrigann's garden until they returned. They didn't plan on being in there for long.

Almera motioned to a pair of dryads lounging around on one end of the great room. The dryads, one silvery-white head to toe and the other triple striped in orange, purple, and brown, walked over to their queen, and Story had to struggle not to stare. Even out of the water they were graceful, ethereal in their movements, as if every step was part of a dance.

Almera took a pile of fabric from each of the dryads and turned to Eirnin and Story, handing one to each of them. Story lifted hers up and could see that it was a tightly woven sarong made out of the softest, lightest fiber she'd ever felt. It was an undulating silver wave pattern set on top of a sea-green background. Eirnin's was the same, only his colors were reversed: sea-green waves on a silver backdrop.

"These sarongs are not like anything you'll encounter on the surface. They are made from silk harvested from bivalve mollusks and then woven into fabrics as you see. I wove these two myself, though obviously not originally for you. One sarong made of mollusk-silk takes many years to make, but the colors were so perfect, I knew they were meant to be yours."

Story, completely overwhelmed by the generosity of the gift, threw a hug around the queen. Eirnin tied his sarong around his waist over his cut-off leggings before thanking the queen with a hug of his own. She whispered something in his ear that Story couldn't hear, and he chuckled before hugging her again.

Pinni decided that would be a good time to belch loudly. The smell of fish wafted over them, and Story felt a bit sick.

Gross.

"Pinni!" Almera admonished the selkie, who didn't seem the least bit concerned. The queen sighed and looked apologetically at Story and Eirnin. "I promise she's fast." Then she asked, "When do you think you'll leave?"

Story pursed her lips. "How soon can we have everything we'll need ready?"

"Now. Not all of us sleep for eight hours in one go."

Eirnin squeezed Story tightly and looked at Almera. "You should try it, your highness. I must admit I've become a fan."

The queen chuckled at that. "Yes, I do seem to recall I didn't mind sleeping so much back when I was in Story's world either. Her da—"

"Okay, so how about those supplies and outfitting the selkies now?" While Story was glad to know that her parents seemed to really enjoy each other's company, she was learning that dryads had a tendency to overshare information that she thought was best left private.

And nobody wants to know that much about their parents!

Almera laughed and raised her hands in defeat. "Fine, fine. You're just like your da. So uptight..."

Story smiled, not minding that comparison at all. Then another thought struck her. "Um, you know how you said you could take me back to my world?"

Almera, Eirnin, and Adair stopped what they were doing. Even the selkies froze.

"Yes..." Almera's face was confused, while Eirnin looked curious but supportive.

"I need to have a letter delivered to a friend of mine. He needs to know I'm alive and well." The fact that Story might not stay that way for much longer didn't matter—Josh deserved to know she was okay, and she needed the closure before she could proceed on to the last leg of her journey. Eirnin smiled at her, an understanding look on his face, and his eyes remained peaceful green, without a hint of brown.

CHAPTER THIRTY-THREE

EYES

STORY AND EIRNIN STARED AT EACH OTHER ACROSS THE FEW feet that separated their selkies. They were both hunkered down in their saddles and pressed tightly to the backs of Pinni and Ped to help streamline themselves in the water. Almera hadn't been lying; the selkies were fast. Very fast. Story felt like a torpedo barreling through the ocean, and looking forward was *not* an option—not if she wanted her eyes intact when they arrived in Faerie Land. Fortunately for her, the view to her side was quite pleasant; Eirnin was still only wearing cut-off leggings.

She shifted in her saddle and felt the scabbard of Eánna's dagger dig into her thigh. Adair had given it to her just before they left, saying that she knew it was a poor replacement for her father's knife, but that Story should have something to defend herself with should the need arise. Eirnin had frowned at that last bit but agreed that it was better to be safe than sorry.

They'd departed, again without fanfare, from Vevila well-stocked with sushi to snack on and a couple of sealed shells filled with plenty of ad'har to last them for over a week, though the trip would only take two days at the most. Story was confused at first as to how to direct the selkies, but despite their silly dog-like dispositions, they were quite intelligent and could understand very basic instructions.

Almera directed them to follow the coastline west until they reached the main river into Faerie Land and then to follow it to its source, the large lake in the mountains there. At that point, it would be up to Story to direct them with her compass to the entrance of the garden.

What could possibly go wrong?

Oddly enough, so far, nothing had. Their first day had passed without incident, with Story and Eirnin taking turns sleeping on the backs of the selkies who never seemed to tire. In fact, aside from Pinni darting toward the occasional school of fish (with Ped always hot on her fins), and a giant squid that they easily out swam, Story was pretty bored.

The sea was beautiful, and at one point she thought she'd seen a mermaid or two, but the selkies were going too fast for her to be sure of what she'd seen or to see anything else of interest. Being with Eirnin was nice, except he couldn't talk. One-sided conversations and being relegated to asking him yes or no questions got old pretty fast, so they ended up just looking at each other more often than not. There were worse ways to spend her time, Story supposed, and it did give her plenty of time to think about, well, everything.

She'd spent her entire life thinking of her mother as a villain: a terrible person who'd abandoned her and her father right after she was born because she didn't want the responsibility or burden of a child. Now it turned out she was a fairly responsible person—as responsible as you could expect a dry-ad to be.

Her dad wasn't completely innocent in the matter either—he'd chosen not to accompany her back to Vevila. Not that Story could blame him, but still… Eilath had also made a similar decision nearly a century ago when he left his love in Ailes to wander the world instead.

If Story was honest with herself, she couldn't be angry with them over the consequences of their choices. If those choices hadn't been made, the twins would never have been adopted, and Adair certainly wouldn't have been born. Story couldn't imagine not having Will, Katie, or Adair in her life; it was simply too painful to fathom. They all brought so much color and vibrancy to everything. Despite the twins' relatively short lives, they'd lived life to the fullest, enjoying every day completely. If Story didn't know better, she would have sworn they were the ones who were part dryad, not her.

So in the end, she wasn't upset with her parents or Eilath—who had become like a surrogate father to her by this point. If anything, she felt sorry for them: sorry that their choices had led them to the relatively lonely lives they had. Sure, her dad and Eilath lived for their children, but who could they share that joy with? And her mother had all the pressure and responsibility of an entire race, with no one to help her ease the burden. No listening ear or comforting shoulder. In many ways, Almera reminded her of Eánna.

Story shuddered, very glad that she was not, nor would ever be, in the position to rule or govern. That was a job she'd never wish on anyone. She'd had the burden of the survival of the elf race on her shoulders for several weeks, and it was more stress than she'd ever experienced. Who would have ever thought that staying alive would be so difficult? At that thought, she felt her face relax; it was almost funny, really.

Eirnin saw her half-smile and widened his eyes curiously.

"*Oh, it's nothing. Just thinking to myself about all the things that have tried to kill me since I've been here. It's not a very visitor-friendly world, you know.*"

Eirnin did not see the humor in her words, and his eyes narrowed, becoming a very unamused reddish-yellow.

"*Oh, calm down. I was just joking.*" Though she really wasn't, but she wasn't about to let Eirnin get worked up over it. "*Why can I see your eyes change color? And Eilath's and Adair's? But not Eánna's or most of the clan leaders?*"

Eirnin looked at her, clearly exasperated, either for the sudden subject change or the fact that he couldn't answer her. Probably both.

"*No, I mean, I remember Eilath saying that elves work very hard to hide their emotions behind their silver eyes. So it's like a control thing, right?*"

Eirnin nodded his head and wiggled his hand in a manner to indicate that she'd gotten it more or less correct.

"*And from what I've guessed, and what he let slip before you cut him off back when I was dying on the beach, you need a strong emotional connection with the person for them to see your emotions. Or completely lose control of your emotions, like Eíbhilin did when Eánna gave you the sword.*"

Eirnin nodded his head, slowly this time. Story smiled to herself, honored that Eilath had chosen to let her into his life so quickly—she'd been able to read his emotions within a few minutes of meeting him. She chuckled when she thought of Adair.

"I'm guessing Adair doesn't bother to hide her emotions from anyone, does she?"

Eirnin's silent laughter and the orange flashes of amusement in his eyes were answer enough. She truly loved his kaleidoscope eyes; they were like a window to his heart. No wonder the elves were so fastidious about keeping their emotions hidden. How easy would it be to manipulate and take advantage of someone if you could read them like an open book? Story's thoughts flitted to the elf maiden who Morrigann had seduced and then taken advantage of in his quest to destroy the elves over a millennium ago.

"That explains why you were so distant with me at first. Too bad it didn't work. I could see your colors almost immediately." Story said the last bit with a smile and a wink.

A rainbow of colors swirled through Eirnin's eyes, and his face contorted in exasperation and frustration. He clearly had something he wanted to say badly, and a simple yes or no response would not be adequate. Finally he reached forward and tapped Ped on the snout before pointing upward. Pinni and Ped zoomed to the surface, and Story was grateful for the ad'har's ability not just to provide them with oxygen, but also to equalize the pressure of the gases in their bodies on their ascent. Otherwise she and Eirnin would have a wicked case of the bends in a few hours, and that would certainly put a damper on their mission.

They breached the surface and tore off the congealed, dried slime in unison. Eirnin flung his away in disgust and inhaled a deep breath of fresh air like it was the nectar of life. Which, Story supposed, it was. It still didn't excuse what he'd just done.

"Are you crazy? What were you thinking bringing us

up to the surface in daylight and blowing our cover like this? What could possibly be worth it?"

Eirnin sidled Ped closer to Pinni and reached a finger out to scoop up the chain around her neck. "It's not that big a risk. The amulets still protect us from being seen by the fey." His finger traced the line of her collarbone and up her neck before cupping her head gently with his hand. He buried his fingers in her braids and traced the line of her jaw with his thumb, sending butterflies through her stomach and distracting Story from her anger.

"As for the rest..." He leaned in. "Do I really need an excuse to want to kiss you?"

His lips were salty, and she ran a hand slowly up the lean muscles of his chest before tracing the now familiar lines of his shoulders. His free hand settled on her waist, and he moved to pull her closer when suddenly a shower of ocean water hit them both in the face.

Pinni's tail slid back into the water, and Ped barked at them loudly over his shoulder.

"Aye, we've got the message you two, thank you very much." Eirnin wiped the salty water out of his eyes and frowned at the selkies. Pinni and Ped moved a few feet apart and barked at each other noisily.

"I guess they want us to focus on the mission?" Story chuckled.

"It would seem so." Eirnin winked at her. "Though I think we'll stay up here for a bit before we re-submerge. I'm enjoying the fresh air." He inhaled deeply again. "Now, to answer your question about elvish eyes, you got it nearly right."

She quirked an eyebrow at him and turned up the corners of her mouth.

"Don't let it go to your head," he said with a laugh. "As you gathered, only those we share a strong emotional connection with can see the colors in our eyes. The stronger the connection, the more colors and variety of emotions you can perceive. And once the connection is made, it can't be broken, so we're very careful about who we share ourselves with."

He leaned in toward her, his eyes a swirl of orange, green, and purple. "In our case, you can see even my most subtle emotions. Barring closing my eyes—though why would I want to do that when seeing your face always brings me happiness—I can hide none of my emotions from you. I trust you to see everything in me."

Story leaned against Pinni's rubbery neck heavily and took a deep breath, overwhelmed by what he'd just told her. Here she'd been so focused on how scared she was to open herself up to someone, when it had to be a thousand times worse for Eirnin.

He smiled at her wryly. "You can see why I was so hesitant at first to get close to you, especially since I felt ensnared by you almost immediately. You were so spunky and different from anyone I'd ever met. You certainly put me in my place. Not even Eáchan could do that."

He nudged Ped closer to Pinni with his knees, and the selkie obliged after a warning flick of its flippers.

"Is that why Eáchan hates me?" Story studied his eyes. "Because I put you in your place? Your words, not mine."

Eirnin chuckled morosely. "It would have been better to leave you believing that she simply didn't think you were the Ailesit." He turned his silvery-pink eyes on her, and unless Story was mistaken, he looked embarrassed. "A while ago, Eáchan wanted to court me. I did not desire it, so Eánna did not give her permission." His eyes flickered with irritated red flashes. "But the thing is, I did not desire to court anyone. Ever."

"But now that you've asked for permission to court me…"

"She picked up on my feelings for you even before that, as soon as we arrived in fact. I kept my eyes averted when we spoke for a reason, but Eáchan is not stupid."

"I'm sorry." She also realized that if he had to keep his eyes averted, that meant he and Eáchan had at least been close enough to have made some sort of connection. She tried not to be jealous. Besides, it was her he wanted to court, right? And wasn't as if she hadn't dated plenty before meeting him.

"Don't be. Nothing has made me happier," he said while taking her hand and interlacing his fingers with hers. "It's funny, I never wanted to fall in love. I was so afraid. It's what killed my father."

Story bit her lip, worried about saying the wrong thing. "I thought you said a troll killed your parents."

"It did."

She looked at him, plainly confused.

"The troll killed my mother. My father died of grief within the year. It was one of the worst things I ever witnessed in my life—like watching a wasting disease grip him, and there was no cure." He closed his eyes for a moment, and she knew they would be a deep blue when he opened them again.

"Bonded elves typically don't outlive each other for very long. The bonding ceremony changes you both, tying you to each other more than just in words, but also in your feelings. Far more than just seeing another elf's emotion in their eyes, with your bondmate you feel echoes of what they feel, especially the stronger emotions like love, anger, happiness, and fear."

Story's eyes widened. No wonder the elves took decades in their courting of each other. You'd want to be absolutely certain of who you were choosing to bond with. It was a lot of risk. She thought of how carelessly people in her culture got married and then divorced, as if marriage was a toy they could play with and then discard when they were tired of it or it ceased to be fun.

She squeezed Eirnin's hand and met his gaze steadily. "Even if my eyes could change color, they'd still be as you see them now. Sea green—perfectly content and happy where I am. It's how I always feel around you."

Eirnin's eyes faded to green, and she knew she'd said the right thing. He smiled mischievously at her. "What? Not even a hint of purple for me?"

"Oh, there's always more than just a hint of purple for you." She flipped her hair at him playfully.

"I won't be satisfied until all of your hair is solidly purple then." Eirnin's eyes darkened, and his mouth crushed down on hers; she drank him in hungrily.

The next thing she knew, they were both surfacing from the water and laughing. The selkies had bucked them both off. Story was about to make a witty remark when Eirnin stared over her shoulder, his eyes orange with excitement. She turned around and saw it, the mouth of the river that led into Faerie Land.

They were almost there.

Chapter Thirty-Four

Salvation

THE SELKIES GLIDED IN SILENTLY TO THE LAKESHORE WHERE Story indicated they should. Not only did her compass point unerringly there, but she also recognized the surrounding landmarks from her dreams. She half expected her hair to suddenly be elbow length again and a purple gossamer dress to appear on her body. But when she stepped onto the shore, she was still wearing one of Adair's smaller two-piece sarongs. While in the water and at Vevila, she felt positively prudish and over-dressed, but standing here next to Eirnin wearing not much more than a swimming suit…

"What?" Story snapped at him when she caught him grinning at her and instantly regretted her tone. She was jittery with nerves and feeling half naked did not help.

"I've just decided that I'm a fan of dryad fashions is all. I'll need to thank your mother and Adair for packing for you." Then with a disarming wink he got to work removing the gear from the selkies and leaving it safely submerged and warded against any fey.

As for the selkies, once free of the packs and saddles they both waddled up on the shore.

Story shook her head at them. "This is hopeless. How my mother expects you two to be of any help I don't know. You'll just need to stay here and wait—" Her words caught in her throat as she witnessed first Pinni then Ped shudder and shift.

There was no other way to explain it. One minute there were two massive seals before her, and the next minute, once their entire bodies were on the dry land, they transformed almost effortlessly into massive dogs. It was like magic.

Well duh! Of course it's magic. And yeah, humans got that legend way wrong...

They looked like a pair of floppy eared Great Danes, and each of them bounded over to Story and Eirnin and greeted them with sloppy kisses. Based on their size and shape, Story would have mistaken them for da'nan had they not been romping around and barking like dogs. As if to prove her point, just then Ped decided to lift his leg and mark an orange tree as his territory.

Story pinched the bridge of her nose and sighed. *So much for sneaking in.*

Eirnin stood next to her and watched the two boisterous dogs speculatively. "Well, if there are any fey here, they can't see or hear us, so as far as they know, it's just two idiot selkies making a mess of their woods. They're a good distraction."

He did have a point, but Story still frowned at them before consulting her compass again. The entrance should be right behind them. She turned around and took a few steps inland, enjoying the feel of the mossy soil on her bare feet. As much as she loved swimming, it was nice to be on solid ground again.

Eirnin followed her deeper into the forest, and judging by the crashing sounds of breaking limbs behind her, so did the selkies. They didn't have to walk far, and after a few feet, suddenly it was there, just like in her dream. The wild orchard, penned in by the living fence, and the open, inviting gates. Story's hand dropped to the dagger strapped to her thigh, as she eyed the unguarded entrance.

This is too easy.

Eirnin followed her gaze, squinted his eyes, and then looked back at her. "What are you staring at?"

"You don't see it?"

"I see a great lot of trees if that's what you mean."

"No, I mean, the gate into Morrigann's garden. Don't you see it?"

Eirnin looked again and then shook his head. "Well, that explains why previous hunting expeditions could never find it."

Pinni sat down next to Story and faced her with her tongue lolled out, breathing heavily. Story scratched her velvety ears and kept staring at the gate.

"Hmmm, it's not guarded."

"Brilliant! Let's go." Eirnin took her hand to pull her forward. "They can't see us—oh!" He stared at the gate.

"You can see it now?"

He let go of her hand and after a moment grabbed it again. "Only if I'm holding your hand it would seem. Which is perfectly acceptable to me."

Story chuckled and shook her head. "Okay, even though they can't see us, let's be careful?"

"Agreed."

Even Pinni and Ped barked their assent. Or maybe they were just barking because it suited them to do so at the moment. In any case, they seemed to have calmed down significantly and were alert and focused.

Good thing there are no flocks of birds nearby, Story thought wryly with a glance in Pinni's direction. Then she squared her shoulders, took a deep breath, and led them through the gate.

Nothing happened.

They weren't attacked, and they weren't denied entrance. Story glanced at Eirnin, and he shrugged his shoulders, just as surprised as she was. She dropped his hand and took out her compass. Just like in her dream it pointed unerringly toward the center of the garden. She looked over at Eirnin again. His left hand gripped the hilt of his sword, ready to draw it, and he was eying the trees with trepidation.

"You can relax, Eirnin. He's not here."

He cocked an eyebrow at her. "How do you know?"

Story raised the compass, showing that it was settled, not spinning.

"Oh, right. I forgot."

She grinned at him. "Ah, so you're not perfect. Come on elf-boy, let's get a move on."

They jogged through the orchard, with Story leading the way, Eirnin right on her heels, and the selkies running alongside soundlessly. It made Story wonder why in the world they'd been so noisy before when they clearly were capable of being quiet.

Silly selkies.

Just like at the gate, nothing attacked them, and nothing hindered their movement—in fact, no branches or roots even got in the way.

This is too easy!

Eventually, Story recognized where they were and dropped her compass safely back into its pouch. They were nearly to the clearing with a quarter mile left to travel at the most. Two more minutes of jogging, and they were there.

She came to an abrupt stop at the edge of the circular space, and Eirnin nearly ran into her back. His words died on his lips as he beheld *The Ailes* for the first time.

"It's real." His whispered words fluttered against Story's ears, and she could feel the wonder and amazement in them.

The selkies wasted no time before gliding into the clearing like wraiths, circling it in less time than Story could take a breath. Satisfied, they barked at her, and given that they had taken great pains to be silent during their actual journey in the garden, she took it to mean that they were alone.

She padded silently over to *The Ailes*, skirting Morrigann's living throne. Eirnin stood next to her, his hand gripping Aiolus's hilt, torn between staring at the skeletal tree and glancing around them in case of an attack. She stared at the tree, a little disappointed. All this time she'd felt such a kinship with the tree, like it was a part of her; now she was here, and she felt nothing at all. It was just a very forlorn, dead-looking tree. But she hadn't come all this way, through such trials, to do nothing.

Story knelt before the tree and drew out Eánna's dagger. She held out her left hand and pressed the sharp point of the blade into the fleshy pad of her index finger.

Just one drop.

A single, crimson drop fell from her fingertip.

Time seemed to slow, and she felt her pulse quicken with anticipation as she watched it fall.

It splashed onto the base of the trunk, staining the bleached white wood a brilliant red for a moment. One moment dragged into two, then three.

And then...

The blood faded into the tree, leaving rich, brown, healthy-looking wood behind it. The spot spread slowly at first and then with exponential speed. Story released a breath she wasn't aware she'd been holding and watched as the tree came to glorious life, silver flowers blossoming on its branches.

She and Eirnin stepped back, and he took her hand and squeezed.

"You've done it."

"*We've* done it," she corrected. "Though it does seem a bit anti-climactic to me. It was so easy." She looked at Eirnin. "Do you feel any different?"

He pondered her question momentarily, before shaking his head. "Not really. But then, who knows if I would?" He smiled and rested his forehead against hers. "Besides, we both know that I don't really care either way. Now that this is done, let's get out of here."

Story felt a smile tug at the corner of her mouth, and she couldn't resist closing that final inch and giving him a quick kiss. At least, she'd intended it to be a quick kiss. But like so often with the two of them, it was like pouring gasoline on a small flame. A bonfire exploded, and the relief and excitement of having lived through it all, of having won, coursed through them both. They kissed and laughed and then kissed some more.

"Bravo, you two, bravo."

Eirnin had his sword out and Story pushed behind him before Morrigann even finished talking. The selkies growled and were on either side of her in an instant.

The Faerie Prince was seated casually in his throne, his gold violin playing a cheerful jig in the air next to him. He was tossing a silver apple from one hand to the other, as if he hadn't just been thwarted by the two of them. He glanced in their general direction and waved an uncaring hand.

"Oh, by all means, don't stop on my account. It's not as if I can really see you; you're a bit hazy. I suppose Eánna had a few more of those amulets hidden away. Pity, I thought I'd managed to get rid of them all."

"Yeah, just like you thought you'd sealed all the gateways between our worlds." Story poked her head out from behind Eirnin and glared at him. If it wouldn't have been too juvenile, she'd have stuck her tongue out at him too. The aloof look on his face irritated her to no end. Did he honestly *not* care that he'd just been beaten?

He stood up languidly and walked toward them, pausing to stretch. Story didn't know if this was because he actually needed to, or if some deluded portion of his mind actually thought she could still be remotely attracted to him, so he was posing for best effect of his looks. The sunlight streamed down on his golden hair, and his skin shimmered as magic radiated from him. He was still gorgeous—perfect even, but she felt nothing but contempt and pity for him.

"Hmm, there's something different about you, Story." He paused and adopted a thoughtful posture. "Let me guess, did you change your hair? Your clothes? Ah, now I see. Where is Daddy's knife?" He smiled like a cat who'd cornered a wounded rabbit.

Eirnin raised Aiolus's point at him, and the selkies bared their fangs, the hair on their neck and back standing on end. Morrigann stopped moving toward them and raised both of his hands in a pacifying gesture. Story noted happily that his empty hand still bore the blackened flesh from her father's knife. She felt a wave of sadness when she thought about the knife, but put it out of her head; she needed to focus on the situation at hand.

"Relax, elfling. I'm not going to hurt anyone right now."

Eirnin lowered his sword, and the selkies stopped growling. Story didn't much consider herself a damsel in distress, but this was a little ridiculous.

"What are you doing? You don't honestly believe him do you?"

Eirnin spared her a quick glance before returning his eyes to the Faerie Prince. "Aye, as a matter of fact I do."

"WHAT?"

"The Sidhe are incapable of lying. Or breaking their word for that matter. It would destroy them." He glared at Morrigann. "Not that I would mind so much if you ceased to exist."

Morrigann narrowed his glittering violet eyes. "Don't push me, elfling. The deed is done. You restored the tree. Now it's time for you to leave my home." He pointed a finger at the elf. "Oh, and word of advice? It's best not to bait beings more powerful than you." He then ignored Eirnin and looked at Story.

Smiling beautifully, he held out the apple. "I brought you a peace offering. No hard feelings, I hope? The game is over now, and I must say, Story, that you did add quite a bit of spice to it." He winked at her, and Story could see Eirnin's forearm muscles clench as he tightened his grip on Aiolus.

"Look, don't, just don't." She stepped around Eirnin and placed a calming hand on his shoulder. The brilliant red in his eyes cooled, though it didn't disappear completely. Satisfied that Eirnin had calmed down enough, she faced Morrigann and ignored the proffered apple.

"Promise you won't do anything to hurt the tree." She indicated it with a nod from her head. Morrigann smiled seductively at her and reached out a hand to touch her cheek. She immediately backed up against Eirnin's chest. He wrapped a protective arm around her waist, and she leaned against him, taking strength from his support. She looked at Morrigann and her expression hardened. "Promise it, and we'll leave."

He rolled his eyes and flopped himself down in his throne. "Fine, I promise I won't hurt your precious tree." He waved a hand in its general direction. "Now go away; you're boring me. You're no fun anymore now that you've taken up with the elfling."

Taking Eirnin by the hand, Story walked away, flanked by the selkies. They were only a few paces away from the Faerie Prince when he called out to them one last time.

"You sure you don't want the apple? It's quite good, I promise." He held it up, and Story just looked at him, incredulous.

"I'm quite sure," she said through gritted teeth. "I don't want a peace offering from you. I'd just as soon never see you again."

"Suit yourself." He bit into the apple, its silver skin crunching loudly under his teeth.

Story shook her head and made a disgusted sound before turning and walking back into the woods, leaving him to sulk on his throne alone.

Chapter Thirty-Five

Death

WELL, HE'S QUITE THE WINNER. I CAN SEE WHY YOU FELL FOR him." Eirnin's eyes were a swirl of brown, red, and yellow. Story sighed and bit back the cutting retort on the tip of her tongue. He was just scared of losing her, angry with Morrigann—and probably himself—and still a bit jealous. Though why he would be, she had no idea.

She faced him and took his face in both of her hands. "Yeah, well, you never had to be-spell me to make me like you. I like you just as you are. You have so much more to offer me than he ever could." She laid a feather soft kiss on his lips before smiling against them. "Besides, you never tried to kill me, so that's got to count for something, right?"

Eirnin chuckled, and she watched his eyes settle. The colors didn't completely fade, but they did become more subdued. He pulled her into a tight embrace, and she rested her chin on his shoulder.

"What am I going to do with you?" His breath rustled against her hair, sending a shiver up her spine.

"Whatever you'd like. Just so long as it involves me being with you."

He leaned back and looked her in the eyes, and when he saw that she meant it, he raised an eyebrow at her.

"What? You can't even come up with your own silly lines to express your feelings for me?"

"I figured if I had to suffer through them, so did you."

He laughed and kissed the tip of her nose. "Right, let's get out of here and back to your seashell. I feel like we could both use a nice, long night of... sleep." He waggled his eyebrows at her, and Story elbowed him in the ribs with a chuckle.

She pulled out her compass to get a good bearing on which way they should go to get back to the lakeshore; she certainly wasn't going to ask Morrigann for directions. She looked through the glass surface of her compass and froze. They were far enough away from the Faerie Prince that it should have been working properly; sure enough, it wasn't spinning. But it also wasn't pointing back the way they'd come. Instead, it was pointing unerringly to her right; perpendicular to the clearing they were just in.

"What's wrong?"

Story held up a hand, silencing Eirnin and the selkies. She looked in the direction the compass pointed. At first, she saw nothing and probably never would have seen anything had Eánna not gifted her with elf sight. But then, a hundred meters or so away, she saw it: the sickly-looking apple tree, incongruous with the healthy trees around it. It was weighed down with several dead and dying branches, and a few silver apples were hanging from one, sickly, yet living limb.

She felt as if she'd been struck by a lightening bolt, and in an instant, she knew.

The Ailes.

She raced toward it without a second thought, ignoring Eirnin's calls and the selkies' barks. She would only have one chance at this. Her mother had warned her. Eánna had warned her. She knew better. Morrigann would never have allowed himself to be so easily beaten, and he always had a trick up his sleeve. Always.

This time the garden was not so accommodating. Roots rose up out of nowhere to trip her, branches tangled in her hair and scratched her skin, but she didn't care. She ran. Story spared a quick glance over her shoulder just in time to see two trees move to block Eirnin and the selkies from her. He was hacking at limbs with Aiolus, and Pinni and Ped were tearing branches off with their powerful jaws and claws. But she couldn't wait for them, she was nearly there.

She looked ahead at the tree and pumped her arms harder, forcing her legs to move faster. Her calves and hamstrings protested—she was not a sprinter—but she ignored them. *The Ailes*—and she was completely certain that it was—drew nearer, beckoning to her.

Twenty feet.

Ten feet.

Five feet.

A swirl of golden sparks coalesced in front of her and Morrigann appeared.

"You should have taken the apple, Story."

He thrust out with his arm, and she felt a sharp tug in her exposed abdomen. He twisted his wrist and pulled out his gleaming obsidian blade, covered in her blood, careful not to let a single drop near *The Ailes*.

Despite the sudden ringing in her ears, she could hear Eirnin screaming her name and the selkies howling in the background. She collapsed against the Faerie Prince, having lost all sensation from the waist down, and he cradled her in a morbid lover's embrace. Morrigann lowered her carefully to the ground and pulled the amulet from her neck.

"That's better; now I can see your pretty face properly." He placed a silencing finger gently over her mouth, tracing the contours of her lips with his fingertips.

"Shhh, talking will only hasten it and make you more un-comfortable. Besides, isn't this what you want? Now you'll get to be with your precious family again." He smiled at her be-fore leaning over and kissing her gently on the lips. She batted at him with ineffectual hands, trying to push him away, but she was already too weak. He smiled down at her once again and cleaned his blade with her sarong. Then he looked back at her frantic companions.

"I'll even do you one last favor. I'll send the elfling to meet you in the hereafter, or whatever it is you mortals supposedly have." Then he left her, discarded like a broken seashell.

Story struggled to get up to call out a warning to Eirnin, but her body refused to cooperate, and her lungs seized with every breath as if she was being smothered with a wet towel. She looked down at her hands and saw that they were com-pletely coated in red, and something that should not have been poking out of her abdomen most definitely was.

Pain exploded through her body as she pressed a hand against her stomach, pushing back in what was threatening to spill out. She wanted to simultaneously throw up and pass out. Instead, she covered the wound with her palm as best she could, though the blood still flowed freely between her fingers. As she fought her clouding vision, Story's world narrowed to perfect focus on one goal; she started dragging herself the remaining five feet to *The Ailes*.

Morrigann may have fatally wounded her, but if she could just reach the tree, Eirnin would regain the ability to wield magic again, and maybe, just maybe, that would be enough for him to get away. Enough for him to live. Besides, she'd be damned if she died without a fight.

Spurned on by her determination, she covered the most difficult and most important five feet of her short life. The sounds of a fight raged on behind her, and worry for Eirnin intruded, distracting her, but she forced herself to focus and have faith in his fighting ability, the amulet's protection, and in Aiolus's sting.

Three feet. Her head felt heavy, as if it suddenly weighed twenty pounds.

Two Feet. She couldn't feel her fingers.

One foot. Her entire body burned as if it was on fire.

Six inches. She had to rest.

Her breath was labored, her vision completely blurred, and red stained mud coated the skin of her legs as they dragged behind her through a trail of her own blood. She clung to the edges of her remaining consciousness, reaching toward the nearest root of the dying tree with her crimson stained hand. Pain burned through her abdomen, and she nearly passed out from the agony it caused her. She could feel her wound tear and grow from the stretch, but she didn't care.

Just.

One.

More.

Inch.

Her fingertips grazed the dead wood, and it was enough.

Story fell onto her back and saw the single living branch bearing the silver apples over her head. A mighty crack rent the air, and the earth shook as if it was being torn in two. As soon as it started, it was over, and the silence was deafening. All she could hear was the sound of her own labored, gurgling breath. And then, in a moment of perfect clarity, she watched as the silver apple turned into a bright red one.

She knew then; it was finished. The elves had been saved.

Eirnin has a chance, she thought with a pained smile.

And then, Story died.

CHAPTER THIRTY-SIX

FATHER

A s I was a goin', o'er the far famed Kerry mountains…"
Story groaned and pulled her pillow over her head.

Marine or not, her dad should respect the sanctity of sleeping in on a Saturday morning.

"I met with Captain Farrell, and his money he was countin'…"

She cursed under her breath and sat up in her bed. It was hopeless. He was going to sing that stupid "Whiskey in the Jar" song as obnoxiously as he could until she got up. It was cruel and unusual punishment really.

"I first produced me pistol, and I then produced me rapier…"

She shoved her feet into her tattered, old, sock-monkey slippers and donned her skull and crossbones bathrobe over her sleep pants and faded race t-shirt from a 10K she'd run a few years ago.

"Sayin' 'Stand and deliver, for I am your bold deceiver'!"

She jerked open her bedroom door and stomped down the hall into the kitchen, glaring. She might be up, but she wasn't going to be happy about it.

"Whack for my daddy-o, There's whiskey in the jar!" Her dad looked up and beamed at her. "Good mornin', kiddo!" He popped a hot waffle off the iron and onto a plate. "Mind gettin' Thing One and Thing Two from outside? They're buildin' a snow fort to attack you from later."

She grunted her acknowledgement and trudged outside, shivering against the snow flurries. Why did her dad seem to think that just because *he* was awake, everyone else should be too? It was so unfair, and she had been having the nicest dream. At least, she thought it was nice, though sometimes it wasn't. Or was it? She couldn't really remember. Something about a guy with tattoos (that her dad never would have approved of), and apples, and sushi? She hated sushi. She shivered as a cold wind blew through the cabin's porch.

"Will! Katie!" Story scanned the snow-covered tree line at the edge of the yard for two hiding shapes. "Come on you guys, Dad made waffles." She sighed and then stifled a yawn. The twins were every bit of their mischievous thirteen years, and they were willing to eat a cold breakfast if it meant pelting her with slushy ice.

"I'm not coming to get you," she called over her shoulder as she turned around to walk back inside the cabin. A ball of melting snow crashed into her ear, the cold ice burning as it trickled down her neck and into her shirt. She ran off the open porch and ducked behind a large tree stump. "That's not funny you guys!"

"Yes it is!" Will's pre-pubescent voice cracked, and she smiled—not because he had been particularly clever in his re-tort, but because he'd just given her a good idea of where they were attacking from. It helped that Katie was hissing at him to shut-up—that he was giving away their hiding spot. Story could see them easily now, crouched behind a bush only a few feet away. There was nothing for it then but to brave the snow and assault them first.

She hastily formed two snowballs, threw them as a distraction, and then launched herself at the twins, knocking them backward into the snowdrifts. Before she realized what she'd unleashed, she was engaged in a full-fledged snow-wrestling match with her two younger siblings. Two against one were never good odds.

Will was laughing with wild delight as he piled snow all over her while Katie pinned her down with tickles.

"Stop!" Story shrieked through giggles. "Please stop! Uncle! Uncle! You win! I give up!"

"Hmm." Will paused with an enormous pile of snow in his hands and looked over at his twin. Katie met his eyes and they shared a feral grin.

Uh-oh. She'd seen those grins before and it never ended well for her.

Katie opened her mouth to list her demands, standing there with her hands on her hips like a little general, when Will dropped his snow pile and pointed.

"Story, what happened?

She looked down and felt a pain in her gut. She touched her hand to it, wincing at the tenderness, and her fingers came away tinged with blood.

"Will, Katie. Come eat your breakfast." Their father's voice brooked no argument, and the twins obediently trotted over to the cabin. Her father stood over Story and extended his arm, helping her to her feet. "Sorry, kiddo, I thought we had a bit more time. Guess not."

THEY WERE IN STORY'S ROOM, SITTING ON HER BED, AND STARING out the window at the snow-covered peaks beyond. At least Milton was; Story's eyes were riveted on the blood staining her hand.

She remembered everything now.

"Dad?"

"Yes?"

"Am I dead?"

"Kinda."

She faced him and frowned, exasperated. "How can I be kinda dead? Either I am or I'm not."

He chuckled and ran a hand over the day's worth of stubble showing on his face. "Kiddo, you're gonna find that not everything is as black and white as you think it is."

"I don't understand."

"I don't expect you too. Hell, I don't fully understand it either."

"Are you dead?"

"Yup."

Story swallowed. "Then, is this heaven?"

"Nope. But don't worry, it ain't the *bad* place either." He grinned at her. "This is more of a waitin' place. While we're here, we learn and continue to grow as people. I mean, the twins were only thirteen when they died—they still had lives that needed livin'. Hearts needin' to be broken, cookies to burn, and songs to sing. Just 'cause you die, it don't mean you stop livin'."

"Then why are you here?"

"I'm waitin' for your mom. Plus I've still got lots to learn too."

"I met her."

"I know."

Story bit her lower lip. "Dad, what you and mom did… Not staying together… That was really stupid."

"I know. I told you, I've still got lots to learn."

"But you loved each other."

"Still do."

"Then why? You could have been so much happier together."

He father shrugged. "People do stupid things, especially when they put themselves or their own desires before the person they love. All I can do is hope that my children learn from my mistakes." He looked at Story meaningfully.

She changed the subject. "You said you were waiting for mom. Does that mean heaven is the same for all of us? Humans, elves, dryads, and gnomes?"

Milton nodded his head. "Yup, and everything else in-between. There's only one Creator, you know, which kinda makes us all siblings if you think about it. We all grew up in different places, and this here's just a big family reunion. Which reminds me, the twins want to have a barbeque tonight."

Story had so many questions, but before she could ask any of them her dad raised a callused hand. "No, I don't understand how it all works. I told ya, I'm still learnin'."

"So, do I wait here now? With you?"

"What for?" Her dad looked at her curiously.

"Well, I mean, I'm dying. I saved the tree, which means I saved the elves, right? So now I can wait here for… oh no." Story's face fell, and she felt like she'd been sucker punched.

"What's wrong, kiddo?"

"The elves. They're immortal now. There's one, well, he's kind of special to me." She felt so guilty for wishing for Eirnin's death so that she could see him again, even if only for a moment, but if she was dying, and he was immortal, they were a hopeless case.

"Oh yeah, that Eirnin fellow. Don't know how I feel about all those tattoos, but he's a nice enough boy, and he's put the first real smile on your face that I've seen in a long time. Plus your mom approves of him, and we both know she's got impeccable taste." He winked at her.

Story sighed and scrubbed her face with her hands. "Dad, it's great that you approve, really, it is, but I think you're missing the point. He's there, I'm here. And I don't really see that changing."

Milt chuckled to himself. "You see, kiddo, that's where you're wrong. Two things: one," he raised his index finger. "It's true, you did save the elves but maybe not in the way y'all thought you would. Two," he raised a second finger. "Nothin's keepin' you here but you."

She let that sink in for a bit. "You mean I can go back?"

"If you want to."

Story's mind was reeling. She could go back! Of course she would go back. Back to Eirnin and her newly-discovered dryad family. Back home.

And then her heart sank. She'd have to leave her father and the twins in order to do so. All she wanted when her family died was to get them back. And now she had them. But the cost would be her sister, her mother, and—she finally admitted to herself—the elf she loved. No matter what she chose, she'd lose. Tears pricked her eyes, and she felt her father's warm embrace, comforting her like a blanket on a frigid night.

"Story, loss and sadness are what make happiness and joy possible. You can't have one without the other." He gave her a squeeze and kissed the crown of her head. "I just want my little girl to be happy. Do you understand what I'm sayin'?"

Story soaked up the feeling of her father hugging her

again then slowly nodded her head against his chest and rubbed her runny nose with the back of her hand.

"I love you, Daddy," she smiled up at him through her tears.

"I love you too, kiddo." He pulled away from her gently and pressed his old knife into her hand with a gleam in his hazel eyes. "By the way, I think you lost this."

Chapter Thirty-Seven

The Cage

STORY OPENED HER EYES. THE BRANCH OF AN APPLE TREE slowly came into focus.

She was back in the garden, covered in her own blood and dirt, but she was alive. She could breathe unhindered, and her abdomen was whole, with only drying, flaking blood attesting to the fact that she'd ever been stabbed.

But when?

How long had she been *there*? It could have been seconds, or it could have been years for all she knew. Who was to say that time worked the same way there?

Then she heard it—the sound of a selkie howling in pain and weapons clashing.

He's still alive!

Story surged to her feet, momentarily stunned by her sudden influx of power. It was as if Ailionora knew she needed to stand, and it had helped her up. Eánna's gift had improved her vision and hearing, but now, it was like she had been blind and deaf before. She held her hands up in front of her face and knew that, if she really tried, she could see beyond the skin, beyond the bone and tissue, into the very makeup of her body on a molecular level.

Ailionora was lending her the strength of a world.

She didn't know how long it would last, so she ran. It was effortless, and the trees bent out of her way as she flew by. In a heartbeat, she was at the edge of the clearing, taking in the scene before her, her father's knife in hand.

Pinni lay near her feet, dead. Ped was a few paces beyond, also on the ground and breathing heavily, silver blood oozing from a clean stab wound to his ribs. Her mind processed the horror, and her eyes frantically sought out Eirnin.

There!

Dagger and sword locked over the Faerie Prince's throne, Morrigann and Eirnin were mere inches apart. Morrigann uppercut Eirnin in the jaw with his free elbow, knocking the elf away and to the ground, his amulet long since gone now. The sidhe held out his gleaming black dagger and circled Eirnin slowly.

"You know, it didn't have to be like this."

Eirnin moved his jaw experimentally, then stood up slowly, Aiolus held at the ready. "Yes it did. All you've tried to do from the moment she got here was kill her."

He lunged at the Faerie Prince, nicking his biceps in the process and sending golden sparks of magic flying.

Morrigann winced at Aiolus's cut and spun away. "But that's where you're wrong, elfling. So very wrong." A cruel smile crept across his face. He was enjoying tormenting the elf.

"If she would have just taken the apple, she'd still be alive, and you two would have had a nice, long, elf-length life together." He resumed circling Eirnin, who kept his sword angled toward him.

"What do you mean?" His eyes were wild, red hot, and swirled with black.

Morrigann shrugged. "The apple would have transformed her. She would have become like you, and in doing so, ceased to have been the Ailesit. But she would have still been alive, and you would have had everything you wanted." The Faerie Prince's face hardened and his violet eyes glittered with menace. "But she was too stupid to leave well enough alone."

His words had the desired effect. Eirnin bellowed incoherently, rage and grief consuming him, and he attacked Morrigann blindly. He hacked with Aiolus, driving the Faerie Prince back at first. Eirnin was powerful, but he was also reckless. He was going to lose, and so, Story acted. With the strength of the world behind her, she threw her father's knife and knew it would fly true.

Time slowed as the iron blade twirled end over end through the air. Aiolus was knocked out of Eirnin's hands, and Morrigann raised his obsidian dagger to strike.

A loud thump sounded as Story's knife buried itself up to hilt, and Morrigann looked at her with shock, amazement, and finally, fear.

"STORY!" Eirnin was dazed, confused, and then gleeful. He sprang to his feet and raced to her side. She spared him a quick smile, but then returned her hard gaze to the Faerie Prince. His face had resumed its bland, bored expression, and his eyes ticked down to the knife stuck firmly in the ground at his feet.

"You missed."

Story quirked an eyebrow at him and raised her hand. "Did I?"

The earth started to rumble and shake, causing Ped to whine in pain. Eirnin looked at Story, as if to ensure she was really there, and then ran over to help the selkie. Morrigann stared apprehensively at the ground around him and backed away, right into his throne.

Iron poles burst from the earth all around him in a hale of dirt and rocks. Story guided them with her will and Ailionora's loaned strength. The poles, about six inches apart at the base, came together at the top in a twist, caging the Faerie Prince.

"You can't do this!" Morrigann approached one of the bars, but dared not touch it—even proximity to the pure iron was making him sweat.

Story ignored him and knelt by Ped's side. The selkie had lost a lot of blood, and the silver ichor soaked into the ground around them. He breathed weakly and whined when she removed Eirnin's hand from the wound, replacing it with her own. Still gripping Eirnin's fingers tightly, she closed her eyes and focused. She could feel Ailionora's strength ebbing from her, but perhaps she still had enough for this.

A glow spread from her fingertips around the selkie's skin, and in a moment it was done—arteries, muscle, tissue, and sinew repaired. Ped stood shakily on his feet and gifted her with a slobbery kiss before making his way over to Pinni's body with a morose whine. He nudged her with his nose, and when she didn't move, Ped tilted his head back and gave a heart-wrenching howl.

Story sagged against Eirnin, completely drained.

"Are you all right?" His voice caught in his throat as he

pulled her close to him, holding her tightly there on the blood-soaked ground.

Story laughed, almost manically. "Yes. No. I died. That was weird. I saw my family. But all I wanted was you. So I came back."

"You can do that?"

"Apparently." She buried her face in the skin of his neck and breathed in his familiar spicy, cinnamon smell. "Though I think it will only work just the one time. And it's an experience I'd rather not repeat. At least, not for a very long time."

Eirnin ran his hands over her arms, shoulders, and hair, as if touching her was the only way he could convince himself that she was really there, alive. "And how long is a long time?"

Story bit her lower lip and considered. "Well, I am part dryad, and they seem to live a while. Plus now there's my blood bond with *The Ailes*—it changed us both. So in all honesty, I don't really know. But I think it's safe to say that it'll be much longer than a typical human lifespan."

Eirnin pressed a kiss to her head and breathed her in deeply. "What are you?"

Story chuckled—even though it hurt to laugh—as those words brought back memories of their first day together. "I have no idea anymore. Something new, that's for sure. Something different."

"You were always different."

"Hey!" Story slapped lightly at his chest.

"I'm sorry. Was I supposed to say you were always special?" Eirnin's eyes glittered, orange and purple.

"What kind of boyfriend are you?"

"The kind who likes to kiss you." And so, suiting action to words, he did.

An annoyed cough sounded from behind them, and they broke apart reluctantly. Eirnin sighed and gently helped Story to her feet, pulling out a few leaves that had gotten stuck in her hair during her initial battle with the Faerie Prince.

"If you two are quite finished, would you mind letting me out?" The Faerie Prince glared at them with a superior, even haughty, demeanor, but Story could see the fear in his eyes. She quirked up one corner of her mouth in a half-smile and reached inside the cage for her knife. She pulled it free from the earth and held it loosely in one hand. Morrigann took a step back, nearly tripping on his throne again.

"Relax, princeling. I'm not going to hurt anyone right now." She slid the knife back in its scabbard. "But I am going to leave you here for a while. Give you time to think about what you've done. It's what my dad used to do with his naughty children—he made them sit in a corner and think about their actions."

"Then you're not going to destroy me?"

"No."

Morrigann visibly relaxed.

"But it's not because I don't think you should be punished for your crimes, because I totally do."

He was on his feet and pacing the length of his prison in agitation. "My crimes, you say? *My crimes?* Oh how very little you still know about our world." He stopped in front of her and narrowed his eyes. "Simple-minded still. You have *no* idea what you've unleashed. Of what is to come." Then his expression softened, and he looked at Story almost with tenderness.

"Why not stay here with me? What I promised you before can still be. I could give you immortality, eternal youth, and rule over my dominion." He snapped his fingers, and his violin started playing her lullaby. "What could the elfling possibly offer you that I cannot?" He reached his hand toward her, but she stepped away before he could touch her.

"Forever young? Do you really want to live forever, Morrigann? It doesn't seem to have brought you any happiness. You have nothing that I want." She took Eirnin's hand in hers, gaining strength from his touch. "And in answer to your question, what you can never give me?" She looked at Eirnin with a smile. "Home."

She faced *The Ailes*, now in full bloom, a riot of crimson flowers and vibrant silver leaves. It was beautiful. She placed her hand on the trunk of the tree and felt the familiar kinship there.

"Thank you." She knew the tree understood and felt its strength flow through her. They were tied to each other now, both changed on a physical level by the bond they shared. She didn't know what it meant, but she wasn't afraid anymore.

"I made him promise to never hurt you again." She pulled a bright red apple from the tree and held it close. "But just in case? I'm taking a bit of insurance."

With that, she turned on her heel and jogged toward the lakeshore where Eirnin and Ped were waiting.

Chapter Thirty-Eight

The Summer Queen

STORY DIDN'T KNOW WHAT WAS THE HARDEST: TELLING HER mother that Pinni had been returned to the sea, her body transforming into foam once reunited with the ocean, or that she'd seen her father again. Regardless, Almera was taking it remarkably well, given the circumstances.

She sat heavily on her coral-encased bed, clutching the worn photo of Milton. She traced the contours of his face with her fingertips, and then closed her eyes, as tears slid out of one corner.

"Did he… did he say anything… about me?"

Story sat down next to her and wrapped a hesitant arm around the queen's waist. "Actually he did. He said he's still in love with you." She didn't know if telling her mother that had been the wisest thing, but it seemed to help. Almera laid her head on Story's shoulder and took a deep, shuddering breath.

"Thank you, Daughter."

Story just stroked her mother's hair soothingly in response, and it felt natural to do so. She was still getting used to the idea of having her mother back in her life but had determined she would make an effort to really get to know her.

"What will you do now?"

Her mother's question surprised her. She thought the answer was pretty obvious.

"We need to go back to Ailes. It's already been over a week, and I've got an apple that needs planting, and another queen I need to report back to."

"So you'll be leaving soon?" Sadness and loss tinged her mother's voice.

"Why don't you come with us? It would be nice to spend more time with you, and I'm sure Eilath would enjoy seeing you again." Story still had no idea what the deal with the two of them was, though it was clear they were no longer romantically involved.

Almera sat up and raised an eyebrow. "While I would love to see Eilath again—if anyone could be called my greatest friend, he would be it—there are others who would not wish to see me."

Story eyed her mother and then sighed. "Do what you think is best. But we do need to go soon. I promise I'll come back and visit for longer."

Her mother brightened. "Just promise me one other thing, Daughter."

"What's that?"

"I'd better get an invite to the bonding ceremony."

"Mom!"

"What? A mother's got to think ahead."

"We're just courting!"

"Right. And you left your father and siblings behind because you missed me and Adair?"

Story couldn't meet her eyes. "Well, yeah, I mean, I just found you guys, and I had seventeen years with Dad, so..."

Almera smirked at her, while her sea-green eyes glittered knowingly.

"Um, I think I need to go. You know, tell Adair to pack, and stuff. Yeah. Bye." Story fled from the room, her mother chuckling behind her.

THE THREE OF THEM GLIDED UP THE CANAL TOWARD EÁNNA'S PALACE on their selkies. Ped had refused to leave Eirnin's side ever since Pinni's death—which had made any attempts at even hugging awkward. But after Eirnin forcefully pointed at the water opening in the floor and threatened to throw him out of Story's room if he didn't behave, Ped stopped trying to interrupt them every time they kissed or cuddled. He'd even taken to sleeping on the floor next to her bed, and she found his loud snoring comforting in a way.

As much as Eirnin had teased her about "sleeping" when they got back, there seemed to be an unvoiced agreement that things would remain as they had been between them before their journey to Morrigann's garden. Eirnin passed every night in Story's room, either cuddled with her while she slept (and he caught a few hours of sleep himself) or reading one of the sea scrolls from her mother's extensive collection. They still kissed a lot, but that was it, and there was no pressure on either side for more than that.

For that she was grateful. So much had changed in her life already that having one thing remain the same was nice. And she was still definitely *not* ready for that level of intimacy yet—and to be honest, she didn't know if Eirnin was either.

Elf culture was drastically different from dryad and human, especially when it came to views on physical intimacy.

Ped barked at her, and she realized that they'd been stopped in front of the palace's dock for a few moments now while she had been lost in thought. She stepped nimbly off of the selkie and adjusted the sarong her mother had given her. It hung delicately to her knees, and the silver waves gleamed in the sunlight. Eirnin tried to help Adair off of Otarii, but she waved him away.

"I'm not an invalid, you know. Even if my arm never grew back, I'd be fully capable of getting off a selkie on my own." She pointed at the skinny, infant-sized arm hanging from her shoulder, and Story suppressed a shudder. It was great that Adair could grow back a limb but kind of creepy to watch happen.

Eirnin gave Story an imploring look, and she shrugged. Adair was at that age where no one could tell her what to do, so, best to just let her fall (as long as it wouldn't permanently hurt her). Ped splashed out of the water noisily and began his transformation once he was on the dock. Clearly, he was still not letting Eirnin out of his sight.

Good thing I like big dogs, Story thought with a wry smile as she eyed the selkie's head, level with her own. Eirnin slipped his hand into hers, once again dressed in his old hunting garb, and she found that she really missed his cut-off leggings. He seemed to know what she was thinking and winked at her with a quick flash of purple in his eyes.

"Are you ready for this?"

She looked at the still shiny, red apple in her free hand. "Nope."

"Me neither."

"Perfect. Let's go."

They stepped off toward the palace entrance, and Story

looked at Eirnin out of the corner of her eye. He didn't appear any different outwardly to her, but something had definitely changed about him. He was already strong and fast (and now she could nearly match him—something else she attributed to her bond with *The Ailes*), so that was nothing new. It was almost as if he had a closer connection to the world around them. He'd tried to explain it to Story.

"It's like a sixth sense. Like I was blind before, and now I can see; only I didn't know that I was blind before. Does that make sense?"

She'd nodded her head because, during the brief time when she'd been infused with Ailionora's strength, she'd experienced that on a much larger scale. As it was, she still felt very different and was certain all the elves did too. It would be some time before their bodies settled out, and they fully understood the changes that had been wrought upon them.

They walked down the marble hallways silently, each lost in their own thoughts, and even Ped kept quiet, padding along beside his master. Story had no idea what she was going to say to the council, or even what to expect. She somehow doubted that Eáchan would be thrilled to see her alive. And therefore, none of the other clans that fell under her sway would either. At least the queen and Eídolin's clans would be happy to see her.

The corridors had been empty of anyone, just as before, yet somehow the queen seemed to know they were coming. Two handmaidens waited on either side of the great doors that lead into the council hall. They pushed them open effortlessly, and Story and Eirnin walked in, followed by Adair and Ped. Eirnin did not relinquish Story's hand, and she watched Eáchan's face harden when she saw them. Still, her eyes remained placid silver, at least as far as Story could see.

"Da!" Adair shoved past them and threw herself into her

father's waiting arms. Story was glad that Eánna had thought to invite Eilath to the gathering as well, despite his unpopular presence there. She smiled as Eilath's eyebrows shot up to his hairline when he saw Adair's tiny arm and watched as she leaned up to whisper in her father's ear. Eirnin squeezed her hand, directing her attention to the front of the room.

Who the heck is that? Story shot a questioning look at Eirnin, and he gave a fractional shake of his head as if to say *"later."*

A girl of about ten or eleven stood before the council. She was swathed in a creamy orange silk slip dress that fluttered to the ground, a delicate flower embroidered train trailing behind it. Her curly, copper colored hair fell about her unevenly in haphazard layers, while a crown of living wildflowers and vines graced her brow. Her skin was deeply tanned, as if she never left the sunshine, and if Morrigann's skin shimmered with magic, hers positively sparkled and radiated it in waves of pure heat.

"I was not the only power released when the earth shook and our chains were broken." Her voice, young like a child's, reverberated throughout the room. She pointed at the queen with an intricately carved wooden flute. "Winter is coming, and Winter brings Chaos."

The queen inclined her head respectfully toward the girl. "Thank you, Rhiannonn. We appreciate what this costs you to deliver this message in person."

The girl held her head high and did not return the bow. "I have a long memory. We have always been on good terms. There was a time when I called your predecessors 'friend'." She glanced at the council leaders and narrowed her eyes slightly. "Though you are all so very different now."

"Mortality does tend to change a society's outlook on life," Eánna countered gently.

Rhiannonn pursed her lips before nodding her head slightly. "Yes, so it would seem." She twirled her flute expertly between her fingers. "There is someone else I need to see now. Goodbye, elf queen." Her gaze flitted over the others, as if she had weighed and measured them and found them lacking. "Council."

The elves came to their feet in unison and bowed their heads respectfully as the girl, without a second glance, turned and walked away. Story could feel the heat emanating from her as she neared, and had she still had human eyes, she would have needed to shade them, so great was the glow coming from the girl's skin. Instead of departing, Rhiannonn stopped in front of Story and Eirnin and tilted her face up to look at them.

Only the strength of Eirnin's hand on her back kept Story from taking an automatic step away from her burning gaze. The girl's irises were flames that smoldered and burned as they locked onto Story's. This slip of a girl scared Story. Scared her more than any other creature she'd ever beheld. She was raw, barely-contained power, and her perfectly sculpted childlike face beamed in a self-possessed smile that did more to frighten Story than anything else had in this world.

"Well played, Ailesit. Well played."

Then she walked away, and Story prayed she'd never have the full force of that gaze on her again.

"Who was that?" she whispered to Eirnin, her voice shaky.

"The Summer Queen. Morrigann's mother." His voice was just as subdued as hers, and she could hear a quiver in it.

Story felt something she'd never thought she'd feel: sympathy for the Faerie Prince. "Poor Morrigann."

"You have no idea." Eirnin ran his fingers shakily through his hair. "I thought she and the rest of her family—outside of

Morrigann—were legends too. But I guess, if the legend of *The Ailes* is true, then so is everything else." The worried look on his face concerned Story—there was just so much that she still didn't know. What other surprises were still in store?

CHAPTER THIRTY-NINE

HOME

A GENTLE CLEARING OF THE THROAT IMMEDIATELY GARNERED Eirnin and Story's attention. Momentarily embarrassed, they both approached the council, hand in hand. Once they reached the dais, Story released his hand and stepped before the queen.

"I bring you an apple from *The Ailes*." She placed it in Eánna's open hands and inclined her head respectfully.

The queen's eyes widened as she beheld the apple. "It's red? Curious."

"Yes. I'm not really sure what happened, but it seems as though the tree and I exchanged a few things in addition to blood." Story smiled ruefully at her.

Eánna's face turned thoughtful, and she nodded her head as if that made perfect sense.

"This is insulting! How long will you allow this sham to go on?" Eáchan was still standing before her throne, as were her other three clan leaders. Eíswin looked like he was torn between standing and sitting as his gaze ticked between his fellow council member and his queen.

The queen raised a querying eyebrow at Eáchan, who was doing a remarkable job at not letting her emotions show.

"My queen, how can you listen to these falsehoods when the evidence lies before us?"

Eánna gazed at her with impenetrable eyes. "Council, it is the evidence before me that leads me to know that the Ailesit was indeed successful."

Eáchan scoffed and pointed at the throne were Eídolin sat, or rather where he should have sat. In the overwhelming presence of the Summer Queen, Story had failed to notice that a different elf now occupied the seat of her dotty old champion.

"The Ailesit was supposed to restore not just our magic, but *also* our immortality. How then, do you explain Eídolin dying of 'natural causes' three days after the great earth shake?"

The council burst into a torrent of yells and angry voices, the two factions trying to shout each other down to prove their point, and all Story could think of was that Eídolin had died. It should have been impossible. He was immortal now. She knew she had restored *The Ailes*, she knew it with every fiber of her being.

"*It's true, you did save the elves, but maybe not in the way y'all thought you would.*" Her father's words haunted her, and she struggled to understand him. What did he mean? If they weren't immortal, then they would still die out as a race. She hadn't saved them at all.

The queen came to her feet gracefully, and all conversations and arguments ceased when she raised a single hand. At a glance from her they all took their seats quietly.

"While it is a fact that Eídolin has sailed across the Ailes Sea to join his loved ones, he knew—as I do—that our race had been saved, and he died content and happy." She raised her hand again when Eáchan opened her mouth to speak. "Story was correct when she said that *The Ailes* took more than just her blood. In fact, it is her human blood that gave us immortality of a different sort."

The entire council was staring at her now, riveted. Story was confused. What could she mean? Immortality of a different sort?

"Eilath has sired a second child." The queen's hand drifted down and rested gently on her abdomen.

Story's jaw dropped. Eilath and Eánna! Of course! It all made sense now, and she wanted to smack herself on the forehead for not seeing it sooner.

Eánna smiled over at Eilath, who beamed back at her. Their love for each other was palpable. "We are bonded. It was witnessed by Eídolin and Eásphor. It is done."

Adair looked from her father to the queen and let loose a loud squeal as she ran into Eánna's arms. "I get another sister!"

Her stepmother laughed and patted the girl on her back. "So you do, young one. So you do."

A low murmur rose up from the council, some of it happy, some of it upset, and all of it shocked. Story knew what they must be feeling; all these centuries they believed that they would be returned to the state they were in before, and now it hadn't happened that way. Some would see it as her fault, while others would view her as a savior. She didn't want either. Perhaps she'd go back to Vevila sooner than she'd planned, and from there she could head back to her own world.

With Eirnin, of course, she thought with a smile. It would be interesting to see how he adjusted to human culture and lifestyle. *And entertaining.*

At a look from the queen, the council quieted, but Story knew that this was not the end of that drama. She was glad she would be going safely home. She'd done her part, and that was enough. Adair gave Eánna one last hug and then skipped back over to her father, who was happier than Story had ever seen him. His eyes had no hint of blue in them at all; they remained a vibrant emerald green.

As the queen took her seat, Eirnin stepped forward and kneeled, holding Aiolus out to her with both hands.

"My queen, Aiolus fought well, though the hands of its wielder were untrained. Thank you for your gift. I return it humbly."

Eánna reached out with both of her hands, as if to take the sword, but instead pushed it back toward him gently.

"Keep it. We will need a leader in the coming war."

He stood and held the sword aloft in his hands before sliding it back into its scabbard with finality. "I am no warrior, my queen. I am a hunter." He stepped toward Eáchan and her seated council leaders. "If you mean to win, we must all be united in this." He inclined his head toward Eíbhilin and proffered Aiolus to him. The warrior clan leader hesitated and looked at Eáchan questioningly. She nodded her head, stood up, and moved to stand behind his throne.

Standing, Eíbhilin took the sword in his hand. He inclined his head toward Eirnin, formally acknowledging his act, and then moved in front of Eáchan's now vacant throne. Eíbhilin bowed to the queen and then his fellow council members.

"My queen, it is with great honor that I act as your war chief. My clan, and clan of my clan are with you."

Clan of my clan? Story realized what had just happened— power had shifted among the clan leaders. Now that the hunting clan was no longer needed as much, and with the looming battles to come, the warrior clan had come to pre-eminence. And it had all happened without drama, fighting, or voting.

"Thank you, Eíbhilin." The queen turned her liquid silver

gaze toward Eirnin and smiled. "You show great wisdom despite your tender years, cousin."

Eirnin met her gaze with a smile and nodded his head in thanks.

"And now it seems we must have a war council." The queen stood, followed by her council of twelve. "But first, tonight we must celebrate in honor of the Ailesit."

STORY SWUNG HER LEGS LAZILY IN THE OPEN AIR BELOW THEM AND leaned her forehead against one of the skinny marble pillars that made up her balcony's railing. The moonlight reflected off the water's surface in a silver haze that reminded her of elvish eyes. She yawned—it had been a long night.

The celebration to honor her had been… well, to put it honestly, boring. A formal dinner was held in a massive dining hall where every elf in Ailes had come to meet her. Her hand was still sore from shaking nearly a thousand others. Eásphor's clan had supplied lovely, soothing, background music, and Eícene's clan had spread the long dining table with more variety and delicious aromas than she'd ever seen or tasted. But there was no dancing, and the talking was subdued, and—from what Story could tell—usually wrapped up in political intrigue. The elves she'd met either revered her or sent angry glances in her direction. Only a small handful treated her normally.

One, Eínlin—a mage clan leader with an ailach that looked like a black pinwheel around his left eye—had approached her. "Good evening, Ailesit."

"Please call me Story."

"Ailesit, I wonder if I might ask you a question?" He had cocked a bushy, white eyebrow and continued when she'd nodded her head—too tired to push the name issue. "I have heard you are a dreamwalker."

"Huh?" *Who told him that? Surely Eirnin wouldn't... but Eánna would, if she thought it would help her people...*

"I have been told that you can walk the dreamscape unfettered." He'd stroked the long, thin Fu Manchu-style mustache and goatee that hung nearly to his belt, reminding Story of an old kung-fu master she'd seen in films growing up.

She'd thought back to all the very real dreams she'd had since arriving in Ailionora and all the vivid dreams she'd had as a child. *Could it be?*

"I might be... Maybe. I'm not even sure what a dreamwalker is. I'm still trying to figure all this out."

He'd smiled then, creasing his almond-shaped eyes at the corners, held out his hand to her, and she'd taken it automatically. "As we all are, Ailesit. In my mage clan, we are the dreamwalkers, and while we have studied the theory of it for the last thousand years, only in the past few days have we been able to attempt it. We have the knowledge, and you have the experience. Would you be interested in learning from each other?"

She didn't answer him right off, but instead watched Eirnin move about the crowd with the queen, working to get the elves to unite under their common cause. She'd realized then that he would not be leaving this world any time soon. She bit her lower lip and gave a small smile. *Just like Dad—he's dedicated himself to the defense of his people.* Eínlin followed her gaze and then smiled knowingly.

"No need to answer now, Ailesit." He'd released her hand and indicated the door. "You look tired. You should go to your rooms and rest. I will let the queen know you have left. There is no reason for you to stay for the war council—they will just argue tonight."

Story had smiled at him gratefully and made a quiet exit, bringing her here to her room now where she sat enjoying the cool night air and reflecting on how much her life had changed and how far she had come. She still missed her family, and always would, but she'd felt the joy of new love, and had discovered more family here in Ailionora. She found she was no longer constantly angry, and she was glad for it. She felt like an enormous weight she hadn't even known she was carrying had been removed from her back.

Just as she was going to call it a night and get some sleep, she heard her door open and then close again. Eirnin sat down next to her and threaded his legs through the railings, swinging them back and forth in rhythm with hers.

"Is the war council done then?" Story stifled a yawn.

"Hardly," Eirnin snorted. "Claiming that the clans are unified is one thing. Actually acting unified is another completely."

He interlaced his fingers with hers, and they leaned back against their elbows, staring at the stars in companionable silence for a time.

"Eirnin?"

"Hmm?"

"How come you were tied up when I first met you?"

Eirnin laughed softly. "You remember that, do you?"

"How could I forget? You were a complete jerk to me."

He gazed at her, and even in the darkness she could see the blue filling his eyes. "I'm sorry for that. The truth is, I was completely embarrassed. At first for being caught by the little blighters, and then for needing to be rescued—by an overgrown gnome at that."

Story grinned at him. "Yeah, I'd figured that much out on my own. What I want to know is *how* you got caught."

He flushed, a bluish tinge creeping up his neck. "Hmpf. That."

"Yes, that. Come on, elf-boy, tell me. It's only fair."

"How is telling you how I got caught fair?"

"Oh, just tell me. Quit being a baby about it."

"Fine." Eirnin returned his gaze to the stars in the velvet sky overhead. "If you must know, I fell asleep."

"And?"

"That's it. I fell asleep. And when I woke up, I was tied up."

She started laughing. "You forgot to put up a ward, didn't you?"

"Maybe…" Eirnin refused to meet her gaze. "Not to change the subject, but—"

She snorted.

"Could you please be serious for five minutes?"

"All at once?" Story answered straight-faced.

He sat up and looked at her. Sensing his serious shift in mood, she did as well. Was he about to ask her to bond with him? Her heart raced. She wasn't ready yet. That wasn't to say she didn't want to be with him forever, but really, they'd just started courting. It still felt too soon, too sudden. She needed more time to get used to the idea. Though, she knew that if he asked, she'd say yes, and be glad to… but she hoped he wouldn't ask her. Yet.

"Story, I… I can't go with you to your world. There is so much going on in Ailionora, and I must stay until the coming war is over." He sighed before continuing, "I have a responsibility not just to my people, but also to every living creature of my world. So much more is at stake than just one race. I can't turn my back on my world when she needs me the most." He placed his warm hand on her cheek, and Story leaned into it.

"After it's over, I'll come to you and spend the rest of my days in your company. That is, if you'll allow it."

She took his hand in hers and smiled at him. "I know. That's why I'm staying here with you."

Surprise crossed his features. "But I thought you wanted to go home?"

"I am home." Story leaned in until their faces were mere inches apart. "I don't want to live in a world you're not in. I love you."

Eirnin's face blossomed into a wide smile. "Thank you."

She smacked his shoulder and narrowed her eyes.

"Ow! Okay, fine. Thanks a lot."

She quirked a smile at him "You are never going to make things easy, are you?"

"Nope."

"Good." She rested her forehead against his. "Otherwise life with you would be boring." She kissed him and felt him smile against her lips as he kissed her back.

Story was happy. Story was home.

Pronunciation Guide

Adair	Aa-dye-ear
Ad'har	Aa-dar
Ailach	Eye-la
Ailionora	Eye-le-o-nor-rah
Ailes	Eye-lees
Aiolus	Eye-o-loos
Ainen	Eye-nen
Aisras	Eyes-ras
Ailanthu	Eye-lun-thu
Aiden	Eye-den
Aiblins	Eye-blins
Ailesit	Eye-lay-sit
Almera	All-mee-rah
Borgmester	Borg-mess-ter
Brygerri	Bree-gerry
Da'nan	Da-naan
Eánna	Ay-un-aa
Eáchan	Ay-uh-shun
Eámonn	Ay-uh-moon

Eásphor	Ay-us-for
Eavon	Ay-vun
Eínlin	Ay-een-leen
Eíswin	Ay-ee-swin
Eídolin	Ay-ee-doe-leen
Eíbhilin	Ay-ee-bee-leen
Eícene	Ay-ee-seen
Eilath	Ay-lath
Eisrus	Ayz-russ
Eirnin	Air-nin
Faolán	Fow-lan
Fuath	Foo-aath
Jord	Jord
Keelin	Key-lin
Morrigann	More-gaan
Rhiannonn	Ree-an-non
Sh'yla	Shy-la
Tilpasse	Till-pass-ee
Vevila	Ve-vee-la

ACKNOWLEDGEMENTS

I have to admit, I was a bit worried about writing this section, because I just KNOW I'm going to forget someone AND THEY WILL NEVER FORGIVE ME. So, can I just cheat and thank everyone in the whole wide world who had anything to do with my book both directly and indirectly?

No?

Dang. Well, here goes…

First off, a great big thank you to YOU my readers.

Thank you to everyone who read my drafts and gave me honest feedback through all the different phases (especially those of you who read it in its first draft *HORROR*): Erin C., Sam Evans, Mandy Hortenski, Melanie Faustino, Kathy Johnson, Michelle Kinseth, Conley Lyons, Tonya Mayberry, Megan "Alpha" Snyder, Caitlin Shindler, Lil Watson, and Laura Williamson.

Thank you to my writing buddies who went on this journey with me and put up with my constant calling to bounce my ideas off of you (and reading of my early drafts): Bryan Young, Maggie Masetti, and Y.M. Rivadeneira.

Thank you to my publishing team, without whom I could not have done this: Kelli Neier (editor/print layout), Rich Sigfrit (webmaster/designer), and Betsy Waddell (cover and interior artist).

Thank you to my mentors, Aaron Allston and Michael A. Stackpole, for always believing in me and for all the great advice throughout this journey.

Thank you to Elizabeth and Jimmy for allowing Ron and me to take part in Will's life.

Thank you to my parents for always believing in me and supporting me in every challenge I've undertaken.

Thank you to my dear, sweet husband Ron, for, well, everything.

Thank you Will, Katie, and Milton for all the lives you touched. We love and miss you.

Last, but certainly not least, thank you to my Heavenly Father, without whom, none of this would be possible.

Music

As with most things I do, be it running, sewing, driving, etc., I love to listen to music. It can really set the mood and also motivate me. Of course I listened to a LOT of music while I wrote this novel, and while some songs had a direct impact on the book, others just helped keep me trucking along with their fast dance beats (thanks running playlist!). Some bands/artists in general got played a lot: The Beatles, Muse, Coldplay, Enya, The Cranberries, among many others. I've listed some songs that had a direct impact on this story—but I'll leave it to you to decide what sections they might have applied to. In no particular order:

1- "Bolero", Simon Standage
2- "Clocks", Twelve Girls Band
3- "The Call", Regina Spektor
4- "Twist and Shout", The Beatles
5- "Forever Young", Youth Group
6- "When I'm With You", JJ Heller
7- "Everything I Own", Bread
8- "Beggin'", Madcon
9- "You Found Me", The Fray
10- "Whiskey in the Jar", Traditional Irish folk song
11- "Fire and Rain", James Taylor
12- "Book of Days", Enya
13- "I Want It That Way", Backstreet Boys
14- "The Mummers' Dance", Loreena McKennitt
15- "This Is Home", Switchfoot
16- "Fireflies", Owl City
17- "I Won't Say (I'm in Love)", Megara & the Muses
18- "Lucy Meets Mr. Tumnus", Harry Gregson-Williams

BOOKS IN THE WAR OF THE SEASONS SERIES

ABOUT THE AUTHOR

Janine K. Spendlove is a KC-130 pilot in the United States Marine Corps. In the Science Fiction and Fantasy World she is primarily known for her best-selling series, *War of the Seasons*. She has several short stories published in various speculative fiction anthologies, to include *Time Traveled Tales*, *Athena's Daughters*, and *War Stories*. Janine is also a member of Women in Aerospace (WIA), BroadUniverse, and is a co-founder of GeekGirlsRun, a community for geek girls (and guys) who just want to run, share, have fun, and encourage each other. A graduate of Brigham Young University, Janine loves pugs, enjoys knitting, making costumes, playing Beatles tunes on her guitar, and spending time with her family. She resides with her husband and daughter in Eastern North Carolina. She is currently at work on her next novel.

CONNECT WITH ME ONLINE

Twitter: @JanineSpendlove
Facebook: www.facebook.com/JanineSpendlove
Blog: www.waroftheseasons.com

www.ingramcontent.com/pod-product-compliance
Lightning Source LLC
Chambersburg PA
CBHW021431240626
47153CB00001B/105